The
STORMS
OF WAR

KATE WILLIAMS

First published in Great Britain in 2014 by Orion Books,
an imprint of The Orion Publishing Group Ltd
Orion House, 5 Upper Saint Martin's Lane
London WC2H 9EA

An Hachette UK Company

1 3 5 7 9 10 8 6 4 2

A CIP catalogue record for this book is
available from the British Library.

ISBN (Hardback) 978 1 4091 3988 1
ISBN (Export Trade Paperback) 978 1 4091 3992 8
ISBN (Ebook) 978 1 4091 3987 4

Typeset at The Spartan Press Ltd,
Lymington, Hants

Printed and bound in Great Britain by
Clays Ltd, St Ives plc

The Orion Publishing Group's policy is to use papers that
are natural, renewable and recyclable products and made from
wood grown in sustainable forests. The logging and manufacturing
processes are expected to conform to the environmental
regulations of the country of origin.

www.orionbooks.co.uk

The de Witt Family and their Circle

Rudolf de Witt – meat dealer, father of the de Witt family and owner of Stoneythorpe

Verena de Witt – Rudolf's wife, the daughter of Lady Deerhurst

Arthur de Witt – their oldest child, living in Paris

Michael de Witt – student at Cambridge University

Emmeline de Witt – due to be married to Sir Hugh Bradshaw

Celia de Witt – their youngest daughter

Tom Cotton – assistant groom to the de Witts

Mrs Cotton – his mother, a former servant of the family

Mary and Missy Cotton – Tom's sisters

Jonathan Corrigan – Michael's university friend, from New York

Stanley Smithson – footman

John Thompson – footman

Jennie Christmas – parlourmaid

Miss Wilton – lady's maid

Christopher Marks – groom

Samuel Janus – Celia's summer tutor, a former schoolmaster

Sir Hugh Bradshaw – local aristocrat, fiancé of Emmeline and owner of Callerton Hall

Rufus Sparks – university friend of Mr Janus

Jemima Webb – university friend of Mr Janus and political campaigner

Lance Corporal Bilks – former Derby factory foreman, successful soldier

Lance Corporal Orchard – lance corporal fighting in the Western Front

Lady Deerhurst – Verena's mother

Matthew – Verena's nephew and Celia's cousin

Louisa – Verena's niece and Celia's cousin

Heinrich de Witt – Rudolf's cousin

Lotte de Witt – Heinrich's wife

Johann and Hilde de Witt – children of Heinrich and Lotte de Witt

Elizabeth Shepherd – novice ambulance driver

Professor Punter – Michael's tutor at Magdalene

PROLOGUE

Michael was shaking. If he held his hand, then it was his leg; if he stilled that, then his back wobbled, like a string waved about from one end only. He sat at the back of the trench and felt his body quiver in the freezing air. The whole place was quiet save for the movements of the men, the scrabbling of the rats over the discarded bits of food. Only he was making sounds: his knees knocking together, his teeth chattering. What a joke that normally was – knees knocking. He had laughed at actors playing fake fear on stage, hands popped over mouths, legs quavering. And now here he was, a caricature, and none of it was funny because he just couldn't stop. A tin can fell to the floor and he jumped in horror. The scream was out of his mouth before he knew it. The men turned around. He looked down and a large rat had knocked over Orchard's billy mug. The men turned back to their positions. That was the most shaming thing of all. Now they hardly noticed him, took it for granted.

It was even worse when there were no bombs. When there was shelling, all the men were shaking, even Orchard. In the silence, it was just him.

Orchard manoeuvred himself beside him. 'It's coming up to time, sir,' he said, tapping his watch. 'No orders to the contrary so far?' He was a squat, cheerful man, worked for the fire brigade in Wapping. Michael knew he was beyond fortunate with his second in command. 'Don't you worry, sir,' Orchard said when Michael was holding his gun upside down or had sent the men the wrong way. 'You'll pick it up in half a tick.' Michael made himself do things he hated, so as not to let down Orchard and his beaming face.

I

'No, Orchard. No orders to the contrary.'

'Right, chaps! Attention. Corporal Witt wishes to issue a command.' The trench was silent. From a distance, you could just hear the French shouting on parade and the boom of the miners making another trench. Michael thought – just for a moment – that he heard a woman singing. Perhaps one of the cooks, although it sounded too delicate for a domestic. He strained for the notes, but there was a gust of wind and they were lost.

Orchard looked at his watch. Michael tried to still his shaking hands. 'Over!' a voice shouted. 'Over the top, men!' It was his. It wasn't loud enough.

'Don't worry, sir,' said Sergeant Orchard. 'The wind ate up your voice that time. I will give it a proper shout so the chaps know what's what.'

'Thank you,' Michael tried to say. But his voice was shaking too and it could not get out.

Orchard stood up. 'All right, men,' he shouted. 'We're going over. As the captain said, we'll have fire cover from the top and the barbed wire will be cut. You'll be as safe as houses.' He put up his arms. 'One, two, three, GO!'

Michael held his gun, willed himself to go forward.

1914

ONE

Stoneythorpe, Hampshire, Saturday 1st August 1914

'There you are!' Emmeline was pulling apart the willow branches, poking in her perfect, entirely regular nose. 'Mama wants you. Michael's American friend has arrived early. And she's fussing about the party.'

Celia looked to the side so the white and silver of the pond was sharp on her eyes. 'I'll come in a moment.'

'Now, Mama says.' Emmeline kicked at the soil with her boot. 'Come along. I think I was good to even try to find you back here. It's so *dirty*.' Celia pulled herself out of the willows, ignoring Emmeline's hand. 'I don't know what Mama is thinking, allowing Michael to invite this Jonathan person. We've quite enough to do, with the party and my wedding.'

None of us cares about your stupid wedding, Celia wanted to say. Not that it would be true. 'Let them try to mock us now,' Rudolf had said, pulling on his beard. 'My wife was the daughter of Lord Deerhurst and my daughter is to be Lady Bradshaw.' She scraped her boots in the grass and followed her sister up to the house.

Emmeline walked ahead, her pale pink skirt snaking after her – she was wearing out her old dresses in preparation for her trousseau. The house beckoned to them, the squat frontage of the servants' hall, the breakfast and dining rooms and the back of the sitting room, its long, pale windows glinting in the sun, the Hampshire stone flashing coolly behind. In summer, Celia would usually be in the Black Forest, visiting her second cousins, Hilde and Johann. 'We will make a longer visit next year,' Rudolf had said. 'When the international situation has calmed.' She blushed to herself that she had been secretly relieved. From the age of eight, she had spent two weeks there with her siblings, but now they said they were too old for it, and last year Celia had gone alone. They had done the things that would look like fun to anyone seeing them from outside: fishing for sticks in the river by their house, taking rides with their groom and listening to the gramophone in the parlour. But Johann had been awkward with her and Hilde had wanted to be alone and not talk. 'She is just growing, dear,' Aunt Lotte had said. 'She wishes to be quiet to think.'

Uncle Heinrich sat her down at the table and talked about the family tree, how Wolfgang de Witt had come from Holland in the seventeenth century, married Anna and never returned to his home country – ever. 'Like your father, Celia,' he said. 'Rudolf will never leave England.' Then he asked her questions about home – even about Tom, though he had never met him.

Now, the sight of Hilde's letters, neatly written on pink-edged paper, illustrated with flowers around the edges, arriving every three weeks or so, made her feel embarrassed for the friendship that they no longer seemed to have, since they were grown. She stuffed them into one of her drawers, guilty also that a cancelled visit meant she could spend the summer months with Tom. That was, if Emmeline would let her escape the discussions about her wedding.

'Come along,' said Emmeline. 'Why are you always so slow? Mama is waiting. She will be pulling her hair out. Well, not literally. But she says she wants to.' Their mother's great pride was her chestnut hair, still as thick as when she was nineteen, Rudolf said.

'Mama is always worrying about the party.'

'You know her, every year she says she will never be able to get everything done. And every year it's a success. Anyway, what were you *doing* down there?'

'I was thinking about Princess May, actually.'

'Hmm. If you ask me, she must have felt lucky to marry the King. She was very plain and her mother had a figure like Mrs Rolls. I shall see them when Sir Hugh takes me to court and introduces me. I simply don't believe she was the ideal bride.'

'I think it was romantic that he chose her when his brother died. But I still don't see why anyone would want to get married, even to the King.' Celia was lying. She'd been thinking of Countess Sophie, the lady-in-waiting, courted by Franz Ferdinand, everybody thinking he wanted to marry one of the princesses of the house.

'Well, he wouldn't marry you. You always have dirty knees.' She was right: Celia did usually have some dust or grime over her dress.

Emmeline was too beautiful, that was the problem. Her fair hair was pinned up by Miss Wilton into a great cloud around her head, and her eyes were so large that they drew your attention away from the rest of her face. She looked like Mixie, Verena's doll from when she was a child, without flaws. Celia knew that, if you looked closer at her sister's cheeks, there were slight bumps, dry patches, and that made them pink. But no one ever did look, apart from her.

Emmeline had always taken the lead roles in plays at school – finishing with Miranda in *The Tempest*. In Eversley, the nearest big village, she was like a kingfisher, striking people silent when they saw her height, slender figure and mass of pale hair. Celia sometimes looked in the mirror and wondered how different her days would have been if her reflection had been like Emmeline's, the snub nose, pale eyelashes and thin frizzy hair replaced by her sister's easy loveliness. 'You have a happy face,' a teacher had once said to her. Not beautiful. If she looked like her sister, people might follow her in the street, as they did Emmeline, offer her biscuits and cakes or ribbons as gifts in shops. Like Emmeline, she could say what she wished and no one would reprimand her, be cross or remember her angry words.

Celia had been a plump child and now she was too tall, too thin, like a lanky bird plopped out of its nest, Michael teased her. Her nose was too wide and her grey eyes too small, and when she smiled, her eyes crinkled smaller and her nose got wider. She tried hard not to envy her sister's mass of hair, for her own lay flat on her head, fell out of buns and clips, dropped over her face. None of her clothes fitted because the waist was always wrong, and there seemed to be a permanent thin line of dirt under her nails. If they wore the same gown, it would look pristine on Emmeline, creased and out of shape on Celia, within a week thinned at the elbows and grey. 'Why can't you just be elegant?' her mother said.

Still, she thought, if all beauty got for you was marrying Sir Hugh, perhaps it wasn't worth so very much. Sir Hugh was grass-thin and looked about a hundred, even though Verena said he was forty (old enough, Celia thought). He dressed so neatly that Rudolf said even King Edward would have approved of his buttons. He wore wide ties over his shirts, expansive, shimmering silk, their generous show a dark shock against the rest of him. Last year, after days of fiddling with their gowns, Emmeline and Verena had gone to Lady Redroad's ball at her house ten miles away. They came back talking of Sir Hugh. A week afterwards, he came to visit, sat upright in their parlour, said nothing. Verena was jubilant. All the mothers had been looking at Sir Hugh, she said, and he was visiting *them*.

Celia took one skip – why did they always have to *walk* – towards Stoneythorpe. The dark red stone of the house shone above them in the afternoon sun, the three peaks on the roof and their turrets and towers reaching almost to the clouds, the whole of the back spread with ivy. As a child, she'd count out each of the twenty great windows and try to guess what might be happening behind the leaded panes of glass, whether the furniture was dancing when they weren't looking. Now she only wondered that about her own room. She knew the house was grandest at the front, with its four main rounded windows and the ornate façade with the handsome carvings over the porch and on the roof. But the back was her favourite, she liked its humbler windows, the chips in the stone.

'Here she is, Mama,' said Emmeline wearily, as they arrived on the lawn in front of the back windows, just at the base of the slope. Closer up, the windows looked slightly fogged around the edges. They'd have to clean them again before the party. The footmen had dragged out a ring of chairs, but only Verena and Rudolf were seated, Rudolf asleep under his hat, legs stretched out in front of him. Michael was lying on a blanket on the grass, staring up at the sky, and a tall man in a boater was sitting next to him.

Arthur was the only one missing, their handsome, know-it-all older brother, in Paris since last year and saying he had no plans to come back. Without him, there was always a quiet spot, a hole where he would have sat in the middle, talked the most. Celia felt ashamed that she didn't miss him, felt relieved not to be on edge from his sharp jokes. Her first memory of Arthur was when she was four, running away as she tried to catch up, laughing and shouting, 'Go away!'

Emmeline swept herself into the empty chair by her mother. 'I found her sitting in the dirt, as usual. No one would believe her fifteen.' Verena tipped her glasses back on her nose and gave Celia a vague smile. She was sitting bolt upright as ever, her long neck extending out of her ruffled white blouse and blue jacket, glasses glittering on her pale nose under her puff of brown hair. *Your mother pays a lot of attention to her clothes*, a woman at a Winterbourne parents' tea party had said to Celia. Verena did. She wore things that didn't match on purpose, combined dark blouses with pale skirts. Rudolf teased her that sometimes she still thought herself dancing as a doll in *Sleeping Beauty*, wanted always to stand out.

Verena had small eyes, like Celia – it was Rudolf who had the great doe eyes Michael and Emmeline had inherited. Wrinkles snaked out from the sides, down her cheeks, up to her ears. When Celia was younger, she'd traced them on her mother's face, drawing a map, touching the soft skin where it dipped and fell. 'You really should not run off so often, Celia.'

The man in the boater stood and made a mock bow. His skin was sunburnt brown, the colour of Michael's shoes.

'Well, hello,' he said. 'You must be Celia. Short for Cordelia, I understand?' His drawling voice sounded so ridiculous that Celia could almost think he'd invented it for effect. 'I'm Jonathan Corrigan.'

'You're Michael's friend from Cambridge, I know,' Celia finished for him. He was so white and blond, the sun behind him so bright that her eyes were watering just from looking at him. 'And no one calls me that name. It's too long.' Verena cleared her throat, her usual signal, and Celia dropped her eyes to her boots. Michael had talked endlessly about Jonathan for the past two weeks: his father's two large homes in Boston, summers by the sea, his house in New York where the buildings were as high as the sky. Before Michael went to Cambridge, Celia had imagined him coming back with friends who looked like him, who would want to talk to her as much as he did: tall, thin young men with glasses and Michael's dark hair, smiles that made their whole faces bright, like his. Michael was clever, shy, sometimes nervous; he bit his nails down so they were ragged and the skin underneath showed, fiddled with his clothes in company. She did not think he would have a friend like Jonathan, with his big round face and smile. Jonathan was like Gwendolyn King at school, the type of person who thought everyone was his friend.

Michael waved his hand. 'Now, sis, be nice. Jonathan has driven all the way from Cambridge in time for the Bank Holiday.' He pulled at his tie, his fingers flickering.

Celia shrugged. *I didn't ask him*, she wanted to say. *I didn't ask him and his buttery smile to come here.* Jonathan was staying for three weeks – almost half her holidays. He would be taking her brother off to walk in the gardens, talk and read, leaving her alone. She hated the fact that men like Jonathan saw a side of Michael she did not. She had hopes – so far secret from her parents – that she would go to Cambridge herself, sit in rooms full of books, discussing ideas with other girls just like her. They would toast muffins by the fire and discuss the philosophy of religion. Then she would go on to Paris, read books about philosophy and be cleverer than any boy.

Jonathan turned to Michael. 'You didn't tell me you had such a pretty younger sister.' He had a thick gold ring on his little finger. Celia had never seen a man wear jewellery.

Emmeline laughed. 'You jest, Mr Corrigan.'

'I'd like to paint you, Miss de Witt, if I might be permitted.'

Celia gave him a polite smile. What was worst of all was that Michael had said to her last week that he might go to America one day. If Michael went to New York on a boat, so far away, he would be surrounded by shops with glass windows, and theatrical shows, and he might never come back.

'I don't know why you fancy yourself a painter,' said Michael, nudging his friend's leg with his hand. 'Shouldn't you stick to poetry? Darned hard enough to do that, if you ask me.'

'If I see something or someone that requires depiction, I do so,' replied Jonathan, his voice sounding more ridiculous to Celia by the minute. 'I'd compose you against the house, Miss de Witt, the large oak tree to your side.'

He gave Celia a wink. She sat down by Michael and looked away, towards the house, hoping that Jonathan would see her eyes watering and so his idea of the portrait would be ruined. Michael nudged her shoulder in the way he always did, their sign of secret friendship amidst it all. Michael's hands had patches of red that flared up from time to time. Verena had said they all had it as babies but Michael worst of all. She had tied his hands together to stop him from scratching.

'How about it?' said Jonathan.

'Celia does not have time to sit for paintings.' Verena's mouth was narrowed, her words taut. 'She has much to do in assisting preparations for the party. She has been given dispensation from her lessons from her tutor in order to help us.'

Jonathan nodded, switched immediately to Verena. 'Of course, Mrs de Witt. The party. Michael promised I'd see a real English village in full swing. That's if he can drag himself away from Professor Punter's reading list. It might just be you and me, Mrs de Witt, if Seneca proves as captivating as usual.'

Celia watched her mother's mouth soften under the light of Jonathan's smile. In the pictures of ships going over the sea she'd seen, there was always a tall man walking with a group of ladies. That was exactly what she could see him doing, striding over the deck every morning, looking forward to arriving in England, where he probably thought people still dressed like they did in the

Queen's time. All the while, Michael was reading, Celia thought, preparing for his meetings with Professor Punter, to sit in his room and discuss great thoughts.

'You certainly shall see an English party,' said Verena, pushing her glasses up her nose. 'If I get these lists completed in time.'

'I do wish you would stop fussing, Mother,' Emmeline said, stretching out her skirts so her shiny boots protruded, her delicate calves almost on show, taking care to look away from Jonathan. 'Every year you get in such a turvy over it all.'

Verena shook her head fondly. 'Dear. You young people think great events arise from nowhere.' She patted her bodice and returned to her lists. Verena had wanted to be a ballerina when she was a child, but grew too quickly, she said, even though they all knew that no girl of her family would have been allowed to flutter her way across a hot stage in front of people of the town. Sometimes, when Celia saw her mother presiding over plans, she tried to think of her as a dancer, directed by a gentleman in a suit, but could not. Everything about Verena was stiff, restrained, as if she were a peg doll grown tall and watchful. 'I have much to do. Especially with Mrs Bell away.' Their housekeeper had gone to visit a niece, whose children had promptly fallen ill with measles. The doctor had told her she must remain with them for at least two weeks.

'Mama, my wedding is more important than a party for the village. Those children throw stones, and their parents only come to pocket as much food as they can.'

Verena did not reply.

'You care more about those children than your own daughter's wedding.' Emmeline tossed her hair. Celia wished she could throw a paper aeroplane at her. For Emmeline, every party list inched her further away from her ideal self, resplendent in ivory silk from Worth, intricate beading billowing out from her tiny waist, a glassy tiara propped over her veil, glimmering with the beautiful future ahead of her.

'It is our duty to entertain the village,' said Rudolf from beneath his hat, the consonants catching on his words.

'Mama! Are you listening to me?'

'Emmeline, your wedding is not for another three months. There is plenty of time.' Verena did not look up. The dark brooch on her lace-covered bosom glinted in the light.

'But you haven't ordered the decorations. I asked you to.' Celia had heard every detail, she thought, a hundred thousand times: the flowers for the church, the tents they would erect across the lawns, the menu of lobster, beef and more ornate cakes than King George V's. For the last six months, Celia had watched Emmeline complain, slam doors and cry about bridesmaids, lace and not having the reception at Claridges. She pinched Michael's knee and he rolled his eyes. Emmeline had threatened that if Arthur didn't come back from Paris, she would go there herself and get him. *Try to be patient, Celia*, Verena sighed when she complained.

Soon, Celia told herself, Emmeline would put on the mauve going-away suit ordered by Verena and take the train to Dover, in order to honeymoon in Paris and the Italian Lakes. She would be Lady Bradshaw and Celia would be free.

'As I said, there is plenty of time.'

'Time I greatly require to save for the expense,' snorted Rudolf from under his hat. They all turned to look at him. 'Celia. Might you go and ask Tom to join us here for tea?'

Verena's voice cooled. 'Dear. Marks needs him in the stables. He is without a second groom.'

'Oh, poor Tom has surely worked sufficiently by now. It is so warm today. Celia, go and ask him.' Celia watched her parents. Tom had come up for tea before, but only when Verena was inside with a headache. She looked at her mother, then her father. She felt their wants tussling over her head. Then her mother sat back and looked at her lists once more. 'Go on, Celia,' said Rudolf.

'You humour her,' said Emmeline. 'She's too old to be playing with the servants.'

Michael propped himself up on his arm. 'Better play with lords, you mean?' His voice caught around the first word. When he was a child, he had had a heavy stutter and Verena and the governesses had practised correct speech with him, over and over again. Still,

Celia heard him reciting at night, bs, rs, ps, stopping and starting for hours.

Emmeline turned to Verena. 'Next thing Father will be inviting Tom Cotton and all his family to sit in the front pew at my wedding.'

'Lord Snootypants might like that,' Celia said, jumping to the side so her sister could not reach her.

Emmeline swung out her hand for Celia's skirts. 'Papa! Did you hear what she said?'

'Oh, leave her be,' said Michael, dropping back to the grass. 'She's right. Sir Hugh detests the fact that he needs our German money, our *canned meat* money, to patch up his precious old pile of a house.'

'Nothing wrong with a bit of canned meat,' said Rudolf. 'We've got a new range in next week, straight from Alsace. Sir Hugh should try some.'

'It might do his pinch nose some good.'

Emmeline struggled to her feet through her tangled skirts. 'You're hateful! Well, when I'm married and living at Callerton Manor, I shall only invite Mama. And if you think I'm going to find a husband for her' – she gestured at Celia – 'you are quite wrong. Just look at her hair! And all that grime under her nails. I would rather die than introduce her to Sir Hugh's friends.'

'Never mind, Emmy,' said Michael. 'We could all turn up as organ grinders and do a German spot at your ball. Crown you the Canned Meat Queen.'

Jonathan spat out a laugh.

'I've had enough,' said Emmeline, her hand on her pink silk hip. 'You can all stay and mock. I'm the only one in this family actually *doing* something. *You* spend more time at Cambridge playing cards than anything else, and heaven only knows what Arthur is doing in France, and Celia looks like a tramp, and nobody cares! Well, I give up on you all!' She turned and hurried up the lawn, stumbling into her skirts.

'Oh, let her go,' said Rudolf to his wife, who was beginning to follow. 'She will cry it out, then Miss Wilton will arrange her hair and it will all be better.' Verena inclined her head, sat down again. Celia watched her sister hurry up towards the house, her shoulders dipped, the thick curl of hair behind her head bobbing in time with her feet. She looked too big for Stoneythorpe already. She could preside over whole ballrooms at Callerton, smiling graciously at queues of Sir Hugh's hunting friends.

'May I go to find Tom now?'

'If you must,' said Verena at the same time as Rudolf smiled and said, 'Right this minute!'

Celia leapt up and hurried away. She could hear Michael shouting that Sir Hugh wanted to wring them dry, declaring that lords and ladies would be nothing in the future. Verena was trying to calm him, Rudolf shrugging it off, Jonathan making some joke about rich Americans.

Secretly, alone, hoping that God could not read her thoughts, Celia sometimes imagined Sir Hugh changing his mind about Emmeline. Then things would go back to how they used to be, and Michael and her father wouldn't be arguing all the time. Then she chastised herself for being cruel to her sister. All Emmeline had ever wanted was to be a society bride.

'The future is a ham in a can!' sang Celia to herself, softly. She had never tasted a de Witt ham. Verena said they were for the poor, and young ladies and gentlemen should never eat them. But Celia followed what her father said about his products and felt a swell of pride every time they used to pass the large advertisement on the boards near the church in Hampstead. 'De Witt, de Witt, keeps you fit,' she sang as she ran.

TWO

Celia ran across the garden, hurried out through the hedge at the side of the lawn, down the dry grass by the willows and cut past the edge of the forest to the stables. She heard the horses first, kicking and whinnying in the heat. She could just see Silver through the door, nuzzling the hay bale. Marks was speaking loudly. A hand hit a flank and she crept closer to the door.

'You staying here, hanging around this lot, wasting yourself.'

'And you'd know.' Tom's voice was high and angry. He'd worked in the stables during his holidays from school for as long as Celia could remember. It was a special school founded by a lord for boys without much money; it took Tom an hour to walk there every morning. In the holidays, he worked at Stoneythorpe to earn the money for his books.

'Your loyalty is old-fashioned, Cotton. You can do better than this.'

'Why should I care what you think?'

She could hear Tom walking towards the door, so she leapt forward and knocked.

'Tom!' she said, entering, seeing both their faces redden. Marks dipped his sunburnt face towards the side of Moonlight, Emmeline's brown mare. Each of the children had their own horse: Moonlight for Emmeline, Red for Arthur, Arrow for Michael, and Celia had Silver. She had ridden Silver for three years now, since she'd been allowed to have a proper-sized horse. She walked over to her stall and held her close. 'Hello, beautiful,' she said. She had ridden her out yesterday, escorted by Tom. Last summer, she and Tom had spent almost every day together after she returned from the Black Forest, when he was not working in the stables. Yesterday morning, he had taken her out into the fields outside

Stoneythorpe, where there had been no one but them. She'd spurred Silver into a gallop and he'd followed her on Red, Arthur's stallion, who needed exercise now his owner was away.

She'd thought the pair of them speeding through the bare grass could be the standard-bearers for a medieval king, hurrying forward to check the land so the soldiers behind could move forward and conquer. She'd hoped, afterwards, that he might have been free so they could go to the pond and look for frogspawn. Last summer they had found piles of the stuff and dropped it into the old stone trough by the back kitchen door. She'd planned out the afternoon, thinking they might beg scraps from Mrs Rolls for a picnic and sit under the trees behind the stables. But he said he had to go back to the horses, and she'd had to wander back to the house alone. This summer, she thought, things were different: she could not always think of what to say to him. Sometimes, words she had thought quite ordinary would make him turn angry and quiet, his eyes smaller, as if they were focusing on arrows sent from far away.

'Did you want a ride, miss?' said Marks, his tone not as polite as his words.

She held Silver tighter. 'No, I'm coming with a message. Tom, Father asks if you can join us for tea.'

'Like this?' He looked down at his dirty breeches. 'I can't.' Marks sniggered.

'I'm sure it won't matter.' Tom always looked smart, the material of his clothes undarned, his shoes without holes. Silver. The horse nuzzled her cheek and Celia wondered if it was possible to love anything more than she did Silver. Papa had taken her to choose a horse at the farm. The minute she'd seen Silver, grey, dappled, she knew she was the one. She had gone to stroke her nose and the horse had shuffled up to be nearer, closed her eyes as if to say *I'm your friend.*

'Better obey the master,' said Marks slyly behind Tom, his bad eye flickering. Celia wished she could push him hard, send his cold smile away.

Tom's mouth twisted. Then he straightened. 'Well, I shall come then. Mrs Rolls will let me wash my hands in her kitchen.'

'Enjoy your silver forks, my lad,' said Marks. 'And you too, my lady.'

Celia kissed Silver's nose. 'I will come and ride you tomorrow,' she whispered, then turned away from Marks and out of the door. A few moments later, Tom came to join her.

'I don't know why Father keeps Marks on,' she said.

'Good with the horses,' he shrugged, looking ahead. His eyes were so pale, they seemed to reflect the air in front of them. When he had arrived, she had been the same height as him. Now he was almost as tall as Michael, able to look down on her. He had grown up in so many other ways. He was sixteen to her fifteen. His skin had lost the spots that had sprouted the previous year, and his face had grown thinner. Tom's great feature was his nose, everyone said that. It wasn't snub like Celia's or too big like Michael's (and Emmeline's, even though she would never admit it). It was what the art history teacher, Miss Quinn, would call a Roman nose. She might want to paint him.

'The horses like you more than Marks. Silver does.'

'I must obey him,' he replied. 'Like you have to obey your father.'

'Emmeline is being terrible about her wedding,' she declared. The forest loomed above them. She never went in there, forbidden by Rudolf. Arthur used to, took two friends from school there years ago; they all came back screaming that they'd seen a ghost.

'You'll be bridesmaid,' he said, smiling.

The sun beamed into her eyes and she covered her forehead. 'I have to.'

'You'll wear orange blossom in your hair and a fancy dress.' He drew his hands to his head, as if there were flowers there.

'The dress is awful.'

'What a pretty girl you'll be. Sir Hugh's friends will think you *quite* the young lady.'

'Stop that!'

She stretched out for him, laughing. He jumped to the side. 'So *ladylike*.' He danced away from her towards the pond. 'Pretty

Celia!' He started to run and she picked up her skirts and hurtled after him. He ran around the tree, laughing, and then into the shrubbery, shouting out all the time. She hurried after him, past the old trees, over the grass, and when they were both breathless he let her catch him and they fell to the ground, laughing. 'Pretty,' he called out one last time. The willow tree over them touched their faces.

'Why don't you write to me when I'm at school?' she said, when they were both lying on the ground.

The leaves cast shapes on his cheeks. 'I wouldn't know what to write.'

'Don't say that. Anything you wrote would interest me. You don't know what it's like there. Day after day of the same thing. It's terrible.' Winterbourne was full of people. Girls, teachers, even gardeners, all of them, everywhere: behind trees, doors, the cupboards of books, all the places she tried to hide.

He turned on to his back, looking up at the sky. 'Those school-marms wouldn't have it, me writing to you.'

'No one would know.' Her voice came out weak. She wouldn't tell the girls at Winterbourne that she was writing to him. She'd once tried to tell Gwen King about him, only for her to laugh that Celia was friends with a *servant*. She wished she could say: *Your father might have died early and then you might be poor too!* But she knew that even if Rudolf died, there would be money for them. She quashed the thought, horrified that she had even considered the idea of his death.

'They'd all know I was writing.'

She squeezed his hand. 'I hate it there. I don't want to go back.'

'Plenty of people wouldn't mind having a good education like that.' Celia blushed. It would be Tom's last year at school and then, he said, he had no idea what he might do; he couldn't go to university. Celia secretly hoped he might work at Stoneythorpe, but she knew that was selfish.

Tom shook his head. 'You're dreaming, miss.' His voice was all sarcasm.

'Don't call me miss.' They'd agreed between them that he would only call her that when there were others around. 'Anyway, it's not the books I mind. It's the girls, the whole place. It smells of fish.' The boarding house was tiny and always dusty, and it was so hard to sleep with the sound of the other girls snuffling and crying around her. Without the English teacher, Miss Lowen, who lent Celia books meant for the sixth formers, Celia thought she might go mad.

'What else do you want? Stay here and have Mr Janus teach you instead?'

'No thank *you*! Mr Janus is dull, he says the same things every day. All he really wants to do is moon after Emmeline.' Pale-haired Mr Janus walked over from Helmingham, the next town. He had been a master at the boys' school there until he had caught a virus that meant he could not get out of bed for weeks. Working with Celia was his steps towards recovery, as Verena put it. He was Celia's first tutor, and she preferred him to the governesses who had gone before – until, that is, he had started following Emmeline around with his eyes.

'Don't let your mother hear you say that. She won't let him back if she thinks he is being disrespectful to the future Lady Hugh.'

'I know, I know.'

Tom got to his feet. 'Well now. In a few years, you can marry like Miss Emmeline herself and then you'll never have to go to school again.'

Celia hit her hand on the grass. 'It is a chain, just like those lady demonstrators say. If you are married, you are your husband's thing; that's why he votes for you.'

'You don't know a thing about politics, Celia.'

'I do! Well, I could if I wanted to.'

'I think your father would be pretty cross if you started burning down tea rooms in Kew Gardens. Or cutting up the paintings in the National Gallery.'

'Well, the King should let ladies vote then.' The women had stepped up their campaign recently, wrapping up bricks in paper, arrested and re-arrested by the police.

'Your father will make you marry, you know that. You're his pet.

He'll have you dressed up in white and being presented by your sister to the Queen before you know it. You'll be deb of the year, like in those magazines.'

'Stop it. You're beastly sometimes, Tom.'

His face clouded. 'Celia, you have to marry. Women must.'

'Women only need husbands if they have babies,' she said stoutly. Marriage, if you asked her, didn't seem to do much that was good. The King and Queen, of course, were very happy, and her parents, but not many other people seemed to be so content. Mrs Cotton was married, and the few times Celia saw her, she saw only unhappiness.

Tom nodded. The sun dropped through the branches on to his face. He hardly ever talked of his mother – and never of his father. She thought: if only I knew the right question, he might tell me. 'Anyway, it was not your mother's fault that your father ran away and deserted her. He was a man of little moral worth, obviously. She married him properly.'

He flushed. 'Yes. Come, your father is expecting us.'

She stood up and squeezed his arm. 'One day he'll come back from far-off lands and you'll be a family again.'

'Celia, let's talk of something else.'

She dusted down her dress, not that it did much good, forced herself to put the subject out of her mind. 'Will you take me riding tomorrow?'

'If Marks says I can.' The rose garden in front of them was hysterical with colour, so much that you'd think it had been daubed all over by a child equipped with a new paintbox. It was a great pond of pinks, yellows and reds. The flowers were curling at the edges, Celia knew. The summer was too hot for them, made them thin, brown, thirsty.

'Life is about improvement,' her father often said. 'The human race must go forward.' When they'd arrived, Verena had applied herself to the grounds, appointing Mr Camlett from London to regulate the overgrown wilderness behind the house with an open array of flowers and ornamental hedges. But even Verena could not turn the grounds of Stoneythorpe into the fantasy of a

Versailles-like eighteenth-century garden, with strips of paving, neat flower beds and rectangles of grass. It was too old, the shrubs were too dug down and Rudolf said he would not disturb the historic plants at the back. Verena had to confine Mr Camlett and his men to the first hundred metres, planting grass and making out paths of small pale stones. Instead of Versailles, a gentle slope led to a perfect lawn, shrubs cut into neat rounds standing like toy soldiers next to the paths, a stone fountain in the middle, fed by a tiny canal coming from the pond behind the trees. Celia thought you could imagine Marie Antoinette walking around it, never even needing to lift up the silk material of her gown. She jumped over the strip of grass that was to her the channel, the break between her garden – overgrown roses, willows and old ponds – and the ornamental perfection of her mother's.

'I'll ask Marks if I can go with you.' Soon, she supposed, she would have to ride side-saddle like a proper lady. Verena was already talking about letting down her skirts. She could not bear the thought of it, the heavy material down to her feet, making it impossible to walk or run or do anything, ever. She wouldn't be able to catch tadpoles with Tom then.

Tom walked ahead. 'No. Celia, don't. He won't like it.'

She shrugged. 'If you say so.' She would ask Rudolf to ask Marks. Then Tom would be allowed.

He smiled at her. 'Are you looking forward to the party?'

'Mama is fussing. I don't know why. It's the same thing every year. Mrs Rolls does it all.'

'You enjoy it. You'll do it yourself when you're a grand madam in charge of a house like this.' They edged past one of Verena's ornamental flower beds. Tom drew his hand lightly over the fountain. 'Even this stone's hot,' he said, absently.

She nudged him. 'I shall go to live in Paris and read books. I told you.' On their last shopping trip to London, she'd bought a copy of a book on dreams by Sigmund Freud by hiding it under a copy of *The Water-Babies*. Some of it did not seem very clear to her, but she was determined to reach the end. 'I shall take an apartment by the river and discuss ideas.' She would find her own

Professor Punter, who would tell her clever things. What was the point of sending her to Winterbourne and hiring Mr Janus (and his predecessors every summer before) if they really only wanted her to get married?

'You'd have to make your own tea if you lived in Paris.'

'I can make tea, thank you.' Although really, she had to admit to herself, she rather hoped that she would be the type of rich lady intellectual who would have everything done for her, so she could think only of books.

'Not once seen you do it.'

'And since when did you know it all?' She hopped over to the other side of the ornamental canal, hoping she sounded brave, hoping he would not dare her to go to the kitchens and show him.

'True. Never.' He nodded, and then stepped back so that she could walk up the path first. 'Looking good, the Hall,' he said.

'Is it?' Celia looked up at the back of the house.

'Your father had the roof done again while you were away. He redid the windows and the guttering. It must have cost him a fortune.'

She gazed at the windows and they did look shinier. 'I suppose it was to impress Sir Hugh. I wish Father would stop building.' As soon as they had moved in, Rudolf had set about what he called modernising the house. He had repainted it, put up new wallpaper and even installed electric lights in the parlour, the dining room and the front hall. Verena, however, tended to decline to turn them on, and the staff were afraid of them – Smithson told Celia that they had heard that an electric light in a house near Winchester had burst and cast yellow stuff all over the entire company under it, and they were burnt quite to a cinder. Rudolf had also recently installed a telephone in a special small booth in the hall, even though no one had yet used it and Verena complained bitterly about the expense. Celia sometimes crept to look at it when nobody else was around. She would pick up the receiver and speak into it. 'Hello,' she whispered. 'Is there anyone there?' The line crackled and fizzed; no one spoke.

'I think the place looks better for all his work. If you've got the money, why not spend it, I say?'

Something caught her heart then, and she could not help herself. She pulled his hand. 'Tom.' She could almost feel urgency flooding between her lips. 'You will never leave. Promise me you won't leave.'

He looked up at the sky, away from her. 'I won't. I don't have anywhere to go. You will, though. You'll go somewhere else.'

'No. Say it to me, promise me. If we leave, we go together.' She stared at the grime on the back of his hand, begging him to answer.

'Life is different for me.'

'What makes you so sure? Please, Tom. Promise me you won't leave.'

He shifted on to the other foot. 'I promise. Things will always stay the same.'

That was enough. She pulled her hand free and took three steps away. 'Race you first!' she cried at him, waving, and then gathered her dress in her hand and began running, hurtling headlong to Stoneythorpe.

Thompson was coming towards them, dragging his bad leg behind him, his souvenir from the Boer War, he said. The rest of the family were no longer sitting at the back of the house. Tom and Celia were running so fast they almost crashed into him.

'Hello, miss,' he said. 'I was looking for you. Your father asked me to tell you. There has been a change. They have returned inside and they are not taking tea.' He looked at Tom. 'He asked me to convey his apologies.'

'What do you mean, there is no tea?'

'That is the case, miss.'

She was about to protest again, but Tom put his hand on her arm. 'Don't, Miss Celia. There is no space for me when Sir Hugh might be near, that is all. It is not Mr Thompson's fault.' His voice was calm but his face was red with fury.

'Why did my father not wait to explain?' Celia demanded. 'It's unfair. He should be here to tell us.'

Tom squeezed her arm harder. 'I'm going back now. Good day, miss. Wishing you a pleasant evening.' She heard the sarcasm in his voice as he turned. She stood next to Thompson and watched Tom run across the lawn to the side exit in the hedge. *I hate Sir Hugh Bradshaw!* she wanted to cry, so loud that the noise bounced around the fountain, echoed as far as the back of the garden.

'What was that you said, miss?' Thompson asked.

'Nothing. You go inside. I will come in one minute.' The windows at the back glittered hard, shining out over the ivy that was already creeping past.

THREE

'I have an announcement,' Rudolf had declared. They had been eating fish in puffed pastry around the heavy table in their Hampstead dining room, five years previously. Celia had been allowed to stay up late to dinner, even though she was only ten. 'I have found us a Jacobean house in Hampshire. In fact, I have told the owner, Lady Lenley, that I wish to buy it.'

Verena dropped her fork. Emmeline shrieked.

'Stoneythorpe Hall is in a beautiful … spot,' Rudolf continued, his words faltering in his excitement. 'It is the house I have always dreamed of. We will be lords and ladies of the manor.'

'I don't want to leave London!' said Emmeline, her handsome face pale in the fog of the table light.

'You will once you see it, dear. I promise.'

'We will never be lords of the manor,' said Arthur from the corner. 'We'll never be anything other than meat sellers.'

'Better a meat seller than a gambling wastrel.' Rudolf patted his stomach. 'People like that can no longer afford such a house.'

'I thought these houses never came on the market. I thought you said you were never going to succeed!' said Emmeline, casting an angry glance at Verena. Rudolf had been searching for a manor house for nearly three years. He had contacted agents in Surrey, Hampshire, Berkshire and Kent, but they always declared they had nothing to sell.

'Stoneythorpe is different. Lady Lenley, the widow of the lord, has no children – and there are none in the extended family who could inherit. The sale will be a quiet one as she does not wish to attract publicity. She desires to meet us first, to decide if she feels able to accept my offer.'

'But—' Verena began.

'I have invited Lady Lenley to tea,' said Rudolf, firmly. 'Three o'clock. I expect us all to be there.'

Lady Lenley did not look to Celia like a lady at all. She was small and bent, dressed in black, her nervous eyes sunk deep into her face. She huddled in the chair and clutched the cup of tea proffered by Violet, the parlourmaid. Rudolf asked her about her journey and she answered in a quavering whisper, as if the very act of speech caused her pain. Rudolf had told Michael and Emmeline to remain silent, and Celia was too young to speak at any visit. Arthur had refused to attend, lolloped out, thin and long-legged, to see a friend from school. Rudolf conducted the conversation; Verena sat beside him, her face stoically composed.

'Do you often come to London?' asked Rudolf.

Lady Lenley's face creased with terror. She shook her head.

'You prefer to stay in Hampshire?'

She nodded and looked at her hands, folded in her lap.

'I thought it a most handsome village. The houses are most excellently kept.'

Lady Lenley looked up and blinked a little, then dropped her gaze.

'The church must be very old,' he tried once more.

She nodded. Silence descended. Violet offered biscuits. Lady Lenley fiddled with her skirt. Michael made a comment about stained glass. No one answered. Verena offered a few words about the village school. Celia watched her father's face redden as he continued to attempt to make conversation, and every attempt failed. Finally, when it seemed to Celia as if there could be nothing more to say, Lady Lenley looked up at Rudolf. 'I am very fond of the garden,' she whispered. 'I have always loved it.'

'But of course, Lady Lenley,' said Rudolf. 'My wife is very fond of gardening too. Are you not, Verena? You direct our current gardeners with great skill.'

Verena gave a frosty smile. 'Very fond.'

Lady Lenley stared at Rudolf and then returned her glance to her hands. 'I would not wish my roses to die.'

Rudolf looked at the window, smiled.

Within a few days of Lady Lenley's visit, the house was a riot of packing. The housekeeper, Mrs Dew, and the butler, Mr Gregory, hurried between the rooms. Verena shut herself in the parlour and emerged only for meals. Mr Gregory and Mrs Mount, the cook, had refused to leave their families in London, and all the lower maids and footmen would never wish to go so far. Verena burst into tears at tea with the strain. 'A whole new staff to be appointed!' she wept on to Emmeline's shoulder. Celia walked downstairs one morning and saw a line of men waiting to be interviewed as their new butler. Letters piled up on the hall table with recommendations of cooks. 'Tom's mother could work for us,' Celia suggested one day. Mrs Cotton had been a parlourmaid for the family but had left before Celia was born, because she was ill, Rudolf had said. Verena turned, her pen poised and directed towards Celia. 'I don't think so, dear.' She shook her head and that was that.

Celia stood at her bedroom window, pretending to dress for Sir Hugh. Just under the ledge, she knew, ivy was creeping thickly over the walls. Every spring, after the house clean, Rudolf would send for twelve men from the village to put up ladders and scramble over the front, trying to cut it back and pull it down. Otherwise, he said, the leaves would work their way into the gaps between the stone, pinching their way into the hollows and forcing the stones loose. For two weeks men tugged and cut and shouted out to each other, throwing great strips of stems on to piles at their feet. The leaves lay confused and browning, ants and spiders clambering through the maze, before the men took the piles to the back of the garden at the end of the day, set them alight and let the flames blaze. After they had finished, for a month or so the pale front of the upper part of the house shone out to the road. The stone looked so painfully naked, with only a few wisps of stems left unbattered by rain, that Celia almost felt she had to avert her eyes coming home. Its clean bareness felt like a challenge: who are you, to live here?

'Stoneythorpe is ours now,' Rudolf had said, when they had drawn up in the car for the first time. 'And when I am dead, it will come to Arthur.' Teams of men had arrived from Winchester to knock out the walls to widen the rooms, install a new kitchen in the basement with a working oven, put in new bathrooms on every floor, and paint and paper over the damp and mould of the walls. Celia stood at her window and watched the carters take away Lady Lenley's Victorian furniture to be burned. The drawing room was covered in silk hangings from London, the dining room decorated with antiques bought from a shop in St James's. Verena instructed workmen to pull down the back wall and replace it with glass doors, so that they could throw them open after parties, she said. Rudolf had even tried to paint the front of the house, but the stone would not take the colour. Now, after five years, he declared himself nearly satisfied.

Celia drew a circle in the mist on the window. She opened the lacquer box on the windowsill, her box of leaves. Every year she had saved a piece of ivy from the cutting-down. She let the leaves dry on her windowsill and then stored them in the box, which Michael had bought her in a market in London. She touched the top one, thinking of how they were like pieces of skin a snake might cast off, dry with months of accumulated life. The oldest was turning into a skeleton, the dried leaf flaking off the intricate frame each time she picked it up.

Verena had to scale back her plans for a Versailles garden in the end for Rudolf couldn't spare the money from his factories. She ruled off the back of the lawn with a hedge, the tiniest of gaps in the centre to allow one person only to pass. Beyond that, the garden billowed, a riot of thorny rose beds flanked by shrubs that not even Mr Camlett recognised, so overgrown that you could not tell where one ended and the next began. The oldest trees Celia had ever seen in a garden grew around it, the bottom of their trunks thick and furled with age. Behind it all was an old pond, with a dried-out fountain in the middle, green and stagnant, the edges untidy with weeds and frizzed with grass, a great willow tree hanging over the water. Verena hated it all; she fenced it off with the hedge and planted trees in front so she would not have to see it from her bedroom. It was like the room with all the broken things in a house, the door you did not open, and it was Celia's favourite place. If she just crept under the willow next to the pond and past the red flowering bush, there was a patch of soil and a rock where she could sit. Even though she had grown two inches since last summer, she could still just about perch herself there without the shrub scratching her eyes. She loved the darkness and the smell of soil, the feeling that what she had was hers alone. In the spring, daffodils flowered next to the stone, and in summer, she watched the violets bud by the moss. She could stay for years, she thought, emerge and still be the same, while everyone else had become aged and grown. When she was younger, she had thought it was a place where fairies played, their tiny feet touching the stones, leaving no trace.

She stared at the leaf in her hand. In the flower press on her windowsill, she had two pansies from her spot in the garden. She had picked them yesterday, delighted by how the more you stared at them, the more it seemed quite amazing how perfectly joined together was the whole thing: stem linked to leaves and petals dropping from their green tip behind. She thought she had never seen anything quite as marvellous as a pansy. She touched the screws on the edge of the flower press. She would just open them, see how it was getting on, even though she knew it would spoil the effect.

There was a heavy knock on the door and Jennie poked her head around. 'Come on, miss! They will all be waiting!' She bustled into the room and started pulling at Celia's dress. 'Sir Hugh will be here in a minute!'

'Is this a German dish?' Sir Hugh poked at the plate in front of him. 'I fail to recognise it.' He sat poker upright, eyes crinkled around his monocle, his moustache quivering as he spoke.

'It is chicken in wine,' Verena replied. 'French influenced.'

'The whole thing tastes German to me. The seasoning is too strong.' His plate was hardly touched. Celia thought he never really ate anything, just pushed the food around almost as if it were poisoned.

Thompson, standing at the side, moved forward, but Verena was quicker. She passed him the gravy boat – the best fine china one. 'Try a little gravy, Sir Hugh.' She had put her hair into a particularly elaborate style. The curls dropped around the diamond earrings that Rudolf had given her for special occasions. Celia looked at the slight quiver in her mouth and knew immediately that her mother wanted to bite her nails.

Sir Hugh nudged the meat with his knife. 'I think the thing cannot be salvaged. Your cook has too heavy a hand.'

Celia hated how Sir Hugh hardly ever called her mother Mrs de Witt. She detested how Verena flurried around him, asking him his opinion, humiliating herself, she thought, in her desperation to please. They all had to agree with whatever Sir Hugh said, as if the King himself was at dinner. Although the King, she thought, would surely be nicer to her father than Sir Hugh was. Sometimes she even yearned for Arthur, who might have been rude to Sir Hugh, laughed in his face as he did to everybody.

She kicked the table. Now she hated Sir Hugh even more. Without him, Tom might have been here.

'Sir Hugh will be your brother,' her mother had said to her once, when she had tried to tell her not to fuss around him so. 'You must learn to love him.'

She tried to write a list of all the things you might like about Sir Hugh, but in the end could only think of two: he was about to marry Emmeline, and he had a large house.

'I find seasoning ruins the flavour of properly good meat. I think it is only intended to cover up the taste of the really poor cut. That is the kind of meat that people put in cans. As your customers find. Disgusting stuff.' He turned to Rudolf. 'I did send you some beef from my estate, did I not?'

'Oh yes,' rushed in Verena. 'It was quite marvellous. We were delighted with it.'

Sir Hugh inclined his head graciously. 'I shall ask Carmichael to send further.'

'That would be so terribly kind of you.' Celia wanted to kick her mother under the table.

They had visited Callerton Manor at the beginning of the year. Celia had hated every moment of it: the preparations, her mother bustling and flurrying, Emmeline vowing never to speak again to Michael if he teased Sir Hugh and despairing over everybody's dress but her own. Then the journey, during which their mother told Celia that if she did not behave, she would not have pudding for two weeks. The huge, cold house had more windows than you could imagine. Stiff servants propped up every corner like vases. They took tea with Sir Hugh's mother, who to Celia looked older than the oak tree in the back garden, staring at everyone through her lorgnette. And then there were hours spent wandering the frosty gardens, Verena cooing over even the tiniest flower bed. Every vowel of Sir Hugh's declamations spoke of his endless family tree, informed them that however many elocution classes they took, they could never make their voices sound like his.

During the visit, Michael kept his head bowed, asked attentive questions of Sir Hugh's mother, winked at Celia when none of them were looking. Then, in June, Rudolf had bought a new Rolls-Royce motor car. He said it was what a man should have for the country lanes. Celia thought he'd bought it to impress Sir Hugh – who had two motor cars, one all the way from France. One afternoon when Rudolf was away, Michael had taken the keys and driven Celia down the lane and out to the village. Then, after she had begged him, they changed places. He showed her how to push down the clutch, set the accelerator. She stopped, started, stopped, started. 'Push that one!' he said. 'More carefully. Think of it like a horse.' She thought of Silver – and then they were away. She was driving, and they were free. 'Let's go to stupid old Callerton Manor!' Michael said. 'Come on, Celia. Turn right!'

She followed his directions, wobbling around until they came round the corner to the great iron gates of Callerton. 'Go faster!' Michael shouted. 'You are a dreary old windbag, Sir Hugh!' he cried. Celia laughed so much she almost took her hands off the wheel. She thought of it, Michael shouting, the wind battering her hair. He hadn't laughed much since then.

'The Callerton game is most superior,' said Emmeline, graciously. Celia had to admit that her sister looked handsome, the jewels in her fair hair glittering in the light, the pink and white of her face set off by the peacock colour of her dress. The shadows from the candlelight made her eyes glow larger than ever. Jonathan, sitting next to her, looked at her, and Celia knew, as if she could read his mind, that he wished to speak to her but thought her too beautiful. Something in her stomach sharpened.

'The news from Europe is shocking,' said Sir Hugh, putting down his knife. He did not wait for a reply. 'The Kaiser continues his aggression. First his man shoots the Archduke and now he threatens Belgium.'

'The shooting had nothing to do with Germany,' said Michael. 'You know it's at Serbia's door.'

'I read that the Archduke was actually sympathetic to the desire of the Bosnian Serbs to rule themselves. Rather ironic,' said Jonathan, smiling, as if he had put an excellent point in a tutorial, Celia thought.

'Poor Emperor Franz Joseph,' Rudolf was shaking his head. 'As if losing a son and a wife was not enough, now his heir.'

Sir Hugh laughed. 'The Austrians deserve no pity. They and the Kaiser go hand in hand to war. Our idiot politicians speak to them in a kindly fashion as if they were babies, while all the while they plan to kill us.'

'You're wrong.' Michael had a heavy scar on his forehead from when he had fallen off a wall as a child. It grew redder and stood out when he was angry. Celia watched it pulse under the skin.

'They are all Bismarck's heirs. Such people will stop at nothing before the entire world is part of Germany.'

'And what qualifies you to state this, sir?'

Verena was staring at Michael, trying to quiet him, but he was looking only at Sir Hugh, his eyes bright with anger.

'Everybody knows it. The Germans shot him, I am certain of it. They will not be content until they have started a war. It's time Mr Asquith stopped dallying and showed them how to behave. Europe is really in a shocking mess. We need to sort it out.'

'We have left the wars behind, thank God,' interrupted Rudolf. 'That was last century. Now what is important is the Irish question. It is uppermost in the mind of Mr Asquith, I am sure.' He spoke with certainty, in the same way he might recite a speech from *Henry V*.

Sir Hugh dropped his face to smirk. Celia blushed at herself for being ashamed of how her father pronounced God as Gott.

Rudolf picked up his fork and set about the meat. 'My dear, remind me that I must write to the managers of my factories in Berlin tomorrow.'

Verena nodded stiffly. Sir Hugh failed to hide another smile. 'It would be so convenient for the Germans who live in England if there was no war,' he said. 'After all, in a conflict, who would they choose?'

Michael thumped his fist on the table. 'We are English, sir.'

Sir Hugh raised an eyebrow. 'Oh, of course.'

'There will be no war,' repeated Rudolf. 'No more. The Queen waged too many.'

'I think a war might be rather exciting,' said Emmeline. 'Shake things up a bit.'

'Everybody was very afraid of British power,' said Celia, remembering Miss Jacques's history lessons at school. She thought of poor Sophie again, her husband, the Archduke, begging her not to die. Why wouldn't Sir Hugh stop? Why was Rudolf letting him continue like this? She wanted to stand up and cry out, *My sister could marry anyone she liked, so we don't need you!*

'Quite so, Miss de Witt. The Germans were particularly afraid of British power. Intimidated, rather. I expect the same is true now,' said Sir Hugh, curling his lip. Michael was almost standing, his face angry. Jonathan watched, his demeanour calm. Celia almost wanted to throw her bread roll at him, as he sat there saving up stories to laugh about with people in New York.

'Now, Michael, let us discuss another subject,' Verena began.

'No, Mother. I shall say it. Our loyalties are to the King. If there was a war, I would join the army. I would sign up to fight as soon as I could.'

Verena's hand was on her mouth. 'You would not. You would not.'

Sir Hugh curled his lip. 'I would like to see that. Anyway, one doubts that the British army would require any further assistance. In this country we do not need men from foreign countries to fight. We have professionals. That is why we win.'

Michael was clasping his knife. Then Jonathan gripped his hand and stood. 'I think us Americans have much to learn from you Europeans,' he said, his voice smooth. 'We have a lot to consider about diplomacy. I am sure the future is one of Europe united.'

'Under Germany, if they get their way,' replied Sir Hugh.

Verena signalled to the footmen and they bent to clear the plates. 'Dessert?' she said, brightly. 'We have jellies. Then let me tell you about our latest plans for the summer party, Sir Hugh. I'm sure it will be our best yet. The village needs a little treat.'

Five years ago, on the drive to Hampshire, Celia had drawn pictures of what Stoneythorpe Hall might look like: castles with turrets, long, flat white houses with no chimneys, big square pale brown boxes with pretty doors, a cottage but ten times larger, one great tower. When they arrived at the top of the long drive, the house looked nothing like her drawings. It was huge and heavy, red ornamental stone flanking the great pale doorway and carved porch. The two front wings were set forward from the door, the windows drew up to three triangular gables on the roof, the chimneys over it all. The windows were cracked, trees straggly. The place looked old and untidy – and, to her, beautiful.

'This is a manor?' said Emmeline beside her. 'And we left London for this? Where am I supposed to wear my gowns?' Arthur was laughing behind his hand.

'It was built in the seventeenth century for the earl at the time,' said their father. 'It was a great house in the local area. The land even features in the Domesday Book. You will be impressed when you enter, my dear.' The Lenley family had been the wealthy associates of royals from the thirteenth century, Rudolf said, but they became most powerful under Elizabeth I, and bought this great estate to celebrate. The Queen had visited once for hunting. 'Imagine, Emmeline,' he said. 'Elizabeth I came here on a progress.' Emmeline kicked her heels on the floor of the car.

Rudolf often told them that he had come over to London from Berlin as a young man to make his fortune – and because he had read so many English books. In his twenties, he said, he could recite every word of Shakespeare's most famous works. He called his first son after a king, his youngest daughter after a heroine in Shakespeare. Verena chose the names of the middle two to be modern. From the beginning, Rudolf told his family, he knew that he had to fit in by pretending he had forgotten everything about Germany: the flecks on the alphabet, trams in Berlin, freezing snow at Christmas, slow boats on the Rhine. People were unforgiving of such things, and if you let the memory of past places remain, you could never escape. He threw his precious copy of Goethe from the boat on the way over. Verena had instructed the children from very young that they must not tell him that his accent retained Germanic inflections and always betrayed him: the quick endings of words and the tripping around 't' and 'd'.

'I am more English than the English,' he was fond of saying in Hampstead, as he stepped out to his club in his neat suit, hat and silver-tipped walking stick, returning in the evening to his fireside surrounded by prints of the countryside. They lived on the same road as that great English poet, John Keats, after all. Rudolf was always proud of the fact that he never grew fat, like some meat dealers did. 'The Englishman keeps his figure.' He said that if you kept yourself quick and upright, life would not catch you.

After the first journey there, Emmeline's lip quivered as she gazed at the front of Stoneythorpe Hall. 'I won't go in.'

Celia did. In those days, Emmeline and their mother complained almost daily about poor plumbing, holes between the bricks, cracks in the floorboards, the birds in the roof. Celia saw Stoneythorpe for what it really was: the grand house she had read of in her books about princesses. She loved everything about it: the unkempt grounds, the stone drive. She begged her father not to change it.

On the day of their arrival, Celia had hurtled ahead of the others so that she could enter Stoneythorpe first. She stood in the hall and then began running down the corridor to the side, into the two large rooms to the left, and up the stairs. She wanted to see and touch all the rooms before anybody else did. She hurried into every bedroom, sped back down the stairs, and pushed past her mother to run into the kitchen.

'Have you found the library yet, Celia?' said her father as she ran breathless to the top of the stairs. 'Turn right, then left and it's at the end of the corridor.' She dashed off again, following his directions, and reached a heavy dark door. She turned the stiff key and pushed it open. Inside were more books than she had ever seen in her life. Red, brown, blue spines were everywhere, across the walls, in piles up to the ceiling, stacked on the desks. She could not credit that Lady Lenley might not have wanted some of them. She walked up to the shelves and touched the leather. She moved her hand over the desk in the corner, too in awe to seat herself in the chair. Her father had been right. Stoneythorpe was perfect. She threw out her arms and twirled in front of the leaded window, catching the last light of the sun.

The party had been Rudolf's idea. They had been living at Stoneythorpe for about two months, not successfully. The villagers shuffled past them without bowing or smiling, they were ignored at church, addressed peremptorily even by the vicar, unable to find servants without paying nearly one and a half times the given wage, distrusted. 'They hate us because we're German,' sniffed Emmeline, often. 'Why can't we go back to London?' Michael stayed in his room, reading, and Arthur shot birds in the garden, even when Rudolf told him not to. Verena began to cry in the mornings once more.

'I have a solution,' Rudolf had said. 'Your mother and I will host a party for the village. Everyone will come.' He meant Eversley as well as Bramshill and all the little clusters of houses in between. It would be a great celebration.

For the next four weeks, the house was a flurry of activity and planning. The servants brought in furniture and the new cook, Mrs Rolls, was put to work on cakes and pastries. Verena fussed over the arrangements and table settings. The day began with cloud but then the sun broke out, everyone in the village arrived and the grounds filled with children. Even Arthur played ring o' roses with the little ones.

'We shall do this every year,' said Rudolf, surveying the detritus of cakes and food on the tables, hands on hips, pleased with his plan. In the village, people bowed to them, and they were greeted by the vicar, who ushered them to the front pew in the church. *Lords and ladies.*

The jellies glistened green and pink in their glasses. Celia took a small bite, unconvinced by Verena's plan of combining gooseberry and raspberry in the same glass. Rudolf ate noisily, clanking his cutlery on his glass. Verena was talking about the roof of the village church. Emmeline was stroking the top of her dessert with her spoon, not eating it. Celia looked up idly and gazed straight into Sir Hugh's face. She started, for something seemed to change in his mouth; it twisted, opened.

'You, sir.' He turned his attention to Rudolf. 'You support the Kaiser?'

Rudolf looked up from scraping the last spots of jelly from the glass. He pondered. 'Well, Sir Hugh, I do not give much thought to politics.'

'In other words, you do. You support the most evil man in Europe. It's something in the German character, if you ask me. I've never met a German who was not motivated by greed.'

Michael was struggling to his feet again. Jonathan was pulling him down.

'There are many good Germans,' said Rudolf.

'And a lot of power-hungry ones who will stop at nothing. We'll be at war in a month. And we'll watch the Germans die in shame.'

Michael shook free of Jonathan's grip and darted around the table. In a second, he was standing over Sir Hugh, grasping his clothes, Jonathan shouting at him to stop. Emmeline started from her chair and stood frozen against the wall. And then Thompson stepped forward and was trying to prise Michael's hands away when Sir Hugh sprang up and grasped Thompson's hair. 'You're nothing but a servant!' he was shouting. 'How dare you touch me?' Smithson leapt forward. Thompson turned.

No one could agree what happened next. Emmeline and Verena thought Thompson was about to punch Sir Hugh; Celia and Rudolf thought he put up his hand to defend himself. They were saved a fight: Jonathan ran around the table, threw Thompson aside and managed to get his arms around Sir Hugh.

'This has got to stop!' he said.

Sir Hugh looked at them all, his hair across his forehead, his face red and angry. 'I am at a loss why I ever came here.' He coughed for breath, holding his chest. 'You are below my observation.' He looked over at Emmeline, who was still standing against the wall. 'I am most sorry for you, Miss de Witt. You seem like a pleasant young lady, caught in a disgraceful family. I wish you goodbye. The rest of you are no better than animals.'

He turned and left the room. Smithson hurried after him

Emmeline looked around the table and burst into tears. She swept her hand out and her jelly glass fell to the floor. 'What have you done?' She ran around them and out of the door. Rudolf started up.

'Leave her,' said Verena. 'Leave her to weep. Sir Hugh will return. It is just a little disagreement.'

Rudolf looked over at Jonathan. 'I apologise, Mr Corrigan.'

Jonathan shook his head, still standing over by Thompson. 'Nothing to apologise for.'

Verena sat up very straight. 'Thompson, I suggest you depart this instant.' He nodded and turned to leave the room, dragging his leg so painfully that Celia could not watch.

Rudolf dropped his head into his hands.

'I'm going to bed,' said Celia. She left the table without asking and strode past them all, trying to walk tall when she wanted to sink into the floor. She could not bear to stay in the house a single moment longer. She crept down the corridor and out of the back door by the servants' quarters. Emmeline's voice echoed behind her. She hurried out into the garden.

The air was cool on her face and arms. She sat for a while, just letting it drift over her. The same air that they would have breathed a hundred, two hundred years ago. The trees were sweeping the water of the pond, gently. There was no other noise. She began to walk towards her spot under the willow.

Behind her, the lights of Stoneythorpe Hall glittered through the darkness. Her parents would be moving about inside, talking over the evening as her mother poured her father a glass of brandy. Rudolf would be saying that it would come to nothing, as he always did. She walked on.

The garden looked like a different thing at night, cool and angry, the magnolias and roses showing spots of colour through the gloom, the grass shimmering with rain. There was something magical about it. By day, it was a neatly trimmed piece of grass, edged with her mother's prize flowers – hydrangeas, rhododendrons, camellias. At night, it erupted into disorder. The flowers grew greater and stranger, the trees bent and strained towards the moon, the shot light of the stars picked out cruel veins of colour on the petals. If you stayed there too long, Celia imagined, it would capture you and turn you into something. At night, the rockery where she sat sedately watching Michael play cricket became a stage where goblins might dance when no one was looking. The fairies hid from her, peeking through the trees, their eyes sparkling like beads. The flowers bent to stare at her, the roses clattered up to the sun and laughed. The insects crawled out from under their stones and grew large. She crept around, quietly.

Even though she knew she was too old, she hoped to catch an unsuspecting fairy. If she caught one, it would grant her wish. For things never to change.

'Well, hello there.'

She looked up at Jonathan's face in the darkness. 'What are you doing here?'

'Taking a little air. Like you, I imagine.'

'Don't you get air in America?' She could not help being rude to him. The little smile he wore was infuriating.

'Oh, plenty. But I wanted to try some English air. Perhaps you could guide me as to where it might be best?' The leaves on the trees behind them played in the breeze. 'Or the stars? They look different here somehow. I am sure you know a lot about the stars.'

'Why don't you look somewhere else? Haven't you seen enough of our family already?' He had to move first. If she went towards her dell, he would know all about it. If she walked away, he might pull aside the tree and see it for himself.

'Oh, that's forgotten. These things happen. Sure he'll come back for as fine a girl as your sister.'

'I wish they wouldn't let him in.'

'They want your sister to make a good marriage, I can see that. He's a man of great status.'

'Still, he expects Papa to give him thousands. I've heard the discussions.'

'I think that's the way it works.'

'I wish ...' She could not say it.

Jonathan's cigarette burned in the darkness. 'It's not easy being the youngest, is it? Everyone growing up around you.'

'I like being the youngest. I just wish they weren't always so eager to please Sir Hugh.'

'People are nice to you in life if you are rich.'

'But he is horrid to everyone.'

'A girl like your sister needs a rich husband.'

Celia felt the grass dampening her feet through her shoes. 'I wish Michael wouldn't talk about fighting. Does he talk like this at college?'

'Not really. No more than the rest of them. He's doing it more now. Maybe they all are. I suppose you're out here to think. I hear you're a great reader?'

She knew he was trying to change the subject. She wouldn't answer.

'I'm fond of books myself.' He came a little closer. 'When I was your age, I was always reading. My father said no to novels and poetry. He allowed only biographies and serious works of history.' His ring gleamed as he waved his hand.

She shrugged her shoulders. Her parents let her read what she liked. 'At least it keeps her quiet,' Verena said.

'You are named after a very wise heroine, you know. You should use your full name sometimes, don't you think? Cordelia is very pretty.'

'It's too long.' She waited for him to describe the play. That was the most wearisome thing about her name: that people would always keep telling her the story of 'King Lear'. *Noble Cordelia*, they would say, *standing by her principles. Well, I'm not like her,* she wanted to cry. *I don't even know who I am yet. My father simply chose the name because he no longer wished to be German.*

Go on, she willed Jonathan Corrigan. *Tell me about Goneril and Regan.*

He did not. 'Michael is always talking about you at college, you know. He's very fond of you.'

She started and blushed a little at the thought of those fine young men who took boats on the river discussing her.

'I don't have a kid sister,' he continued. 'I always wanted one. It's just me and my dad in my big old house. I'm the youngest, like you. My brother and sister are miles away. I envy you de Witts, always together. Almost the first thing Michael said when I met him was how close he was to his family.'

She nodded. She wasn't going to tell him that she dreamt of there just being Michael, Tom and her, without Emmeline, or Arthur, who was even worse than Emmeline.

'Bet you miss your big brother,' he said, as if reading her mind.

'Arthur? Yes.' *No. Not at all.* 'He's in Paris.' At least Emmeline was just rude with words. Even at the farewell dinner they'd had for Arthur in February, he'd teased her and pulled her hair. She'd turned on him, said, 'You won't see me for a long time. Why can't you just be nice to me?' He'd only laughed.

'You should go and visit him. Wouldn't you like Paris?'

'You should go and talk to Emmeline,' she said. She knew she was being rude.

He shrugged and winked. 'Your sister's not my style of broad. Too showy.'

She knew that he wanted her to say, *What is your type of girl?* 'Arthur and Emmeline got all the looks.' She walked on, but he followed her. His cigarette had gone out. He took out some matches, relit it. The end flamed and subsided.

'Such a beautiful place you have here. So much green, it's almost indecent. You know, every time I look out of my window, it's as if time has stopped. The whole place is like it must have been in Tudor times. When I arrived in London, I couldn't believe it. All those houses crammed together. All the rooms are so tiny. It's one big museum, this country.'

She stepped aside to avoid a snail crawling along the grass, its white trail glittering in the moonlight. 'Papa says America isn't up to much. He says it's just full of advertisements.'

'Perhaps you should come see for yourself.'

She shook her head. 'I wouldn't like it.'

'I'd show you around.' He gave her a smile, and looked so sure of himself that she felt even more annoyed. 'Americans,' her father had tutted. 'They are coming to take over.' One of his friends had already received offers for his factory. 'They think they can buy everything with their dollars.'

She wanted to walk in the garden alone. She wanted to find Tom, even though Verena would never allow it. 'I've much better places to go than America.'

He drew on his cigarette again, blew out the smoke. 'Your brother told me that you had spirit.' He said something so quietly she barely caught it – *Little German fräulein!* – then, in a moment that she could hardly comprehend, he swooped down. She had no idea what was happening, and her body was not her own – and he was kissing her. She felt herself stiffen and then grow loose. He drew away and she stared at him.

'I wasn't sure I would have another chance,' he said. 'I leave early tomorrow. With everything that is blowing up in Europe, my uncle would expect me back in New York. I should go before he summons me.'

'What are you doing?' she said, brushing off his words. No one had kissed her before. She had heard some of the girls at school say that you should never let a man near you, and if you did, you would be cast out. She tried to say it, stammered and blushed. 'It's wrong.'

His face changed in the darkness. 'I'm sorry. I shouldn't have. I didn't think. Please, Celia. Forgive me.'

The stars were hanging too low, scraping the trees. 'I don't understand.'

'Celia, I'm sorry. I don't know – I didn't mean it. It was just that … you looked so pretty in the light. I wasn't thinking.'

'You want to ask me not to tell my parents, don't you?'

'I'm sorry, Celia, I shouldn't have. May I walk with you back to the house?'

She shook her head. 'I want to stay here.'

'On your own? You sure it's safe?'

She stared at him, saw him blush through the gloom. 'Sorry.' He hesitated for a moment, and then turned to walk up the hill. 'Sleep well, Celia.' He looked at her; she thought he was hoping she would say something. She did not, and he turned away.

She watched him saunter towards the house. As soon as she knew he was far enough, she ducked under the tree and huddled on to her stone. But it was not as it had always been before. The leaves above her mocked, the stone below her was shifting. The blackness did not feel comforting. *How could this have happened?* she wanted to say. How could Michael's friend have seized her and kissed her like this when she didn't even like him? Everything had been sent the wrong way: the arguing, Michael being so strange, now this kissing in the garden. Last year, she had felt she was in a sort of sleepwalk, that the small things around her were nothing compared to the greatness of what she expected to happen. Now, things were beginning – and she wanted them to stop.

A loud shriek from a fox at the end of the garden made her start, and her head turned. It was no use. She stood, bending to avoid the tree, and made her way back into the garden. Outside her dell, she waited for a moment and looked up towards her room. All at once, it was terrifying. The dark trees were looming, the grass was long and threatening and there were strange shadows in the clouds. She was convinced there was someone in the trees. Someone watching her. She picked up her skirts and ran towards the house, praying that she was leaving the dark shadows and the monsters behind her. Her mind careened with images. Jonathan putting his hand out for her, the smoke winding up into the night. She looked towards Stoneythorpe, hoping it would open its arms and let her in, like she was a little girl. But it stayed dark, unseeing, even though she was waving, running towards it, holding up her arms.

FOUR

—◦—

'I shall go to London tomorrow to discuss my trip to the Berlin factories,' Rudolf was saying as Celia walked into the breakfast room. No one else was there but her mother. Celia sent a prayer of thanks and seated herself at the table. 'I have been meaning to visit for some time, and now, with these concerning events, matters seem more pressing. Mr Lewis tells me the London Stock Exchange continues closed. We need to plan business for when the Bank re-opens on Tuesday.'

'My dear, I hardly think it the time,' murmured Verena. Celia reached for a piece of toast.

'I stand by what I said last night. This assassination will lead to nothing. But still, if it does, surely now is the time for me to travel, before anything that might occur. As I was already going to meet Lord Smith about our contract, it seems an opportune time to investigate a visit to Berlin.'

Verena fingered her teacup. 'You must wait until after the party, at least.'

'Of course, my dear. But the party is in two days. Then I shall go to Germany. We must look at every situation. If there is to be a conflict, we may be of use. Armies need feeding, after all – and what could be more ideal than canned meat?'

'Arthur should come home,' Verena said. 'He should come home tomorrow. I shall write to him. France might be dangerous.'

'Could I come with you to Germany, Papa?' asked Celia. Away from Jonathan and Emmeline and all of them.

'Of course not. What an idea.'

'We didn't see Hilde and Johann this year.'

'Next year. Anyway, you're needed here. You should help your mother.' Celia kicked the table, hard. Rudolf turned to Verena.

'My dear, I shall discuss it with the managers. But I feel it is imperative that I go.'

'Michael could go in your place, dear. I am sure he could be an ambassador for you.'

Rudolf applied himself to his egg. 'Perhaps. But at present I am in charge and it is my responsibility. Michael has his studies. I shall go.' He put his hand on the table. It was his signal: the conversation was at an end. Celia watched her mother's fingers flurry at the side of her plate.

'Is Emmeline still asleep, Mama?'

'Poor girl is exhausted after last night,' said Verena.

'Ah, love is tiring to the young,' said Rudolf. 'He will return today with apologies for all of us and devotion for my beautiful daughter.'

Verena raised an eyebrow. 'He was very unhappy in his words last night, husband.'

'I am sure he is sorry. He knows we have nothing to do with the Kaiser. And he loves Emmeline and wishes to marry her. You have often said that the British aristocracy are very eccentric. What about your own departed cousin who used to roll in the mud at the lake every morning?'

'He did, that is true. I hope you are correct, husband. It was an ugly scene.'

'All forgotten. I shall speak to him about it, offer something to make amends.'

'Where are Michael and Jonathan?' asked Celia.

'Still in bed too, I think.'

'You are my little early riser,' said Rudolf.

'Jonathan has not gone?' she asked, unable to help herself.

Verena shook her head. 'Why would he be gone?'

She ducked to hide the blush. 'I thought I heard him say it, that's all.'

Verena passed the toast to her husband. 'No, no, Celia. He remains. After all, we are to show him a proper English village party. He has volunteered to give out the prizes.' She gazed at Celia. 'It would be terrible if he had gone. Do not say such things.'

Her eyes were glassy. Celia kicked herself inwardly for touching her mother's nerves, letting the butterfly of uncertainty flutter around her heart. She hated it when her mother asked her begging questions, more frequent recently. *What did I do wrong? Mother told me I would be a great hostess.*

'The first encounter between the village and an American,' said Rudolf. 'It might be almost as stimulating as their first meeting with a German.'

Verena put her hand over Rudolf's. 'How lucky they are.'

'May I leave the table?' Verena nodded and Celia hopped down. If she went upstairs, she might encounter Jonathan coming to breakfast. She turned around and headed down the hallway. Her heart was full of confusion and fear. Everything from the night before was mixed up – the argument with Sir Hugh, the fight, the darkness, Jonathan reaching out for her and the movement of his mouth on hers.

I leave early tomorrow, he'd said. That morning she'd been eager to dress herself before Miss Wilton arrived and began pushing and pulling at her, trying to force her waist into looking like that of a proper young lady, as she said every time. She didn't want her coming close, as if what had happened last night was still there, somewhere on her skin. She tugged her hair into a bun, pulled on her boots and was just opening the door when Miss Wilton entered, as grey-faced and cross-looking as ever. Celia thought she looked like one of those long pointed shells you picked up on the beach, spiky. On Celia's thirteenth birthday, Verena had told her that Miss Wilton would be dressing her and doing her hair every morning, and sometimes in the evening if there was an event.

'Surely she has enough to do with you and Emmeline?' Celia ventured. Verena didn't reply and so she tried again. 'I think she'd prefer to be just your maid.'

'You're growing up, Celia,' said her mother, absently. Ever since then, Miss Wilton had wrestled with Celia's tangled hair, tugged her skewed buttons and hems as Celia watched the clock, desperate for her to depart.

'I'm already dressed, thank you,' she said this time, hurriedly.

Miss Wilton raised an eyebrow. 'So I see.'

'I prefer to dress myself. You can go back to fixing Mama's gown for the party or whatever you were doing.'

Miss Wilton nodded her small head. 'Don't mind if I do return. I have six gowns to alter.'

'I'll wait here.' Miss Wilton had brushed past her, the musty smell of her black dress filling Celia's nostrils. She had remained upstairs in her room until she was sure Jonathan must have gone and it was safe to come down, and still she had been first to breakfast. Surely he would have said farewell to her parents if he had left, so he must *still be in the house*. She hurried off towards the garden. He wouldn't hunt her out there a second time.

She rushed past the women from the village scrubbing at the windows and the floor, supervised by Jennie, and pushed open the glass doors into the garden. Thompson and Smithson had already been there, marking out where they would put the tables and the sections for children's play. Mr Vine was scaling it out by paces, his head bent in concentration. She ran down the lawn, turned and gazed at the house, forcing herself not to look at Jonathan's window. She could just see her mother and father in the breakfast room. Rudolf rose, patted Verena's shoulder and left the room. Her mother looked down again – presumably at her lists.

Celia ambled through the garden, past the markings for the placements for the party, thinking vaguely of how Rudolf might let her hand out a few prizes this year, or even oversee the cricket match.

And then her heart jolted. Jonathan had rushed out and was running, on the far side of the lawn, heading to the house. He had been in her spot, behind the hedge.

She hurried down, cut through the opening in the hedge. Had he been waiting there for her? 'Morning, Celia.' Michael was standing by the pond. He gestured to his cigarette. 'Don't tell Mama.' His hands were always worse in the summer; the sun made the bitten flesh flame even redder.

'Was that Jonathan?' She heard his voice in her head. *Well, hello there.*

Michael did not reply, turned his gaze back to the dried-up fountain.

'When did you start smoking?'

He kicked at a leaf on the ground, avoiding her eyes. 'All the chaps do at college.'

'Can I try?' She wished she could put her hand in his as she had done when she was a child. He used to help her play with her dolls. They had once set up a whole hospital in his room at Hampstead.

'Of course not.'

'I'll tell Mama.'

He glanced up at her and smiled, crinkling his eyes and looking more handsome than ever. 'Don't try it.'

'Mama would forgive you anything.' Michael was everyone's favourite now, that she knew. *My son attends Magdalene College. He has a scholarship*, Rudolf boasted to those men in business who looked down on him for not having a degree. Celia watched her parents' eyes follow Michael out of rooms when they did not do the same for her any more, or Emmeline or Arthur. She had vowed that if she had children, she would not have a favourite. But, then, she knew, if she had four children like them, she would like Michael best. He was the kindest and most interesting person she'd ever met. She felt so fortunate to be his sister – and she hated Cambridge for taking him away.

She watched the grey mist curve up into the sky. 'Does it feel nice to smoke?'

'Sometimes.'

'You're sad.'

'Do you know,' he said, 'where the word "toady" comes from? You would think it's because a man has to suck up, like a toad. But it's not that. It comes from "toad eater", a job. Professor Punter told us. In the seventeenth century, the pedlars who toured the country used toad eaters to sell their wares. When the pedlar had his crowd assembled, the man would eat a toad and then fall to the floor, quivering with poison. The quack would cure him with his potion – and sell bottles to the village. An advertisement. Imagine that. Paid to eat poison every day. To be reviled by everyone.' He scratched at his hand, reached up under the cuff to rub at the parts of it hidden by his sleeve.

'I didn't know that.'

'Dying and reviving every day.' He puffed again. 'Jonathan's going to London. We've just had an argument.'

'For how long?' She hoped there was no expression showing on her face.

He shrugged. 'Don't know when he's coming back.' He bit savagely at his thumbnail.

'He's leaving now?'

'So he says.'

'You could stop him, couldn't you?' She said it reluctantly, for the last thing she wanted was Jonathan hanging around. But Michael's face was so sad, she could not help it. 'Go and say you are sorry.'

'We argued about the war. I can't take back what I said. It's not just about German aggression.'

'Oh well. Maybe he was going anyway.'

'Last night was awful too. I don't regret what I said, not at all, but I wish I hadn't done it like that. I wish I'd taken Sir Hugh out, spoken to him like a man.' He blew out more smoke. 'Jonathan's a great chap at college, Ceels. Everyone thinks him splendid. I was pretty taken aback when he picked me out as a friend. He could choose anyone.' He held one hand with the other, and she knew he was trying to stop himself pulling at his fingernail.

'So could you!' She thought of the pair of them, wandering out on to the college lawn, books under their arms, joining in with games of croquet. The sun broke out over their heads and glittered on their hands.

He shook his head. 'You're kind to me, Ceels. Now I think he's changed his mind. Something about us he doesn't like.'

No, she wanted to say, gripping his hand. *He said it was about Europe. And then he kissed me. Why did he do that?*

'Let's walk a while,' Michael said. He offered his arm, and she took it as if she was a real lady.

'I was glad you shouted at Sir Hugh, though,' she said. 'He's awful.'

She expected him to laugh, but he did not. 'Emmeline's very unhappy.'

'It was his fault. He wanted someone to shout at him.'

'Maybe.'

He fell silent again. They walked on. A year ago, he had allowed her to visit him in Cambridge, staying with a friend of Verena's who lived near the station. Celia had thought she had never been happier. He took her for tea and to the covered market in the city. There was a shop there selling fine hats in which sewing women sat in the window, just as they had done hundreds of years ago. She'd admired the young ladies walking to lectures with armfuls of books; promised herself that she would one day do the same.

'How many children do you think we will get this year?'

'Who knows?'

'I think more than ever. Forty, fifty?'

He shrugged and they walked on. She wanted to go back to the house, forget she had ever seen him.

'You know there won't be a war,' she said. 'It's all talk.'

'More's the shame.'

'Peace is better.'

'What is the use of a man if he cannot defend his country, does not fight?'

She smiled at him but he did not look up. His face was still furious.

'Would you play going to Paris with me?' Last summer, it had been her favourite game with Michael. They'd both pretended to be writers living in Paris, walking along, discussing the latest theories. Exactly the opposite of what they knew Arthur would be doing. Sometimes they would discuss the founding of the world.

'No. I don't much like that game any more.'

'Desert explorers, then.' That had used to be his favourite.

'We are too old for that.' He turned to the house. 'I'm going in now. I shall see you later, Celia.'

Please, she wanted to cry out after him. *Please come back.*

She stood for a while, watching him. *Will I be less lonely as a grown-up?* she wondered. But who could tell her? She brushed the grass off her skirts and began to follow him back to the house. Just at the brink, he cut off to the side, as if to walk around to the front. She watched him go, wishing she could follow. He didn't want her with him, and anyway, she was not allowed around the front of the house without permission, not until she was eighteen, Rudolf had said.

'So you were right, young lady,' said Verena, as she walked into the front room. 'Jonathan has gone. He said goodbye just now; apparently his uncle requires him. How did you know?'

Celia blushed. 'It was a lucky guess, Mama.'

Verena's face was pained. 'But why would he leave? We were planning a party.' Celia could not bear to look at the hurt etched on her face. She had been so proud that Michael had finally brought home a friend.

'Well, as he said, his uncle, I suppose. I think the situation in Europe or something like that.' Celia blushed again, hard.

'But what have we to do with that? I don't understand.' Verena shook her head, and Celia saw the nerves fluttering over her skin. 'You know, dear, I wish you would invite girls from Winterbourne to stay in the holidays.'

'They are always away, in places like France and Switzerland,' Celia lied. Really, she did not want Gertie or Gwen King or anyone like them at Stoneythorpe, fingering and mocking her books, wanting to ride Silver. Verena wished her to make friends so she could stay with them, meet their brothers and then one day find a husband. But Celia didn't want to pass the summers in their houses. She wanted to be at Stoneythorpe, with Tom.

Verena touched her hair. 'I just don't understand why Jonathan would leave so suddenly.' *I don't know*, Celia wanted to cry. *You're*

53

the mother! I wish we could go back to the days when you were all powerful, knew everything.

As if she had heard, Verena snapped tall. 'Anyway, I have a task for you. I'm sending Thompson to town to collect some more elaborate gifts. He was supposed to be wrapping the presents for the lucky dip today. I wondered if you might do it?'

'Of course!'

Verena ushered her to the parlour, where there was a pile of presents and some crackled tissue paper and ribbon. 'Do be careful. I asked Emmeline but she has the dressmaker with her.' She picked up a box of sweets and wrapped it in paper and ribbon, showing Celia how to tie the neat bow on the top.

There was a knock, and Smithson appeared at the door. 'Madam, Miss Wilton wishes to discuss a matter with you.'

Verena sighed. 'It is impossible. I simply cannot settle to anything. Now, Celia, do try to leave them looking tidy. I'm trusting you.'

She shut the door behind her. *Don't think of Jonathan,* Celia told herself. *Think about something else!*

Celia's father liked to tell them, usually at Christmas and on her mother's birthday, about how hard he had tried to gain Verena's affections. They had met at a ball, and Rudolf had gone to visit her family every Wednesday afternoon in London, and then followed them to Norfolk.

'Your mother was the girl for me,' he was fond of saying. 'I simply had to persuade her. Lady Deerhurst said to me, "I have not spent years on my daughter's education and finished her in Paris, only for her to marry into canned meat!" But I knew I would win them all round in the end.' Celia had seen a daguerreotype of her mother as a bride, delicate and smiling, her hair a great nest on her head. 'Well,' Verena said once, 'the pictures make it look more dignified. Cousin Sarah had a cold and sniffed all the way through the ceremony and the photographs. And my corset was so tight I could barely breathe.'

Last time they had visited Grandmother Deerhurst had been two years ago, in the little house she lived in near the estate. There had been many more photographs of Celia's English cousins, Matthew and Louisa, than of the de Witts. Verena had complained and asked what was wrong with her children. Since then Lady Deerhurst had not issued any invitations. Verena shrugged and said she was too angry about the Kaiser and would get over it one day.

Grandmother Deerhurst was tall and stern, her bosom jangling with jet beads. When she spoke to Celia, she looked at her through an eyeglass and talked thinly of the different dress of girls in her day. Celia could not imagine her being won round. But then she could not imagine her mother or father as young as she was – or her father ever having to fight for anything.

'I think my mother believed Papa was going to whip me away to Germany and I would never return,' said Verena, smiling. Celia thought that her mother liked that, the idea of being taken away entirely. And yet she did return, numerous times, for Verena often mentioned the Deerhursts, meeting the Queen as a debutante, reminding them that she was an aristocrat. When Sir Hugh proposed, she had said to them all at the table, 'He saw the *right blood*, that is it.'

Celia sat on the floor. She took the crackled tissue paper and the ribbon and began sorting through the presents. There were cones of sweets, boxes of nuts, two little brown bears, a skipping rope, a wooden top and stick. For one lucky boy there was a toy train engine, and for one girl a large china doll with yellow hair and a green silk dress and hat. Celia held her out of her box, against the light, decided to wrap her up last. 'You will be Belinda,' she said, under her breath. 'And Missy Cotton will take you.'

She longed to meet Tom's sisters; Missy, six, and Mary, who was fourteen and – Tom said – fond of her own way. But Tom refused to bring them to the house and they had never come to the summer party. Michael had pointed out their house in the village once, but it had been shuttered up, no sign of anybody there at all.

Once, when they lived in London, she had been driving in

a cab with her father through another part of the city. Where Hampstead was made up of rows of great houses, bearing down on the road like grandfather clocks, these houses were squat and small, red-brick and huddled together on the dirty roads. After some minutes, they came to a wider road, where the houses had small gates and painted fronts. A little girl walked past holding the hand of her mother.

'This is the home of the Cotton family,' Rudolf said abruptly, gesturing at the road. A carriage clattered past them, obscuring Celia's view.

She grasped the window pane. 'Which one, Papa? Show me.'

Her father looked vague. 'One of those.' He sat back against the seat, his face disinterested.

'But which one? Can we stop?' She'd pressed her face on the window, trying to smell what was outside. She wanted to hear the children sing. 'Let's go and say hello.'

He shook his head. 'They wouldn't like it.'

She turned to him. 'But I want to see where Tom lives. Tell me which one the house is!'

'Now, Celia, your mother is expecting us.'

The carriage rolled on. 'Let's go back!' she cried, but Rudolf shook his head. Celia craned, trying to see the houses, in the hope that Tom might come out, or one of his sisters.

When Rudolf had said they would be moving to Stoneythorpe, Celia's first question had been: 'What about Tom?'

She could not be without Tom. Whenever she attended the parties of the other little girls in Hampstead, she yearned to escape the flurry of lemon and pink, dresses and cakes and presents, so that she could play with Tom. They did everything together, from pretending hospitals and schools to racing in the garden.

Rudolf looked down at her and his face was pure confusion. Then it cleared. 'He shall come too.'

Verena drew in her breath. 'Now, dear, Tom would wish to stay with his family.'

Rudolf nodded. 'Well then, all the Cottons shall move to

Eversley, just nearby.' Celia clapped her hands. Tom, his mother, his sisters, all together in the manor house.

Verena's face flamed. Celia saw her clench her fist. 'But my dear. Surely not?'

Rudolf patted his knees. 'If they wish to come, they shall. We shall find them a cottage nearby, or something similar.'

'That's you, Papa,' cried Emmeline, standing. 'All you care about is the servants.'

'Or at least the Cottons,' Celia heard Arthur say under his breath. She had given her father a wide smile. In the country, she and Tom could spend every day together.

Celia tied a bow around a small bunny rabbit and looked at Belinda. She imagined Missy seizing her with a cry of joy, clutching her to her heart, thanking Celia shyly – and then Tom would invite her round for tea. She would sit at the table with Tom's mother, telling them jokes that made them all laugh. She looked down at her wrappings, the parcels resplendent in tissue and gold. Even Marina Evershold, the neatest girl in the class at Winterbourne, could not have done a better job. Surely her mother could not fail to be pleased with that.

FIVE

Next day, Rudolf went to London, early, before any of them rose. The day was theirs – to plan the party and for Celia to get in everybody's way. 'Oh, Celia,' Verena sighed, as she looked at a tangled section of bunting Celia had been trying to deck over the tables. 'You are always so *clumsy.*' She'd written two letters to Arthur so far, had them all sign both. She said Celia's signature was wobbly.

Celia fled to the kitchen. It was her second favourite part of the house, after the library. She loved the coolness of the white surfaces, the stone of the floor under her feet and the high glass jars full of sugar and flour. Sometimes Mrs Rolls would show her the recipes and give her scraps of cake mix or raw pastry. Not today. The kitchen was all activity. Ellie was sieving flour, and all around them were meat pies in stages of preparation. There were two empty pastry cases on the side, alongside a bowl of raw meat, chopped eggs and chopped parsley. Jennie and Sarah, the housemaids, were hunting for a tin, taking out piles from the cupboard, deep in conversation.

Celia supposed her mother wanted one to play apple bobbing or some type of party game. Jennie she was most devoted to, tall and thin like a candle, with a pale face and a shock of yellow curly hair she could never control. She was like you had drawn her picture on a piece of paper and slotted it into a top and made it run very fast: she hurried everywhere, talked a thousand words a minute, did everything quickly. 'More haste, less speed,' Mrs Bell called after her, hopelessly, because Jennie was always rushing. Once Jennie had even fallen down the stairs, she had been so determined to dust them in double-quick time. Celia had come out from the parlour just as she fell, hands flailing, landing on the bottom step with a bump. 'No harm done, miss!' she called out, then leapt to her feet and hurried off. A ball, that was what she was, a yellow rubber ball that never stopped.

'More pies? I cannot credit it.' Mrs Rolls beat the pastry circle with her plump hands. 'As if I don't have enough to do. After all that fuss on Tuesday over French soup and ice stacks, and Sir Hugh returning my chicken almost untouched.' Celia pulled herself up to perch on one of the surfaces, kicking at the morning light with her feet.

'Mama worries when Sir Hugh comes.'

'And now she is demanding enough for this party to feed the whole of Africa.' The cook's face was the plumpest of all, a big moon under her tight bun of brown hair streaked with grey. Celia wondered if cooks were ever thin. Mrs Rolls held up her hand and counted off. 'Meat pies, plum cakes, hams, a pig's head and apple tarts. That alongside the normal meals, and however many other visitors plan to descend.'

'I could help,' said Celia, thinking of red and amber jam tarts and plum cake mix.

'You? Whatever next.' Mrs Rolls brushed her face with a floury hand.

'Someone's after my job,' said Ellie, smiling at Celia. 'I could swap and marry an aristocrat like Miss Emmeline.' She was a tiny girl from the village with red hair in a plait and bright green eyes – too pretty to be a kitchen maid, Mrs Rolls had complained when she first arrived.

Mrs Rolls continued to beat her pastry circle. 'Less of that, my girl.'

'I might be good at chopping,' pushed Celia.

'I'm sure, miss. Get along with you now. Come back in half an hour or so and you can have the pastry ends.'

'No one will play with me. Even Tom is too busy.'

'Well,' said Mrs Rolls, banging the pastry with her pin. 'That is no bad thing, Miss Celia.' She spoke carefully. 'You are getting to be a young lady now, no need to play with boys.'

'Tom and I have always played together.'

'That's what I mean.'

'*She*'d make sure you did,' said Ellie.

'Who do you mean?' asked Celia.

'*Her*, you know. Madam Cotton,' said Ellie. '*Mrs*, oh yes.'

'Ellie!' Mrs Rolls brought down the rolling pin. 'Stop that talk, right away. Get to those pans before I give you something proper to do.'

Celia shook her head. 'I don't understand.'

'I'm warning you, Ellie!' called Mrs Rolls. 'Miss de Witt, time for you to go back upstairs.' She turned to Ellie. 'To the scullery pots for you, my girl.'

Celia was about to go when Jennie burst out: 'Sarah, you mustn't let him!' They all turned to her. 'Sorry, Mrs Rolls,' she said, dropping her voice. 'It's just that Sarah said she would gladly give her brother to the King. She shouldn't, should she?'

Mrs Rolls put a hand to her forehead. 'Well...'

'King needs men,' said Sarah. She looked up. 'He'd need your Davey too, Mrs Rolls, if he had a mind to it.' Sarah was small and dark, the opposite of Jennie, Celia supposed. At Christmas, she dressed up as a gypsy and told their fortunes until Rudolf stopped it, said God would not approve.

Mrs Rolls held up her rolling pin. 'Davey wouldn't want to fight.'

'Who?' asked Celia. 'What does the King need?'

Mrs Rolls beat the pastry hard. 'To come and eat here, if you ask me. Twenty pies in three days, can't make them before because they won't stay fresh, then the cakes and all the rest later and goodness knows what. Every year Mrs de Witt asks more from us.'

'Amazing how much those children can eat,' said Jennie. 'Pockets full of the stuff, bulging. I've seen.'

Mrs Rolls shook her head at Jennie, but Sarah was already looking up, her face hot. 'Not mine!' Sarah's four brothers and sisters always came to the party, along with Ellie's little sister. Mrs Rolls and Jennie both lived in the house. Celia thought Jennie came from a village half an hour away, but of Mrs Rolls she was not sure. Her mother had placed an advertisement in *The Lady* for exactly the type of chef she wished for, able to cater for large and fine parties as well as cook for a polite family. She had even interviewed a few Frenchmen, who arrived at the house in black suits, patted Celia absently. Probably best that they hadn't come to Stoneythorpe in the end, Celia thought. They probably wouldn't like cooking for the yearly party.

'I'll eat the leftovers, Mrs Rolls. Michael too. Anyway, what were you talking of? Who does the King need?'

'Men for the war. But I don't believe a word of it,' said Jennie. 'It's just to sell papers, they just make up all these words.'

'We have to teach the Kaiser a lesson,' said Sarah. 'We need to do it now.'

'I don't believe we'll have a war either,' said Celia. 'The Kaiser doesn't mean it. His people won't support it.' How could they? Not Hilde and Johann and their family.

Mrs Rolls straightened at that and looked up. 'Indeed, miss. Quite so. Sure all the Kaiser's subjects are decent, law-abiding people.' Celia watched Sarah's eyes flicker as she turned to her pans. Mrs Rolls held out her hand. 'Why don't you have this pastry, dear? And then run and tell Mrs de Witt that we are proceeding well with the pies and will start on the cakes in an hour or so. Time we all got back to work.'

'Yes, Mrs Rolls.' Celia turned, walked to the door. She wanted to say it again: the people do not want war. But it was all too much and too complicated, so she hurried into the corridor with her pastry, eating it there next to the small window, feeling the dough fill her mouth so she did not have to think about war or Germany or Hilde and Johann running by the stream in the Black Forest, throwing sticks in the water in the sun, without her.

She often had to remind herself that others saw her as German. It had been a shock to her when they had started German lessons at school and Frau Gritt had expected her to recite a poem in the first lesson.

'My father told us to learn another language,' she said, blushing to the entire class. Frau Gritt told her to go on, and she stumbled her way through the words and the rhymes, watching surprise and disappointment spread across the mistress's face. She knew the words, but she couldn't say them, unnerved by the beam of Frau Gritt's attention. After that, she was inattentive and lazy in German on purpose, feeling disloyal to her aunt Lotte who had practised sentences with her at the kitchen table in the Black Forest. But despite herself, she found the language flowing from her pen. She knew the words, recognised them, understood the sentences. 'It must be in your blood,' said the mistress later, looking over Celia's excellent exam.

Rudolf had hated Latin and French at school. 'If my children like,' he had said, 'they can learn. But I don't see the point. English is the language of the world now. In fifty years' time, no one will remember German. We will all be part of England.'

Verena had travelled to Germany, with Rudolf, in a second trip after their honeymoon. But not long afterwards, Rudolf's parents had both died and his cousin, Heinrich, whom he said was like a brother, moved to the Black Forest. Celia imagined a big country full of mountains, thick with dark trees, and a house that looked as if it were made of gingerbread. It was something of a disappointment when she did visit to find that it was really not so different to England after all.

Celia walked past the village women cleaning the paintwork now. Down the hall, she saw Mr Vine, the butler, flurrying about, his feet clapping the floor like a dancer's. Everyone would be busy today – her mother scouring her lists, Michael helping move tables, Mrs Rolls chopping and stirring, the maids polishing, her father going to London. She had no lessons, so that she could help, but there was nothing to do. She didn't even want to go to the library. Around the corner in the lower part of the servants' hall, Smithson and Thompson were setting up the children's games.

'I wish I could carry things too,' she said to Smithson. Celia often occupied herself trying to work out who was her favourite footman of the two. Smithson liked to listen to her jokes and let her chat. But Thompson sometimes gave her a jawbreaker sweet he had bought in the village. Even though she often ran their names together in her mind, like twins, Smithson and Thompson looked very unalike. Thompson was tall and broad, with dark hair, and some visitors said he had an Italian air. He told her his bad leg had been crushed by a falling horse in a battle on a huge plain where they heard lions roar through the fighting; that he came home ashamed to have been injured in such a cowardly way. He was devoted to Michael, followed him everywhere, brought him little biscuits from the pantry and left them in his room in the afternoons. Smithson was a wiry, straw-haired little man with a great round face and a noisy voice that Rudolf complained you could hear through the entire house. Celia was his favourite. She liked him too: admired the way he screwed his face into a ball when he was concentrating.

'Quicker if we do it, miss,' Smithson said, tying a coconut to the frame.

'I wish I could help you tomorrow.'

'That's our job too.' They were to have more games this year than ever before: a coconut shy, apple bobbing, pin the tail on the donkey, of course, and races with eggs and spoons.

'They are talking about war in the kitchen,' she said.

'Is Miss Jennie down there?' Smithson was sweet on Jennie, hopelessly so, Mrs Rolls said, since Jennie saw herself as destined for better, although who knew who *that* would be. Sometimes she allowed him to walk with her to church or ask her questions about her family, and then he behaved as if a goddess had touched him. Celia looked at his eyes, dark with love, and wondered if anyone would ever feel the same about her.

Smithson peered at her. 'Are you quite well, miss? You look a little pale.'

She nodded. 'I don't like the idea of war, that's all.'

He shrugged. 'Not up to us, though, is it, miss?'

Celia wandered to the front room and walked out on to the grass, a little dewy already. Tomorrow it would be teeming with children, rushing around, clutching cakes in their hands, gobbling gingerbread, waving to their parents (stuffing their pockets, Jennie would say). Every year, Celia grew impatient with the lists and the preparations, and then she took it all back when she saw the wonders her mother had created: long tables strewn with bunting and flowers, the great bins waiting to be filled with the lucky dip, the spots for pin the tail on the donkey, the coconut shy, the skittles to knock over, the gold stars strung on the trees, the flowers sparkling and shining up at the sun. It was handsome, the kind of place some of the more romantic girls at school like Gertie or Laura would have called 'fairy tale'. One year, it had been raining and so they had all transferred into the dusty old ballroom at the back, which Verena otherwise locked up. That, secretly, had been Celia's favourite year of all, watching the children skidding up and down the once-polished floor.

The day always proceeded in a set way: the children arrived, most with their parents, or older sisters, and were welcomed by Jennie and Smithson, then through to the back garden. Every year Celia looked at them, thinking how much work had gone into their outfits, hours of sewing new dresses, scrubbing socks, plunging the children into the bath – for once before their father, who was usually first in line for the clean water. Their cheeks shone pink, hair newly plaited or combed, and their aprons had been scrubbed so hard that they shone white. In the garden, Michael, Tom, Smithson, Thompson and Jennie would divide the children into age groups and set them playing games: tag, hide and seek, egg and spoon races and jumping to begin with, then, after an hour or so, pin the tail on the donkey and blind man's buff.

Last year's party had been magnificent. More than forty children had come, the little ones racing around the lawn, the older girls watching them to make sure they didn't fall, the big boys lounging in groups by the trees, pretending not to be interested in the babyish games. Everybody had been there, apart from the baker's children, who were suffering from chickenpox. Even little Johnny came, the son of the village beggar, who never went anywhere because he was mocked and teased. He hid from the other children, watched them from a distance, along with Lizzie, the girl who had lost her arm to a farm scythe and whose mother kept her home for fear she would lose anything more. Celia sat with Verena and Emmeline, as Michael and Tom ran the games. She watched Bill Smith winning pin the tail on the donkey and the Lyon sisters winning blind man's buff. Finally, at half past three, Mrs Rolls brought out the big cakes and pies and the children settled around the table. Emmeline ate half a sandwich and then drank only tea, so Celia had her piece of ginger cake, treacle tart, scones and shortbread biscuits. 'You'll get fat,' Emmeline had said, poking her in the ribs.

'You will first.'

After tea, the bigger boys took part in the tug of war, supervised by Smithson and Thompson. Michael was allowed to play too, and Celia watched him, on a different side to Tom, both boys pulling hard. Tom's side won. Then Rudolf stood up and thanked all the children for coming and the maids gave out paper bags of cakes and biscuits for them to take home. Smithson brought out the lucky dip and Jennie supervised the children as they came, one by one. Celia watched them tearing open the parcels, flinging the paper on the floor in their excitement at finding tops, hoops, dolls, bears.

'Goodbye!' they cried. 'Thank you!' Rudolf and Verena accepted their thanks, upstanding, taller than any of the village parents. They walked inside, stately, followed by Emmeline. The last children hung around – Jessie and John, whose father beat them harder than most, said Mrs Rolls, and the little boy whose name Celia always forgot. Jennie shooed the rest of them away and then scurried inside herself, crying that she needed a cup of tea before she could do *anything at all*. Smithson and Thompson shouldered in a table, but once inside, they did not come out either, and Celia had the garden to herself.

In previous years, her mother had forced her to accompany her and Emmeline back to the drawing room, where they would ring for tea and Verena would luxuriate in a lengthy discussion about the afternoon, in which every avenue led back to the same conclusion: it had all been a splendid success. 'You have excelled yourself, my dear,' Rudolf would say. It had been even grander than the party two years ago, made a coronation party to celebrate the King, when each of the children took home a present of a cake bearing three tiny silver balls – the King, the Queen and the Prince of Wales. Last year, without warning, Verena had shrugged her shoulders and said to Celia, 'You can stay to help the maids if you like.' Celia could have hugged herself with delight. The whole place was her playground – for as long as it took before Smithson and Thompson returned. She walked up to the tables and poked a finger into the chocolate iced cake, stuck it in her mouth, then took a strawberry biscuit, the fruit bruised and sunken. Close up, the cakes looked sunburned, touched by too many hands. The ones she had really wanted – shortbread chocolate hearts – had all been eaten. She wandered to the lucky dip and plunged her hands into the bundles of newspaper, then, after looking around, pulled the bin down to the grass and put her head inside, smelling newsprint and the paper from the presents.

That day she had been like a princess, she thought, who came down to a banquet after everybody had gone, fingered the plates, picked up the flowers. After righting the bin, she had taken another biscuit and set off towards the games, played pin the tail on the donkey. After a while, Smithson had come out and called to her to help him pull down the banners from the tables, if she wouldn't mind, and the spell was broken because he was complaining about Thompson not helping enough and dropping a plate on his foot.

Celia wandered down to her dell and sat on her rock, trying to make up poems about the willow sweeping the pond. But she couldn't find the right words, and her mind kept returning to Jonathan's mouth on hers, the terrible argument with Sir Hugh. *Think of the party*, she told herself. *That will make everything happy again.*

After a few hours had passed, the air cooled and it struck her that she might have missed lunch. Verena would be cross with her if she had. She ran up the garden and into the front room.

The corridor was deserted, no Smithson and Thompson, no one cleaning.

She walked further. Rudolf was coming towards her. He stopped and blinked slightly as if he did not know her. 'Celia,' he said, finally. 'My dear.'

'Hello, Papa. I didn't hear you come back. You are early.'

He rubbed his eyes. 'Of course. I would not miss the party.'

She tried to smile, to cover up the unease she felt nearly every time she was with him now. As a child, she had run to him whenever she saw him, always before her sisters and brothers, and she knew she was his favourite. He used to take her on long walks and point out the butterflies and the flowers. Now she could not see him without a creeping sense of embarrassment about the changes that were happening to her. It seemed impossible to her that he could love the adult as he had the child. She thought he must feel a similar sense of cringing shame.

Talking with him, just the two of them, made her nervous. 'You had a good trip?'

'Lord Smith's man, Mr Gregson, did not arrive, nor my other appointment. I passed useful time in the offices, though.' He shrugged. 'Unaccountable, really. Mr Gregson is always so punctual. I will go back next week.'

She nodded. He fell into step with her and she listened to the touch of his heel on the hall floor. 'A big day tomorrow.'

'Mama's favourite.' She paused. 'Do you think Sir Hugh will come?'

'Oh, undoubtedly. The young have hot tempers. He has already forgotten, I am sure. Now, my dear, I have something to show you. Come to my study.'

She followed, waited as he opened the door and pulled something out from behind it. 'Look! It is supposed to be drying, but I could not resist.' He held the great piece of paper across his body. A donkey, painted brown, its eyes wide and comical, its mouth open in a sort of smile.

'It is excellent, Papa.'

The donkey was her father's tradition. Every year he drew it for the pin-the-tail competition. 'English children love this game,' he said, as he sketched the lines of it and filled them with paint ordered from London, carefully stroking out the mane and skin.

'I still need to do some work on the face,' he said now. 'Not quite perfect yet. But he will come. You could come and help me paint him later. I know how you like colouring the tail. I think him a very good donkey, do not you?'

Verena enjoyed the success of the parties, the planning, the feeling of work well done, but Rudolf loved the actual event, the children dashing around his chair, the bold ones coming up and asking silly questions or patting him on the knee. His face pinked with pleasure, his eyes followed the littlest ones as they hurtled around the garden.

'Why didn't you have more children?' Celia had asked him after the party two years ago. 'The Queen had nine.'

Rudolf patted her head. 'You know your mother was very ill with you.' As Celia had been told so many times, her mother had almost died, sick the whole way through the pregnancy, hardly able to drink water, and then so bad after her confinement that the doctor had called Rudolf to sit by her day and night, in case she died. 'You were our miracle baby,' he said. 'Our last one.'

'It is a very good donkey, Papa.' She could not help it. 'Just the one to get Emmeline married.'

He caught her hand. 'You are young, Celia, you do not understand. The marriage is important to Emmeline, to us. In just a few years, you will be leaving school and you will be looking for a husband. Emmeline, as Lady Bradshaw, could do so much for you. She could introduce you, give you a proper debutante season. You will be the young lady of a great family, fulfil the promise of your mother.'

'I do not wish for it.' She had heard it from her father too many times, and from her mother. *Stand up straight! Think of your deportment. Brush your hair one hundred times every night or it will dull. You must prepare for the future.*

He smiled. 'You will change your mind. Imagine the gowns, the parties.' He clasped her hand again, his palm dry around hers.

'I will tell you, Celia, just between us. It is my dearest wish that you be presented to society. Who knows what a brilliant match you might make?'

'I would like to go to Paris,' she said.

'Perhaps we might be able to send you for a few months or so, when the situation is calmer.'

That wasn't what she'd meant, but it was a start.

SIX

Celia stood between her just-open curtains, wearing her night-dress. It was the day of the party, and the sun was glistening over the garden, touching the trees and flowers with gold. The maids and footmen were hurrying about, rearranging the tables, moving the chairs so they were in a better position. She dressed herself quickly and went down to breakfast. Everybody else had gone and there was no Thompson or Smithson by the tray of food. She ate her eggs and her mother came into the room.

'We forgot everything last night,' she said, holding her hand to her head. 'I did not ask Miss Wilton to put your hair in curl papers.' Celia had hugged herself with pleasure at not having to sleep in curl papers, for you could never get settled on the pillow with them on your head. 'Well, she shall have to do it with extra strength today. I've sent her to your room. Run upstairs and sit for her, there's a good girl.'

Celia made a face but obeyed, hurrying up the stairs to her room. Miss Wilton was already standing there, holding out her hands, her tight fingers outstretched. 'I can't wait for ever, miss,' she said as Celia flung open the door.

Celia dipped her head. She could not arrange her own hair; she was clumsy-fingered and it slipped between her hands when she tried to plait it at school. She sat down and Miss Wilton began to brush it, pulling hard on the first tangle she found.

By two o'clock, everyone was ready. Celia walked down the stairs – carefully, because Miss Wilton was watching – feeling the house almost trembling with excitement around her. The children would already be gathering outside at the front, jostling and gig-gling as Jennie and Smithson kept them in line. Mr Vine stood ready to take up his position in the gardens. Downstairs, Mrs

Rolls was putting the last touches to the cakes, while the maids were patting their hair, ready to load up trays of pies, cakes and biscuits and carry them into the sun. Celia loved the house most at such moments; when it was waiting.

She pushed open the door of the parlour, the last one to arrive. Her head still aching from Miss Wilton's nails and the hat pins digging deep into her head, she admired her handsome family: her father, his head almost touching the lights; and Michael, smart in his blue suit, his fair hair brushed over his forehead, one edge just touching his eyebrow, his hands hidden behind his back. Emmeline wore the pink scalloped gown the dressmaker had delivered last week. Despite herself, Celia admired the embroidery over the hem, the fake pearls sewn on to the bodice. Emmeline looked like the doll Belinda, great blue eyes open wide as if she was always surprised, with eyelashes that looked as if water had been dripped on them, circles of pink on her white cheeks. Celia was even slightly saddened that Arthur was not there, that he was smiling his flashy smile around Paris instead.

'That dress is perfect for you, Emmeline.'

Her sister opened her eyes wide. 'I've had a very kind letter from Sir Hugh,' she whispered. 'He's been called away on business so he cannot attend, but he hopes the party proceeds well, and then we can return to the proper business of the wedding. He sent a basket of game.'

Celia squeezed her hand. 'It is all forgotten, then.'

'Come along, girls,' said Verena. She was the mother Celia knew again; not lost-faced as she had been in her room the day before, but serene and upstanding, like a magazine fashion plate in her new green skirt and waistcoat, the cameo given to her on her eighteenth birthday at her throat. Miss Wilton had coiled her hair up around her head in an elaborate style, pinned it and arranged it, dressed it with oil and rose water, left it tamed and silken. Emmeline's was bound up in what looked like a hundred little plaits.

Miss Wilton had worked hard on Celia's thin hair, combed and puffed it until it looked halfway decent, and she had kept her blue dress unspotted on the journey from her bedroom to the front room. It covered her knees, made them seem less gawky. 'Hey,' said Michael, nudging her. Verena and Emmeline were deep in a conversation about the drape of the dress's material. Rudolf was listening to them, smiling. 'You might be getting a pretty girl in your old age,' Michael said under his breath. 'Not bad at all.'

'Why would I care about being pretty?'

'So you can marry the Prince of Wales.'

'He is an old man!'

'But another German too. We'd have a lot in common.'

'Michael!' scolded Verena. 'Such a way to speak about our future King.'

'It's true, though. No one complains at them for their accent, do they? No one says they are Kaiser-lovers.'

Rudolf turned to him. 'This is not the place for such discussion, Michael. We are about to celebrate.'

Michael drew himself up. 'But when will we discuss it? You always say it is not the time. But you are fine, are you not; you are a great businessman, everyone respects you. And Emmeline is beautiful and for a woman it does not matter – a husband makes her his own. But what about me? In a year, I will be finished at Magdalene. Then you all want me to go in to the law. Do you think any of those firms of solicitors would employ me?'

'Of course they would, Michael. With your degree.'

'But they can hear a German accent.'

'Of course they cannot. None of us have a German accent.'

'They can see my foreign surname. They know it.'

'Then they're not good people to work for,' said Celia, more staunchly than she felt. Michael twitched slightly, did not look at her, as if she was not worth regarding.

'We should change our name,' he said, flatly. 'I've said it before. Why do we still have this name? We could be de Wills or something and be French. Or better still, take on Mother's name, Deerhurst.' As Michael talked, Celia thought, Rudolf grew smaller, as if he was a plant drying up in the sun. *Answer*, she wanted to will him. *Say something!*

Verena stepped forward. 'Michael. That's enough. I did not marry your father to stay a Deerhurst.'

Rudolf looked up from the floor. 'Yes, my dear, quite right. We are the de Witts. Come along, let us go into the garden and greet the children.'

Verena gave a pale smile that was not really a smile at all. 'If only Arthur were here. Then we would be a proper family.'

'He will return soon, my dear.' Rudolf took Verena's arm and led them all out of the open French windows into the lower part of the garden. Michael shrugged at Celia and raked his foot on the carpet. 'You first,' he said, plunging his hands in his pockets, waiting by the door. She stepped out into the sun. Thompson and Smithson stood by the tables along with another footman. They bowed, pulled out chairs, and Verena, Emmeline and Celia sat down first.

'The children will be here in a matter of minutes,' said Rudolf, smiling around. 'They will be playing and enjoying themselves.' His face was red, expectant. Celia thought of a schoolboy waiting to receive his accolade at prizegiving. She sat upright and smiled, trying to imitate Emmeline's carriage. On the table in front of her was a small vase of roses and carnations, pinks and reds. The flowers were perfect, billowing out their petals, not one of them drooping or browned. Jennie or one of the other maids must have just picked them. Celia put her finger out towards the flower nearest to her, fingered the pink frilled edge.

Even the sky was still. It too was waiting.

Fifteen minutes or so must have passed. Then footsteps were coming around the house. 'Ah,' said Rudolf, pulling himself up and beaming. 'Here they are.'

Jennie appeared at the side of the house. Celia, watching her father, saw his smile drop. Jennie was alone. Her face was red, her curly hair springing from her cap. She walked towards them, not looking at anyone. *Where is Tom?* Celia cried in her head. *Where is he?*

'We're still attending them, sir,' Jennie said to Rudolf.

'Well, it is still early. Why don't you bring around the ones who are here? Let's let the early birds catch their worm.'

'I can't, sir.'

'Nonsense, of course you can, Jennie. Just bring them round. Even if it is only ten or so, we should get the games started. The rest can come on later.'

'But sir—'

Verena broke in. 'Now, Jennie, this is not like you. Just go back and ask Smithson to bring them, if you can't.'

The maid stared at the ground.

'Jennie, don't be upset.' Rudolf's tone softened. 'If only a few are here, it does not matter. How many do we have?'

Jennie said nothing.

'Come now, my girl. Ten?'

She shook her head. Celia gazed at the petal in front of her. She was watching everything in slow time. She could see it coming. Michael was tensing next to her. The great fire was on its way.

Rudolf gave a jovial smile, but his voice was strained. 'Eight?'

Jennie shook her head again.

'Five?'

She stared at the floor.

'Come on, girl, tell us. How many?'

At last she looked up. 'None, sir.'

'None?' Now Rudolf shook his head. 'That cannot be. They must be there. They must be.'

Celia sat, her smile fixed. Her shoulder was hurting. The pale icing on the cake in front of them was melting, as if it might fall down the side, on to the plate. It would spoil soon, not be nice at all. Mrs Rolls always complained that she was forced to bring the food outside too early, but Rudolf wanted it to be on display when the children arrived.

'They must be,' Rudolf was saying. 'The parents surely have made a mistake. They must have thought we would collect them from the village. Yes, that's it. Jennie, ask Smithson to go to the village and fetch them. I am certain they are waiting by the green.'

'Father—' Michael began.

Emmeline broke in. 'Yes, I'm sure Papa is right,' glaring at Celia and Michael. 'A mistake has been made.'

The cameo was trembling at Verena's throat. 'Yes, Smithson could walk up to the village while Jennie waits here in case any arrive. Let us do that. Go back and tell Smithson, thank you, Jennie.'

The girl turned and began her long walk across the garden.

'Well,' said Rudolf. 'What a little error. What a small mistake.' He gave them a wide smile. 'We shall have to put the party back by twenty minutes. If any of you would like a brief walk while we wait, please do. Perhaps we might take some of the sandwiches.' He held out a plate to Verena. 'My dear?'

Verena took a sandwich containing cucumber. She fingered it. 'The bread is not light,' she said. 'When Mrs Rolls makes bread in summer, it is not light.'

Rudolf was looking out towards the gate. Michael put his head in his hands. 'We are like puppets!' he said. 'Dressed-up puppets in finery.'

Emmeline gave him an angry stare, even though he was not looking. Celia almost wanted to pat her sister on the knee.

Rudolf smiled again. 'These look like excellent sandwiches. But I shall not indulge just yet. I shall take a short walk to verify that everything is in order for when we must begin once more.' He stood up and headed towards the games tables, his back bent slightly as he made his way across the grass. The bright flowers shone in Celia's eyes.

Michael looked after him. 'Papa fools himself,' he said. Verena turned quickly to face him and then manoeuvred herself up, grasping the chair as she did so. She stood and followed Rudolf, her green skirt trailing in the grass.

Michael's head was still in his hands. 'Why do you say such things?' spat Emmeline.

'It's the truth.'

'What would you know?'

'All you care about is what Sir Hugh might think. This whole thing is ridiculous. Everybody hates us.'

'Stop it!' said Celia. 'Stop saying it.'

'You as well.' He stood up. 'I'm leaving you all to it.' He hurried off, and they heard the door slam as he entered the house.

'Go on,' said Emmeline. 'Aren't you going to run after him like you always do?'

'I'm waiting with Papa and Mama. I hope the children will come.'

'Of course they will.' Emmeline reached up to adjust her hat, and gazed out, her face calm. Her eyes looked larger than ever. Celia could almost imagine that you might trust in her beauty so much that it would make everything fine and happy once more, which, she supposed, was what men thought when they picked women like Emmeline. 'We must wait. Things come to those who wait. We'll look back in the future and smile at the mistake we made this afternoon in sending the children to the green.'

I'm afraid, Celia wanted to say, but you couldn't say anything like that to Emmeline. She supposed there must be sisters who told each other such things, confided their inner secrets, were like friends. But Emmeline could not give her the answer to what she really needed to know: *Where is Tom?* He should be standing by the tables, with his sister clutching his hand, too shy to speak. *Help me!* Celia wanted to beg her sister. But she couldn't say any of it. Instead, she stared at the cake, the icing dripping now on to the plate, leaving bare patches over the top. Emmeline continued to gaze forward, as if willing everything to turn out right. Celia was trying to think of something to say to please her, generous words about her hat, when she saw Rudolf and Verena turn and walk towards them again.

'Now, girls, have you left the cake alone?'

'Yes, Papa,' said Celia.

'Well, we shall tuck in now. The children should be on their way. Let us sit.'

'Celia, run in and find Michael,' said Verena. 'Tell him we need him here.'

Celia nodded and hurried off into the house, her skirts flurrying around her legs as they always did when she was trying to do *anything*.

Michael was not in the parlour. She called his name, walking to the library, but he was not there either. She started upstairs and then on the first landing she heard the sound of thumping, something being hit over and over. It was coming from Michael's room. She hurried up. His door was shut. She knocked and put her ear against the dark wood. The sound wasn't stopping.

'Michael!'

No reply came. She hardly ever went into his room. In the old days, they had the big sunny room upstairs as a playroom, with all their bears, his toy trains and their Noah's ark. Michael had told her that Verena had talked of making it the schoolroom, but they had begged her not to, so she had changed her mind and appointed the smaller room next door that had previously been used as a place to store her gowns and Rudolf's boxes of maps and books. Whenever she went into the playroom, Celia sat in front of the stained-glass window that coloured the light blue and green and thanked Verena for giving them this room. Even from the age of six or so, she felt certain Michael would not want to play ark with her, or bears' hospital – their favourite – in a poky, darkened room. He was so tall and handsome, everything about him made of light. She was lucky he played with her at all.

She called again at the door. 'What are you doing?'

He didn't answer. She grasped the handle and pushed, expecting the door to be locked. It fell forward in her hand and she stood at the threshold of the room. Michael was lying face down on his bed, banging his hand into his pillow. He was making a terrible coughing sound, almost like a sob. She was about to speak when her eye was drawn upwards. The movement of the opening door was fluttering the air – and the dozens of little wooden planes hanging from the ceiling.

'What are those?' she asked, gazing at the ceiling. 'Did you make them?'

He didn't look up.

'They must have taken *ages*.' She wanted to touch them. Over by the far wall was a chair and a desk covered in books and papers, the only untidiness in his spotless room. She wanted to hoist herself up on the chair and hold one of the little planes. 'Did you really make them all?'

He punched the pillow again. 'Who cares about the bloody planes?'

'But this one here. The wings are all lacy.' He had carved out holes and frilled edges on the plane. 'When *did* you do them?'

He turned over and looked up at her, his face reddened and angry. 'Why are you asking about planes? You are as bad as them, fiddling about with that ridiculous bunting.'

'Why are you being so mean? The local children love the party, you know that. And Papa is so happy when he gives it. Mama too.'

He let out a groan and pushed himself up on his arm. 'You just don't see, do you? There isn't going to be a party. There isn't going to be anything. We are going to war. And everybody hates us, they already do.'

'Sir Hugh has sent a letter to Emmeline. He is content again.'

'Not just him. Everybody.'

'Not true,' she said. But weakly, for her head was filling with Sir Hugh's words and digging backwards, further backwards, to pictures of Cambridge that one time, of men waving at Michael and smiling, but turning their faces and laughing when they thought she couldn't see.

'I won't go back to college, you know,' he said, and her mind jumped – caught by the shock that they had both been thinking of Cambridge. 'They probably won't have me anyway.'

'But you have to go. You *must!*' Rudolf's pride in his son's achievements, his delight, the money poured into buying Michael books, papers, paying for the succession of tutors in Latin and history and the rest, the house hushed, Celia not allowed to run or even call out because Michael was *working*. For as long as she could remember, Rudolf had had three etchings on his wall. She found out early on that the best way of putting off bedtime or anything else that Verena wanted from her was by asking him about the pictures. 'St John's, Magdalene and Christ's,' he told her.

'The best colleges. They are full of the greatest brains. The men from them rule the world.'

Arthur had never been a candidate: lazy, relying on being handsome; interested only in European cafés, Lady Deerhurst had snorted. But Michael had always been different – Rudolf said he knew his son would be a Cambridge man on the day after his third birthday. 'He simply took down *Pilgrim's Progress* and read five lines of it. From nothing to sentences!' No one needed to look back with Michael, wonder if, as they did with Arthur, they should have altered something, sent him to a different school, given him a different tutor. The Harrow reports spilled praise, the trunks full of pristine exercise books arrived home, Michael applied himself in the holidays in a disciplined fashion and exams came and went, always the same, each one scored just a tiny bit higher. And then Cambridge, the whole place bathed in gold, in Celia's imagination. Rudolf accompanied him on the drive there and returned unable to speak, not from pain but because he had gained everything. No one would be able to stop Michael now.

'You can't,' she said now. 'What about Papa?' Then she felt drier land under her feet. 'What about your scholarship? How hard you worked.'

'Not really. I did it to please everyone here. That big shiny scholarship, all that work and what's the use of it? It can't change anything.'

'But it's not supposed to change anything. It's once you have it. Then you can do what you like. Business, politics, change things that way.' Her head was ringing now with the rooms and rooms of girl students sitting at desks, looking over locked gardens, reading books about literature or history. 'You have to go back.'

He shrugged. 'I've made my decision. When the world is like this, there is no point to verbs and declensions, listing the dates, the history of building projects in Rome. It's irrelevant stuff. You know, we don't even learn about the things themselves. That's not the point. What you are supposed to do is argue with the writers of books, say they have taken the wrong approach, that they cite the wrong books by other people. That's it.'

'Lots of people wanted your place.'

'They can have it.'

She gazed up at the aeroplanes. 'So what will you do instead? Make more of these?'

'No. Of course not. In fact...' He caught her eye then and stared at her. She watched his eyes, round and blue, so blue. His voice softened. 'Poor Ceels. Always the youngest. Maybe you can go to college, if you like.'

'I have to go to balls first. Lots of balls. I might get to go to college when I'm *thirty*, maybe.'

He smiled. 'That's not so old. Anyway, what did you come here for? To ask me to come down, I suppose?'

'That's right. Mama wants you.'

'Tell her I'm ill.'

'That would be lying.'

'Well then you can tell her the truth. That I can't bear to watch this charade. I don't want to. I'll come down after it's all over. It's inviting disaster.'

'But they're expecting you.'

'They have you to keep them company. And dear Emmeline. Surely that is the point of having four children. Always one or two of them around.'

'Why are you being like this? It's not fair.'

'Honestly, Celia, going through all the family stuff just seems like a lie at the moment. We might all be dead next year. The whole country might be dead.'

'So you won't come down, then?'

'No.'

She took a step towards him. 'Not even for me?'

'No.' He flushed. 'Celia, I can't. If I could, I would. You know you're my favourite. You are. But I can't. Not today.' There was a tear beginning in his eye, glimmering at the corner. She did not want to look at it. As she walked out of the door, he turned and thrust his face into the pillow again.

Let everybody be there, she bargained, as she walked down the stairs. 'Let them all be playing and eating and laughing. Please

God.' She promised to do anything: be kinder to Miss Evans, the French teacher at school, not complain at Miss Wilton, think sweeter thoughts about Emmeline. Anything – if all the children would only be there.

She walked through the doors of the garden room, still bargaining and offering. She looked out. Rudolf and Verena sat, erect, smiling, their faces fixed. The sandwiches were wilting, the bunting drooping. Emmeline was staring at her nails. Just over to the side, by the donkey picture, stood Tom, holding hands with a little girl of six or so. Her pale face had been scrubbed hard, and dark hair hung in a long plait down her back. Tom's face looked thinner all of a sudden, sickly.

'Come on, Missy,' he was saying. 'Close your eyes and put in the pin.' The child was holding the pin with the tail limp in her hand, looking around, her face fearful. Every adult in the garden was staring at her: Rudolf, Verena, Jennie, Smithson, Thompson. Even Emmeline was gazing, through the curtain of her looped fringe.

'Look, Missy,' he said again. 'Close your eyes, that's all you have to do.'

She clutched his hand, her eyes wide. Celia felt as if her heart was burning in her chest. Rudolf was statue-still, watching. *Daddy!* she wanted to cry. *It does not matter! We still have next year.* Tom's voice was high and unnatural, like Madeline Smith's in the school play when she suddenly got frightened on the stage in the midst of pretending to be Peter Pan and burst into tears. Celia longed to rush over to him and throw her arms around him.

Jennie was standing beside Tom and the girl, blinking fast. Celia could see she was itching to put her hand out and place the tail.

'Look,' said Tom. 'I will show you again. I will do it.' He closed his eyes and they all watched. Then he pinned the tail, next to the donkey's foot. The little girl was still clutching his other hand.

'Oh no!' he said, opening his eyes. 'What have I done? It is miles away. Silly me! Can you do better, Missy?' He held out the tail to her, but she shook her head. 'Please,' he said.

They all watched. Celia knew that no one had even seen her

come out. Missy put out her hand and then seized it back. Her dress was clean, but darned and shabby. It couldn't be her best one.

There was the sound of a scraping chair and they all looked around to see Rudolf getting slowly to his feet. 'Please, Miss Cotton,' he said, his voice cracking around her name. 'It would mean so much to me.'

She gazed back at him and then held out a trembling hand to Tom. He gave her the tail and she reached up for it, closed her eyes. The air was still as she held it out, circling around the animal's feet. They watched as she moved her hand over the paper. Then she pinned the tail, pushed it in. 'Good girl!' cried Tom. It was right where the donkey's heart would be. She opened her eyes and stared. Rudolf, still standing, lifted his hands and began to clap. They all joined in so that it was a proper round of applause. The child stood there, holding tight to her brother, and very quickly started to cry.

'She's only young,' Tom said, drawing her to him. 'She's not used to parties.'

Rudolf smiled. 'Oh, we quite understand. A party is a lot for a little girl.'

Tom held Missy as her hiccups quietened and her back shook. 'There we go,' he said. 'There we go.' Celia had seen him do the same to the horses.

He smiled out at them. 'All better now.'

'Well done,' said Rudolf. 'Now, perhaps you would like to try the skittles?'

The child shook her head, tears on her face. 'Later, then, later. Perhaps a little food?'

Tom nodded. 'That would be a good idea. Come along, Missy. How about some cake?'

She hung back. 'Now then, dear,' said Verena, standing up. 'We have all the cakes you might want: cream-iced, Victoria sponge, jam, and Mrs Rolls made special biscuits with fairy wings on, just for little girls like you. Right over here.' She gestured to the children's table next to theirs.

Tom propelled Missy forward. Smithson pulled out a chair for her and Tom patted her legs. She scrambled up and sat down. Tom seated himself beside her. Smithson passed her a plate of biscuits and she took one, trembling, placed it on her plate. She refused a cake and another biscuit, shook her head to a sandwich. She picked up the biscuit, took one tiny bite, looking around at the adults as she chewed. Then she picked it up again, bit once more. The adults watched the child as she took regular bites, concentrating entirely on the biscuit before her. She ate neatly and dutifully, and as she did so, Rudolf passed a cake to Verena, who took it with her delicate fingers and perched it on her plate. Celia looked up at Emmeline and saw tears forming in her eyes.

Celia sat at the table with her parents. They barely seemed to see her. Verena was holding the side of the table so tightly that her knuckles had gone white.

After Missy had eaten two biscuits and half a sandwich, she whispered to her brother. Tom turned to them and spoke. He had never had such a transfixed audience, Celia supposed. 'My sister would like to leave the table.'

'Have you eaten sufficiently, Miss Cotton?' Rudolf called over.

Missy gave him a mute nod.

'Well of course then, you may.'

Tom and Missy stood by the tables, both staring over at Rudolf and Verena. Let them go, Celia willed. Of course, the party had to continue as planned.

'Still don't fancy the skittles?' said Rudolf. 'It has been a busy afternoon. I think that now we have played and we have eaten, it is time for our final celebration. Let us begin the tug of war. Smithson, perhaps you would like to take the other end to Tom?'

Smithson walked over and took up his end of the rope. Tom shook off Missy's panicked hands and stepped up.

'Come here, Missy,' said Emmeline. 'Watch with me.' The child scuttled over to her side and held her chair.

'I want to play too,' Celia heard herself cry. She leapt down from her own chair and hurried over, ignoring Verena's call to come back. She stood by Tom, held the rope in her hands.

'Two against one, eh?' said Smithson, pretending to flex his arm muscles. 'I will have to pull my hardest.'

Rudolf stood up. 'So here we go. One. Two. Three. Go!'

Celia pulled and pulled, feeling Tom do the same behind her. They were tugging Smithson over the line. She pulled again. Then Smithson fell forward, shouting, 'I give up!'

'The winners!' called Rudolf. 'Congratulations! Come to receive your prize.'

Celia wanted to smile at Tom, but he jumped ahead of her. Rudolf held out a large wrapped package. Tom stared at him for a moment, then took it in his hands. He pulled open the paper and held up a big cricket bat, new and perfectly polished. 'Thank you,' he said, looking down. It was the fine bat that Rudolf gave every year, destined for the village cricket team.

'It is for you,' said Rudolf. 'Now, Miss Cotton, are you ready for the skittles?'

Missy shot Tom a pained look. 'My sister's ill,' Tom said. 'She was too much in the sun this morning. Our mother might miss us.'

Verena bowed her head. Celia, standing by the rope with Smithson, wanted to throw everything in the air and see it come down perfect and proper once more.

'Oh quite, quite,' Rudolf mumbled.

'Thank you, sir, for the lovely party,' burbled the girl as she scrambled from Emmeline's chair to her brother's side.

'You cannot leave without trying the lucky dip,' said Rudolf. 'Celia, dear, help Miss Cotton to the lucky dip.'

Thompson waited, smartly, by the barrel. Celia walked over, Tom and Missy behind her. She tipped the lucky dip so that Missy could reach inside. The child bent over, uncertain, and grasped a small parcel.

'No,' hissed Celia, and dug into the newspaper until she found the big parcel she knew was the doll, and thrust it into Missy's hands. Missy took it, but as she did so, Celia regretted her actions. The child's face was full of fear. 'Have them both,' Celia cried, but Missy shook her head. The tears were coming again.

'I didn't mean to frighten her,' Celia said, looking at Tom.

'You didn't. She's tired. It's a long day for her.' He wasn't really looking at her, she knew. He was looking away.

'Why isn't she wearing her best dress?' She knew why. If he'd walked from Eversley with Missy in her Sunday dress, everyone would have known they were coming to the party. 'You're ashamed of us.'

He shrugged. 'Everybody thinks I'm one of your lot anyway.' She hardly recognised his voice, tinged with anger.

'You *are* one of us!'

He stared at her, his eyes full of an expression she could not place. His lip curled. 'I'm your servant.' He looked beyond her. 'Thank you, sir, madam, Miss de Witt, for the party. We enjoyed ourselves very much.' He did not go closer, did not walk up to Rudolf or give him a chance to deliver his speech. 'Thank you very much,' said Missy. She bobbed a curtsey, shyly, then lifted her apron to rub at her eyes.

They turned and walked away, followed by Jennie to let them out. The de Witts watched them, Celia, Emmeline, Verena and Rudolf, the cakes melting around them, the bunting slipping from its pinning on the tables.

Rudolf stood up. 'Let us take a walk,' he said. They gazed up at him, blankly. 'Come along. Let us walk. Walking is good for the soul.'

'I don't want to walk, Papa,' said Emmeline.

'I think we all should go.'

'Go where?'

'To the village, of course!'

Verena gripped his hand. 'But we cannot do that.'

'It is surely all a very easily solved mystery, I think. Let us go and investigate.'

'Please, Papa.' Emmeline put her hand over her face. 'Please.'

'Come along!' He clapped his hands. 'Chop, chop!' Celia stood up, followed them. Emmeline's head was drooping. Rudolf was parading ahead. Celia could not bear it. She broke forward and began to run. She cut around the edge of the building, through the side path and out on to the front drive. She ran to the end. And then she looked. And again. There was red paint daubed over the drive. Huge capitals, scrawled across like blood: GERMANS GO HOME.

She dropped to her knees and began scrubbing at it with her bare hands, ignoring the pain. 'Celia!' she heard her father shout. 'Stop that!' She felt Emmeline's arms around her, pulling her back.

There was no dinner that night. After the party they usually had a supper of cold cuts, to give Mrs Rolls and the girls a rest. But this time, when Celia came down at eight, changed into a white gown Verena liked, there was no one there but Smithson.

'I think most of them are dining in their rooms, miss,' he told her. 'You can do the same if you like, I would think.'

'I think I'll stay here.' Her room looked out on to the party tables, still waiting for children. She sat down in front of the great piles of meat and wondered how she was supposed to eat any of it. Smithson ladled ham and cold potatoes on to her plate and stood back from her, gazing into the garden. She ate slowly. The words on the drive blazed in her mind.

'I will not go to bed just yet,' she said. 'I'm not tired.'

'As you wish, miss.'

She did not even want to go into the garden. She sat in the dining room, after Smithson had cleared away the plates, her mind tumbling. Eventually she put her head in her hands and felt a dozing sleep overtake her.

'Oh, it's you, miss.' Smithson was at the door. She lifted her head, sleep making her heavy. 'I'd forgotten you were here.'

'I think I fell asleep,' she said, dizzily.

'There is a gentleman on the telephone for Mr de Witt. Someone from London. I can't find Mr Vine anywhere.'

'Oh.'

'Your father said he was not to be disturbed.'

'Where is he?'

'I last saw him in his study. If the gentleman says it is urgent, I think we must find him.'

'I will go,' said Celia. 'Don't worry.' She hurried out to the corridor, to Rudolf's study, and knocked on the door. 'Papa?' There was no answer. She pushed open the door. He was not there.

Smithson stood behind her. 'I think he may be sleeping, miss.'

Celia had not been into her parents' bedroom since she was a child with nightmares. 'You go to wake him up,' she said. 'I'll ask the man to wait.'

She walked along the corridor to the room where Rudolf kept the telephone. Smithson had left the door open. She pushed through and stood at the booth. She picked up the telephone, cool in her hands. The line crackled. 'Hello?' she said, down the receiver. 'Mr de Witt is just coming.'

'Mrs de Witt?'

She was about to say no, but the voice continued. 'It's Edward Lewis here, from the London office, Mrs de Witt.'

'Hello, Mr Lewis.'

'I am sorry to disturb you, Mrs de Witt. I'm calling from the house of a friend in Westminster. London is quite overcome. There are people everywhere, cheering outside the Palace and trying to get to Downing Street. They are crying out for the King. Mr Asquith has put down an ultimatum. If Germany does not retreat from Belgium by eleven tonight, we are at war.'

'What time is it now?'

'Nearly eleven.'

Celia strained to hear. 'What do you think will happen?'

'Word is that Germany will not respond. We have spoken of getting in place an emergency plan, to protect the interests here and in Germany. We can lose no time. Can you tell your husband? It is imperative that we speak.'

'Yes.'

'Ah. Mrs de Witt, can you hear? I'll hold the telephone at the window.'

She strained at the crackle down the line. A clanging sound, very faint. It was the strike of Big Ben. She sat in silence and listened. Ten strikes – eleven. At the final one, there were cheers.

'I don't know, Mrs de Witt. I think perhaps we are at war. Let me go to see.'

There was a bump as he put the telephone down. Celia sat quietly, holding the receiver, staring at it. Where was her father? After five minutes or so, Mr Lewis came back, breathless. 'The street is full of people cheering and shouting that we are going to war. It's not certain, of course, but I think... I think...'

'Oh.'

'Everybody is calling for the King. Mrs de Witt, can you hear?' His voice was excited, in spite of himself.

'I can hear faintly.'

'Well, I should leave you now. I will go to the Palace to see if there is an announcement. I will call again from the office tomorrow morning. Goodbye, Mrs de Witt.'

'Goodbye.' She heard the click as he put the telephone down. The line fuzzed. She continued to listen, hearing only noise that meant nothing.

There were footsteps. Rudolf with Smithson. Her father was gathering his dressing gown around him. 'What is it?' he said. 'Is Mr Lewis there?'

'He's gone to Buckingham Palace.'

'Gone to Buckingham Palace? But why on earth would he do that?'

'Because he says we are at war with Germany.'

Rudolf looked at her, his face paling.

'I must speak to him. Was he in the offices?'

'No, at a friend's house. He has gone out now.'

'And what is the telephone number?'

'I don't know.' She felt a tinge of fear. Her father's face was angry.

'How can you not know the number, Celia? What is wrong with you?'

'I'm sorry, Papa.' He had never been so angry with her before. She had no idea what to say.

'Well you should be! Such carelessness!'

Hot tears sprang to her eyes. She turned and rushed up the stairs.

On the second corridor, near the turn for Emmeline's room, she heard the sound of a man's voice. She saw that the window was open and crept closer. It was Tom's voice. He was outside in the garden, just underneath where she stood.

'What are you talking about, Michael? Good at sport? What can that possibly matter?'

Someone replied – Michael. Celia could not catch his words.

'You don't mean that.'

Celia edged forward, and as she did so, she knocked the table decked with her mother's photographs of the family. They rattled flat; five fell off.

'What's that?' said Tom.

'Someone is up there,' said Michael. 'You should go.'

'Michael! Tom! It's me!' Celia called from the window. She saw them look up.

'What are you doing there?' hissed Michael. 'Go on, Tom, go.' Tom hurried away, not glancing back. Michael looked up at her. 'Celia. You should be in bed.'

'What were you talking about?'

She wished she could have jumped from the window and followed Tom. Instead, she got to her knees and started picking up the silver-framed photographs: Lady Deerhurst, Arthur as a baby. She put them back on the table, even though she could barely see and knew they were going back in the wrong order, out of place.

SEVEN

Michael pulled apart the fronds of the trees where Celia was sitting. 'Take a walk with me, Ceels?' She had an hour and a half before lessons with Mr Janus started again, after a whole morning of equations. She was supposed to go up to her room for a rest after luncheon, but instead she ran out to sit on her stone under the trees, her place. She didn't want to be in the house anyway.

It was Friday, three days after the party, the tables cleared, the food thrown away because Verena did not want to see it. Celia had thrust her dress to the back of the wardrobe.

Jennie had brought in women from the village to scrub the drive. But cleaning wasn't enough; they couldn't take the house back to what it had been. Rudolf paced around, tried to use the telephone, talked of going to London. He said the government had banned export of animals, though it probably wouldn't make meat cheaper in the end, because there wouldn't be any more imports; the most important thing was that the factories kept going. He talked of writing to the *Mail* to tell them to stop printing tips on how to economise. 'Now is not the time to economise,' he roared. 'It is the time to spend!' Verena quivered on the brink of tears. 'I know it will be over by Christmas,' she said. 'But Christmas is so far away.'

Mr Vine had fallen ill on the word of the war and had retired to bed. They had never been without their butler for so long. Rudolf said he had requested permission to visit his relatives in Surrey – a thing he had never asked for before. Mrs Bell had begged to remain with her niece, whose husband was planning to sign up. 'She will never return,' said Verena dully. She and Rudolf had until the seventeenth to register at the police station. Verena was refusing to go. 'I am no alien,' she snapped. 'Neither are you, husband. You're a better subject than Mr Asquith himself.' On the day before, Verena had gripped Celia's hand, holding tight as if she could not see anyone, and started talking about how her father had always said it was the responsibility of the British Empire to balance the power in Europe before it was too late. 'And that was in 1880!' she said, pained. The servants were under orders not to let anyone in.

'Come on, Ceels, what do you think? A wander into Eversley?'

'I could do.' She would normally have leapt at it, but she wouldn't this time; she wanted to show him that he was wrong to have hidden himself in his room on the day of the party. 'Where do you want to go?'

'Let's go down to the village green.'

'Michael! We can't! They didn't come to our party.'

'No one cares about parties any more. We are at war now.'

'I don't think Mama would like it.'

'She is in her bedroom with a headache. She won't know. Listen, Ceels, I don't have all day. If you don't want to come, then I'll go alone.'

'I'm coming.' She jumped to her feet and the two of them set off towards the side gate, nodding at the gardeners as they walked through. There were traces of red paint on the stone and the gateposts of the drive. Rudolf had said the rain would wash the last of it away.

'Who do you think did this to us?' Celia asked.

'Who cares? They all think it.'

'But someone must have!' Someone must have found the paint – bought it, even – carried it down to their drive, scrawled the words, not caring who saw them.

'Stop it, Celia. I don't think it's worth thinking about.'

Out on the road, Michael was quiet. Celia asked him about the aeroplanes, but he shrugged off her questions. She wanted to talk to him about so many things: the war, whether the factories would do well, and Hilde and Johann. But he dug his hands in his pockets and didn't look at her, walking fast so she had to skip every five steps or so to keep up with him. The sun was very hot. No cars passed them, or even carts. As they came closer to the village, the houses thickened along the road: low cottages, the scrubs of grass outside piled up with broken chairs, rubbish, an old pan, left there in the hope that someone might take them away. There were goats and sheep tethered to the front of some, pigs tumbling in dirt by others. Outside one with a roof that was losing its thatch, two women were talking, arms folded, a baby in a basket at the foot of one, three children of about four or so poking at the ground with a stick, a bored-looking older girl supervising them, her pinafore grimy with dirt. As Celia and Michael passed, the women stopped talking and stared at them. The children halted too and gazed. You could have come to the party, Celia wanted to say.

'Look away,' hissed Michael in her ear. 'Stop staring at them.' Celia tore her eyes away from the round-eyed children on the ground, the stern-faced women. He gripped her arm. 'Do you want them to come after us?'

'They are only children,' she protested when they were clear of the house.

'Their mothers aren't. I really don't think you understand a thing, Celia.'

'I do! I understand everything.' But she faltered as she was saying the words.

They turned a corner and came to the village green. It was, Celia thought, surely one of the prettiest in the area, the pond at the centre, the houses dotted around, the spire of the church visible over the tops of the pubs and the few shops: a baker's, butcher's, greengrocer's, haberdashery and dry goods. The two pubs either side of the pond, the Drake and Duck and the Bell, were full. Men and women spilled out over the grass in front, holding glasses as they leant on tables and talked in the sun. To the side of the Bell was another big crowd of men.

'It looks like it is a holiday day.'

'We are all at war. It is a holiday for them, Celia, don't you see that? Keep walking.'

They were heading towards the White Hart. 'You don't want to go to the pub, do you?' she said, suddenly panicked. 'We can't!' The men were red-faced, their arms slung around the women. Pubs were for working men, servants. The whole world would fall down if people like Michael and Celia went to one.

'Of course not. We are just walking.' He hurried on to the path across the green, making for the White Hart. She clutched his hand but he threw her off. About three yards away from the crowd of men, they stopped. 'Look,' he said. 'What do you think of that?' Celia could see men in bright red jackets sitting behind a table. Their buttons shone silver. 'Don't you think that is marvellous?'

'What is it?'

'The men are signing up to go to war. They set up tables here yesterday evening. Tom Cotton told me. They'll probably be in France in a week, fighting for the King.'

'But ...' She couldn't say what she wanted to, somehow couldn't explain that it didn't seem fair to have a stall right next to the pub. 'They might get killed.'

'Thousands are signing up across the country. Imagine how proud they are. Don't you think it's exciting?'

She realised she did, a little: there it was, a surge in her heart, like before the school play started or when Rudolf had taken her to a concert in London and the big trumpets began playing.

'Look at those other men at the pub, just standing there. They must feel like cowards.'

'I'd be afraid.'

He tossed his head. 'But you are a girl, of course, Celia. Why would you think otherwise?'

'Don't say that!'

But he didn't seem to hear. He stood there staring at the men in red jackets, who were holding out papers, talking, offering pens. She was reminded of their school trip to the National Gallery, and how Miss Grey, the history teacher they all mocked for her escaping hair and flappy ways, had gazed at the portrait of Olympia, her eyes yearning.

Celia waited next to him, dipping her head because the men and women in the pub were staring at them, her face flushed. The sun was burning her hair. Still Michael did not speak to her, and she felt afraid that he might tell her to go home, walk back alone, past the houses and the women watching.

Finally he brought himself back. 'We should leave. Come on home now. Mr Janus will want you soon.'

She turned, glad to leave the red-coated men behind. 'What were you and Tom talking of that night after the party? I heard you.'

'Oh, this and that.'

'It was something!' She could not bear the idea that they had a secret from her.

'Really, Celia, it was nothing.' He strode forward, making her run again to keep up. He did not talk to her on the way home. At the house with the falling-down roof, the three children were still outside with the stick but the women and the older girl had gone. They could hear the sound of a woman crying and begging, a man shouting back. Celia wanted to stop, to smile at the children, but Michael pulled her on.

Back at the house, they walked around the side and Emmeline was there. Celia had seen her very little over the past few days. The change in her appearance was painful. Her beautiful eyes were rimmed with deep purple and her cheeks were hollow and grey. She was wearing her favourite apple-green and lace gown, but it looked as if she had worn it yesterday as well, maybe even the day before, for it was dirty around the neck and the hemline.

'Where have you been? To the village?'

Celia nodded. 'There were men at the pub.'

'Did you see Sir Hugh anywhere?' Her voice was almost cracking in her desperation.

Michael put his hand on Emmeline's arm. 'No, we didn't, but you know, Ems, he wouldn't be around the village green. You mustn't worry. He'll come. He must be busy with something. You'll look back and smile at this when you're married.'

A tear was forming in Emmeline's eye. 'I just wish he would write. The country's at war and he hasn't written to me.'

'I'm sure he is occupied. He is probably still away on business,' said Michael. 'Really, that's all it is.'

'Yes,' said Celia, nodding too hard, she thought. 'It will be a business thing for him. With the war, he might have to apply himself to something like that.'

Emmeline shook her head. 'This is his favourite gown, you know.' She touched her neckline. 'He likes the lace here.'

'You look very pretty,' said Michael, patting her arm again.

'Sir Hugh will be pleased when he comes,' said Celia, looking at her sister's pained face and feeling guilty at having detested Sir Hugh so.

'Well there you are, Miss Celia!' Mr Janus came around the corner. He saw Emmeline and his face changed. 'Good morning, Miss de Witt.' His sharp voice softened and he gazed at her. Celia had once asked him what had caused his illness, and he had blushed, said he had caught a chill. He still looked unwell, Celia thought, thin and pale, his hair fine as if it had only recently grown back, like a rabbit that had been underground too long. And yet, she had to admit, when they were supposed to be doing history and he was distracted by philosophy and started talking about how economies had been dominated by kings, he was very passionate. You could see that he might have been interesting, before he was ill.

Emmeline barely shrugged. 'Good morning.' She turned her face away from him.

Celia could see that Mr Janus was itching to say how beautiful Emmeline looked, how he admired the dress, her hair. She was staring at the floor, trying to hide the tears in her eyes. Michael stood there, looking at them all. 'Celia, you should go to your lessons now,' he said. 'Will you take her, Mr Janus?'

Mr Janus snapped to attention. 'Of course, Mr de Witt. Come along, Miss Celia. Let us make a start on Louis XIV.' He walked away, Celia following him. All afternoon Mr Janus droned on about Cardinal Mazarin, and wouldn't be distracted into discussing the inequality of people and kings.

After lessons, Jennie came to collect Celia as usual. 'There will be a proper dinner tonight, miss,' she said. 'Mr de Witt has said. Seven sharp. Miss Wilton will come to you at six.'

Celia had not mourned three days without Miss Wilton's harsh fingers. But then a dinner meant that things were returning to how they had been, making the party a thing of the past, like Cardinal Mazarin.

'Is Sir Hugh coming?'

'I don't think so, miss.'

They walked back to Celia's room together, the noise of the house flowing around them: a maid clattering up the stairs; Thompson or someone moving furniture around; Miss Wilton knocking at Verena's door. Things were going back to how they had been before.

'I think the bravest thing a man can do is to fight!' Michael had drunk six of the crystal glasses of wine – Celia had been counting. His face was red and his hair was falling over his forehead. 'If everyone else is going, he should go too.'

'But everyone else is not going, dear,' Verena said, patiently. Rudolf was concentrating on eating, his knife cutting the meat in swift strokes. 'It's all just talk in the newspapers. They say that people are running out to sign up, but I just don't believe it. We have a plentiful army in this country. That is enough.'

'What do you know, Mother?'

'Dear. I have seen many wars. Always the same. There is a big fanfare at the start and then it all ends in a damp squib.'

'This is different.'

'That is why I have told the ladies' committee that Stoneythorpe cannot be given up under any circumstances. I had a letter from Lady Redroad requesting the use of the Hall as a place for men to recuperate. Not for the wounded, because of course there will not be many; just for those men who are tired after the war and wish to rest. She said we had an ideal position for the railway station and the kind of ground-floor rooms needed. Warbrook is just as good, if you ask me. She might surrender her own house before she starts asking others.'

'Imagine,' said Rudolf. 'Stoneythorpe full of nurses.'

'We've enough to do with this ridiculous demand to give up the car.'

'I think—' Celia wanted to say that she thought it would be splendid, that ladies at Stoneythorpe tending poor soldiers would be great and heroic. But Verena shot her a look.

Emmeline was staring at the table, fiddling with the lace on her collar. She had eaten nothing as far as Celia could tell, just pushed her meat and potatoes around the plate.

Michael was still full of questions. 'What about Smithson and Thompson, then? Shouldn't they be allowed to go?'

'They wouldn't want to,' said Rudolf. 'They have important work here. They don't need a job.'

'The men aren't signing up because they need a job.'

'We saw them—' Celia began. Michael kicked her hard under the table.

'You saw what, Celia dear?' said Verena.

Michael was glowering at her. 'Birds,' she said, improvising wildly. 'We saw a beautiful flock of birds over the garden. They were not fighting.'

'You should be more like your sister,' Rudolf said, putting down his knife. 'Think of birds, not soldiers.'

Out in the cooler air of the garden, when Rudolf and Verena had retired to the parlour and Emmeline had walked heavily to her room, Celia ran through the dinner in her mind. Michael and Rudolf picking away at each other with words, Michael hurrying into the garden after it was all over. Celia had felt sure she had seen the glow of a cigarette just ahead, but when she walked on, there was no sign of anyone. She looked back at the house, scattered windows lit and dark clouds skating over the roof. Tomorrow, she decided, tomorrow she would tell them about how they had gone to see the soldiers in the village. She would say to Rudolf that he should let Michael just talk about it, that he wouldn't really do anything. If her father wasn't so quick to anger, Michael would be calmer.

She walked a little further, feeling the evening wetness of

the ground on the soles of her feet. If only things could be as straightforward as gardens. Flowers grew, insects ate them and trees drank the water from the soil. It was all simple, the same thing over and over.

'I'm going to pretend you don't exist, war,' she said, out loud. She would not think about it. She walked on, her feet padding in the damp grass.

'Celia!' Tom's voice. 'Celia, over here!' His shadow was cast against the great oak tree.

'What are you doing down there?' She trod carefully through the wet leaves.

'I'm waiting for you!' He sprang up in front of her, the smile on his face so wide that she could see it in the gloom. It surprised her when he stood up so quickly, tall and broad, not a little boy any more.

'I thought you might come to the garden,' he hissed.

'Were you *hiding*?'

'Some might say the same about you!' He was giggling, his eyes wide in the dark. 'Are *you* hiding?'

'No! I was thinking about the war.'

'Grand thing, isn't it? And over soon.'

'Shouldn't you have gone home by now?'

'I thought I'd stay! See the stars.' He waved a leg from behind the tree. 'Dance with me?'

'I don't know how.' She was blushing in the dark.

'You must! They must teach you something at that school of yours.' And then, laughing, he came from behind the tree and seized her around the waist. 'Let's sing!' he cried.

'Papa will hear,' she hissed.

But Tom wasn't listening; he was singing out to the stars. He caught her and danced her around, whirling her to and fro, laughing. She could not remember who tripped, whether it was her or Tom, but then they were tangled on the ground, laughing and breathless. He propped himself up and leaned over her. 'You are a very pretty girl,' he said solemnly. His eyes were bright.

Something was going to happen, she felt it. But then he dropped and lay beside her.

'I've a secret. There's something I'm going to do. I want to tell you but I can't.'

'Maybe I don't want to know.' Michael's refusal to tell her what they had been talking about was rankling. 'I think I've heard enough secrets.' Jonathan saying that Emmeline wasn't his type of broad, that he would go in the morning. Michael wanting to leave college. Verena and her worries; what Sarah had said about the King needing men. The girls at school were always swapping secrets, using them to leave people out, especially Celia, and when she heard them, they were nothing more than silly things, jokes about teachers or nasty words about someone's hair. 'I think I want to know them but then I don't. If secrets really matter, you don't tell them to anyone.'

'Please. If I die—'

'Why would you die? You're only a year older than me.' She clasped his hand.

He smiled up at her. 'You're right. Why would I die?'

He brought himself up again. Then he bent over and his face touched hers, and before she understood anything, he was kissing her. She stiffened – and then reached for him. The darkness behind them leaned down and wrapped them in its arms.

The next morning, Celia woke with her head heavy and groggy from the night before. What had she been doing dancing around the garden with Tom? Rudolf and Verena would surely have heard, seen. She buried her head in the pillow. The feeling of Tom's hand was burned on to her skin. And his words.

She turned on to her back, gazing up at the stripes of light coming through the curtains as they shifted on the ceiling.

Then there was a sound, a terrible cry, half suppressed, something like an animal being strangled. She swung herself out of bed, hurried her gown on and ran into the hall. The person was weeping now, great hiccupping sobs. The sound was coming from Michael's room. She ran then, tripping over the cord of her gown as the noise subsided into low, awful wails. She turned the corner and there was her mother, holding on to Miss Wilton, her head buried in her maid's arm. Rudolf in his blue dressing gown was dashing red-faced up the stairs, Emmeline behind him, her features suddenly tiny in her pale face.

Michael's door was open.

'What is it?' shouted Rudolf above the noise. 'Wife, what is happening?'

She did not look round, cried even more loudly.

'What is wrong?'

Miss Wilton turned to face him. 'It is Mr de Witt, sir. He's gone.'

Rudolf's face drained white, as pale as Emmeline's. 'What do you mean, gone?'

Verena lifted her head and gazed at them all, Celia on one side, Rudolf and Emmeline on the other. Her face was ravaged by tears. 'Michael is gone! Gone to die!'

'What is this?' said Rudolf, pushing past Verena and Miss Wilton through the open door. Then he too let out a terrible wail. Celia rushed forward. Her father was sitting on Michael's bed, head in his hands, holding a piece of paper. Above him, the planes were dancing, clopping in the air from the open window. He looked up at her. 'Your mother is right. Michael has gone to fight.'

She leaped towards him, hardly knowing how she did so, and seized the paper from his hands. It was a long letter, and she could barely make out some of the words. She turned it over, picking them out as they flashed before her eyes. *Truth... love... bravery... the King. I want to really feel alive. To live for real, not just in this pretend world. Do not worry about me. I will be in the open air, hearing the birds sing and feeling the soil of France under my feet. I will bring peace.*

'Papa,' she said. And then she looked at the final line of the letter. *I will not be alone.*

Oh God help us. Fear filled her mind. She put the letter back in her father's hands, backed out of the room, past her weeping mother, and then she ran. 'Celia!' her father was calling. She did not turn back. She hurried to her room, pulled on a shabby woollen winter gown that buttoned at the front and Verena never let her wear except for when she was painting, then her old pair of boots, fingers stumbling over the laces, begging her hands to hurry, slapping the laces for not obeying. Finally clothed, she ran out of the door, down the stairs, through the hallway, past the parlour, the dining room, the other sitting room, towards the kitchen and out into the garden. She ran, ran up the hill, turning past the flower beds and flinging herself at the stable door.

'Marks! Where are you?'

Marks emerged, rubbing his eyes. 'Very early for a ride, miss.'

'I don't want a ride. Is Tom here?'

He stood looking at her. His delay was unbearable, entirely unbearable. 'Tom?'

'Tom Cotton!'

He raised an eyebrow. 'The young lady of the house enquiring for Tom at this time of the morning? Wouldn't credit it.'

'Is he?'

He drew his shoulder up slowly and dropped it again. 'Who knows?'

'He's not, is he?' As soon as the words were out of her mouth, she started to back away. She heard him laugh, but she did not care; she was running, running, careening down the hill, falling over a lace that had become untied, dashing around the side of the house and out into the road – where she had never been alone before. She knew where to go. She hurried past early-morning labourers and women collecting water, children awake early and playing, old people stumbling along; turned down the cobbled road and right, then left, to a row of low houses with white fronts. She flung herself at the door. 'Mrs Cotton! Let me in!'

Two old men sitting together at the far end of the row of houses stared, enjoying the show. A shutter on the other side opened and a man's head peered out. Celia thought, in that moment, how strange she must look, red-faced, her heart hot in her mouth, desperate and afraid.

'Mrs Cotton! It's me, Celia!'

The door opened a crack and a dark-haired woman in an apron peered out. Celia had not seen her since they were in London – she had grown even thinner, and her body was bent over. Little Missy clung to her waist. As soon as she saw Celia, she tried to close the door.

Celia put her hand against it. 'No! Please let me in. Missy!'

She banged again and the door opened. Mrs Cotton stepped back. The corridor behind her was dark. Celia blushed at her boldness, arriving at the door like this.

'What are you doing here, Miss de Witt?' said Mrs Cotton evenly. 'You shouldn't be here.' Missy gazed up, her great eyes wide in the gloom. Celia could hardly believe how close the place was, the corridor cluttered with wooden things. It smelled damp. So many times she had thought of Tom's house, thought of him living in a pretty country cottage like the ones in the stories. She had not imagined it would look like this: dirty, peeling paint on the walls.

'Is Tom here?'

'No. He spent the night at the Hall, so to be better up with the horses.'

'May I see his room?'

'I think you should leave, miss.' Celia saw the fear in the woman's eyes. She realised then that Mrs Cotton was afraid of what would happen if Rudolf found that Celia had been in the house. A cruel instinct of how to get what she wanted came to her. 'If you will not let me up to his room, I will tell my father that Tom told me I had to come here!' Mrs Cotton dropped her head into her hands, backed away. 'Where is it?' Celia cried.

'Up there,' said Missy, pointing.

Celia clambered up the narrow steps, putting her hand on the damp wall and then snatching it back. One room with the door thrust open was clearly that of girls, dresses strewn over the bed. The doll from the lucky dip had been thrown on to the floor, leg in the air. Celia forced herself not to look. She flung open the door of the next one – and knew it was Tom's. The bed was neatly made, the thin blanket pulled over. A set of books on the small table. He had so few things, it was what Celia might have thought a prison cell would be like. She had thought Tom's room would be more like hers, looking out over a neat kitchen garden.

Mrs Cotton, Missy and another, older, red-haired girl were standing behind her. Celia looked at the older girl. She was surely Mary, the one Tom said always wanted her own way. 'What is missing?' she cried at them. 'What's not here that should be?'

Mary considered. 'I can't see his boots. Maybe some books.'

There was no wardrobe, but a pile of clothes on the chair. 'No coat,' Celia said.

'What is all this about?' said Mary. She had a pretty, turned-up nose. At school, Celia would have been jealous of her for her nose.

Celia turned and began pulling the blanket off the bed. 'Michael, my brother, has gone to fight,' she said. 'He wrote that he was not alone.' She looked back at them. 'There has to be a letter!'

Mary paled. 'You think Tom is with him?' A strangled cry came from Mrs Cotton.

'Where would he leave a letter?'

Mary stepped forward, so close to Celia that she could have gripped her hair. She bent to the row of books and picked out one with a leather binding. 'Your father gave him this.' She opened it, and a sheet of paper fell to the ground. Mrs Cotton cried out and dived for it; Mary snatched it first and held it up. She touched the sentences. Mrs Cotton crouched on the floor. *I will read it!* Celia wanted to shout. How could they be so slow? 'Miss de Witt is right, Mother. Tom has gone to France. He says he wants to fight for glory. He says we must not worry about him.'

There was an awful wail, and suddenly Mrs Cotton was grasping at Celia, Missy was shrieking and Mary was grabbing her mother's other hand. 'Stop, Ma, stop!' But Mrs Cotton was strong, pulling Celia down. 'You've taken everything!' she was weeping. 'Your family has taken everything.'

Mary was talking fast to her mother. 'Let her go now, Ma! Stop!' Celia felt herself being hauled up. 'Stop it!' She scrambled to her feet, away from the girl and her mother in a tangle on the floor. Mary looked up. 'Go! Go now! And don't come back.'

Missy was staring at her. Celia meant to run, but instead she put her arms around the child and held her close. 'I'm sorry,' she whispered. Then, as she heard Mrs Cotton push up to her feet, she began to run, down the stairs, out of the door and into the rising sun of the street.

EIGHT

On the way home from Winterbourne for the holidays – had it only been three weeks ago? – Celia had made a resolution. Every day she would choose a new word from the dictionary and use it at least three times, without anybody spotting. At night she would write down the word and the sentences used. In her first six days, she found susurrus, diaphanous, ephemeral, grandiloquent, emaciated and exiguous. No one noticed. She had told only Michael of her plans. 'I would like just an exiguous spreading of butter,' she said to Thompson at breakfast, hoping he might look up and smile. He did not. Well, she told herself, the words would be pleased about it. They sat side by side in her notebook, happily neat, like soldiers.

There were two more words that she had learned, too special to share. Anaphora – the art of beginning repeated sentences with the same word. And her favourite of all, anadiplosis – using the last word of the sentence to begin the next. Words were like that, they would obey. You could put them in a circle, beginning sentences over and over, and they would follow your wishes. She had been choosing new long words every day, since the end of school. She could slip a word in here and there and no one would know, she thought, as if she had shouted out a word in fairy language in the middle of it all.

On the day that Jonathan arrived, she had a new word: misconjugated, which was particularly appealing as it didn't repeat a single letter. But with everything happening that day she'd forgotten to use it. Since then she had barely looked at the dictionary. Now, she thought, what was the use of all those words? Not without Michael and Tom. She could learn five thousand new words, and still Michael would not come home. And it wasn't as if she was going back to school in September. Verena wanted her at home. 'Without Michael and Arthur, I need my daughters with me,' she said. 'Anyway, you are better off here. You know what girls are like. No doubt the German teacher has been sent away and you would not be welcome.'

Celia's form teacher had written her a letter saying they were sorry she would not be returning. Others had written too, all fizzing with excitement about the start of the war. Celia had replied, but when they had written again, she hadn't the heart to keep up the correspondence. What was there to say? She would not be going back to Winterbourne, and she had nothing to do but wait for letters from Michael and Tom. Being told there was a letter for her only to discover that it was one of her classmates updating her on things that did not matter – well, she would not be able to bear that. The whole house was quivering, waiting for news. Mrs Rolls had been crying into her food, and it tasted bad. She blamed the fact that there wasn't much sugar.

When he was at school, Michael had sent her long letters, about the other boys, the masters, the thick custard on the apple sponge at lunch, the silly pranks played by a boy called Elkins. She used to squirrel them away, just for her, savour them in her room. He gave her so many details that she often felt she could imagine herself in the school, eating the puddings, running around the sports field and throwing paper aeroplanes back at Elkins under the desks.

From Magdalene he had sent letters that were more varied, sometimes quite short, other times long, full of his thoughts about the history books he was reading and the essays he was writing. She remembered one letter, bursting with his ideas about the Wars of the Roses, whether it was more than just a family rivalry. She had read it over and over under the cover of her prep books at Winterbourne, touching every word, pondering the questions about Edward IV and Richard III, ready for the debate they might have when they were both home. Within a fortnight, of course, his letters were about Henry VII. She always felt as if she was hurrying to catch him up, then. Now, she took out those letters, read them over and over, as if by looking at his words she might grow closer to him in France.

On the afternoon after Michael and Tom left, the house was in chaos, Rudolf writing letters, Verena alternately weeping and demanding of Thompson, Smithson and Jennie what they knew. Mr Vine grew upset and demanded to leave even earlier to see his relatives in Surrey, and Rudolf let him go. Celia crept away, up the garden and towards the stables. They were empty; Marks was not there. The horses were pacing and blowing hot wind from their nostrils. She went to Silver and touched her. Silver shivered slightly and Celia stroked her side. 'There, girl,' she said. 'There.' Silver shuffled around so that her flank was next to the door. Celia stroked her again. 'Good girl. Good girl.' The other horses were moving around as well. Michael's horse and Emmeline's were turning in their stables. 'Marks will come soon.'

She put her head on Silver's flank. 'Tom will come back to us.' She thought of his room, the few books, the thin pillows on the bed. The tears were rolling down her face on to Silver's coat. 'He will come. Soon.'

She was still there when Marks arrived. His clothes looked rougher than ever.

'You know you are not allowed in here, miss.' His lip wrinkled at her red face, the tears in her eyes.

She was angry at the world, at Tom, at everyone. 'It doesn't matter any more. Tom's gone to war.'

He raised his eyebrow. 'Has he now? Mind you, doesn't matter for him. He knows that you lot will have a job waiting for him whatever he does.'

'He'll come back covered in glory.'

'Or be shot to bits by a dirty Hun. Take your hands off that horse. You're upsetting her.'

She couldn't help it; the angry words seized her. 'You should go to war too.'

'Well I might just do that, you know. Much better money fight-ing. And then where would your precious father be? In the state we are in now, you wouldn't find anyone to look after the horses. They'd have to go.'

'I could look after them!'

'You're a child.'

'I am not.' She leant down to seize a fork. 'I'll show you!' She opened Silver's door and began forking up piles of Silver's straw. The horse watched, quietly.

'Ha! Very good, miss. Let's just see how long you last.' Marks gestured at the saddles. 'You could polish those next.' He walked out. Celia carried on forking. 'Good girl, Silver,' she said. 'Good girl.' She could feel the sadness rising in her, the anger against everyone, and she tried to fight it down. But then Silver backed up against her and knocked her with her foot, and that was the end of it. The tears started in her eyes and she slumped against the side of the stable. She was so angry and afraid, she wanted to scream.

Marks arrived back at the door. 'Given up already?' He was smiling, showing all his teeth.

Celia jumped to her feet and pushed past him, tears blurring her vision as she ran back to the house.

Every day since, she had woken up, seen the sun slipping through the curtains and thought of rising. Then she would remember that Tom and Michael had gone and she would begin to weep. She tried to tell herself that those tears should be her only ones of the day, but they kept seeping out, sliding down her cheeks in the afternoons and pooling in her eyes when she lay down to sleep.

Mr Lewis had a friend with contacts in the War Office who had told them that he expected Michael would be training in England for a few months, although he could not say where. Rudolf had written to the War Office, but as Mr Lewis's friend said, it was likely to be months before he received a reply. He had even gone to the headquarters in Winchester, but when he arrived, the men had already left, and no one could tell him if Michael had been there or not. He came home that night bowed, his shoulders bent.

Now, he did not go anywhere. Instead he read the newspaper

every morning and told them the news. Outside, Celia realised, the war was growing, creating, becoming great, the thing that they did everything for. The newspapers talked of troop movements to France, the terror of the Germans. Celia read hopelessly, avidly: descriptions of the discussions back and forth, the late-night Cabinet meetings, the letters to the King, the German ambassador refusing to reply, everything that had brought them to the moment of war. Mr Lewis had told her about the people swarming around Buckingham Palace to cheer for the King, but she still read about it, imagining herself there, looking up at the Queen. The newspapers reported many spies. *Does signing as an alien take the malice out of a man?* was in the *Daily Mail*.

'I've had a letter about the horses,' Rudolf said, over a cold-cut dinner. 'From someone who says he's the local commissioner. He says he understands we must submit them to the war effort.'

'No!' Celia pitched forward. 'You can't let them.'

'Quite, Celia,' said Verena, sharply. 'They're ours. The children need them.' Rudolf raised an eyebrow. 'All of them,' she snapped.

'Wife, we must be shown to support.'

Celia stared at her father, stricken. Silver carrying things over the channel on a boat. 'Papa, she might *die*.'

'They wouldn't be the most useful of horses, I suppose,' Rudolf said. 'They have been trained to trot around and carry ladies. Not go to fight.' He pondered, staring at his plate. Celia beseeched him silently. He looked up, slapping the table. 'I know. I shall offer my car instead.'

'Oh Papa, would you?' Celia's heart swelled.

He shrugged. 'I expect it is only a matter of time with the car, you know. They say no aliens should have a car. So I might as well.'

Three days later, two policemen came and drove the Rolls Royce away.

Rudolf was pleased by the news. 'The modern war is an excellent idea,' he said. 'No one hurt.' He told them that men were amassing in France to fight. Both armies had begun digging long holes in the ground, from which they would attack the other side. They would be guarded by rolls of barbed wire, and it would be the particular responsibility of teams of men to check on this wire every night. *The Times* said there would be none of the casualties of the Boer War or the Crimea. The trenches would allow the British to assemble in an efficient fashion and prove their superiority over the Germans before they all came home at Christmas.

After a week, the newspapers had changed, no longer discussing troops and Asquith meeting the King, but relating terrible stories from Belgium about children shot along with adults, and churches burned down with babies inside them. Verena fretted about Arthur in Paris, seized the newspapers from Celia when she saw them, but Celia was a fast reader; she rushed past the housekeeping and economising tips, took in all the stories of babies without their mothers, soldiers shooting little boys for fun.

'Why can we not help them?' she said to Mr Janus.

He shrugged. 'I suppose Asquith thinks the entirety of Belgium will come and live here if we do. We haven't space for everyone. Anyway, maybe the Germans will follow.' Mr Janus was the only man unenthusiastic about the new modern war. 'Now, Celia, back to Richelieu. No point following the war. It proceeds badly, as history tends to show us.'

'The Germans can't come here!'

'They might.'

That night, Celia practised barricading her door with her desk and her chest of drawers. If the Germans came, they would have to hammer through her doors, and by then she would have jumped out of the window. She packed a small bag: clothes, her favourite horse ornament and two books. She stole a packet of raisins from the kitchen and stuffed that in too.

'You must put the wardrobe in front of your door,' she said to Verena. 'Then, if they come for us, you can climb out and we can all meet in the garden to run away.'

'Dear me, Celia,' said Verena. 'We are quite safe here.'

Emmeline shook her head. 'I am not running anywhere.'

There had been no word from Sir Hugh since the party. Two days earlier, Rudolf had intervened by sending a letter himself. He and Verena had sat together at breakfast, not speaking to Celia but talking together in low voices. 'But what if I push him the wrong way?' said Rudolf, anguished. 'I could anger him.'

Finally Verena got to her feet. 'It must be done. There is no question. Not a letter asking about his intentions, no need for that, not yet. Just an invitation to dine here on Saturday. It is simple enough, husband.'

Rudolf stood up heavily. 'As you will.' He closed the door after him and they heard his footsteps padding to the study. Emmeline spent that day in her room and refused to come out for dinner.

There had been nothing from Michael either. Celia wanted never to leave the house in case a letter came – or, she dreamed, a visit from Michael himself. He would walk in the door, holding out his hand. 'The Germans have agreed not to fight,' he said. 'So I have come home!'

'Come, Celia. You must accompany me. It is Lady Redroad's sewing committee at Warbrook.' Verena stood in the door of the bedroom. The brave look on her pale face pierced Celia's heart. Just over two weeks since Tom and Michael had gone, and Verena believed that things could be the same again if only she kept faith in the future. She was standing perfectly erect and still, her blouse spotlessly white, her hair so neatly arranged. Only the pearl brooch at her neck quivered a little, betraying her.

Celia was sitting on her bed, book open on her lap, although she had not been reading. She had been trying to write to Tom, in her mind. *I'm waiting for you. We hope we'll see you soon. As I told you before, Marks says he might go to war, so he could take your place.*

'Miss Wilton has arranged your hair nicely, as I asked her to. Now, put on your blue dress with the edging and come out with me. It is important we present ourselves at the sewing committee. Lady Redroad said it is for the poor people of Belgium.'

'Why can't Emmeline go?'

'She is not well, dear. She has a headache. You know she's been very tired.'

Celia stood up with ill grace. 'Well, if Emmeline won't come then I suppose I have to.'

'Good. I will meet you downstairs and we will take the carriage.'

The footman announced them as they entered: 'Mrs de Witt. Miss de Witt.' Celia felt she heard an edge of scorn in his voice. Seven ladies turned to look at them, all erect in silk dresses more exotic than anything even Emmeline would wear. The walls were striped blue and gold and hung with portraits of august-looking old men, glaring out over heavy vases on tables.

The footman gestured towards two chairs. Celia wanted to seize her mother's hand and say: 'Sorry, Lady Redroad. We have a prior appointment.' Instead they stood there, feeling the terrible late August heat, made worse because Lady Redroad would never open the windows, for that would mean the beginning of the end.

In the centre was a great pile of white sheets, and each lady had one on her lap. Maids stood around the walls. Celia wondered, guiltily, if the maids weren't faster at sewing than all of them, but she knew they were there to serve tea, stand to attention. Maids doing the sewing while they got their own tea was not the point.

'Welcome,' said Lady Redroad, a tall woman with thinning hair, dressed in green. Her voice was cool. 'We have here Lady Stormont, Lady Martens and Miss Martens, Mrs Fitzgerald, Mrs James and' – she gestured towards an older woman in the corner – 'the Dowager Lady Redroad. The sheets and the thread are on the table. Mary, pass Mrs and Miss de Witt their work.'

'Thank you so much,' said Verena, too fast and too eager. Celia blushed for her. It was only due to the Dowager Lady Redroad that they had been invited at all. She had met Verena at a charity drive a few years ago and sent her intermittent invitations, usually late, a few days before the event started. Still, they had her to thank for the meeting with Sir Hugh.

The maid passed two sheets and cotton. Celia had no idea what to do with it, not really. She had learned how to sew from their governesses and then at school, but that was embroidery and fancy sewing. She didn't know how to edge a sheet. The maid bent down to show her that the edges had already been tacked up with big looping stitches. 'There, miss.' She pointed at the spot where she should begin. Celia put her hand there. At school, the teachers had despaired of her sewing. Gwendolyn produced perfect squares of embroidered cotton; Celia's came out greying and frayed, squeezed where she had pulled the thread too tight. She gazed at one of the maids, tiny, neat hands held in front of her apron. She, surely, would be a thousand times better.

'How are your three further children, Mrs de Witt?' asked Lady Redroad, without enthusiasm.

'Arthur, my eldest boy, is studying in Paris.' Once, her mother had swelled with pride at the words. Now her voice faltered.

'Indeed. Surely he will be on his way home now.'

'I believe Paris is quite safe. Michael is my younger boy. I have also Emmeline, who is nineteen.'

'Nineteen? She must be quite out.'

'The elder Miss de Witt is something of a beauty, I understand,' piped up the Dowager from the corner.

Verena nodded.

'And due to be married to Sir Hugh Bradshaw, no less.'

Celia dipped her head, stared at her sewing, on which she had not done a single stitch.

Verena nodded again. Previously she would have talked at length about the wedding, Sir Hugh, Callerton Manor. 'Yes, she is.' Her voice was tiny.

'Quite a match,' said one of the women coolly. Lady Martens, Celia thought.

Verena did not reply. Finally a new conversation started up about the relative heights of Lady Martens' and the other women's children. Verena bent her head to her sewing; Celia watched her needle darting in and out of the material. Piles of sheets to go to the men in France. Celia knew she was ridiculous to imagine that Tom might touch the sheet she had sewn – there were so many men there – but she couldn't help it.

Miss Martens, an insipid girl of thirteen or so, smirked at her. Celia looked back with the stare she used when she played at being a witch to put a spell on Emmeline. *Don't look at me*, she wanted to say.

The conversation about the heights faded. 'You did not tell us about your younger son, Mrs de Witt,' said Lady Redroad, breaking the silence.

Verena's needle halted.

'Is he also at school?'

'Michael was at Cambridge. Magdalene.'

'I see. But no longer.'

'He is going to France for the King.' She stumbled over the last word.

'How very patriotic,' exclaimed the Dowager. 'Marvellous! Those young gentlemen who choose to volunteer are the backbone of this country. At the end of the Crimea, they were talking of forcing men to fight – can you imagine? We are very lucky to have young men who will lead the way.' Celia turned to smile at her, hoping it wasn't too disrespectful.

'I was horrified to read of the rush of ordinary men to sign up,' said Lady Redroad. 'We have a trained army. Men who come from the serving classes will only muddle things. Which regiment is your son with, Mrs de Witt? One of the Hampshires?'

'No. No, he is not.'

'A London regiment?'

'No.'

'Well, which one is he in exactly?'

'I confess I cannot remember.'

'You cannot remember. Dear me. But it is surely Lord Crichton's. I believe Lord MacAdam's son is an officer in that regiment. He must know him. I shall ask Lord MacAdam when I next see him.'

Verena held herself still. 'In truth, Lady Redroad, we do not believe he is an officer. We are not entirely sure.'

'You are not entirely sure?'

'No, we are not. His departure was a surprise.'

'Do you mean, Mrs de Witt,' said Lady Martens, 'that he has gone off with one of the ordinary battalions?' Celia had her witch stare ready, but it wasn't working. Just when she needed a spell, none came.

'A Pals battalion?' said another woman, her mouth open.

Verena was still holding the needle in her hand. It was trembling so that Celia thought she might drop it. 'I don't think so.' Men with nothing in common but living in the same village or town. *Mixing of classes*, Verena had said in horror.

'Oh no, no,' said the Dowager. 'The Pals are for men from the *north*.'

'Well,' said Lady Redroad, looking around. 'Not an officer.'

'Very brave.'

'Quite. We need every man we can enlist to fight the enemy. Such atrocities committed against the poor Belgians.'

'Children burned alive, I understand,' said Lady Redroad.

'Mrs Phelps is planning a bazaar for them,' said the Dowager.

'Mrs Phelps could not run a bazaar if she tried. We shall have to take the lead. I was thinking that we might engage in some first-aid classes, ladies.'

'An excellent idea,' said Lady Martens, soothingly.

'And some educational lectures. How to distinguish a spy.'

'They are everywhere, Lady Redroad. Yesterday I even read that one man took a cake at a tearoom in London and dropped down dead.' Lady Martens lowered her voice. 'Poisoned.' The women all gasped, and gazed at Verena and Celia.

'Shocking,' said Lady Stormont. 'They have tried to flood the country with special toothbrushes from which all the bristles fall out and then you choke to death, I read. Ladies, tell your servants. If they see anyone loitering near the river, they must report it, for they might try to poison the water supply!'

Lady Martens fingered the thin material of her blue sleeve. 'I heard that they were trying to put something in newsprint so that every time you read a newspaper you would get the stuff on your hands and die. They hate *The Times*.'

Lady Redroad was warming to her subject. 'Ladies, if you ever visit a house with German servants, refuse all food and drink.'

'Oh come now, Gertrude,' said the Dowager. 'They said this

kind of thing in the Crimea when we were all wearing crinolines. Nothing happened.'

'Mama, *dear*, we are not in the Crimea any more.' She shrugged. 'The Dowager Countess sometimes forgets that our dear Queen is no longer with us.'

Lady Martens sniffed. 'Mr Asquith needs to act. These people should be immediately taken into prison. And then, when the war is over in October, they should all be sent back to that horrid little country and see how they like it.'

The Dowager shook her needlework. 'That would mean that we would have to arrest the royal family, Gertrude, dear. I would like to see someone try with Queen Mary.'

'Terrifying,' said the woman who Celia thought was Mrs Fitzgerald. 'Trying to get the Queen into a prison!'

'Do not be ridiculous, Mama. You can't possibly talk about arresting the royal family. His Majesty is not German.'

'The Queen is,' said Celia. She sensed Verena stiffen beside her.

Lady Redroad stared at her. Finally she spoke. 'Her Majesty is as English as I.'

'A whole school of children might be dead from a poisoned well before Mr Asquith acts on the enemy within,' said Lady Martens. 'Lord Martens has written to *The Times* about it.'

'Quite right, Lady Martens.'

'But of course, Mrs de Witt, no one would mean your family,' said the Dowager Countess, kindly. 'The ladies here are talking about the other Germans.'

'Yes,' said Lady Redroad, icily. 'Of course not. The other Germans.'

'Thank you,' said Verena. Celia hated her mother for saying those words. She dipped her head and began sewing. She would not shame herself. She would sew as neatly as Gwendolyn.

'Why did you make us go?' she hissed at her mother on the way back to Stoneythorpe. 'Why?'

'We had to go. It is the effort for the war.'

'We should sew at home, then. All day long. I will never go again.'

'You don't understand, Celia. We must be seen to be doing it.'

They arrived back at the house. Smithson met them at the door. 'There has been a letter from Callerton Manor, my lady.' He held out the platter, elaborately polite.

'I should wait for your father,' Verena said to Celia. Rudolf had travelled up to Winchester to visit his bank.

Celia looked at the envelope. 'I think you should open it now. Emmeline can't wait.'

Smithson's hand was shaking slightly as he held the platter.

'You are right, Celia. I shall read it now.' Normally Verena took her letters to the parlour and Rudolf took his to the study. This time, she seized the letter and ripped it open.

'What is it, Mama?' said Celia, watching her eyes scan the paper. Verena's face was filled with fear. 'Tell me!'

Verena dropped her hand, the letter drooping.

'What does it say, Mama? Please.'

Verena turned to her. 'It's not good news, Celia. I must go and speak to Emmeline now. Not good news at all. Smithson, please leave us.'

'He won't come for dinner?' Celia felt panic rising.

'Worse. I don't think he will ever come again. I must speak to Emmeline.'

'I'll come with you!'

'I don't think so, dear. I must talk to her alone. Wait in your room.' Verena turned and walked up the stairs. Celia hurried up behind her.

But Emmeline had already heard them and was out of the door. Her hair was undone and she was still wearing her nightdress. 'What is it? Why are you coming? Have you a letter?'

'I need to talk to you, my dear,' said Verena. 'Let us go and sit down.'

'I don't want to sit down! What is it? Tell me!'

'Please, Emmeline. Let us go to your room and talk.'

'Mama, tell me now! Give me the letter!' She reached out and tried to clutch the paper. Verena held it up. 'Emmeline! Stop this!'

'Give it to me! Tell me!' Tears were rolling down Emmeline's face. 'Please.'

'Very well, let us sit here. On the floor. That is it.' Verena held the banister as she lowered herself to the ground. She coughed. 'It is some time since I sat on the floor.'

Emmeline sat and put her legs out in front of her, the way no debutante ever should. 'Tell me, Mama. He won't come to dinner?'

Verena shook her head. 'No.'

'But he will come again?'

Verena shook her head. 'He says not. I suppose he means only in friendship.'

Emmeline opened her mouth and began screaming. Her screams filled the hallway. She paused, looked at them both and screamed again.

'Emmeline, please stop.'

She lay down, curled into a ball and screamed there, into the floor.

Verena gestured to Celia. 'Go and fetch Smithson. Or Thompson. Anyone.'

Celia hurried to the stairs. Jennie was already walking up. 'Were you in need of help, miss?'

Celia nodded. She grasped Jennie's hand and hurried her forward. Jennie crouched down by Emmeline, who was still wailing. 'Come now, miss, come on now.' She slipped her arms under her and steadied her as she rose. 'Good girl.' Emmeline put her arms around Jennie's shoulders and buried her face in her chest. 'Let us go to your room. Come on now.'

Celia followed and opened the door to Emmeline's room. She hadn't been in it for weeks. It was strewn with clothes, stockings, shawls.

'Come, miss.' Jennie laid Emmeline down in the bed and put the blankets over her. She smoothed her hair. 'That's it, have a good cry now. Get it all out.' She looked up at Celia. 'It's all right, miss. Leave us now. Miss Emmeline will be fine with me.'

Celia closed the door and walked along the landing. Verena was still sitting there, her head against the wall, her eyes closed.

Celia put her arms around her but Verena did not flinch. 'Mama, I think Emmeline is getting better.' Verena made no reply. Celia held her. Finally, Verena opened her eyes. 'Thank you, dear. Now, surely Mr Janus will be waiting for you downstairs. You should go to your lessons.'

'Yes, Mama.' She set off towards the hall. Mr Janus was there, leaning against Rudolf's shelf of ornaments. He was gazing at the reproduction Turner on the wall.

'I am sorry to keep you waiting, Mr Janus.'

'Good afternoon, Miss de Witt. Time for history.'

She nodded.

'Are you quite well, Miss de Witt? You look rather pale, if I may say so. I thought I heard noises earlier of some distress.'

'The noise was because one of the maids received some bad news. I'm just tired.'

'History will wake you up. How is Miss Emmeline?'

'She is sleeping.'

'That is nice to hear. Sleep is good for beauty.'

Verena knew that her mother would have stopped him saying such things, but she did not know how to do so. She was still trying to think of the right words when Mr Janus said, 'To the Wars of the Roses, Miss de Witt.'

'I wish we didn't have to study war, Mr Janus. Why is there so much of it in history?'

'Because people think it's glorious. Perhaps you are right, Miss de Witt, we have covered enough war. Let us turn a little further forward. The fiscal policy of Henry VII.'

NINE

Celia was awake before she even realised she had fallen asleep. After two hours of Henry VII, she had run upstairs and thrown herself on her bed, tired out by holding her tongue at Lady Redroad's. She had been dreaming about a horse galloping towards her on a racecourse, everyone shouting in the stands. She was crying out, but no one could hear her. She sat up, tears running down her face. She reached to her table and the tin of emergency boiled sweets that Verena did not know she had. Something to eat would make her feel better, surely. She took a red sweet, but it tasted of tin and did not improve her headache. She wiped the tears from her eyes, reached for another sweet. She was just taking a third one to cram in her mouth when she heard footsteps clattering past her, and a sobbing sound.

She hurried to the door and pulled it open. Her sister was at the end of the corridor. 'Emmeline! Where are you going?'

Emmeline didn't turn; she ran around the corner and Celia could not see her. 'Emmeline. Come back!' She set off in her stockings, running after her. Around the corner and then into the second corridor. Emmeline reached the ladder that led on to the roof and started up it. 'What on earth are you doing?' cried Celia to the back of her sister's head. Emmeline did not reply, continued clambering up the ladder.

Celia followed her, struggling to keep her footing on the wood, cursing herself for not wearing shoes. Emmeline hauled herself through the door on to the roof and Celia followed her. She had not been on the roof since she had been a child. Michael used to bring her up as a game. Then, she had thought it fun to chase about. Now her feet were slipping and she was afraid. She clasped a turret. 'Where are you going, Emmeline? Wait for me. Please.'

Emmeline, still wearing her nightgown, was stumbling over the roof, weaving between the chimneys and the turrets. 'Stop, please! Please!' Celia looked at the expanse of garden beneath them, the hills rolling further away. The wind was swallowing her words. 'Emmeline,' she cried. 'I'm frightened.'

Emmeline was still picking her way forward. She fell against a chimney, carried on. Celia felt a flash of pain as she cut her foot on a tile. She knew then, in a moment of terrifying clarity, what Emmeline was doing. She was walking to the edge. 'No!' she cried. 'Emmeline, come back.' She gripped a chimney, pulled herself to the next one. *Go to the edge*, she was telling herself. *You have to help.*

Emmeline was nearly at the lip of the roof. 'Wait for me!' Celia cried. 'Please.' She was scrambling now, trying to catch up. She dropped to her knees and began crawling.

'Go away, Celia,' Emmeline shouted over her shoulder. 'Just go away.'

'I'm staying.'

'Go away. You're a baby.'

'You're my sister. Please come down with me.' Celia was crying now. 'I love you, Emmeline.'

'Be quiet.'

'He's only one person. Someone better will ask you to marry him.'

'A girl who is jilted once is never asked again. That's it now. Everyone's laughing at me. I'll never marry.'

'Emmeline, that's not true.'

'Stop talking!'

Emmeline wouldn't turn around. Celia was afraid to touch her, in case she moved. Only half a foot or so and Emmeline would be falling through the sky. Celia crawled to the edge. The drop was dizzying. Sickness lurched in her. If she spoke, Emmeline might be angry and pitch herself forward. But she might do that even if she didn't speak. Emmeline's white nightdress was tangled around her legs. Her feet looked unbearably tiny. 'Please,' Celia said. But the wind swallowed up her voice.

Celia looked out, feeling as if her whole body was shaking. Then her heart jumped. Walking past the rose bed below them, only a little way away, was Mr Janus, hands in his pockets. She had to catch his attention. If she shouted, Emmeline might react badly. She lifted her hand and waved. He was gazing at the roses. She begged him in her mind. *Mr Janus. Please.*

Emmeline was still standing, clutching the chimney. She wasn't looking at Celia. The wind was probably in her ears. That gave Celia an idea. She reached out for a loose tile, lying on the roof next to her after being blown off in a winter storm, she assumed. She clutched it in her hand and then threw it towards Mr Janus, as hard as she could. It landed on the grass just by his feet. He looked up at the roof. She gestured frantically, waving and putting her finger to her lips. But he was hardly looking at her. He was staring at Emmeline. Celia waved at him again and beckoned, mouthed, *Please help us! Send Thompson and Smithson and Jennie, help us!* He put up his hand and dashed into the house.

Emmeline had noticed none of it. Celia put her head against the chimney. Mr Janus would go and tell Smithson, Thompson and Jennie, and they would all be up in a moment. She just had to try to speak to Emmeline, keep her from moving off the edge. She supposed she should give her something to look forward to. Instead, she found herself talking about Emmeline's dresses.

'I saw your gowns on the floor.' Emmeline did not move. 'My favourite's the blue one; I think it very pretty. You really do look beautiful in it.' She cast around vainly in her memory. 'You've a blue hat that goes with it, I think? That's very pretty too. Although sometimes you wear the yellow, and that one with the lace can be really splendid.'

Emmeline was not turning around, but she was not moving closer to the edge either, so perhaps it was working. If only Celia had paid more attention to gowns before. 'I should take your advice on dresses now that I am growing older. I tell you which other one I really like – the pale peach.' She was getting desperate now, didn't even know if Emmeline had a pale peach dress or not. But she had to keep talking.

Then a noise came from behind her. She turned and saw Mr

Janus stumbling over the tiles. *No*, she wanted to say. *Not you! We need Smithson and Jennie.*

'Miss de Witt!' She heard his voice, reedy and high over the wind. 'Miss de Witt!' She stared at him. He would have to do.

Come closer, she mouthed. *Can't you get Smithson?* He didn't seem to notice.

She watched him clamber over the tiles, ungainly and uncoordinated. Even in shoes, he was slower than she had been. He came closer and stood behind Emmeline.

'Miss de Witt. I don't mean to scare you. It is Mr Janus here.'

Celia saw her sister's shoulder twitch. Her own stomach lurched. But Emmeline did not move forward.

'I came to talk to you, Miss de Witt,' said Mr Janus. 'I thought we could speak.'

Again, Emmeline did not move her body. But she turned her head, very slightly. Celia knew she was listening.

'You're very beautiful, Miss de Witt. Forgive me for saying it, but it's true. You are the most beautiful woman I have ever seen. If you had grown up differently, you could have been on the stage, mesmerising the audience with your handsome eyes.'

A strand of hair blew over Emmeline's ear. She reached up to brush it back. Celia knew from that that she must be listening. Why had she not thought of saying such words about her sister's looks? She knew it was ludicrous to be annoyed with Mr Janus, since Emmeline seemed to be listening, but still, she was. From the way he was speaking, it was clear that he had guessed that Sir Hugh had broken things off. Perhaps it had been easy enough, since the wait for the letter had consumed the whole house.

'Miss de Witt, you live in a country village, where you see few people. If you were in London on a regular basis, I promise you that people would not be able to countenance your beauty. They'd be thrilled, they would follow you, they'd talk of you. You could wear a sack and still people would adore you. Forgive me once more for speaking so boldly, but the truth is that hundreds of men would be captivated by you and wish to marry you.'

Celia could see a little colour spreading up to her sister's cheek. She wanted to reach out for her, but she held back.

'When you marry, which you will soon, you will go through life meeting thousands of men who will wish you had married them. There are only a few women in every hundred years who look like you. I don't doubt you could marry the Prince of Wales if you were interested in being a princess.'

Celia's mouth dropped open as Emmeline shrugged. 'I wouldn't want the Prince of Wales.' Her voice was quiet, but still, she had spoken.

'So he would dream of you and never earn you. Like thousands of other men. Miss de Witt, I speak God's truth. You are the most beautiful woman anyone has ever seen. You have a gift. You must show people your beauty. It is practically a duty.'

She still did not turn, but Celia noticed she gripped the chimney next to her harder. 'I was told I was beautiful before, but I think he was lying. If I am so handsome, why did he not want to marry me?'

'Because he is wrong – stupid. Because he will spend the rest of his life regretting losing you. He will end up in a loveless marriage with a woman he cannot endure. And then he will see you, beautiful, adored, happy, surrounded by children, and he will be ashamed for what he has done. A man such as that is not worthy of you.'

'I don't feel so very beautiful at the moment. Miss Wilton has not styled my hair for days. My face is a mess.'

'That is just wrong. Looks like yours cannot be undermined. They shine through. Do you know, Miss de Witt, if you were to turn your face towards me, I would be quite stunned by your beauty, as I always am.'

Emmeline's shoulder was moving. Celia's heart was beating so loudly that she thought the other two could surely hear it. What if Emmeline turned too quickly and fell? She wanted to reach out and grasp her sister. She could see that Mr Janus wanted to do the same. 'Come now,' he was saying. 'That's it. Turn around to look at me. That's it.'

Emmeline manoeuvred herself around, clutching the chimney.

'See!' he said, staring at her. 'You're the most beautiful woman I have ever seen. The most beautiful anyone has ever seen.' He held out a hand. 'May I come a little closer?'

She nodded.

He edged nearer. 'Anyone who has lost you is a fool, knows nothing. He will regret it. Truly.'

She began to cry, great round tears dropping on to her cheeks.

He smiled. 'Only you, Miss de Witt, could look handsome when you cry. May I come closer?'

She nodded again, and he worked his way forward. He gave Celia a quick nod and a gesture, and she realised that he meant her to go to where Emmeline had been, so that she could not run to the edge. Celia hesitated. If she moved to stand there and Emmeline panicked or barrelled back, she would fall. Mr Janus nodded again, and she knew she had to do it. She made her way gingerly over the tiles, afraid of making a noise that might startle her sister.

'Your beauty is wasted on me, you know, Miss de Witt,' the tutor was saying. 'You should be showing it in London. You should be at the theatre and the opera, dancing. You would be discussed in the magazines; other ladies would wish to copy your dress.' He paused, and then, emboldened, carried on. 'We should make a plan so that this will be the case, so that you will be launched truly upon the world.' He nodded, repeated the words that were like a chorus. 'You are so very beautiful.' He looked entranced. Celia could make a good guess that he was acting, pretending at how he would have been if they were not balanced on a roof, for she knew he was full of fear. 'Could you move closer to me, Miss Emmeline? So I can see your eyes? Did you know they have tiny flecks of amber in the blue? They are like spots of gold under the sea.'

Emmeline shook her head.

'No? Well, you must go to the mirror and look. They are like jewels, lapis lazuli showing a little of their gold.'

Celia could see Emmeline was intrigued. It would be wrong to kill oneself if one did not know exactly the nature of one's eyes.

'Flecks of gold?' she asked.

'The most divine you can imagine. Your eyes are magnificent. And yet they are assisted in this by their setting, you see. Your skin is the finest one can imagine. Can you come closer to me so that I can regard it better?'

She nodded.

'There is the most wonderful curve from cheekbone to ear. Did you know that? It is perfectly symmetrical on each side.'

Emmeline reached up her hand to touch her cheek.

'And then did you know that the side of your mouth matches perfectly with that line? It is really incredible. You should be painted, over and over again. A portrait of you in the Summer Exhibition would be the most popular piece. You would be part of history. Like the greatest female models. I would be honoured to have you sit for me.'

'Can you paint?' asked Emmeline, fingers still on her face.

'I try a little. But I'm not so talented. I have friends who do, though, in London. Mrs de Witt would never permit you to visit them, of course. But perhaps they could come here.'

Celia blushed uncomfortably. Mr Janus was correct, of course he was. But he was saying rather a lot. She was so used to him droning about history that she found his words oddly intimate, as if she had seen him coming out of the bath. And she knew that Verena would not have allowed them.

'They could come here and paint you,' he was continuing. 'And then – imagine – their portraits would take their place in the Summer Exhibition. One day, in the National Gallery. You will be celebrated, Miss de Witt, take my word for it.' At this, he stretched out his hand. 'Come, Miss de Witt, come. Let us prepare. Let us begin on our plan.'

Emmeline reached out her hand and Mr Janus grasped it. 'Will you come down?' he said. 'Will you come down with me?'

Emmeline nodded. He called over to Celia. 'Come, Miss de

Witt, we are going to go down now. Can you take your sister's other arm?'

Celia clasped Emmeline's arm and felt the warmth of her body. 'Let us go forward,' Mr Janus said. 'Come.' And so they did, tripping over tiles and the chimneys, bumping each other and muddling their feet. Celia fell more than the other two, even over the turret, blushing, although neither of them seemed to notice. 'Come on now,' he said, lifting Emmeline through the entrance. He left Celia to clamber down on her own. When she reached the bottom of the ladder, hot and irritated with him for not helping her, Mr Janus was still holding Emmeline, her head resting on his chest. Neither of them was looking at her. Celia knew she should not be there, none of them should, but now how could things be the same again?

'What about lessons?' she asked.

Mr Janus stroked Emmeline's hair. 'Perhaps we could all read some poetry. Yes. Let us sit outside and read poetry.'

Emmeline nodded against his chest.

'I think we should go now,' said Celia. *Before anyone finds us,* she wanted to add, *before Mama or Jennie comes up to Emmeline's room and finds her not there.*

'If you say so, Miss de Witt,' shrugged Mr Janus. Celia saw Emmeline smile. In that moment, she thought, they had both crossed over to another side, together, without her.

TEN

It rained that afternoon, so they sat in the schoolroom to read poetry. Celia was relieved – Verena would be angry if she saw the three of them outside. Mr Janus read them 'The Lady of Shalott' and Browning. Emmeline listened and took some of the parts, Celia too. At five, he was due to walk back to the next town, where he was lodging. 'Tomorrow, ladies,' he said, although Celia knew he was not speaking to her. She trotted after Emmeline, talking about poetry. On the stairs, her sister turned around. 'Celia, you don't have to follow me, you know. Don't worry, nothing will happen now.'

That evening, Emmeline did not come to dinner, but Verena reported that she had been content when Jennie took her tray up. Her mother squeezed Celia's hand under the table.

'I heard you and Emmeline talking about poetry,' said Rudolf. 'I was always a great admirer of Browning.'

She knew she was being thanked, that they were pleased and thought she was the one responsible for Emmeline's smile because she had talked about poetry, distracted her from thoughts of Sir Hugh. Celia felt a hot shame that she was being wrongly chosen, and still more that the truth was something she could never tell her parents, not ever.

At dinner, Rudolf was talking about the factories. Mr Lewis was saying they had had a surge in orders for meat pies and sausages.

'That is excellent news, husband.'

'Prices are soaring. I expect people think there will be shortages. And the soldiers need supplies. Mr Lewis is going to the War Office to discuss the contracts with the army.'

'That would be a fine thing. A contract with the army to supply meats.'

'Yes, apparently they are frantic for new suppliers. Mr Lewis thinks we may be lucky.'

Celia had only seen her father's factory once. He had given her a tour, but she had begged him to take her out after ten minutes or so. The smell of meat was so strong. He patted her hand, said he spent most of his time in the office or meeting with people who wished to buy his meats, rather than in the factory itself. That made Celia feel better. The thought of the factory, the smell of blood and bone and the dripping carcasses, was too horrible. She was glad he hardly went near it. They had five shops – three in London – and even they were too much for her. When she was younger, the other girls teased her: 'Your papa is a butcher!' She hated herself for wishing he sold something else for, as her mother said, it was good work, honest work. His office was piled up with account books, correspondence, evidence of his industry. The meat they were eating had to come from *somewhere*.

'Surely you should go to the War Office yourself to discuss such a matter, husband.'

'Not for the moment. Mr Lewis considers it better that I stay here. After all, there is all that business about registering and if we do that, then we won't be able to travel.'

'Yes, husband, but they don't mean you. They mean waiters in London, that sort of thing. I remember we had a rather odd one in the Savoy once.'

'Are you sure they don't mean us, Papa?' asked Celia.

'They will have to take Queen Mary first.'

Celia stared at her plate. She had a cruel thought in her head. Why couldn't her father just be English? Then they would have none of this; she could read articles about the poor Belgians and the terrible Kaiser and it would all be clear in her head. But if her father was English, then she would not be Celia – she would be someone else. And if you said the Germans were evil, that made Hilde and Johann evil too, and how could that be right? Surely, she thought, surely, if they just asked the Kaiser to stop? Sarah's voice rang in her head: *teach the Kaiser a lesson.*

Before this year, Celia had been secretly a little proud of being

German. It was something that made her more exotic, more interesting than the other girls at school, those like Gwendolyn and Marion who never went anywhere in their school holidays. It explained why she was tall; one teacher had said that Germans always had height. She had seen it as making her more English, not less; it made her more like Queen Victoria. The Queen's mother had hurried away from Germany so that Victoria could be born, just in time, at Kensington Palace; she had read it all in a book. Her and Albert's eldest daughter, Princess Victoria, was her favourite, good at lessons, married a German. The Queen shook so much at the wedding that they could not take her photograph; she wept even though she was happy. And now the Princess's brother was King and the Queen was dead, her son the Kaiser. It was too interlinked, too confused.

'Are you eating your beef, Celia?' said Verena. 'Plenty of children would be glad to have it. Especially in Belgium.'

What did Michael think? she wondered. Practising to fight against Germans, and yet he was one? Her head was spinning. She looked at her father and felt, for a moment, a flash of pure resentment against him.

Seven years ago, Rudolf had bundled her into a carriage, collected Tom from the next street corner and told them not to tell Verena. They travelled all the way to a giant glass building that he said was the Crystal Palace, surrounded by what looked like thousands of people. 'Do you remember from your book about the Queen?' Rudolf said. 'We are here to see a show I saw advertised in *The Times*. It's about the future of the English village. They say it is very good.' Past the ticket barrier were rows and rows of seats around which Celia realised was a whole life-sized model of a village, with actual flower beds planted with tulips, a duck pond, a church, and shops selling what looked like real bread, meat and haberdashery. There were people there, milling around, women taking down the bread and passing it over to be bought, men sauntering around the pond. Two women chatted over a perambulator and four girls played hopscotch in front of the shops. Over the top of it was a network of wires, supported by thick posts on each corner.

'I wish we could go down and play with them,' Celia said to Rudolf. He did not seem to hear.

A man with glasses had folded his newspaper and stood up. 'Welcome to our village,' he said, and walked over to stand by the women with perambulators. 'It is the summer of 1907,' he called out. 'People in Englandsfield are enjoying a fine Saturday afternoon. The children look forward to their future. And then something arrives on the horizon.'

Celia clutched her father's hand. 'Papa!' From the top of the wires at the side, three great model aeroplanes dropped down. 'Oh, nice machines!' said Tom, with satisfaction. The people in the village looked up and began to cry out. 'God save us!' a woman wailed. A great explosion of smoke appeared on the green. Some girls at the front were shrieking.

Celia was ashamed of her earlier panic. 'This is a very silly play,' she said, more bravely than she felt. The children in front of her were pretending to be scared, she thought.

There was the sound of trumpets. A group of soldiers arrived on the village green. 'We are German,' they shouted. 'We are coming for you!'

Rudolf smiled broadly. 'We Germans are always the bad man in the pantomime!' He grinned happily around at the other spectators. And yet, Celia thought, they were not laughing. People were still as stone, their faces afraid or shouting insults.

There were two more explosions of smoke on the green. 'I think they are meant to be bombs,' said Tom. 'You can look up, Celia, no one is injured.'

She lifted her head. The planes were still hanging. The people in the village were still crying, the women clutching each other as they sheltered by the sides of the shops. Then she jumped. 'Here they come again!' The planes were swooping down. 'Most ingenious,' said Rudolf, peering up.

From the other side of the seating there was the sound of marching, and men's voices counting out the steps.

'Here come the army,' sighed Tom. Thirty or so men in uniform marched in formation through the streets and on to the green. The German soldiers turned and fled, shouting, 'We have been discovered!' in thick accents that Celia thought did not sound German at all.

The British raised their guns into the air. 'The Germans will not come back,' called one, turning around so that all sides of the audience could see him. 'Never again will English children feel afraid of German planes or armies.' The people around Celia were jumping to their feet and clapping, cheering and shouting. 'Hooray for Britain!' Tom tugged her up. 'Come, Celia,' he said. 'We must join in.' She tried to call out with them, her voice weak and cracked in her ears. She heard other words. 'The Kaiser can lick my boots!' 'Kill the lot of them!'

Rudolf remained sitting, entirely still and straight, looking out. 'Mr de Witt,' said Tom. 'You must stand up.' Rudolf looked up, bewildered. It was as if, Celia thought, he did not know Tom at all. Tom pulled his arm, not gently, and Rudolf got unsteadily to his feet. 'Shout it,' Tom hissed into his ear. 'Shout hooray!'

Rudolf did. Celia heard his voice, even shakier than her own. 'Hooray! Hooray for the King and the army!'

On the way back, Rudolf patted her knee. 'It is a play, little one. Do not think of it. Admittedly, I thought it was about the English village, but it was only a play.'

Celia had forgotten it, put it out of her mind, but now she thought about it again, felt it more important than she had re-membered, looked back at that day and saw herself saying to her father: we should not stay here. We should go somewhere else! But where? They could not go to Germany – and where else was there? America, with Jonathan Corrigan? She pushed the idea from her mind.

Next day, Celia sat in Emmeline's room. Verena and Rudolf had gone to register at the police station. Verena said the police wouldn't care that they were two weeks later than the due date. 'I am the daughter of Lady Deerhurst and Rudolf is exempt as a creator of industry. We'll get there and they'll send us away, just you wait.'

Celia watched Emmeline as she took out the gowns ordered for the honeymoon and her life as Lady Hugh and put them in the trunk she had used for school, throwing in silk and lace and lamé, uncaring, until they looked like one great sea monster trying to get out of a box. They dragged it outside the door. 'I will ask Smithson to take it to one of the storage rooms,' Emmeline said, crossly. 'I don't wish to see any of it.'

'You might use it again.'

'*If* I choose to marry, it will be all out of fashion by then. I will have to have another set. And you don't want them, do you?'

'They wouldn't suit me.'

Emmeline cocked her head. 'True. You are not right for pale colours. Dark blue and dark red, pink are what pale girls like you should wear. Even black.'

Celia couldn't help herself. 'Do you think so?'

'Definitely. Dark blue and dark pink. Or black.' They continued with the gloves and the stockings. 'I want none of it,' Emmeline said.

Celia threw handfuls of gauze into another box. 'What if Sir Hugh changes his mind?' As soon as the words were out of her mouth, she regretted them. Emmeline stopped, brought her hands to her face. 'I'm sorry, Emmeline, I'm sorry.'

Emmeline shook her head. 'I don't know.'

'He might,' said Celia.

'But I think Michael was right. People see us as Germans.' Emmeline dropped a pair of evening gloves into the box. 'If the war hadn't broken out for another few months or so, I would be married to him.' She seized up an evening bag and threw it aside.

'But the war will be over in a few months and everything will go back to normal. Then Sir Hugh will write to you and be different.'

'Maybe.'

'Yes.' Celia turned to the shawls because she could feel tears starting in her eyes. 'Do you think he will come back?'

'Who? Michael? Of course he will!'

'But he'll go to fight soon. He might die.' She held up a peculiarly fine cashmere shawl, pink and white, that Emmeline had been most fond of. She thought of asking for it, then stuffed it quickly in the box.

'No, no, that's what the working men risk. Men like Michael will be in charge of the planning, so he will be safe.'

Celia turned her attention to the hats. 'But I don't think he's an officer. Mama isn't sure. We don't even know where they are.'

'But why would he just be fighting with the ordinary men? That's impossible.'

'Why hasn't he written, then?'

'Perhaps they don't let them send letters. I don't know. But Celia, he'll be back before you know it, back at Cambridge, same old Michael.'

'Tom is there too.'

Emmeline tossed a hat in the box. 'He is a servant, Celia, remember. We can't talk about him in the same conversation as Michael.'

Celia felt an old flash of anger with her sister, the feeling that had flooded her when she was sitting in the garden and Emmeline had laughed at the idea of Tom at her wedding.

'Don't think about him, Celia. All very well to play together as children but you are a young lady now. And don't worry about Michael, he will be back soon. Now pass me that straw hat.' Celia threw it over with ill grace. Only the thought of Emmeline, her thin legs balancing near the edge of the roof, the nightdress caught around her body, held her back from arguing. Unkind words about Mr Janus rose up in her, but she squashed those too.

'Well, I want them both to come back,' she said, quietly.

'Whoever said they wouldn't? At least they are doing something. At least they are out there and feeling alive, rather than putting clothes in boxes.'

We're missing you a lot, Celia said to Tom and Michael in her head. *I wish you'd come home. We're doing a play you might like.* She could think of nothing to ask him, so she started again about herself, knowing it was not really polite to do so. *Mama and Papa went to register and the policeman was angry with them that they didn't do it before. He said he'd have to mark Papa's file for the War Office. Papa said they have to say that sort of thing to sound stern.*

Every day after that, Emmeline called at the schoolroom. Sometimes she listened to Celia's lessons, other times they recited poetry or plays together. Celia told herself that Emmeline was simply looking for company, but her heart was flooded with guilt. Emmeline came down to dinner, calm and smiling, and Verena clutched Celia's hand under the table, squeezed it, all gratitude. Celia blushed, miserably.

Four days later, Emmeline had an idea. They were studying *Henry V* and reading out the parts. 'I know!' she said. 'Why don't we put on a play!'

'A play?'

'I think it might cheer up Mama and Papa, don't you?'

When they were children, they had put on Christmas plays for their parents, dressed up in Verena's old curtains and her leftover gowns and hats. Arthur was Herod one year; the next, Emmeline played Cinderella, with Arthur as Prince Charming. That seemed so long ago now. They hadn't done a play for eight years or so. But Emmeline had a glint in her eyes – the same look as when she had been determined to get the role of Cinderella.

'It will be wonderful!' she cried.

'But Emmeline, I don't know if Mama and Papa would like it.' Celia felt as if she was caught in a train that was not stopping.

Emmeline cocked her head. 'Well then, we'll put on a show for the village and raise money for the war.'

'I think that is an excellent idea, Miss de Witt,' said Mr Janus. 'Quite superb.'

'Oh, you would think that,' snapped Celia.

'What do you want to do instead? Go to the sewing committee?'

'It would certainly be a good way to raise money,' said Mr Janus. 'It would really remind the village what good patriots you are.'

'I don't want to do it.'

'Well, then,' said Emmeline. 'We will put on the play without you.'

Celia thought of her sister parading with Mr Janus, one of the gold curtains they used to play with swathed around her. 'Oh, very well. I will do it too.'

'I've an idea. *A Midsummer Night's Dream.*'

'That's impossible, Emmeline. We are only three.'

'You need to have more imagination, sister. We will play most of the parts.'

'You'll be Titania.'

'Of course. Now, Mr Janus, we have a copy of the play, do we not?

'We do, but I know a lot of the lines. For example: "I pray thee, gentle mortal, sing again/Mine ear is much enamoured of thy note."'

Every day after that, the three of them closed the door in the schoolroom and rehearsed *A Midsummer Night's Dream*. Emmeline was Titania, Helena, all the beautiful roles, and Mr Janus her partner. Celia played the secondary roles. She was the watcher, the fairies, as the other two danced around her. She found herself enjoying it, even when Emmeline complained about her too-fast delivery and made her give the speeches again. Certainly it was more fun than reciting dates as Mr Janus stared out of the window – a thought she admitted with a shiver of guilt for Rudolf and his determination that she would be educated.

I am busy in a play, she wrote to Tom, in her head. *Emmeline seems very happy doing it.* But sometimes it seemed very strange to her that there was war and dying Belgians outside, and here they were putting on a play. *Do you get much time to read?* she asked Tom. *Perhaps you are too busy. If you wrote to me, then I would have a better idea of what it is you're doing. I'd be very interested.* She waited for him to say something in reply, but he was quiet. *Are you cold, being outside so much?* she said. *I would knit you something, really I would, if I knew where you were.*

On the fourth day of doing the play, something very odd

happened. They were halfway through when suddenly Mr Janus said some strange words. Celia and Emmeline stared at him. He repeated them, smiling.

'I do not know what you mean,' said Emmeline. He smiled again, said something else and returned to the play.

Later, Celia went to her room to find a shawl that they wanted to use for Puck. It took her longer than usual to find it in the piles of clothes in the drawers in her wardrobe. When she returned, Emmeline and Mr Janus were crouched over the floor with a piece of paper. It was covered in rows of letters in Mr Janus's writing. He was pointing to them and Emmeline was nodding.

'Ah, Celia,' he said, starting when she walked in. 'There you are.' Emmeline clambered to her feet, a little red. Mr Janus stood, brushing himself down, holding the paper. 'Let us resume the play.'

When they had finished that day, Celia was leaving the room when she saw Mr Janus give Emmeline the paper with the letters on it. 'Study it well,' he said. Emmeline smiled and took it in her hand.

The next day, Mr Janus spoke the strange words again. This time, Emmeline replied in the same tongue, slowly and a little haltingly, her face growing pinker. Mr Janus patted her hand. 'Good!' he said, and said some more, slowly. Emmeline answered. He touched her hand again and a smile spread over her face, gradually, like sunlight coming into a room.

'What are you saying?' demanded Celia. 'Are you talking about me?' Mr Janus shook his head. 'Tell me!'

Emmeline looked at Mr Janus. He turned and patted Celia's arm. 'Don't fear, Celia. Once Emmeline knows the language fully, then we shall teach it to you.'

That night, she lay in bed, spoke to Tom. *They are always talking in this language, it is very odd. I have tried to understand it but it seems confusing. I don't think it's fair that they are always leaving me out.* Then she thought better of it. *Still, we are probably much warmer than you. Is it very hard there?*

A week later, and the play was going well. Celia had been learning her lines in bed before she got up to dress, and Emmeline had conceded that her speaking voice had improved. Celia thought it apt that in the same way that everyone in the story had become caught up in their night-time playings, the three of them had grown entirely absorbed. It was as if Emmeline had never tried to throw herself off the roof. Sometimes Celia even found herself so caught up in the poetry that she forgot about Michael and Tom and how they must be already in France.

When Emmeline and Mr Janus began in their strange language, Celia simply took the time to think over some of her speeches in her head. She had decided that she didn't really care if they explained it to her or not. She thought it was probably the same as some of the made-up languages the girls at school used. Once you knew it, it was completely dull. Occasionally Emmeline forgot it and Mr Janus had to write down letters on a piece of paper to teach her again. He stuffed the papers behind the desk. Celia had taken them out to look at them, but still she could not understand the words they were saying.

She did sometimes question when they were ever going to put the show on for the village. 'Oh, that'll come later!' said Emmeline, every time she raised the question of when they should stage it, or even where, since Thompson had said that they had moved the recruiting station from the green to the village hall.

It was a Friday morning and the sun was dropping through the windows. Emmeline and Mr Janus were playing out their favourite scene. They hardly needed to practise, but still they were insistent on doing so. Emmeline said it had to be perfect.

> My Oberon! what visions have I seen!
> Methought I was enamour'd of an ass.
> …Come my lord, and in our flight
> Tell me how it came this night.

Celia watched them standing there. Mr Janus had opened his mouth but he was not saying the words. He was already holding Emmeline's hand, and now he clutched it to his heart. The air in the schoolroom was shivering, Celia thought, trembling. She gazed at Emmeline. Something was going to happen. Mr Janus took up the hand and kissed it. Then he put his other hand out to her sister's cheek. *No!* Celia thought she should shout, but she did not. Instead, she stood there and watched as he ran his fingers over her sister's face. Emmeline looked up.

Celia stared, the scarlet velvet limp around her body. She could hear nothing but the drumming of blood in her ears. She did not hear the sound of feet walking smartly up the stairs, of someone coming along the corridor, of a hand grasping the door knob and turning it. 'What on earth is going on?'

It was Verena. Celia turned and felt her face flush scarlet. Her mother stood there, tall in her long black skirt and white blouse. She was clutching a piece of paper in her hand. 'What is happening?' Celia looked back at her sister. Mr Janus had dropped his hands and stepped away. Emmeline was gazing at her mother, her face frozen in horror, the crown awry on her head.

'Mama,' she began.

'No,' Mr Janus broke in. 'I must speak. I am responsible. Mrs de Witt, we were rehearsing a play. We were producing *A Midsummer Night's Dream*, to put on for the village.'

'Indeed.'

'We intended to raise money for the war effort.'

Verena folded her arms. 'And you, Emmeline? I presume you are Titania?'

Emmeline nodded.

'What role are you playing, Mr Janus?'

'Oberon.' He dropped his head, shame-faced.

'I see. And you, Celia. What is your role in all of this?'

'I'm acting too.'

'Really? It rather seems to me that your presence makes it appear as if lessons are going on. Which is some way from the case, is it not?'

Mr Janus opened his mouth and began to speak. Verena held up her hand. 'Actually, Mr Janus, I do not wish to hear from you. I came up to the room to find Celia. I had looked in Emmeline's room and found her not there, so I presumed she was in the garden. I wished to speak to both my daughters to show them this letter.'

Celia felt her heart rise. 'Michael!' she exclaimed. 'It's Michael!' She jumped forward. 'Oh, Mama!'

Verena held the letter away. 'It is indeed from Michael. If you might remember, daughters, he left us to fight. The country is at war. Your father is very concerned for us. But you two – indeed, three – are carrying on as if you are living in some kind of . . .' She waved her hand. 'Photograph!' she ended triumphantly.

Celia fought to control a flush of laughter at her mother's choice of words, dipped her head.

'I am glad you find everything so amusing, Celia. I rather think that all of you are in trouble.'

'Please may I look at the letter, Mama?' said Celia. 'How is he?' Michael's words on a piece of paper, so close to her.

'He is alive and not injured, which is all that counts. Your father thinks they are about to continue their training in France. I will perhaps show you later if you can be better behaved. You can spend the rest of the week in your room. Go now.'

Celia crept away, nodding, casting a look at Mr Janus's pale face. Verena didn't watch her go, so she stood quietly at the door.

'I am very shocked and disappointed, Emmeline. This is not the sort of behaviour I expect from you.'

'I'm sorry, Mama.'

'And Mr Janus, I trusted you in our home. My husband trusted you. This is how you have repaid us.'

'I apologise, madam. It was only a play.' *No!* Celia wanted to cry. *Don't talk back to her. Just nod and agree.*

'Indeed, only a play. So you tell me. But how do I know this? And how do I know that if I had not arrived when I did, something else might not have happened? You're fortunate that it was me and not my husband. Now, sir, do you have all your belongings here?'

'My bag is here. My coat is downstairs.'

'Very well. You will collect your bag and you will come

downstairs for your coat. My husband will forward to you the rest of the month's salary. And we will not see you again.'

'Mama!' Emmeline cried.

'I have no interest in what you wish to say, Emmeline. Mr Janus is leaving us.' She turned. 'Celia, I told you to go to your room.'

'But Mama, he rescued—'

'No doubt he did rescue you, dear. From geometry and comprehension and everything else you were supposed to be doing. Rudolf thought that a man would have a better standard of education. You will be taught by governesses in the future.'

'No! You don't understand. He helped—'

'I understand entirely. Go to your room, Celia. If you succeed in behaving yourself for the rest of the day, I might bring you the letter from Michael. Not that you deserve to see it, having forgotten about your poor brother as you have.'

'I didn't!'

'To your room. Or you won't see the letter.'

Celia turned and looked at Emmeline. She was standing there on the pile of books that they had used for a stage. Her golden gown was slipping from her shoulders, her crown had fallen to the floor. Two big tears were falling from her eyes. 'I lose everything I want,' she said, as if to herself. Celia thought she looked sadder than even Cordelia could, the saddest person in any play in the world. Then Verena slammed the door, pushed Celia towards her room and headed downstairs with Mr Janus.

ELEVEN

—◆—

Dear Ma, Pa, Emmy, Ceels,

We are off to France soon. We are getting plenty to eat, so don't worry. Have been marching a lot, the people cheer when they see us and the girls wave their handkerchiefs. When we get to France, we will be going down to the trenches and then we will see the enemy. I think we are taking over the trenches from the French. Perhaps they will leave us some cheese and wine about!

We have a few men who used to be doctors, so we will be in good hands!

Everything seems a long way from Stoneythorpe here. I hope you are all well. I miss you. Send me a kiss. All the chaps say we will be back in England before you know it – a couple of months, we think.

Love
Michael
PS Tell Celia to be good!

Celia gazed at the letter in her hands. 'Is there no more?' It was the morning after Verena had discovered them all playing Shakespeare. Celia had begged so hard that her mother had relented and allowed her to read the letter. She touched the writing. 'But it's so short.'

Verena gave her a sad look. 'Papa thinks that the men can only write so much. That they are told to keep it short.'

Celia ran her finger over the page. She lifted it close to her nose. She thought she could smell carbolic soap and something like rust. She couldn't smell Michael. 'It doesn't sound like him, Mama.' *Tell Celia to be good!* Was that all he was going to say to her?

'Papa says that all their letters are read by the War Office, so they make them simple. He supposes that Michael is also kept busy writing letters for the other men who can't write.'

'He must be an officer, then.' *Where is Tom?* she wanted to cry out to the letter. *Please tell me.* He might be with Michael, the pair of them polishing their boots. Or he might be miles away. She had thought they were together, imagined them marching side by side. But now where were they?

'Papa says that if he was an officer, he would have sent us a different sort of letter. He'd be allowed to write a longer one.'

'When will he be back? Do you really think a couple of months?'

'So the newspapers say. After all this fuss he'll never set a toe in France, I expect. Now, Celia, give me the letter. Your father wishes to keep it.'

Celia could not help it. In a moment, her eyes were full of heavy tears. They were streaming down her face.

'Oh Celia, don't cry.' Verena sat down and put her arms around her. 'Please don't cry. It will all turn out fine, just wait and see. He'll come back and swing you around in the garden, just as he did when you were a little girl. The war will be over and everything will be forgotten.'

Celia wept into Verena's bosom, her tears pooling over her face and on to the dark material of her mother's bodice. She cried and hiccupped, with Verena stroking her hair, saying soft words, just as she had when Celia was a child, until it felt as if there were no more tears. 'Why can't he come back?' she cried. She meant Tom and Michael in one, both of them

'Come now, Celia,' said Verena. 'Things are not so bad. Michael will be home soon. The war will be over before he boards the boat. Now, I should take this letter to Emmeline, and then return it to Rudolf. You will soon feel better.'

Celia felt her head spinning, sickness rising. 'Please, Mama. Please can I go outside?'

Verena gazed at her, then nodded her head, smiling. 'The air will do you good. I am too soft on you, always have been, you know. After that, you are back to your room, do you understand? I haven't forgotten what happened – and I won't.'

'May I write a letter to Michael?'

'Of course. We're all going to write.'

'How is Emmeline?' Celia asked tentatively. She had been lying in her room listening, desperately hoping that she would not hear Emmeline's feet rushing past to the roof once more. She did not know what she would do if she did. Scream and scream, she supposed. 'Don't lock me in,' she had begged Verena, but her mother had been adamant.

'Your sister is quiet. Well.'

'You know, Mr Janus really did save us.'

Verena held up her hand. 'I do not wish to hear it. Stop talking now, Celia, before I reconsider my kind decision to let you go outside.' She turned, and Celia followed her. It was impossible to know what to say. How could she tell Verena what Emmeline had tried to do? Her mother would despair, and never let either of them out of her sight again. And yet if she knew what he had done, she might invite Mr Janus back.

Celia wandered down the stairs and out into the back garden. She didn't feel like playing. She didn't want to go to her little den. She couldn't go to the stables to see Tom. What she wanted to do, more than anything, was to go to the Cottons' house, back to his room, lie in his bed and wait for him to return. But she could not. She gazed around. At that moment, she hated the garden, the place where the whole village had humiliated them by not coming to their party.

She wandered out to the side gate, where she knew she should not go. The same gate that Tom and his sister had come through for the party, where she had walked with Michael on the way to the village. She stood out on the front lawn. There was nobody there but her. She sat down on a rock and gazed at her feet. Princesses got stuck in castles, this she knew. How did they while away the time?

'Celia! Psst! Miss de Witt!' A voice came from the bushes a little lower down the drive. 'Celia! Come over here!'

She stood up and peered down the garden. The yellow and pink flowering bushes, Verena's great pride, were shaking. She could not see who was in there. 'Who is it?'

'Just come over here.' A hand waved from the leaves.

Knowing she shouldn't, she walked to the bushes. Two branches parted and Mr Janus's face poked out.

Celia wanted to laugh. 'What on earth are you doing there?'

'Crouch down!' He was waving his hand frantically. 'Someone might see.'

'You shouldn't be here,' she said as she sat down. 'Mama would be angry.'

'I wanted to ask you something.' He had a big smudge of dirt on his nose.

Then she really did laugh. 'You have been down there all this time waiting for me? But what if I had never come out?'

'I'd have gone to the back garden. I'd have found a way. Miss de Witt, I need you to take this.' He held out a letter. 'Give it to Emmeline.'

She stopped laughing. 'I can't. Mr Janus, you know I can't. Mama would never allow it.'

'This is not about your mother. You must give this to Miss de Witt. It is important.'

She shook her head, feeling it heavy on her shoulders. 'I really can't.'

'You must. Miss de Witt, I cannot emphasise to you how important this is. Your sister's happiness hangs in the balance. Without this letter, she'll suffer. And you know what happened last time she suffered?'

'Yes.' She could only whisper.

'Do you want the same to happen again? Remember, I won't be here this time.'

'No.'

'Well, this is what you must do. Take it, and go. I suppose Emmeline is still confined to her room, so it will be easy enough for you to give it to her.'

She nodded.

'You promise?'

'Yes.' She took the letter. 'What if I read it? I might, you know.'

'You know you shouldn't read other people's letters.'

'Those historians you were always praising to me went peering into the letters of Henry VII and the rest, didn't they?'

'Go on, Celia. Emmeline will be waiting. Hurry. Tell her seven.'

'I can't. What if Mama sees me?'

'You will have to find a way. Remember, your sister needs you to do this. You want her to stay well? You must do it. Now *walk* back, do not run. You must keep the letter on you, do not go straight to her room. Behave as you would normally. Pretend you are in a play.'

'You're not teaching me any more.' But he had gone back into the bush.

Celia walked back to the house, feeling Mr Janus's eyes upon her. The letter was burning her hand, and she thanked the stars there was no sign of her mother. Inside the corridor by the kitchen, she tore the envelope open. The paper fell into her hands. It was all gobbledegook, like the silly words they had spoken in the middle of the plays. She stared at it, trying to get the better of the code, but could not make out a single word.

Up at Emmeline's room, she slipped the paper under the door and heard footsteps on the other side. Then, after ten minutes or so had passed, she knocked. 'Emmeline? Has Mama locked you in?'

'I think she meant to, but she forgot,' Emmeline hissed back. She opened the door a crack and ushered Celia in. Her hair was loose around her shoulders. She was smiling.

Celia looked at her pink cheeks, her bright eyes. 'He said seven. I don't know what he meant.'

Emmeline bent down and gave her the first unprompted kiss on her cheek that Celia could remember for years. 'Thank you. Thank you. Tell him "Yes, K Yknn Eqog. Oggv cv Vgp. Until then."'

'No! I'm not going back. Mama will catch me if I do.'

Emmeline's eyes glittered. 'You have to. You've taken one letter. You're already in this.'

Celia gazed miserably at the paper. She'd started now, she had wound herself into this thing and she could not get out. 'I can't remember that.'

'You will. Repeat it to me.'

Celia tried a few times, and failed.

'Come on, Celia, get it right.'

Finally, after two more attempts, she had it to Emmeline's satisfaction.

'That's not bad. Now, when you say it, start with a "Yes". Tell him "Yes", and then these words. You understand?'

Celia nodded. 'I am not taking any more messages between you, you know.'

Emmeline put her arms around her and held her close. 'It is kind of you, Celia. You know I am grateful. I am your sister, always will be. My dearest little Celia.'

Celia wanted to wriggle out of her embrace. *I'm only four years younger than you!* But she held still, unsure about what Emmeline would do next.

'I remember when you were first born. Papa let me look at you in the crib when Mother was ill. He said I wasn't allowed to touch you, but he let me look at you. I thought I had never seen anything so small. Papa said I had been a baby once too, but I could not believe it.' She patted Celia on the back. 'You should go now. Mr Janus will be waiting. But don't forget it. You are my precious sister.'

Celia hurried down the stairs, reciting the words to herself, over and over. *Yes, K Yknn.* She didn't look around with much caution as she walked out into the garden and around to the bush.

'Well?' he said, peering through the leaves. 'I've been waiting.'

'I don't have a letter. She sent me with a message. She said, "Yes, K Yknn Eqog. Oggv cv Vgp. Until then."'

He listened gravely, nodded. 'Thank you, Miss de Witt.'

Celia stared at him. She had hurried through the house and dared to go past her parents, and all he could do was nod, as if she was reading out an essay about George III.

'I am not taking a message back, you know. I 've done enough.'

'I understand. Instead, just say it to me one more time.'

She repeated it. He smiled.

'I'll go now.' Celia felt rather confused. She had expected him to fall on her, beg her not to stop taking messages. But he was just sitting in the bush, smiling. Still, she thought, reminding herself of the phrase that Rudolf liked: do not look a gift horse in the mouth. She was spared from carrying any more letters. 'Goodbye, Mr Janus.'

She did not knock on Emmeline's door. Instead she arrived back to find Miss Wilton waiting for her. 'Where have you been? Time to arrange your hair for dinner, miss.'

'But I am not supposed to be allowed to dinner.'

'Mrs de Witt has changed her mind. You may come down, she says. Miss Emmeline too.'

But Emmeline was not at dinner – Jennie came through with the word that she had a headache. Celia played with her broccoli on her fork and felt sad for her sister. She must be sitting up there thinking about how she would miss Mr Janus, how she would never see him again. After dinner, she went up to knock on Emmeline's door. 'Sister?' she said. 'I wanted to see how you were.'

There was no answer. She tried again, then walked away. Maybe Emmeline was asleep. In the last of the light, she sat down to write her letter to Michael, feeling a little guilty that she had been distracted by Mr Janus and had not written before.

Dear Michael,

We were glad to get your letter. I miss you very much. Not much is happening here. I'm glad Papa managed to keep the horses but I think he misses the car. It is hot and I have been reading. How is it where you are? What can you see?

She forced herself to keep writing, sending questions, telling him about her day. Then she folded up the letter, ready to give to Smithson to post. She went once more to Emmeline's room, but there was still no answer.

*

That night, Celia did not sleep well. There were odd pictures in her mind, tormenting her and running through her head: a monster chasing her around what felt like a maze, an old man who came up to her and told her he was dying. When she woke next morning, her head hurt.

She went to Emmeline's room again. No answer. A wave of sadness swept over her. 'I will take another letter if you like,' she said at the door. 'I am sorry for saying I wouldn't. I don't mind really.' Still there was no answer. Poor Emmeline, Celia thought, two things taken away from her.

Verena had lifted the curfew, so she was free, but there was nothing to do. She wandered downstairs to talk to Jennie, but she was busy polishing the candlesticks and told Celia she was just getting in her way.

'I can't think of anything to do,' she said dolefully to Smithson when she gave him her letter for Michael.

'Of course you can, miss. What about embroidery?'

'Very funny. You know I hate it. I'm tired of books.'

'Well then, you're clearly missing Mr Janus. If he's not here, you should educate yourself. That is what I think. Go and learn some geography.'

'Why is nothing interesting?'

'Because you don't have enough to do. Think of your brother preparing to go to France.'

She hung her head. 'No.' She looked up, reached for the vase he was dusting. 'You won't go to war, will you?'

He shrugged. 'We'll see. Wouldn't mind a bit of French food.'

'Please don't.'

He smiled and ruffled her hair. 'Just for you, Miss Celia, I won't.' She waved at him as he walked away, not entirely sure she believed him.

Still feeling lethargic, she plodded up the stairs. She had not been to the schoolroom since Verena had sent them all out. She had thought Jennie might come in to clear it, but it was just as they had left it. Emmeline's gold cloak was still on the pile of books. Celia's copy of the play was lying on one of the desks. She sat down and began leafing through it. *Then I must be thy lady: but I know/When thou hast stolen away from fairy land.*

Emmeline as Titania, Mr Janus as Oberon. She put the picture of Emmeline balancing on the roof from her mind and picked up the golden cape. She draped it over her fingers and wandered over to the desk in front of her. Behind it were the pieces of paper. Celia picked one of them up and glanced idly at it. One line of alphabet, one line of other letters. She took a pencil, sat down on the floor with it and traced between the letters with her fingers. A. B. C. And then, almost without knowing it, she was working out Emmeline's message. The pencil moved forward. *Yes. I WILL COME...* She looked again. *MEET AT TEN. Until then!*

Celia threw down the paper. She hurtled out of the room, dashed up the corridor and threw herself at Emmeline's door, flinging it open. The room was empty. The bed looked odd and lumpy. She threw off the covers and saw two pillows, laid out like a person. She spun around, brought her hand to Emmeline's dressing table and her jewellery box. All the rings and pendants were gone, the gold bracelet that Rudolf had given her for her eighteenth birthday.

She dashed from the room and threw herself at the banisters. 'Mama!' she screamed. 'Mama!'

TWELVE

'The factory has been attacked again overnight,' said Rudolf at breakfast. 'Lewis tells me he thinks it is not safe to be there. He is very concerned.' The telephone had rung that morning. 'In other cities, German shops are being set upon.'

'Terrible,' said Verena, as she always did ever since the first attack on the factory in October, just after Emmeline left. That was just daubing, like on their house. Now it was more: windows broken, doors smashed. Last month, the shop in Mayfair had been vandalised by an overnight gang, who stole all the knives. 'So much violence. Is there much damage?'

One day they'd break in, Celia thought, take everything.

'Not too serious. Our guards caught it. But we cannot afford to lose productivity. Certainly not at the moment, when we are on the brink of the government contract.' He nodded. 'I shall not take tea this morning, dear. I shall be too occupied in my study.'

It was early December. Emmeline sent letters, without an address, to Rudolf and Verena, saying that she was well and that they should not try to find her. Rudolf had written to all the addresses they had for Mr Janus and to the school he had taught at before leaving to be a tutor, but none of them knew where he was.

He had even hired a private detective. A little man in a dark suit had come to the house and looked through Emmeline's drawers. He had left with a picture of her, saying that his guess was one of the big cities – Birmingham, Southampton or maybe even London. 'What did I do to deserve these terrible things?' said Verena. 'What did I do to my children?' Celia had confessed her part in the letters, and Verena had been so angry that she had nearly hit her.

Rudolf had said to Verena, 'It's not so important that we find her. What matters is that we make him marry her.' They said these things in front of Celia now. Occasionally Verena declared that Celia must be able to guess where her sister was, since she and Emmeline had spent so much time together. But Celia shook her head and said no. She was telling the truth. It was a great wide world of places, and Emmeline could be anywhere.

Michael had sent three more letters, none of them much longer than the first. She gazed at his words about soldiering and she could not hear his voice. She had written him ten letters, full of questions, and he had not answered any of them, or sent her more than friendly words in the letters addressed to all of them.

'I wonder if I should change the name of the shops for the moment.' The de Witt shops were in London (Hampstead, Kensington and Mayfair), Birmingham and Liverpool. 'To something like Smith Meats.'

Verena clattered her teacup down crossly. 'Husband, I cannot conceive of anything more foolish. To throw away the de Witt name overnight? We would lose every one of our customers. And remember, the royal family have kept *their* name.'

'This is about the mob, not the man who knows what is what.'

'It's too late,' said Celia. 'They've just changed the law. Germans can't change their names now.' She'd read about it in the newspapers at the beginning of the month. Too many spies were escaping detection, said *The Times*.

Verena shook her head. 'First we can't travel and now we can't change our name. I would have thought the government would have something better to do.'

'Anyway, there hasn't been much of a war,' broke in Celia. 'It is not like the Germans have *done* anything.'

Verena leaned across the table and clasped Rudolf's wrist in her hand. 'We need you. You must stay here to protect your factories. You must stay to protect us! What if Emmeline decides to come home? She would expect you to be here.'

Rudolf shrugged. 'Sometimes I think that Britain and Germany have always been at war. Little boys threw stones at me when I was a child.'

Verena picked up her knife. 'All children throw stones.'

'Just you left,' said Smithson. Celia had been spending more time than ever down below with the servants. Upstairs was too sad and slow, Verena sitting in the parlour as the clock ticked round, Rudolf buried in his study. At least in the kitchen they were busy.

'We have standards,' Smithson would tell her as he moved pieces of furniture or supervised Jennie dusting. 'We can't let them slip.' *Even if the master and mistress are* were his unspoken words. Mr Vine and Mrs Bell still hadn't returned. Miss Wilton left soon after Emmeline, pleading that her married sister needed her help after her husband had signed up. Verena was trying to replace them, but the agencies told her that they had hardly anyone on their books. She declared that she would do her and Celia's hair, that actually they didn't *need* a maid.

The ones remaining kept up their routine at Stoneythorpe, airing rooms that no one went in, dusting ornaments no one saw, laying fires that were not lit, setting the table for dinners that never occurred because Rudolf said he had changed his mind and did not wish to eat. Mrs Rolls baked bread and roasted meat that languished by the hearth. She stopped Celia from throwing it away. 'Who would want to eat stale bread?' Celia demanded as the cook packed it into cloth bags and gave them to Smithson to take into town.

'Plenty wouldn't think that stale at all,' Mrs Rolls said, raising her eyebrows. 'Plenty would think it *fresh*.'

Mrs Rolls was always trying to think up new ideas for recipes, in the hope of tempting Rudolf and Verena to the table. She whipped up cakes, preserved fruits, covered apples with meringue, and baked fish soufflés. Celia felt sorry for her, told her that she shouldn't waste her time.

'It is a pleasure for me, miss. Yes, they might not eat it today, but one day they will. Anyways, if the word I hear is right, I might find myself baking without sugar or flour in a month or two. The quality of the stuff is nothing to write home about, but I might as well enjoy myself while I can.'

'If we run out of food, there are always birds to eat,' said Jennie. 'Those girls must be getting all those white feathers from somewhere.'

'They should say what they feel, if you ask me,' said Ellie. 'Why should some men be at home when the others aren't? Mr Smithson?'

Smithson shook his head.

'Hush, girl!' said Mrs Rolls. 'Don't say such a thing! We couldn't run Stoneythorpe without John! We can't send all the men.'

'We can send some of them.' Ellie slid a look at Celia. 'Young Tom from the stables has gone.'

Celia nodded, fighting to control her face. 'Mr Marks talks of signing up too.'

'Well, good riddance, we don't need *his* sort around,' said Mrs Rolls. 'But John is a different matter. What a naughty girl you are, Ellie.'

Ellie shrugged. 'Just saying things how I see them, Mrs Rolls. There's a lot thinks the same as me, I bet.'

'Not in my kitchen they don't. Get along with you to those pans and don't say another word. Time for you to go upstairs, Miss Celia, if you don't mind, thank you. The girls have got work to do.'

At dinner that evening, Rudolf mentioned that he had paid Marks double not to sign up.

'I don't see why,' said Verena, flatly. 'We don't need those horses any more. What are we going to do with them? Moonlight, to start with.'

'Mama! You said you wouldn't! We have to keep the horses for when they all come back.' When she was younger, Emmeline had loved riding more than any of them. Michael had teased her that the only reason she was marrying Sir Hugh was because of his extensive stables.

Verena was playing with her knife, something she never would have done only a year ago. Her hair drooped around her face. 'They are an expense. Lady Redroad says we should donate them all to the war effort.'

'But you promised you wouldn't!'

Verena laid down her knife. 'They are without use, like everything else in this house.'

'My dear.' Rudolf raised his arm. 'Do not say that.'

Verena shook him off. 'It is true! What use am I as a mother if three of them are gone and God knows when they will return?'

'My dear,' Rudolf soothed. 'I will write to Arthur again. I will ask him to come back.'

'It will do no good.' Verena pointed at Celia. 'And she – she wants to go too. I can tell.'

'I do not, Mama!' Celia protested. Guilt wrapped around her heart, for she knew she was lying. There was a world outside Stoneythorpe and she could feel it reaching in to claim her.

'See,' said Rudolf. 'Celia is happy here. She will not leave us. Not my Celia.' He looked at her fondly across the table and the guilt clenched even tighter.

'I will not keep them,' continued Verena. 'If they do not want to live with me, they cannot expect me to keep their things, look after their horses. And I will not.'

'My dear, you must not upset yourself.'

'I do not upset myself. They upset me!' She put her head on the table and began weeping. Rudolf put his arm around her. Celia stood and crept out of the room. Neither of them saw her go.

Smithson left three days later to join the Hampshires. Rudolf forbade Celia from accompanying the other servants to the station to see him off. She sat on the chill front steps and watched them leave in the carriage, their arms full of bags and baskets of food for him from Mrs Rolls, Jennie smart in her hat, holding her handkerchief to her eyes. They waved at Celia as they left, and Smithson raised his hand, and it was a moment she thought would be like a photograph, conserved and stuck in her mind, frozen in brown and cream, something she would never forget. She waved and waved until she could not see the wheels of the carriage, or even hear them, but still she was waving. She did not want to stop.

She stood there on the drive. A piece of stone had fallen out of place and she nudged it back with her foot. She meant to go back to the house and start tidying her books, as Verena had told her. But her feet were carrying her forward and she followed them. Before she knew it, she was out on the road. The cold winter sun beat down on her bare head. She pulled her cloak around herself against the freezing wind. The road curved and she followed, walking on with it, further and further towards the village. She turned off towards the cobbled road and the low houses with white fronts. The Cotton home.

Other houses were open to the road, the women leaning out of the doors, children swarming over the steps. The Cottons' house was closed. When Celia was younger, she often imagined houses with personalities, thought of them as happy or sad, drew them so with the door as the mouth. The Cottons' home had once looked like all the rest, she thought, but now it was shuttered up and downcast, unfriendly. It was as if it wished to turn its back entirely on everyone. And then she chastised herself for childishness, finding faces in things that did not have faces at all. They were at war – Michael and Tom were fighting, and Smithson was on his way. Everybody had to be an adult now.

She needed a position to spy from, of that she was sure. Slightly up a hill was a wall, part of which looked like it had been the surround for a well that had fallen down. She hurried up to it and crouched behind it. She waited. People milled around her, women mainly. A small boy peered at her and hissed, 'What are you doing there?'

'I'm looking for my pet mouse,' she whispered back. She shook her head when he offered help, and he wandered off.

Finally she had her moment. The door of the Cotton house opened and Mrs Cotton came out. Celia felt a stab of remorse when she saw her. Tom's mother's pretty face was crushed and sad. Her dark hair fell unarranged around her face. She dragged her feet as she headed towards the village green.

Still, Celia reminded herself, she could not feel sad for her. She had to act. She jumped out from behind the wall and hurried down to the house. She knocked twice and then walked in. The hall was as dark as it had been before.

'Ma?' came a voice. 'Is that you?' Celia felt sure it was Mary.

'It's me,' she called back. 'Where are you?'

'Who are you?'

But Celia had already located the whereabouts of the voice. She hurried up the stairs and along the corridor to a white-painted door. 'Miss Cotton?' She pushed open the door.

Mary's red hair was untied and frizzy around her shoulders. She was buttoning a pinafore on to Missy. The room was painfully cold without a fire.

'I came to see you,' burst out Celia before the girl had a chance to speak.

'You shouldn't be here, miss. Ma would forbid it.'

'Who's this, Mary?' whispered the child.

Mary pulled the pinafore tight at the top. 'You remember, Missy. You went to her party. She's the lady who came before to tell us Tom had gone.'

'Why's she here?'

'I'd ask her the same.' Mary slotted through the top button and bent to pick up the comb for the child's hair. Celia studied her, but she couldn't see much of Tom in Mary's flat face and small features. The little girl had the same sort of look too: big cheeks, tiny features. Neither of them had Tom's large eyes and mouth.

Celia took a breath. 'I wanted to know if you had heard from Tom. If you had received any letters.'

Mary shrugged. 'Of course he writes. We have had five, I think. No, six.' She cast a sly look. 'Does your brother not write to you, miss?'

'He does. His letters are short. He says they are well, the people are friendly, the food not too bad.'

Mary took a brush and began smoothing out the child's hair. 'He writes, miss. What else can you expect?'

Celia sat down on the bed, even though no one had offered. 'I just can't see it, do you understand? I just can't see where he is. I can't imagine it. He says there is not too much mud and he has got a little sunburn. He doesn't tell me about the other men or what they eat or do or anything.'

Mary was plaiting now, smoothing one skein of hair over another. 'Tom doesn't tell us much either. His letters sound pretty alike.'

Celia did not speak immediately. She took a breath. The words waited in front of her, shining in the air. She could not say them. And then she did. 'Might I see them?' She could not help adding more words. 'I would like to see them.'

Mary paused. 'I don't know where they are.'

'Please. I'd like to see them.'

The plaiting continued, slow and steady. 'Ma says your family has brought us nothing but trouble. She says you think everyone must admire you because you have money.'

'Not me. Please. We were friends. I'd show you my brother's letters if you wanted.' She had no idea how she'd manage to take them from Rudolf's study, but if that was what Mary desired, she would.

'I don't wish to see them.' Mary pulled a skein of hair over, then tugged it tight. She stood still for a moment, thinking.

'Please,' Celia said.

'If it'll make you leave, you can see the last letter he sent. Our mother keeps the others, I don't know where. I'll finish this first.'

Celia sat and watched her pull sections of Missy's hair, wrap them over each other. It just looked brown from this angle, but she supposed it was all colours like hers, little streaks of blond, red, brown and darker brown. The child was humming to herself, occasionally falling towards Mary's hands when she pulled too hard.

'There!' Mary said, tying a piece of ribbon around the end. 'Done. Good girl, Missy.' She dusted her hands. 'The letter is downstairs in the kitchen. You can come if you like.'

Holding Missy, she set off down the rickety stairs. Celia followed, stepping carefully to avoid the piles of cups and spoons and bits of toys. The kitchen was strewn with plates and saucepans, the chairs all out of place, a heap of paper and firewood dumped on the floor. 'Come on in,' said Mary, impatiently. Missy sat on the floor and began fiddling with a dropped potato and a spoon. Mary flicked through the piles of paper on the side. 'Here it is.' She passed a single page over to Celia. 'You can read it here. But quickly. Ma will be back soon.'

Celia's heart shivered as she unfolded the paper. There it was, Tom's handwriting, unmistakable. Rudolf had been so very proud of all the advances Tom had made at school – before Verena had forced him to take him away.

Dear Ma, Mary and Missy,

Hope you are all keeping well. Things are not too bad here. Weather is good and the people are friendly. Captain Elletson says I am doing well and he is glad to have a man with strong hands about, says he is glad he didn't lose me to the horses. One of the other men who has come over here from another battalion was a travelling actor. He gives us a good show in the evenings. He knows all the old songs – remember 'Ellie Mae', that one you used to sing us, Ma? It lifts our spirits. Food isn't too bad here, I can say. Captain Elletson is a fine man. He brought a good breakfast cake, said it's a speciality here. He is pretty strict about cleanliness too, which is good, keeps us men up to scratch because sometimes you are so dog tired that you don't have the energy. But he makes a point of telling his Staff Sergeants to have a good look at the men's feet, as he says that if you don't keep them clean and dry once we're out, you will get a nasty infection and then the foot has to come off. Yesterday he asked me to take over the inspection. You would have laughed, Mary, to see me looking at all those feet! Well, I should get back to the men now. I hope you are all well and Missy that you are good and learning your letters. I send you all a big kiss. I miss you and the news from home.

Your loving
Tom

Celia read it again, savouring the words, looking at Tom's writing. 'He writes much more than my brother does,' she said. 'Maybe he's happier.'

Mary wrinkled her mouth. Missy was trying to pull a pan from the stove. 'Missy, stop that now!' She tugged the child away, turned to Celia. 'Only one of your type could say that,' she said, her eyes blazing. 'Only someone like you would think my brother could be happy in a place like that.'

'I didn't mean—'

'Give me back the letter.' She held out her hand. 'Ma will be home soon, and she will hit the roof if you are here. I should have never let you have it.'

'I am sorry. I—'

'Just go! Really, just go.'

From the floor, Missy cried out, 'Just go!'

Celia passed the letter across, feeling as if it were burning in her hand. 'Thank you,' she said.

'Don't thank me! Just go away.'

Celia held out her hand. 'Please. May I have his address?'

Mary looked as if she was about to burst into tears. 'No! Go now!'

Celia turned then, hurried out of the kitchen, into the hallway and out of the house. Two women at the opposite door stared at her. She dropped her head and rushed back up the road, dreading seeing Mrs Cotton at every step, pushing against the icy wind. Tom's words were pounding in her head: the feet inspections, Captain Elletson and the breakfast cake. *Why does he not write to me?*

She still could not tell if Michael and Tom were together. She had consoled herself in the first days after they had left with the idea that they sat side by side. But now she did not know. She could see that Tom might not mention Michael to his family. But why would Michael not mention Tom? The answer rang through her: Verena would be angry. But how could they be together and not say anything about it? That made their letters into lies. And surely Michael and Tom wouldn't send lies.

THIRTEEN

Christmas was Rudolf's favourite time of year. He said it was the gift the Germans had given to the world. 'It was all thanks to the Prince Consort,' he was fond of saying. 'He decked the Palace with bowers of green and even made the Queen put up a tree.' In the old days, Verena used to tease him that he fancied himself a bit of a Prince Consort.

'Well,' said Rudolf, 'I have certainly had practice in supporting a demanding lady with strong opinions.'

Verena shook her head. 'You shouldn't talk about the Queen like that. Especially not in front of the children.'

'See,' Rudolf shrugged to the table, 'there is no doubt who is Empress of India around here.'

Each Christmas, Rudolf directed Smithson and Thompson in adorning the walls, he supervised the delivery of the tree, he told the four children where to hang the glass and wooden ornaments he had collected over the years. Arthur got to put up the most brilliant decorations, Emmeline placed the star on the top, giggling on the ladder, and Michael strewed the branches with silver ribbon and little silver pieces of string. Then, finally, Celia – who had sat watching in the corner – was allowed to put on the last few baubles. Every year, she wished she could do it all herself.

Now she looked at the tree and her father standing beside it, his eyes full of hope, and was miserably reminded of what Verena used to say: be careful what you wish for. Here she was, with what she had longed for so desperately: four boxes of baubles and ribbons and the star to perch on the top. *I didn't mean it this way*, she pleaded. *I didn't! I meant them just to be doing other things, to be coming home later for Christmas.* Rudolf stood smiling at her eagerly, begging her to smile too, to play the part of all four children, to show him that he had a family.

'Look, Celia,' he said. 'Even in wartime, we have found a beautiful tree.' Thompson had balanced the tree in the corner of the library with the help of Jennie. After two weeks of poring over advertisements and writing to agencies, Verena had given up on trying to replace Smithson. Apparently all those young men who hadn't gone to war preferred to be in the big towns. Jennie and Sarah had to do the pushing and pulling with Thompson. The three of them had dragged the tree through the back door while Rudolf clapped his hands and hugged Celia tight. 'I knew I would find a tree!' he said. He had been hunting for weeks, writing letters and sending Thompson off to Winchester, determined not to be beaten by the shortage of wood.

He gestured towards the boxes of ornaments that Jennie had brought down from the attic. 'What a treat! You can decorate it all yourself!'

'Thank you, Papa,' Celia said, trying to smile. She felt as if her parents were china ornaments, that the merest word from her might smash them – like *Arthur, Emmeline and Michael will stay away! Christmas Day will be just the three of us!* But she knew that Verena had ordered Mrs Rolls to bake ten pies and roast five sides of beef, to recreate two of the cakes that she had baked in August. Verena had no patience with Mrs Rolls talking of the shortages. 'Just pay more!' she said. Rudolf had ordered gifts, especially for Emmeline. Every day he asked Thompson for letters, always hoping for an envelope.

'Well, go ahead then,' he said now. 'The tree needs its decorations from my favourite Celia.'

Celia reached into one of the boxes and picked out another, smaller box. She opened it and pulled out a tiny wooden model of an abacus. Her heart bumped. That one had been Michael's favourite; it had been Rudolf's as a child. As a young boy, Michael had begged Rudolf to allow him to take it up to his room and play with it alone.

'Now, Michael. This one is for everyone,' Rudolf always said.

Michael would position it on the tree, placing it right at the front. 'It must stay here,' he said, firmly. 'No one can move it.'

Celia stood there holding the abacus in her hand. Michael had always taken it down as well, he loved it so. Some part of it was in him, she thought. She wanted to let the tears roll down her face. *I wish Michael had taken this to France.* But she couldn't say that. Instead, she hung it on the front of the tree, reached down for the next.

Michael sent them a Christmas card, which arrived midway through December, a cheap one that Verena suspected was given to the men in bulk to send out to their relatives. It had a chilly-looking robin on the front, sitting on a snowy bough. *Many best wishes for Christmas and the New Year*, he had written. *We hope for peace.* After that, they watched every day for another letter. 'It is probably delayed in the post,' said Rudolf, sagely. Arthur sent a card from Paris with a picture of the Eiffel Tower, saying, again, how he was occupied by his search for business opportunities, how he would definitely come in the spring. Emmeline sent a letter with no address, saying she was well. She told them she was in London and said that the shops looked very pretty, preparing for Christmas. Celia gazed at her sister's regular, rounded vowels and envied her. She hated all her siblings, then, their breezy words: hope you are well, how is Stoneythorpe, what is the weather like? *You have left me here*, she wanted to cry.

'We could ask Mrs Rolls and Jennie and Thompson to eat up here with us on Christmas Day,' Celia had said to her mother, three days before. There had been letters from Smithson, two to Mrs Rolls and Jennie so far (really he just meant Jennie, they all knew), describing the training. Jennie's eyes were red in the morning.

Verena drew herself up, immediately the dignified chatelaine of Stoneythorpe once more. 'Celia! How can you think of such a thing? What if word got out?'

'Don't you think it would be nice?'

'No, I do not! And what is more, they would dislike it. What are you thinking of, Celia? Has the world turned upside down?'

'I wish it would,' sighed Celia, under her breath, so quietly that Verena could not hear.

She went to bed on Christmas Eve past bowers of green and decorations, her heart heavy. She almost could not believe her own thoughts – her wish that Christmas could have been cut from the calendar for the year seemed bizarre, unnatural, but still she felt it. She tried to imagine Michael having a Christmas celebration, but could not.

They drove to church arrayed in their smartest coats and hats, feet cracking through the snow. Everyone stared at them – as they had done at every service since the war had begun. Reverend Martin talked about forgiveness and peace, led prayers for the troops. Celia sat upright, aware of eyes on her back. She longed for the Cottons to be behind her, but when she rose they were nowhere to be seen. On the way out, they were stepping into their carriage when a clump of mud landed on Rudolf's shoe. They looked up as a group of boys ran away over the mound behind the church. 'Filthy Hun!' one shouted. A giggle rose from the crowd outside the church.

'Come, my dear,' murmured Rudolf, grasping Verena's arm. 'Let us go into the carriage. Do not look back. Come, Celia.'

'What's happening?' hissed Celia.

'Nothing. Just children.' Rudolf ushered them both in, shut the door and clapped for Glover to drive on. As the horses turned, Celia felt sure she heard more bolts of mud hit the carriage.

Back at Stoneythorpe, she stood on the drive. 'I want to look at the carriage,' she told Rudolf. 'There is mud there! I heard them!'

'No more than the usual,' he said, shaking his head. 'Only a little.'

'I want to look.'

'No!' He shouted out the word with more anger than she'd expected. 'No, you will not.'

Celia's heart thumped. Rudolf never shouted at her. He prided himself, he said, on not raising his voice to his children. He always said that doing so taught children that violence solved things. Which it didn't, he said, it never did.

She looked at him, expecting him to smile, relent. But he did not. 'You will go in!' he said, loudly and furiously. 'Go inside.'

'Come, Celia.' Verena woke from what had been stillness and took Celia's arm. 'Let us go to the house. It is beginning to snow once more.' Celia sank into her mother's grip and they made their way up the snowy slope to the front door. Thompson was coming to meet them, pushing snow out of their way with a beater.

Celia looked back. Rudolf was leaning against the carriage, crumpled and bent, his head in his hands. Verena jerked her arm. 'Come on, Celia. You must change for lunch.'

The Christmas table was fabulously decorated with evergreens and candles. A great side of beef was the centrepiece, surrounded by pies, mountains of glazed carrots, potatoes, parsnips and beans. Their plates were piled high. Celia stared at them, thinking of the shortages of sugar and meat talked about in the newspapers. 'Mrs Rolls has done marvellous work,' said Verena, smiling beatifically as if there were a dozen people at her huge table, rather than just the three of them spaced around the polished mahogany. 'Do you not think, husband?' Rudolf looked up, his face pale, his eyes bewildered, as if, Celia thought, he were lost. 'Yes, wife,' he said, his voice cracked. She was sure he did not know what he said.

Thompson brought around the gravy boat.

'Let us pray,' said Verena. 'Let us begin. Rudolf.'

Rudolf stared at her dizzily. Then he bowed his head. 'Our Father,' he began. Celia mouthed through the familiar words. Usually she paid no attention, but now she found them wanting. *What do you mean, thy will be done?* she wanted to cry. *How is* this *your will?*

After lunch, little of which Celia could eat, they retired to the parlour to open their presents. She looked at her pile and wanted to weep for all the expressions of joy and gratitude she would have to give, three times as many as she ever had before. Her first gift was a beautifully illustrated copy of *The Water-Babies*. Celia gazed at it. *This is too young for me*, she wanted to say. *And I've already got one that I bought with you in London to hide Freud.* Verena's face was shining, expectant. She was just about to say how much she loved it when there was a great cry from the garden outside.

'What is that?' Verena stiffened.

'It sounds like one of the horses, madam,' said Thompson from the back of the room.

Celia leapt up and her mother craned to look out of the window. 'I can't see anything. Has one got free, do you suppose?'

'Do you think it is Silver?' Celia cried. 'She will freeze!' Her heart flashed guilt then, for she had not been to see Silver for a week now, and her visits had become more and more infrequent before that. She had not had the heart. Everything there reminded her of Tom.

'I shall go and see,' said Thompson. 'Do not worry, madam.' He slipped from the room and they watched him hurry up the garden through the snow to the stables.

Celia returned to her book. 'How beautiful it is, Mama! You have found me such a beautiful thing.' She knew it would be churlish to say *I'm too old for* The Water-Babies! She supposed that it was hard to find good presents these days.

Four parcels later, Thompson came back into the room, red-faced and out of breath.

Verena was already standing. 'What has happened?'

'It's not good, madam. It looks as if Marks has left. I don't know when, perhaps three days ago. More, maybe. I can't think when I last saw him. The horses are very weak and Miss Celia's Silver is so hungry that she has started to bite her own leg. It's incredible that none of us heard them. I don't know what I should do.'

'That cannot be possible!' Verena exclaimed. 'He would have said.'

Celia leant over the fire, her face hot with shame and guilt. What had she done? She had abandoned Silver, left her to starve. The set of bronze hearth tools mocked her.

'I will go up there,' she said. 'I will go up there to look after her.'

'I wouldn't, miss. Not a nice sight.'

'No, Celia,' said Rudolf, his voice weak. 'You are not permitted.'

'I've given them all some hay and water, sir. Jennie has gone up there to try to calm them. I will enquire in the village about finding a man. We might have a job, though: a lot of the good men have signed up and I don't know who to try.'

'Thank you,' said Rudolf. Celia sat down again, stared at her mound of presents. She could feel tears sliding out of her eyes. Thompson closed the door behind him.

'I said that we shouldn't have kept all those horses,' said Verena. 'I said they would never come back.'

'Now, my dear, do not blame yourself.'

'I don't. I blame Arthur, Michael and Emmeline. Going away and leaving us, expecting everything to be the same for them when they return, expecting us to keep things going.'

'They are our children.'

'That is not a licence for doing anything they like.'

Celia waited, in dread, for her mother to berate her as well. But instead she sat back heavily in her chair.

'I wish I could call for tea,' said Verena. There was no one left downstairs who was permitted to serve in the parlour.

Celia sprang up. 'I'll get it, Mama.'

'You know you cannot.' Verena's voice was weaker than her words.

'I'll go,' Celia said. She hurried out of the room and towards the kitchen. Mrs Rolls, Sarah and Ellie looked up as she arrived. Ellie was crying.

'Merry Christmas, miss,' said Mrs Rolls, little joy in her voice.

'I came for the tea,' Celia said. 'Mama would like some tea.' Ellie was trying to wipe away her tears.

'I'll bring it, miss,' said Sarah, straightening up. 'Sorry, miss, we're all a bit low-spirited anyway, and Ellie is terrible fond of horses. I'll just knock and leave the tray outside.'

Celia wanted to say kind words to them that would make them happier, make the kitchen the cheery place she had used to go to as a child. But she could not think of any. 'Merry Christmas!' she said, and ran back up the stairs.

She could hear the raised voices of her parents as she walked to the parlour. She waited outside the door and listened.

'I will not let you!' Verena cried out. 'I will not have it! How can you think of going and leaving me?' She burst into a torrent of tears.

'It is the right thing to do,' Rudolf said. 'Sometimes you have to do the right thing. And do you not agree that it is better for me to go before they come for me? Anyway, I am sure that it is just a case of signing and registering all over again. I will not be imprisoned.'

'How do you know?'

'What sense would there be in sending everyone of German origin to prison? None. Anyway, they're releasing all the men they took in summer already.'

'You are naïve! Why else would they have called you to London?'

'Well, naïve, or not, wife, I must go. Do you suggest I should lock myself in at Stoneythorpe?'

'Yes!' Celia could hear that her mother had stood up.

'I wish you luck in such an endeavour! Now, let us be calm. Celia will come back soon. We cannot let her hear us speaking like this.'

Celia heard Verena sit back down. 'Do not go to London, Rudolf. Please.'

'I do not think I can hide. I am prominent already, through the business. And anyway, someone will be reporting me, you know. It says very clearly I must attend this meeting. There may be nothing you or I can do.' Verena continued to cry. 'Come now, dry your tears. We must make the best of things.'

'But everybody else has left me. You cannot go as well.'

'It is not my choice. Come, wife. It is Christmas Day!'

Sarah was approaching with the tea. Celia knew she could wait no longer. She knocked on the door and entered. Verena was leaning her head on the back of the sofa, hands over her face.

'The tea is coming, Papa,' Celia said.

'Good, good.'

Sarah knocked on the door and Celia hurried to open it. She picked up the tray and brought it through. 'I will pour,' she said.

'That's it,' said Rudolf. 'A good cup of tea. Makes all the difference.' He raised his cup to her. 'Merry Christmas to us all.'

Four days after the start of a miserable New Year, Rudolf left to have his meeting with the gentleman from the Aliens' Office in London. Verena locked herself in her room. Celia asked Mrs Rolls if she could eat her meals in the kitchen, but the cook would not allow it, so she took her lunch to the parlour and ate it in the armchair. There was no one to see, after all.

After she had finished her toad in the hole, she ran to put on her coat and boots. If she could eat in the parlour and escape being told off, she could go to the horses, even though Rudolf and Verena had made her promise not to. She walked up through the melting snow to the stables. She could hear the horses as she arrived, pacing and puffing.

'Hello!' she called. She had stood by this door with Tom; he had held her hand, held it up to feel the wood, taken her to ride on Silver, laughed when she failed to balance.

A man came to the door. Celia didn't recognise him. He must have been found in another village, one that still had some men left. 'You're not allowed in, miss. Some of the horses are not so well.'

'I just wanted to see Silver. I miss her.'

'We have instructions, miss.'

'Please. Just to see Silver.'

Another man came to the door and shrugged. 'You could let her. Might do the horse good if it is hers.'

They opened the door and Celia went inside. The place smelt of illness. Arrow, Michael's horse, was lying down at the back of his stable, and Arthur's Red was also curled up in the corner. Emmeline's Moonlight was standing up, swaying a little, hanging her head, her eyes closing. Her face was tired, her beautiful mane hanging lank.

'That one won't eat much, miss,' the second man said. 'Not good.'

Silver was at the back of the stables. Celia rushed up to her but the man told her to stop. 'She is nervous. Don't go too close too fast.'

Celia wanted to cry when she saw her beautiful horse. Her eyes were open but dull. Her ribs protruded from her skin. Usually Silver smiled and rubbed her feet when Celia arrived. Now, she did not look up.

'I've been neglecting her,' Celia said, filled with shame.

The man shrugged. 'You're not the only one. We don't know how much they were fed even before Mr Marks went away. We've had the surgeon in twice, but he says the medicine this one needs is out of stock. Still, good food and proper care will be enough, I'm sure.'

Celia put her arms around Silver and leant her head on her flank. 'Poor little thing,' she said. Silver hardly moved as she held her.

'Try not to cry, miss,' the man said. 'You will make the horse sad too. No use crying over spilt milk.'

'Do you think she will get better?'

'Hope so, miss. Hold her close and give her some of your spirit.'

Celia was walking up the stairs to her room when Jennie stopped her. 'There is a letter for you, miss,' she said. 'Miss Emmeline sent it to me and asked me to give it to you in secret. She said it was very important. Please don't tell Mrs de Witt.'

Celia shook her head. 'I won't.' She reached out her hand and took the letter.

'Go now, quickly!' said Jennie. 'Go to your room and keep it hidden.'

Dear Celia,

I hope you can keep this letter secret from Mama. I know how her eyes are everywhere. I think of you often there on your own, my poor sister. Papa and Mama are happy to have you, I am sure, but perhaps you are lonely. I am very well here with Mr Janus. I am doing everything that society said I should not, but I tell you, I find nothing wrong in it. It is wartime, and everything is different. London is very interesting, you know, much more in town than Hampstead ever was. There is a lot to see. The troops are always walking around and the railway stations are full of men departing, men arriving and people hanging over the fences just to watch them. I haven't seen the King or Queen, but they waved out over the crowds on the day that war was announced.

Your loving sister
Emmeline

Celia folded the letter, wanting to cry once more. She immediately began to write a reply, knowing she could not send it without an address but needing to get the words down anyway.

Dear Emmeline,

Thank you for your letter. I am very happy to hear from you. Things are not so good here. We don't hear much from Arthur and Michael, and Marks ran away and left the horses to starve.

She could not go on. She put down her pen and lay on her bed. She heard her mother's footsteps hurrying past. 'Everybody leaves me!' Verena was crying. *Not everybody*, Celia wanted to call. *I'm still here!*

She dressed and came down to wait with her mother for Rudolf. No sign of him by ten. 'He must have decided to stay at his club,' Verena said. Celia lay down to sleep and dreamed of fearful things, monsters in caves, faces full of hate. Something like the telephone woke her up, footsteps for it, a man's voice, then footsteps past her door, but it could not be, for who would telephone so late?

Celia sat bolt upright. An explosion in the garden. Bang! Then another. The noise echoed around her room. She screamed and scrambled out of bed. The enemy were coming! She was about to run from the room when she realised she should get dressed first, if the Germans were invading. She pulled on her dress and boots, reached for her jacket and dashed downstairs. Jennie, Sarah and Thompson were in the hallway. As she reached them, there was another terrible explosion. The freezing air was shaking over her head. She clutched Jennie.

'The Germans are coming! We are being invaded!' she said. 'Hurry!'

'No, miss,' said Thompson. 'They are not in Hampshire.' They were standing there as if held to the spot.

'Well what is it, then? We must stop them! They are coming for us! Where is my father?'

There was another awful noise. Celia clapped her hands over her ears, but too late.

'He didn't come back last night. Madam had a telephone call. I took it. Mr Lewis from the factory said they had taken Mr de Witt into custody.'

'Don't stand here!' Celia said. 'Come with me!'

Thompson shook his head. 'No, miss, don't!' He reached to grasp her arm, but she was already running. She hurtled out into the garden and towards the noise. There was another one, the sound ricocheting through the sky. It was coming from near the stables.

'Stop it!' she cried. 'Stop it, whoever you are!' She ran, her heart in her mouth, her face burning. Another one. *This is what war sounds like*, she told herself.

The noise was definitely coming from the stables. She hurried on – and then stopped still. Verena was coming towards her, blouse awry, her hair fallen from its style. She was carrying Rudolf's hunting gun in her hand. She staggered towards Celia and then fell to the ground.

'Mama!' Celia ran towards her, her feet pounding. 'Mama!' Verena was folding into the ground, tears pouring down her face. 'What is it? What has happened?'

Verena looked up at her, eyes full of tears. 'I've done it,' she said. 'No one was ever coming back for them. They've all left me. Now my husband, too. It was a cruelty to keep them alive.'

'What do you mean? Keep who alive?' And then she realised.

She stood up and began walking towards the stables, so slowly she could almost see herself moving. She was about to seize the door – and then Thompson was grasping her and carrying her up in his arms and bearing her away. 'No, miss,' he was saying, as she screamed and fought against him. 'Don't go in. Don't look.'

'I have to! Please!'

Verena had dropped the gun now and was sobbing on the ground. Jennie kicked it out of her reach and crouched down beside her. Thompson carried Celia, crying out and shouting, back to the house. 'Hold on to her,' he said to Mrs Rolls and Sarah, who were standing by the parlour window, white-faced. 'I have to go back. She might not have finished the job.' Celia shook off their hands and watched as he walked back to Verena, took the gun from the ground and set off to the stables.

There was another report and a terrible animal scream. Celia dropped to the floor and put her hands over her ears. 'No!' she cried. 'No!' Mrs Rolls knelt next to her, put her arms around her and rocked her, crooning in her ear. 'There, there,' she was saying. 'There, there, miss. Soon be better now. Soon be better.'

1915

FOURTEEN

Loos, France, May 1915
Twelfth (Eastern) Division 35th Brigade
Suffolk Seventh Battalion

The men were pressing against the door. Michael could almost feel the heat of their bodies: dozens of them, maybe. *Hundreds.* They had pushed him forward. 'Go on, sir!' they shouted. 'Go in first!' He had smiled as the hands jostled him, enjoying the sensation of being moved. He stared at the wood he had slammed shut behind him. He fancied he could see it bulge with the bodies of men – his men – pressing behind it, eager to come in. 'One in, one out!' the old crone had shouted, sticking her head out of the door.

'I have three girls,' she had said when he came through into the musty front room. Two other soldiers he did not recognise were lounging with bottles on a grubby-looking sofa. She had been in the shadows, rose up towards him. Toothless old crone, he thought immediately, and then despised himself for the thought. He stared at her, supposing she must be around his mother's age, or perhaps a little younger. She was bent, her crescent-moon shoulders covered by a grimy red dress. 'Three girls, monsieur.'

'Dark, blonde, and not so blonde!' snorted one of the men from the sofa. 'First one's the best. Youngest one too much of a child for my tastes ...'

Michael shook his head. Why had he come here? Jamieson, a lieutenant from C Company holding his shoulder: 'Go on. It will help you forget.' Their cheers. His own weakness, thinking it would make the men like him, respect him, even.

The woman was advancing towards him. 'I will just stay here,' Michael stammered. 'Have a drink.'

'Oh poor show, my man,' said the soldier on the sofa. The other one had closed his eyes. The woman was advancing towards him, shaking her head. 'Business, monsieur,' she was saying. 'Business.' She held up three fingers. 'Three girls. Which one?'

Michael shook his head, desperately. 'Madame...' The house was so humble that it did not have a hall or an entrance; one just arrived straight in the parlour, such as it was. He backed towards the door. As he did so, there was a great cheer from behind it.

'Oh come on. Get on with it,' shouted the man on the sofa. 'You're holding everybody up.' Michael heard the sound of him swigging drink. 'Have some courage, old chap.'

He backed against the door, sure that he could literally feel the hot bodies on the other side. *Have some courage, old chap.* That was what they kept saying to him. His commanding officer before he sent him off into the field. Bilks as he passed him his gun: 'You can do it, sir. Just show some backbone.' The men didn't see. But they did see; they laughed at him, sidelong, patted him, like Bilks did when he came around with the rum ration: 'Pecker up, old boy. It might never happen.'

But I don't have any courage! he wanted to say. *I don't have any backbone, not even with rum. I shouldn't be here. Bilks should be commanding the men.* Even Andrews would make a better job of it. Michael had been to Winchester and Cambridge, learnt to read Theophrastus and debate ideas. But nothing had taught him how to command the men to go over the top, fill them with confidence, say, *These are the orders approved by Field Marshal French himself. They are correct. We will win the war. Rule Britannia!*

'The men look up to you, sir,' Bilks had said last night in the dugout. 'You are their officer. You have to be what they imagine an officer to be.'

'I don't know what that is.'

'*Pretend* it.' Bilks had two children, been a factory foreman in Derby. He was used to commanding.

Michael had stared at the other officers when he saw them passing. C Company had Derreny-Mills, a tall, athletic man with a voice that surely carried across the whole of no-man's-land. The man reminded him of Stallon, the sports captain at school, who had nothing but contempt for Michael. B Company had Griffin, solid as a doorstop, who looked like he should be dissuading drunk men from entering a pub. Actually he was a solicitor from Croydon and always gave Michael and his men a cheery wave. 'All right, boys?' he shouted. 'Fritz blowing kisses again?' Michael's men always waved back enthusiastically. Michael knew they would be happier under Griffin. 'Cheer up!' Griffin shouted across to Michael, beaming. 'Could be worse. We could be stamping house sales in Croydon.'

Most nights, Michael couldn't sleep. He lay there in the dugout as the bombs crashed around him, wondering: *Why did I think I could do this?* The thin boy who had been no good at games, the one who no one wanted to pick for their team, who crept off to the library rather than play. *De Witt is not a team player,* he remembered one report saying. Rudolf had snorted. 'Pah! Who needs it? The English always want to play in a team.'

He had thought it was just sport. But in Cambridge, where there were men who could not play sports, just as many as those who could, it was no different. He came to understand that the other students tolerated him, allowed him to sit with them in the bars or the public debates. When he contributed something to the argument, they nodded and smiled, talked of another question.

He'd met Jonathan halfway through the second term, happening to sit beside him in a lecture about Plato. He had seen him before, of course, everyone had; big and handsome, Jonathan was always surrounded by other students, laughing at his jokes. He even dared talk to the few girls from Girton at the end of a lecture on the philosophy of mind. He was the man everyone wanted to befriend. 'I've seen you about,' he said, sinking into the seat next to Michael with a pile of books. 'De Witt, is it not? You're a rather hard-working fellow. What do you do for fun?'

After the lecture, instead of going back to his own room to resume study, Michael followed Jonathan to his set, where the bedder had laid the fire and made tea. 'This is a jolly cake,' Jonathan said, sliding a pink-iced confection on to the table. 'Clay's wife makes me one every week; suppose she thinks I need feed-ing up.' He laughed then. *No*, Michael wanted to say. *It's because everyone likes you. Show me how you do it.*

As he finished his cake (better than anything they gave him at Magdalene), he began to panic. He thought he should go; surely there would be someone else Jonathan wished to see. Any minute now, crowds of chums might be coming through the door and he would be as superfluous as ever. He stumbled up, in agonies whether he had already overstayed, bid Jonathan a quick goodbye and hurried out into King's quad. On the way home, he was in torment. What a fool he had made of himself: said the wrong thing, had no idea when to leave. Jonathan must think him a dolt.

Two days later, there was a hearty banging at his door. Michael opened it and Jonathan was standing there, grinning.

'Studying again, old thing? You'll give yourself a headache. Let's go.'

Michael fiddled with his hair, not brushed yet. 'Go where?'

'Don't ask questions; get your coat and come along.' Jonathan seized his hand and began pulling him out of the door. Laughter was bubbling up in Michael, from deep down. 'I haven't finished my essay!'

'I won't hear another word. Come along.' He tugged Michael out and slammed the door behind him, then led him down the stairs, through the quad, out into the street and into a cab. 'To the Plough in Fen Ditton,' he said.

'We're going to a pub?' said Michael as the cab bounced north. 'Wednesday, in the middle of the day?' He thought his voice sounded like his mother's, it was so scandalised.

'Dear chap, these places are no fun at the weekend. Far too full. Now, let's concentrate, look out for any gals from Girton. I might stop and ask them along.'

'No, you simply can't!' His voice came out like Verena's again, this time thickened with misgiving. He didn't want two hearty girls from Girton with big hair buns and baskets of books coming too. Hopefully, he thought, they would be far too busy with their studies to wish to do such a thing.

'Isn't this the life?' said Jonathan, as they sat at the lunch table (thankfully free from Girton girls), looking out to the river. He reached over and laid his hand on Michael's. 'Now, this is why I came here from New York.' He withdrew his palm and put it behind his head.

Michael looked down at his wrist. Surely, he thought, surely, if he looked closer, he would see the imprint there of Jonathan's palm. He wanted to save it.

Within weeks, he and Jonathan went everywhere together. 'What on earth does Corrigan see in de Witt?' he heard someone say, sitting on the lawn, when he was by an open window in the library. 'Corrigan!' they called across. 'Talk of the devil! Bet you're here to see de Witt. What do you see in him?'

'He's the most honest man I have ever met,' Jonathan drawled back. 'Not like you lot.'

Honest! Michael wanted to snort. He was not that. He was a coward, welcoming the new interest in him that came because he was Jonathan Corrigan's friend. Men moved to make a place for him at lunch. Burlington, a brashly handsome son of one of the richest men in Britain, the acknowledged king of Magdalene's social set, called him over to chat at Master's drinks. Even his bedder, Berts, had brought him some potatoes from his garden. 'I'll polish them up for you and make them nice. You can eat them with Mr Corrigan, so you can.'

Michael had invited Celia and Emmeline to come and visit. Celia had been begging him ever since he'd started at Cambridge, and every time he told her he had too much work to do. In the event, Jonathan was away visiting a friend of his mother's on the only weekend Verena would allow Celia to come. Emmeline was too busy taking tea with Sir Hugh. Michael escorted his sister around town, responding to the waves of chaps as they walked. 'You have an awful lot of friends,' she said envyingly.

'Oh, you know.' He waved his hand airily. 'I meet them at lectures.'

He took her to the Plough for dinner. 'This is beautiful,' she said, looking out.

'Jonathan found it,' he replied. He would never have known of it if it was not for him.

That night, as he walked her back to the Newnham home of one of Verena's old deb chums, the only place Verena had deemed safe enough for Celia to stay, she held his arm. 'I am so proud of you, Michael. You've so many friends. You're *happy* here. I will tell Mama how well you are doing. And then she'll let me come here, I'm sure.'

Celia. What was her life like now? The night before he left, he had tried to write her a goodbye letter, failed. He had tried to write one to all of them, his mother, father, Emmeline. He could not. He began and stopped, began and stopped, threw them aside. Then he picked up a paper to write to Jonathan. *Why did you leave me?* he wrote. *Why did you go?*

He had received a letter three days after Jonathan had hurried away, saying he had had to go to New York for business interests, and hoped to be back for the beginning of term. When, on that night by the flower beds, Tom had talked of war, saying they should do it now, before the war was over and they had missed their chance to *live*, he'd thought of Jonathan. *I shall make you proud*, he told him in his mind. *I shall come back from the war a great man and you will be proud of me.*

They ran away from Stoneythorpe in the middle of the night, not saying goodbye to Celia. He thought of her as she must be now, dashing around the summer flowers, singing as she ran, begging anyone to take her out on Silver. In her last letter, Verena had said that Emmeline was married – so Sir Hugh had come back after all. He supposed Celia must take Silver over to Callerton Manor to call on her sister. *We are all well*, Verena wrote to him. *I am well*, he wrote back. His words were a lie, but he knew theirs were truth. They were happy at Stoneythorpe, as they always were.

He had received a letter from Jonathan, forwarded by Thompson.

I didn't hear back from you, dear fellow, suppose the letter has been lost. I wrote to your mother and she said you were on your way to France. They tell me there is an awful lot of mud out there! Well, as I said, I couldn't get a boat out to New York in the end, they were all full of people dashing back home away from the Kaiser. Outlandish prices. Back at Cambridge now, place quiet without you. Seems like there are quite a number of you out there. Do you ever see Peter Burlington? He sends letters to the chaps here saying he's having a bully time, lots of French food. It must be quite a riot out there. Are the girls pretty? Do they dance like I hear they do in Paris? Seriously, I am proud of you, old thing. Terribly brave. The men must really look up to you.

Michael meant to throw the letter away. He crumpled it into a ball. But then he smoothed it out, found himself keeping it, tucked away in his box in the dugout. He looked at the words and hated himself. *Brave. Proud.* Of what? Being a coward, shaking when a bomb flew over, retching when Fritz sent up another explosion. 'Don't worry, sir, none of the men saw,' Bilks would say. If Jonathan saw him, he would pity him, despise him even. 'Surely you can do better than that, old thing?'

Michael had seen Burlington once. 'De Witt!' he had heard. He could hardly bear to turn round. 'Good for you, old thing!' Burlington had shouted over an expanse of land that had recently been bombed. 'We need to get the others out here. Heard anything from Corrigan recently?'

Michael shook his head.

'We must have a drink sometime!' shouted Burlington, as if they were talking across the quad, rather than scrubby land full of smoke dotted with stretcher-bearers scouring the ground for limbs. 'Toodle-oo!'

One other time he saw a boy from school, another shy one, no good at sports, whose name he had lost from his mind. He told Michael that Stallon had gone straight into the army from school, was now terribly high up with the generals.

Of course, Michael had thought. This place was for people like

Stallon: tall, confident, pushing people out of the way. What on earth had made him think that he could go to France? It was a place for leaders, or even for those who could just be cheerful, like Griffin, finding mud and cold more amusing than house sales in Croydon.

Jonathan had written twice more. Michael had replied to neither letter. It was like being back in his room on the night before he left. *Dear Jonathan*, he began; could say no more. What would he say now? *I am in a brothel and I don't know what to do.* Jonathan would know. He had told Michael once that he had been to a brothel in New York. 'The second time, I arrived in one girl's room just when she was reading an article in one of those murder magazines. She stood up, introduced herself – but I could tell she wanted to be back with it. You know how it is when someone pulls you away from something gripping! I said to her, "Miss, why don't you sit yourself down, finish the article first before you think of anyone else?" She was ever so pleased with that, couldn't do enough for me. It was some story about a woman who had been kidnapped from her bed by a monkey, outlandish stuff. I like a reading girl.' He winked. 'What about you, de Witt? Any kept birds for you?' Michael shook his head.

And now here he was by a bulging door, the heat and bodies of men pushing against it, all for these three girls, one for each finger on the old crone's hand. In his pay envelope – in everyone's – there was a section from Kitchener's speech on avoiding wine and women. He'd looked at it, on the boat, wondering who had been given the job of printing it out, stuffing thousands of copies into envelopes.

'Go on, old man.' The soldier on the sofa broke through his thoughts. His voice had turned sharp. 'You're keeping everyone waiting, dilly-dallying like this. The girls need to earn a living.'

Michael was senior to the man, a mere lance corporal. He should have declared that he would report him to his captain for insubordination. But he did not. A coward again. He turned for the stairs.

'Which one?' said the woman, holding up her infernal fingers.

'The eldest,' said Michael. 'What is her name?' The woman shrugged.

'Good choice, my man. She'll tell you her name. Upstairs with you, before the door breaks in.'

Michael tried to speak. His stammer returned. The words stuck in his mouth, would not come out.

'Two shillings with wine,' the woman said. 'Cheap at the price.'

The incredulity must have shown on his face. 'Not really a buyer's market around here, is it, dear boy?' said the soldier. 'These are the best girls for miles.' Michael had seen the other places: small houses with the sign WASHING DONE HERE FOR SOLDIERS, where housewives still in their aprons sat on a couch in the kitchen, flicking brown stuff between their legs in between each customer, the kettle boiling for the men to douse themselves quickly, to stave off the pox.

And now here he was in the room. '*Merci,*' she was saying, sitting on the bed. '*Merci, monsieur.*'

He knew French, he had learnt it. But he could not speak it. *Are you really her daughter?* he wanted to ask. He could not say the words.

'*Viens, monsieur.*' She patted the bed. 'Come.'

Was this your bedroom? he wanted to ask. He thought of Celia's room: pictures on the walls, piles of books on the shelves, trinkets on the desk. This one had nothing: a sparse single bed, a threadbare red cover slung over the top, a pile of boxes in the corner, another box acting as some kind of bedside table. *Did you grow up here? Is that woman really your mother?* The old woman had guided him up the creaky stairs using a candle, had pulled open a dark door (what was this French obsession with dingy wood?). 'Here!' she said. A pale girl with light brown hair and reddish rings under her eyes rose from the bed and smiled. She was very thin, he thought, wearing some sort of pinkish dressing gown, pulled tight around her body. The door slammed behind him and he was alone with her.

'What is your name?' he asked, but she only shook her head,

beckoned to him again. He had no idea of ages; supposed she must be about the same as him, or younger. How young was the other one?

'Why are you doing this?' he said. She did not answer, but he felt from the look in her eyes that she understood. 'This must have been your home. You went to school here. Surely you want to get married.'

She shook her head. '*Merci, monsieur,*' she said again. She lay back on the bed. The dressing gown loosened.

'Don't,' he said. 'I am sorry.' He walked to the window, clung to the frame. It was covered with a dirty sheet. He could hear the men below, roaring out: 'Quicker up there, you bastards! We're waiting.'

'*Monsieur,*' she said. Her voice had hardened. '*Monsieur?*'

He stared at her. There were words in his head and he could not say them. It was like the days of his stammer again; his mouth would not join his brain. She pulled the dressing gown around her and then, in one swift movement, hopped off the bed and came towards him. She clutched the front of his trousers. He jumped in horror. 'Stop!' he shouted. 'Stop.' He pushed her off and she fell back on the bed, her gown flapping open. She started laughing, infernal endless laughter. 'Stop!' he shouted again. 'Stop it now!' and he tore out of the room, down the stairs and back through the parlour, ignoring the men and the crone. He wrenched the door open and threw himself out into the road. A great roar went up from the gang of men outside. Hands were on him. Cries of 'Good on you, old chap!' 'My turn now!' He heard Bilks's voice. He pushed through them, the infernal, shouting mass, and dived into the street, kept running. He turned a corner into a quieter street, leant against the damp wall of a house, breathing deeply.

'Michael!' The voice was above him. He looked up into Tom's face. 'I thought it was you!'

He shook his head, could not speak.

'I thought I saw you come out of that place. I've heard the daughters there are pretty good.'

Michael felt a tear bulge up behind his eye.

'Come on, Michael. I didn't mean to upset you. Nothing to be ashamed of.'

'It's not that,' Michael managed. The last time he had seen Tom had been at Boulogne. Tom had been sent further south, he thought.

Now Tom clapped him on the back. 'Splendid to see you, Michael. I've been wondering how you were getting on. It's been pretty quiet up where I was, so Loos should be a nice change. What's it like here?'

Michael shook his head again. 'I don't know. I really don't know.' He had left his men in the trench singing their hearts out with Private Andrews who said he would have gone on the stage if his father had let him. 'The Grand Old Duke of York': that was him, marching them up to the top of the hill and marching them down again. 'The men are doing well. There's mud. Have you seen the rats? Some of them as big as cats.' That very morning, he had been dreaming of a cat wrapped around his feet and had woken to find a rat there, fat as anything, licking at his socks. He swore the things must feast on corpses.

'But what is the real fighting like, man? We spent most of our time chucking mud out of the trenches with buckets. They made us do it at night so Jerry couldn't spot us, but he never seemed to do much anyway. Honestly, it was more like living on a farm than in a war. The farmers got so used to us, they used to herd their cows past the front of the trenches. We were told by our officers to keep our heads down in case of Jerry, and then a load of cows went mooing past.' He clapped Michael on the back. 'Shame we were split up. I thought they would keep us together. But we're back together again now.'

After they'd joined up, the officer in charge had told them to go home and wait.

'We're a bit full, you see,' he said. 'The top brass didn't expect such a rush.'

'We can't go back. They won't let us leave again. My father

187

would be against it,' said Michael. The officer moved to refuse; Michael cut him off.

The officer went away, came back ten minutes later. 'You can join the group at HQ in Winchester. Look, there's no room here. We're sending you to Bury. Don't tell the rest.'

They piled on to a truck and the officer drove them off. Michael smiled at Tom. 'Thank you!' he shouted, over the wind battering around their ears. 'Thank you!' If it wasn't for Tom, perhaps he wouldn't be there. In the garden, saying *Of course you can do it, Michael, you'll make them proud.*

A girl fluttered past them in the alleyway. 'Come on,' said Tom, 'let's find a café. It's freezing out here.' He linked his arm through Michael's. 'I am so pleased to see you. Thought I might not bump into you for the whole war.' He squeezed. 'It was the right decision, don't you think? For me, definitely. There was nothing back there for me but slaving around under Marks for a few pennies, a job for a boy.'

'And now you are a man?' Michael could not help the bitterness in his tone.

'Why of course! Don't you think so?'

'You want to please my sister.' Tom looked down. Michael knew he had been cruel. The night before they left, Tom had drunk too much and talked of how beautiful he thought Celia was. Michael had sighed. Anyone (except his parents, who were blind) could see that Tom was devoted to Celia, followed her round like a puppy. He knew other things that Tom did not say – that he hated being treated like a servant, thought that going to war would change things, make Celia proud of him. 'My father would never allow it,' he said after Tom had poured out his heart.

'I don't want anything like that. I – well – I can't.'

'Glad you recognise that, at least.'

'Not for the reasons you think!' Tom said, angrily. He glowered at Michael, so much so that Michael felt he had to soothe him, change the subject, return the conversation to the subject of their plans to join up in secret.

This time, Tom was ready for the Celia question. 'No. You were right, I was wrong with all that. I am here for the King, to save us from the Germans. Like you.'

Michael shrugged. 'Our training was pointless, you know.'

At Bury they were given a ticket, then sent off to the stores, where they were handed a set of khakis that didn't look as if they had been darned since the Boer War. They were lucky; some men were training in pyjamas, stores were so low. They had to hew firewood into the shape of rifles, then they were set to marching, round and round, holding, turning, front, back, inspection, learning how to form fours, right wheel, left wheel, supervised by an elderly commander who said he'd fought in India. Then they went to the local park and practised digging trenches. Surely, Michael had wanted to say to the officer in charge, by the time we get there, they'll already be dug. Or are you planning to turn all of France into a trench? He held his tongue, bent over in the August sun, and shovelled mud out of a rose garden that some philanthropist had planted for the benefit of the workers.

After a month, they were given real rifles. One of the old chaps said it wasn't the right sort of rifle; it was a long one, which wasn't what they wanted, apparently. It wasn't loaded and it didn't have any webbing, but still, Michael thought, he had a gun. He held it up and stared at it. It was a deterrent, he told himself. He would use it as a deterrent. He wouldn't need it until the final pitched battle of the war, which would be something like Waterloo, lots of them on horses, the Germans retreating with their hands up in the air.

The town band played them to the station, the girls waving their handkerchiefs, the people cheering. He crammed with the other men on to the train to Southampton, his heart bursting. He would make them proud at home. Hours on the boat, then bundled off at Boulogne. One solitary gendarme with a gun patrolled the dock, nothing more. They piled into a fleet of thirty London omnibuses, their sides papered with rain-sodden advertisements for soap and cereal, fighting to sit at the top – until it started to rain. Most of them were sodden by the time they were turfed out to march. As

Michael stepped down, the officer in charge grasped his shoulder. 'Your corporal has been moved on,' he said. 'Bilks is your lance.'

Fifty minutes on, only ten minutes of rest. Barker and Cook kept falling to the side of the road, begging for water. They wouldn't get up. 'You must leave no one behind,' his commander had said. 'Beat them if they will not move.' Michael made another man cut down a branch from a tree and hit them on the hands until they got up. The twigs slashed at their fingers, caught their faces. When they got up, they were red and angry, did not look at him.

'Why did you do that?' asked the commander when they arrived and he was reporting. 'That was your lance corporal's job. You should oversee.' Michael nodded, wrong already. 'Still, at least you didn't let them take their boots off like Cullen. Half of his men couldn't get them back on again after the lunch stop and had to walk barefoot or with them unlaced. They're in no fit state now.'

They were ready for the bullring: more shooting, throwing grenades and charging at bales of straw with their bayonets. The instructor sergeant said they had to show more teeth, made them charge the straw five times until they were screaming, diving on it, as if to show the truth of Hobbes and his vision of man, Michael thought, standing back.

The trench was, as he'd expected, already dug, shored up with sandbags at the sides. 'There should be boards over the ground,' he said to Bilks. 'The men can't get around like this. Tell them we need boards.'

Bilks shrugged. 'If they give them to us, they'd have to give them to everybody, and they can't spare that. I'll ask, though.'

The commanding officer came back with Bilks and peered down. 'You are asking for wood? We don't have it.'

'Won't the people give it up from their houses?'

'The old woman I asked yesterday said she would rather kill herself than relinquish wood from her house to us. I told her that if it wasn't for us, the Germans would come and take what they wanted. She said the Germans had been here in 1870 and were very well behaved.'

Two days later, it rained hellishly and the whole place was flooded up to the knees. The rats swam untidily along, chasing after floating bits of biscuit, the only way to get that stuff soft, Michael thought. After a morning of trying to bail the water out, he was leaning on the side, exhausted. 'Just you wait till it goes up to your waist!' shouted one man. 'Then you'll have it.'

That day, a young boy called Stembridge fell into the water. Michael, Baker and Bilks had a job pulling him out; he was stuck fast in the mud and kept going under, his arms flopping from their grasp, his mouth filling with water. Michael thought he could have tried harder to scrabble up. 'You have given up, Private!' he shouted. 'Get out.'

Bilks eventually hauled him out and on to his shoulder. 'He needs to rest,' said Michael. 'Take him to the first aid station.' *Before he tries to drown himself again*, he did not say. Stembridge had not yet come back. He'd probably tried to kill himself there too.

'We've been cleaning out the trenches,' he said to Tom.

'That all?'

'I killed a man last night,' he said. 'I did it with my hands.'

It had been sometime past midnight. The CO had sent him and Bilks to check the wire at one of the trenches. 'Watch out,' he said. 'The Germans have it covered.' They sloshed their way through the mud, trying to grip the sandbags without pulling them out. Then they hauled themselves out, lay flat on the soaked ground. To get to the bit they had to check, they would have to cross ground that was quite perfectly lit by the moon. 'Crawl – and go fast,' said the CO. 'Otherwise you will be sitting ducks.'

Bilks went first, dragging himself through the white bath of moonlight. In any other life, you would have thought it was beautiful, a fairy dousing of moon-magic. 'Come on, sir!' he hissed. 'It's safe. Come quickly!' The shelling started again, somewhere over to the left.

Michael's feet felt as if they were mired in mud. 'I can't,' he said. 'They'll spot me.'

'You have to, sir.' Bilks put his hand out. 'You must.'

Michael looked up. The shells were exploding, coming for him. 'Let's go back.'

'No, sir, we need to look at it. Men's safety depends on us.'

Michael nodded and began to pull himself forward. The light bathed his hands. Then they turned dark as he reached Bilks' patch. 'Good,' said Bilks. 'Good, sir. Now come on.'

Michael was pulling his hands through the mud when he heard Bilks cry out. He looked up. A huge German was looming above them. Bilks was on his feet, trying to wrestle the man to the ground. Michael gazed dizzily. The man had a great beard, dark eyes. He looked like an ogre from a children's story. Bilks was trying to pull him down, but the man was too strong for him. 'Help me, sir,' he panted. Bilks had the man's arms, but he was trying to get them free – and to his gun. 'Help me.'

Michael thought he would be sick. He kept on staring. And then a voice in his head said, *You must! If you do not, he will kill you both.* He hauled himself to his feet, kicked the man's legs, first left, then right, so that they fell under him, pushed the man into Bilks's arms. The German was struggling, pulling against Bilks. 'I can't hold him,' he gasped. 'Help me.'

Michael stared.

'Help me.'

The man said something in German. It sounded like 'God is with me.' Michael gazed at him. 'Don't look into his eyes,' panted Bilks. 'Don't.' But Michael could not help it. He gazed into the whites, the pools of the pupils. *Who are you?* he wanted to say. And at that moment, the man broke free of Bilks's arms, brought his hand to his rifle. In that brief second, Michael knew. *He is coming to kill me. And I am here to kill him.* He seized his own bayonet and drove it into the man's chest.

The German gazed at Michael, eyes wide. 'God,' he was saying. 'God.' He dropped to the floor, writhing, hand clutched to his chest.

'Do it again,' said Bilks.

'We don't need to.'

'You can't leave him like this. It is kinder to kill him. Come on, sir.'

Michael reached down and thrust again. The man's eyes blurred, and blood came from his mouth.

'Oh God,' he said, over and over. 'Oh God.'

'That's why we need grenades with us, sir,' said Bilks on the way back. 'They make things cleaner.'

'I killed a man,' he said to Tom. 'I looked into his eyes and I killed him all the same.'

'I need to know all of this,' said Tom. 'Let's go for that drink.'

Michael looked at Tom's face, furious with excitement, and then he pulled away. 'I should return. You know, things to do. Watching the other side build a trench in plain sight while we stand in the dark and hold our fire. Standing about all day. Reading the field. Listening to the BEF laughing at us. Waiting to see when we might be sent to kill someone.'

'Let me walk back with you.'

'No – no. I want to think. Sorry.' He could bear Tom's eager face no longer. He walked away from him, shouting goodbye over his shoulder as he hurried off.

When he got back to the dugout, he threw himself on to his bed, lay there, heart beating hard. The men were still singing outside. One of the Germans on the other side had somehow managed to bring his French horn with him, and he sometimes took requests. Michael could hear Baker shouting for 'Daisy, Daisy'. He knew he should go and stop it, but he could not. He lay there, frozen. He could not say it to Tom. *What have we done?*

An hour or so later, the shelling began. He put his pillow over his head, but they still burst through.

FIFTEEN

Stoneythorpe, May 1915

'Why can't we *do* something?' Celia knew it came out sounding weak, but she could not help herself. 'Other people are doing things. We could offer the use of the house as a hospital, don't you think?'

Verena turned her head on her pillow. 'Don't *talk* so, Celia.'

'But don't you think we could help? Other people are making convalescent homes, that sort of thing, to help the men.'

'We can't. Not Stoneythorpe. Your father would not have it.'

'He's not here to care.'

He was, though. He was everywhere around them. His portrait hung in the dining room and the parlour. The study was just as he had left it, his papers strewn over the table, his boots neatly at the side. His umbrella still sat in the stand by the door.

In fact, Celia thought, all of them were still there. Four months after her father had left to sign on as an alien and never come back. Nine after Michael and Tom had gone, seven after Emmeline, and she could still convince herself, if she just closed her eyes, that they were about to return, that Michael would run in shouting that he was back from Magdalene for a visit, her sister would stamp down the corridor, cross because the washing house had sent her dress back without the belt. Then Tom would come, saying that he had been away for a while in France on a trip to buy horses. And her father would walk through the door. 'Back from Germany,' he would call. 'And the factories are up to excellent standards.'

She stood in the hall and listened to their voices, and happiness flooded her heart. Then she opened her eyes and saw nothing but the walls and the floor. 'Emmeline!' she shouted. 'Michael!' Her voice echoed. No one heard. 'What was all that shouting?' Verena said, occasionally, when Celia came up with her tray. 'It gives me such a headache. Were you practising poetry?'

'Yes, Mother,' she said. 'Of course.'

The War Office had sent Verena a letter saying that Rudolf had been interned as a suspected spy. He would be taken to the coast. If his interrogation proceeded well, he would be allowed to write to them. They might also expect a visit from intelligence officers themselves.

Secretly, Celia longed for a visit from the interrogators, so that she could tell them they were wrong. But they never came. Instead, Verena received a letter from Rudolf saying he was living by the coast, was being well treated and the food was not bad, he was fortunate to be in a hut rather than a tent. When he was taken away, they had told him it was for his own good and he would be safer in the place they had for him – that might be true after all, he said. He had made friends with two German men also from the Black Forest. Onto those small details they had to hold tight.

Mr Lewis wrote occasionally. He had taken over the running of the factories and said he would look after them faithfully until Rudolf came home. Any money that Verena desired, she simply had to ask. But Verena had given up opening his letters – along with those from the Dowager Lady Redroad and all the rest, inviting her to lectures, sewing committees and Refugee Aid. Invitations were piling up for her now that Rudolf had gone. Celia told herself that they pitied Verena for being alone. She saw them stacked up by her mother's bed, gathered them up and took them away.

'I don't think Papa would mind if we made the house into a hospital,' she said. 'Not now.' She tried to smile. 'They could walk around the gardens.' *What else are we doing with the gardens?* she did not say. *Ever since you shot the horses.* Even four months later, Celia still woke with nightmares, sitting bolt upright, the noise of the shooting in her head, the sound of the screaming, the telephone call from Mr Lewis, Verena's tears. She wanted to cry out, but she knew there was no point, for there was no one to hear or comfort her. She would lie back down, attempt to quiet her racing her heart, find sleep again.

Only a year ago, at Winterbourne, Celia was following the school timetable, the day filled with lessons and study. Her classmates, she supposed, were still working hard at French or history, longing for the half-hour free after lunch. Now, she watched the day slip through her fingers, rising late and then waiting around by the door for the postman, not giving up until past eleven, when it was far too late for him to call. She stared at their letter box. *I am waiting for you, Papa*, she willed to wherever he was.

There had been one more letter from Michael, short, saying that he liked France and the people had been pleased to see them. Jonathan Corrigan had sent three letters for Michael. The first one came in October, Celia had seen it and torn it open, hurried her eye down the page, hating all the questions Jonathan asked, his big flourishing handwriting. He was back at Cambridge, he said, missing Michael greatly. Professor Punter sent his regards and said that tutorials were thin stuff without him. Jonathan said he was taking proper notes in lectures, so that when Michael returned, he could read them and be just at the right standard to go straight into the third year.

Celia ripped it in half, hating Jonathan for being in Cambridge, detesting everything about him. How dare he, she thought, come to their house, then leave after one night, casting Verena and Michael down? She blushed with embarrassment when she thought of him seizing her hand, calling her a fräulein. She picked up the pieces of the letter and crumpled them in her hand. Then she felt guilty, for Michael liked him, she knew that, and perhaps he would want a letter from him.

Thompson found the next two letters from Jonathan first and sent them on. Celia felt relief when he told her, free of the choice of whether to tear them up or not. She wondered if Michael wrote back to Jonathan – for he did not write back to them.

'No letters is a good thing,' said Thompson. 'Means they are all still – er – well.'

'Not dead, that's what you mean.'

'Sorry, miss.'

Only Thompson, Mrs Rolls and Jennie were left. Most mornings Celia helped Jennie or Thompson with something in the house. She felt she had become rather good at dusting and polishing. But what she did was just touching the surface. The house was failing. The dust and dirt was mounting up, there were damp patches in the parlour and grime beneath the floorboards. Even with Thompson's best efforts in the garden, the grass had grown long and filled with daisies, the weeds were wild in the flower beds, the hedges jagged and untidy. For a long time after the day with the horses, Celia couldn't go to her dell; now, when she did, it made her sadder. The place had once been her refuge, cut off from the garden, hidden, but now it was as if all of Verena's beautifully laid-out Versailles arrangements were turning into it, unkempt, full of secrets.

By now, Celia knew, they should have torn down the ivy on the outside of the house. It was growing thickly into the cracks of the walls, in between the bricks. They should have called in the men, as Rudolf did every spring, to pull it down. She told herself that it was because there were not enough men left to work, but that was not true. They had not even tried to look.

At lunchtime, she ate soup in the kitchen. She had begged Mrs Rolls to allow her to sit there rather than in the dining room, and finally she had given in. 'I suppose there is no one to see,' she said. After two weeks, Celia had begun asking if she could help with the cooking. 'I think I should learn how to chop things,' she said, watching Mrs Rolls demolish a carrot in a second. 'It would be a very useful skill for if I have to go out in the world.'

'What nonsense! Dear me. You will never cook for yourself, miss.'

'I could *try*.'

'The Kaiser would have to kill me first, young lady.'

Sometimes, after lunch, they would read over Smithson's letters.

They had two from training and one he had written in the boat on his way to the Ottoman Empire with the 13ths. 'Such a long way away,' Mrs Rolls sighed. Then, in the afternoon, Celia walked slowly up the stairs to her mother.

Not long after Rudolf left, Verena took to her bed. She said she was ill with exhaustion and could not get up. In the mornings she slept, and in the afternoons Celia came to read to her. At first Verena had been unsure of what she wanted, and then decided on Jane Austen. So far, Celia had read *Pride and Prejudice* and *Sense and Sensibility*, and they were halfway through *Mansfield Park*. She stared at the pages, hating every minute of reading about Fanny and Miss Crawford and Edmund, for they had each other as a family when she did not. 'Such a *happy* time,' Verena said.

She refused to hear a single word of news, and once, when Celia tried to tell her about what *The Times* had said about the Battle of Champagne, she put her hands over her ears. She didn't want any of the news that, on Christmas Eve, a German plane had dropped a bomb on a Dover man's cabbage patch. Thompson said it was the first attack on Britain since the Spanish Armada but they never even got *close*. Then there was the first Zeppelin in January, a silver looming thing throwing bombs on Great Yarmouth. 'They won't come here,' Thompson said. 'They're only attacking the ports.' But still Celia made him unscrew her shelves of ornaments over her bed. If the house was bombed, they might fall on her head and kill her. She arranged her glass animals over the floor by the door instead, her favourite three coloured swans at the back.

In January and February, Verena would correct her reading, tell her to go faster or slower or add more emphasis. By April, she had stopped trying, and simply lay back against her cushions, eyes closed. Celia opened letters from Mr Lewis saying that the factories were doing well and to alert him if they desired money. She wanted to write back: *But people* do *things with money. We never do anything.*

'Please come for a walk, Mama,' she said, nearly every afternoon. 'Just into the gardens. A little air.' Verena refused, shut her eyes, sent her away and said she would wait for Jennie with her dinner tray. And yet Celia knew that she did walk. At night, when everybody was asleep, she heard Verena pacing up and down the corridor outside her room, her footsteps the only sound in the silent house.

That afternoon in mid May, everything was different. When Celia arrived, Verena was holding a letter. She waved it across the mountain of bedclothes. 'It is from your father,' she said.

Celia jumped at it. 'Show me!'

Verena shook her head. 'He says they have decided he is no longer so dangerous. He has been transferred to Crystal Palace, where visitors are allowed. He says that we might go and visit him this weekend.' She dropped the letter on the eiderdown. Celia itched to pick it up. 'I don't know, Celia. It would be very exhausting to go to London.'

'You have to! Mama, you must!' Celia stamped her foot, know-ing it was childish. 'I will go if you do not.' She rushed to the bed and seized her mother's arm. 'Get up now! We have to go!'

Three days later, they were on the train to London, after hiring a cab from the next village to take them to the station. Verena blushed under her hat, told Celia she felt humiliated by travelling so. On the train, she said she was nervous, and conjured *Mansfield Park* from her bag. Celia began reading about Fanny's choice of chains on which to wear her cross, and her dilemma lasted all the way to London, and then in the cab south to Crystal Palace. Celia stared at the page, unable to bear looking at her mother's eyes, for they were full of fear. Verena had stared at the lady ticket collectors and clerks at Waterloo station, baffled.

They clambered down at the gates and waited in the queue of ladies in shabbier coats and hats than theirs. The sun flashed off the glass front. Sixty-four years ago, Celia thought, ladies had lined up here to see things from all over the Empire. Miss Lowen said her mother had been as a schoolgirl and saw Nelson's ship *Victory* made out of butter. Celia thought of herself, seeing the English village play with Rudolf and Tom. Now, inside one of

those windows, Rudolf was waiting for them. 'So many people.'
For almost half a year, Celia realised, Verena had seen no one but
her and the servants.

Eventually they were ushered into a huge hall. Celia felt her
mother clutching her hand. Men were sitting at tables in rows,
as if they were waiting for a lesson. 'There he is!' said Celia. She
hurried forward. Rudolf was looking up at the swell of people,
wearing a black suit she did not recognise. 'Papa!' she cried, throwing herself in front of him.

He stood up slowly and reached over to her. She felt his arms
around her. Verena came up behind her. 'Husband,' she said,
moving jerkily. 'We've missed you.'

He stared at them both, tears brimming in his eyes. 'Me too.'
He embraced Verena. 'But you are here now.'

'Has it been very terrible?' Celia asked. His eyes were sunken,
with what seemed like hundreds more wrinkles criss-crossing his
face. He was much thinner, older.

He smiled, shook his head. 'Not so very bad. The first place was
a little like school. And this is much better.' He gestured around.
'Look at how many there are here.'

'Every waiter in London, I imagine,' Verena sniffed. 'Surely
there is no one of your class here. I *told* you. If you had listened
to me, you would still be at Stoneythorpe.'

'Did they treat you well at that other place?' Celia asked.

Rudolf shook his head, signalling not to speak of it. 'Of course.
But tell me. How is Stoneythorpe? How is my garden?'

'Very well, Papa,' said Celia, guiltily. 'We are looking after it.
Thompson is. We don't have any gardeners now.' At the table next
to them, the woman – surely the wife – was crying. The husband
reached his hand across, trying to console her, but she shook her
head, thrust her handkerchief to her face.

'Any word from Emmeline?'

'Not much, Papa.'

Verena shrugged. 'She says she is happy.'

'And Michael?'

'He says he is content too. Doing a lot of digging.'

'And how is Tom?'

Verena stiffened. 'I hardly know, husband.'

Celia sat there, stared. The words were in her mouth. *I went to see Tom's family. They showed me his letters; he seems happy too.* She looked at her father, his dark eyes ringed with wrinkles, trying to will him to read her thoughts: *I know! He is doing well.* And the painful thought that struck her when she lay awake in bed at night: that he was happier with the army than he had been with them.

She had thought it had only been her who wanted more from life. She had never really thought that he might wish to be more than a servant. She looked at Thompson and Jennie now and thought: but what else could they do? Surely they were happy? Hers was the kindest family to work for.

Celia's thoughts were wandering. She could hear her father speaking about the hardships people had suffered: that the German waiters who had been dismissed by the London hotels had ended up sleeping in the parks and depending on the Quakers, so most of them were happy to be in Crystal Palace, because at least they had a roof over their heads and regular meals. Verena was complaining about how impossible it was to keep Stoneythorpe in condition since the servants had left. She promised to bring Michael's letter next time and then started to talk about the war, asked how long he thought it would last. Rudolf shook his head, told her she should not, not there.

'Celia.' Her father's voice. 'You are sad! Don't be.' She shook her head, feeling guilty that she had been thinking about servants and Tom rather than her father. He waved his hand. 'Look at all these people. Waiters, tailors, musicians, language teachers, me. There are even a few gentlemen just here on holiday. How can we be a threat? Now that everything has died down – and England is nearly winning – well, how can they want to waste money keeping us? I guarantee that in three weeks or so, we will all be set free – and most of these gentlemen will be on a boat back to Hamburg.'

'Really?' Celia felt a swell of panic. How could they tidy up

Stoneythorpe in time? They would have to get someone in to clean and do the ivy. She clutched Verena's hand, trying to signal to her. Rudolf would be furious if he returned and saw how they had let it slip.

'And you, Celia?' he said. 'Are you keeping up your studies?'

Celia nodded. 'Of course, Papa. I am reading a lot.'

'What have you been reading? Tell me. We are only given the Bible here.'

Mansfield Park, she wanted to say. And *Pride and Prejudice*, *Sense and Sensibility*, and when they had finished those, they would start again, she supposed.

A bell rang and a man stood at the front and told them all it was time to go.

Rudolf smiled. 'You can tell me next week. You will come again?'

'Of course!' Celia nudged Verena.

The bell rang again. They said their goodbyes and were flurried out of the place with the rest of the women, some of them still weeping. The gates slammed behind them.

'I am so tired,' said Verena. 'I could lie down here and sleep.'

Celia stared at the traffic hurrying past. 'I don't know how to find a cab.' All the other women were walking down the road, towards the train station, she supposed. 'Let's walk.'

Verena shook her head. 'Just hail one. You know you can.'

Celia had no idea how to do it. She stared at the traffic, held out her hand, until finally a passing man offered to help her. He flagged one down and handed Verena in.

'What were you two ladies doing there, if you don't mind me asking?'

'Visiting unfortunates,' said Celia, swiftly. 'We come from the Church.'

She sat back against the seat, her head flooded with thoughts. To distract herself, she stared out of the window. There seemed to be hundreds of signs demanding men for the army. Another as they halted made it clear that the Ritz Carlton did not employ any waiters of Austrian or German descent. *Check their passports*, someone had scrawled underneath.

'The minute we get back, we will have to start on the house,' she said. 'We will have to find someone to do the ivy.'

Verena nodded, eyes closed. 'And the spring clean. If only they would give us a proper *date* for when he will come home.'

'He said three weeks. That's all we have.' To reverse months of neglect in three weeks? They would be like dolls on a top, running fast. Celia knew she should feel joy that her father was coming home, but her heart was full of panic. He could not see what they had let Stoneythorpe become. And if he was on his way back because the war was finishing, perhaps Michael would be too. She thought, with crushing shame, what Tom would say if he saw the house as it was now. He loved how Rudolf was always improving it, adding to the building, spending money on it.

'We have let it get into a sad state, Mama.'

Verena's eyes were still closed. 'It will not take us long to tidy it once more. Jennie and Thompson are very capable.'

As they drew close to Waterloo station, the entrance was blocked by a crowd.

'You might have to descend here, ladies,' the driver said. 'I can't see a way through.'

'But what are they all doing? Is it some kind of demonstration?' Verena asked.

'I'd say it was about the news.'

'What is it?' Celia asked. The only news she'd seen was that there was nothing happening on the Western Front.

'My last passenger told me. It's only just come through. Hundreds dead at sea, they are saying. He's a brute, that Kaiser.'

'What's happened?'

'One of our ships full of passengers sunk at sea by the Hun. Mothers and babies, children, the whole lot. Terrible.' He turned and gazed at them. 'It was mere fighting before. But now it's war.'

Verena looked shocked. 'A passenger ship? There must be some mistake.'

'Clear as day, ma'am. There will be riots once it is known. Looks like it's getting that way already. You ladies should stay away from the Huns in that place. They don't deserve your mercy.'

'We will descend now, thank you,' said Celia, staring at her mother's face, which was stricken with horror. 'No need to help us, thank you.' She jumped down, handed her mother and took her arm, fumbled in her bag for money. 'Now,' she whispered, 'we are going to have to walk through them. We must keep very quiet so we can catch our train. Come.'

Verena gripped her arm tightly. Celia thought of vulture's claws, then told herself how cruel that was. She held her mother close and they set off through the crowd. People were shouting about how Germans were evil, child-killers. 'Don't look at them,' she hissed. 'Keep looking forward. Don't listen.' She kept her gaze fixed ahead, not looking at the angry faces of the men and women around her, trying to think about how they would arrange the cleaning of the house, which room would be tidied first.

They were almost on the other side when Verena froze. Celia turned and saw her staring into the face of a man. He was young-ish, dark – and he was reaching a hand out for her. 'Who are you, madam?' he was saying. 'Are you new to London?'

Verena, glassy-eyed, was mesmerised. 'Mama!' Celia hissed. 'Mama!' Verena did not turn. Celia seized her hand and pulled her forward. 'What were you thinking of?' she spat, panicked, as they reached a clear space in the station.

Verena looked at her dizzily. 'He seemed familiar.'

'Would you have told him our name?' Celia heard the fury in her own words and thought better of it. People would stare. 'Come on. Let us find the ladies' waiting room.' A news boy was putting up a board on the wall next to them: HUNDREDS DEAD IN THE IRISH SEA.

The ladies' waiting room was deserted, apart from an old woman crocheting something in pink. Verena gripped Celia's hand as they walked in.

'Perhaps we should go to Germany?' she said. 'Don't you think? When Rudolf and Michael come back and the war is over, we should go to live in Berlin.'

Celia sat down. 'Our lives are here. We aren't German.'

Verena shook her head. 'No, I'm decided. That is exactly the right idea. We should go to Germany. We cannot stay here. When Rudolf returns, we will set off. What do you think, Celia, a new life? A fresh start?'

'Papa loves Stoneythorpe. He loves *England*.'

'We can find a more beautiful house.' She looked sideways at the woman, still intent on her work. 'It is true, Celia. We are not welcome here.'

'Once England has won the war, that will change.'

Verena sat looking calmly ahead. Celia stared at the woman's pink crochet. She thought of Hilde and Johann in the Black Forest, great piles of black bread and butter, how she imagined Berlin. Perhaps it would be better there.

In the mercifully empty train carriage on the way home, she thought more about Germany. By the time they had got into the cab to come to Stoneythorpe, she was sure. They should go, at least for a couple of years. They could persuade Emmeline and Michael too.

They drew up in front of the house. Celia jumped down and again handed Verena out. She looked back at the driver and saw him staring. She followed his gaze. There, scrawled across the drive in front of them, in red paint, just as in August, was the word DROWNED!

Verena turned to her. 'See, I told you so. I am going to start packing.'

'But who could be writing these words?' asked Celia. 'Twice over. And how did the news get here so fast?'

'I do not care!' said Verena. 'We will not be staying long enough to find out.'

A week later, a letter arrived from the government. Verena and Celia had been in Verena's room, packing her gowns, when Jennie brought it up to them.

The letter regretted to inform them that Rudolf de Witt had been reassessed and was to be moved from Crystal Palace to another secure location, where they would be unable to visit. Verena threw it on the floor, burst into tears. 'I will not believe it,' she said. 'I will not!'

A few days later, a letter came from Rudolf himself. *Since the sinking, we are all under suspicion*, he said. *I am told I will not be able to write to you again.*

Verena was already in bed once more. The packing, half finished, was still strewn around the room. 'Read to me,' she said to Celia, tears running down her cheeks. 'Read to me.'

SIXTEEN

Loos, France, September 1915

Forty men were crouched over, sitting on hay bales and planks of wood, talking in low voices as they fiddled with what looked like empty jam tins.

'Anything I can help you with, sir?' said a lance corporal, appearing at his side.

'I just came to look,' said Michael. 'What are they doing?'

'You don't have any matches on you, do you, sir?' Michael shook his head, untruthfully. 'Well, the Krauts have top-hole grenades. We are improvising. We stuff our jam tins with small pieces of metal, hobnails and the rest. One of the men even persuaded the farriers to cut up old horseshoes. Then you put in two pieces of gun cotton, the detonator and the fuse at the other end. Simple.'

'Ingenious. Very ingenious.' Michael gazed at them, wishing he could paint their calm, their sense of purpose, looking for all the world like a ladies' church group knitting quilts for poor children.

'Quite so. A good soldier can throw one thirty yards, so they are useful when the boys can't get close enough to shoot into the trenches. We'll be sending them down to you soon. The only problem is getting them lit when it rains.' He held one up. 'Let me show you.' He brandished a stick. 'Pretend this is a match.'

Michael stared at the jam tin nestled in the man's hand. He would have to take it. The man expected him to. He reached out a finger. It shook. The man saw, and in a split second had drawn back his own hand. 'Let me do it for you, sir. This stick here is a match. You hold the end against the head of the fuse. In one quick go, you strike the edge of the matchbox along the fuse. Then – fast – you have to throw it that very minute.'

'Very clever indeed. Really very so.' Michael held out his hand. 'Would you let me try with your stick?'

The man's eyes narrowed. 'Of course, sir. Perhaps outside.' He moved towards the door, nodding at another man as he passed. Outside, under the sun, two birds pecking at the ground, he held the grenade and matchbox out to Michael. 'Take it carefully, sir.' There was fear in his voice.

Michael reached out, took the grenade. It was curiously warm in his palm. He watched it shake in the quiver of his hand, but objectively, as an observer might. *Nervous man lights a grenade.* If it were a picture, that was how it would be. 'Might I have the stick?' He took it, then stared at the tiny fuse protruding from the tin. It could have been a stray string on a jumper. He touched the stick to the fuse, watching the man quiver a little as he did so, the smile on his face painfully forced. Then he brought the matchbox down. His hand was shaking so much that he had to cup his palm to keep it from falling. 'And that is all I need to do?'

The man nodded. 'Quite. That is all you need to do. I could take it back if you have finished with it, sir.'

'So it makes it cleaner, this type of thing. No more hand-to-hand?'

'Quite so, sir. Now, may I take it from you?'

Michael did not give it back. He held it up high, gazed at it. That was all he needed to do: hold a match against it, then the box, hurl it away. In his hand, he had the means to destroy perhaps ten men, more if they had ammunition with them. They would all be dead. He stared at it – then looked at the man. 'Thank you.' He passed over the grenade. The man's face shone with relief. 'I shall be sure to pass on your lesson to the men. Good day.'

'Good day, sir,' said the man, clutching the bomb.

Michael walked away, back straight, knowing he was being watched. He could do it. He could light a grenade and throw it. Easy. After all, a battle was what they were waiting for, wasn't it? Nearly a year now of nothing but holding the line, repairing the trenches, endlessly cleaning their guns, occasionally going out on investigatory parties. Soon it would be their chance to fight.

'Time for the rum,' Bilks was saying. 'That's it, Andrews, as much as you want.' The silver flask glittered in the sun as Andrews lifted it. 'Remember, if we were working down the mines, Mr Lloyd George wouldn't want us to have it. One perk of the job.'

Bilks was very fond of his rum flask, polished it with his hand-kerchief with any clean water they managed to find. Michael shook his head when Bilks offered it to him. He didn't think an officer should. It was for the men. He and Bilks were leaning against the trench together. Michael had received the orders on a wire. They were clear enough, pretty confident. Walk forward, slowly, following the barrage.

He sat back against the sandbags. There was a pause in the shelling and the birds were singing up a storm. They were often even louder after a night of shelling – protesting, Michael sup-posed. 'Swallows,' said Bilks. 'That's what they sound like to me. I used to be keen on birds as a boy.'

Michael put his head up and stared across towards the German position, searching for the last group of men to have been sent over, smoke from the shelling blurring the view. 'I can't see a thing.'

'Shouldn't put your head up like that, sir.'

'Well, what choice do we have, Bilks?' He scanned the ground in front of him again. If you shut your eyes and listened, it could have been a farmer's field once more, echoing to the singing of the birds. A skinny-looking rabbit sprang up nearby, looked around and hopped away.

'Could do with that for dinner.'

'Put your head down, Bilks. We don't need both of us to get killed.'

Around him were twelve men: Weaver, Andrews, Long, Pie, Wood, Mills, Cook, Ebbots, Porter, Brown, Baker and Tiller. Sometimes he looked at the list of his men in front of him and thought: why did no one bear the surname Soldier, or Fighter? Why were they all Cooks or Butchers or Bakers, when all a man could do here was fight? The command through the wires had been to expect to embark on the German positions at eleven a.m., coffee time at home. At training, they'd said all attacks would happen first thing. He presumed they were trying to catch the Germans unawares.

Long, Pie and Baker were carrying grenades. Michael looked at Baker's jam tin. 'You're sure you know how to light that thing, Baker?'

'Yes, sir.'

'Good.'

He put his head up again. The people at home who thought of the Western Front probably imagined it as something very heroic. Instead, just piles of sandbags, looking for all the world like rubbish dumps, scrubby land in between them dotted with dank puddles filled with bullets, guns and debris, and then the mess of wire on sloppy poles, cows bent over it, farm implements caught up. Just along from them were the foundations of a bombed house, a bit of wall around what was once a garden. Last night, on lookout, he had spotted one rose bush still straining upward, barely touched by the fighting. Now he could see nothing at all, just smoke and what might have been hundreds of men.

'Sir!' said Bilks. 'Come down.'

Michael had passed a poor night. It had been impossible to sleep as the barrage came over. And now they were waiting for the signal to go. The men were growing restless, their packs hanging heavy on their backs. Michael supposed they were being held in reserve. They were to advance towards the Germans, take their position, lob in the grenades and move forward to attack. So many others had gone in front that the way would be clear.

'Why can't we get started, sir?' said Pie. 'The old-timers always have to have first go. There'll be nothing but cleaning up to do when we get there.' He was clutching one of his beloved souvenirs, a German army badge he had stolen from a body at the field hospital.

'We must accomplish any duty bravely,' Michael said, knowing he sounded stiff.

He had scanned their letters before they set off. Wood, Baker and Andrews had told their sweethearts about the next push, so those he held back. Most of the letters were straightforward enough, but Andrews' he hated reading. The man was always fretting about whether his girl, a mill worker called Betty, was off with an old flame who worked at the docks. He'd almost cried on Baker's shoulder when the last lot of leave was cancelled – as leaves usually were – because they needed every man.

'Still no word, sir.' Bilks shrugged. 'All right, men, you know the drill. Keep going forward. And don't stop if a man falls down. The stretcher-bearers will come for him. Walk, always walk. Now, have you all got your gas helmets?' They nodded. 'Remember the orders. Keep them close.' They were horrible hoods that made them look like khaki ghosts, soaked in disgusting stuff. He could never see out of the tiny window, dreaded the day when they'd have to go over the top with them on.

Michael guessed their packs must weigh about sixty pounds. Back home, he supposed, people imagined a platoon as a group of swift-moving men, not a cluster of little turtles stumbling over the grass carrying sandbags, water bottle, mess tin, rations, ground sheet, ammunition, cardigan, rifle – and knife and fork. He often wondered about that one: why did they need a knife and fork? They could eat biscuit and bully beef with their hands. But then if they did, that would make them savages, he supposed. Here they were, Kitchener's army, out in France earlier than most of the others, following behind the regular army, barely thought able to do the job. When they had first arrived, the BEF laughed at them, told them to get back to the farm, hissed and thrown bottles. They were still here, though. The proper army went forth and they followed, cleaning up.

He heard the shrill of whistles and shouts as other men went over the top. He stood, leaning his back against the cold earth of the trench, told himself not to cry out.

'That's it,' said Bilks, as the whistle blew down the line. 'Here we go!' They clambered out of the trenches as best they could. Baker propped himself up on a ladder. Then they began walking forward.

'Not too fast, Baker!' shouted Michael, for the man was moving ahead. He had expected a barrage of firing, but there was little. Instead, their way was blocked by the bodies of men already fallen, and the wounded trying to crawl into the shell holes. 'Come forward!' he shouted. 'Keep going.' A leg was in front of him. Where was the rest of the body? How could he continue?

The sky flashed and the shattering light of artillery shells exploded. 'Move forward if you can.' Bilks shouted it again. 'You'll be safer once we get to the German trenches.' *Don't stop.* There was an animal screaming somewhere, Michael thought, a cow, probably. The gunfire strafed over their head. He could hear a whizz-bang shooting above, landing somewhere behind them. Screams rose behind him. Bilks was next to him. 'Throw off your pack, Bilks,' he said. 'We're targets.' The smoke was so thick he could barely see.

They advanced to the wire. Michael looked ahead and there were dead men hanging from it. It had not been cut. The shells had been on target, but they had just covered the thing with mud. It was impossible even to make out the trench. 'Take cover!' he ordered. Bilks shouted it behind him. He dived for a shell hole, shallow. The ground was soft under him as he lay, eyes closed, waiting for the machine-gun fire over his head. After a while, he reached down and touched flesh. He was lying prone over another man's body, the pair of them in a cross shape, his stomach on the other man's. He groaned, dipped his face into the dirt. Then he felt a soft wetness spreading over the front of his jacket. He knew what it was: the man's stomach had burst, either side of his webbing. Oh God. What the hell were they going to do? Walk into the wire and try to climb over it? Impossible. No orders came. He presumed the commander was dead.

'Sir.' He heard Bilks's voice. 'The men need orders, sir.'

Michael watched another shell hit the wire in front of them, sending the soil around it exploding into the sky, pitching a body into the air. He felt the warmth of the man's stomach spread over his jacket. It was hopeless.

'Retreat,' he said. 'Tell them to retreat.'

'What?'

'You heard me. Tell them to keep their grenades, just in case they need them.'

'Retreat!' shouted Bilks, loud enough that the Germans in the trenches could have heard. 'Back, every man. Go low, keep cover. Don't leave your grenades, retain.'

Michael fell back into the hole. One minute, he told himself. He would wait there for one minute, then emerge with the men. Bilks would take them forward and he would join them. The sounds passed over him. He put his hands on his forehead. Stoneythorpe came into his mind, Celia walking towards him, smiling.

A barrage of artillery and rifle fire exploded above him. Michael looked up, and realised that Bilks had gone. He could not say how much time had passed: five minutes, fifteen, an hour? He crawled forward. A hand seized his arm. 'Please.' It was a tiny private, no more than sixteen, surely, his face half blown away. 'Help me!' He could barely speak, only whisper.

Michael propped his head up and looked back. The young man had lost a leg by the look of it. His uniform was a bloody mess. 'I can't...' Michael began. And then he hated himself for it. 'Come on, then. Quickly.' There wasn't time to look for the leg either. He hauled the boy up on to his back, ignoring his moans, and began to crawl across no-man's-land. 'We'll get there,' he mumbled. 'Don't worry.' The gunfire continued overhead. The boy screamed as a shell landed nearby. 'Don't worry,' Michael repeated. 'I'll get you back. What's your name?'

'Glass, sir.'

'Where are you from, Private Glass?'

'Devon.' One of the soft ones, that was what they said. The toughest soldiers were from the hardest cities: Newcastle, Manchester, and London's East End.

'Nice beaches there?'

'Very.'

'Think of those, won't you?' They crawled forward through the fog. Another bomb landed. Glass groaned and bucked on his back. 'Stop that,' shouted Michael over the gunfire. 'You're not making it any easier.' He caught a stone with his leg and realised his knees were swollen with pain. Glass was slipping to one side. 'Hold on,' he said. Then he had a better idea. He got the man's belt and tied it around his hands, then looped them over his neck. He hauled the string from his pocket and lashed it around him, Glass on to him. The man was only groaning now, a low, hopeless sound. 'Not long now,' said Michael, trying to sound cheerful, and ducked down back on to the muddy ground.

He crawled through the mud, coming up against a tree stump and gathering himself over it. He could see two men on top of each other, crying out. 'I'll come back for you!' he called. 'Hold on, chums.' Despite the cold, the mud and the stuff all over his shirt, the nagging pain in his knees and the weight on his back, he was feeling exhilarated. This was what he had come here for. Surrounded by bodies and machine-gun fire, he was *helping*. He was doing something, not just hauling rats out of the water in the trenches and pushing sandbags back in.

He tucked Glass's body more securely on to his back and pushed forward, pulling himself along like a child on his hands and knees. There were bits of shrapnel and guns everywhere, metal. A dead sheep, legs in the air, a man who looked no more alive across it. He carried on crawling. He might even be going the wrong way. Dozens of men had got lost in no-man's-land before. One chap from C Company had been found screaming 'Where am I?' after walking around for hours – and he had been only six feet from home position. You might think you were going in a straight line, but really you were heading to the side or backwards, going around in a circle, and *you had no idea.*

Michael shook the thought out of his head. Of course he wasn't lost. He was going forward. 'All right up there, chum?' he shouted. He could speak in any way he liked out here. No one was listening, commenting, saying *Witt doesn't sound much like an officer.* No one could ask about his odd name, say, *What does your father do again?* This was fighting. This was war. He was bringing his comrade home. 'Keep going!' he shouted, aware even as he did so that he was bucking himself up as much as the man. 'We're nearly there.' In truth he had no idea where he was. The smoke was even thicker now. He only had the glitter of shell fire to guide him – which sparked so randomly, it hardly gave him anything.

He moved towards an area where the bodies were sparser, thinking that that was surely nearer home. Home! What a word for that jigsaw of mud. But still, that was what it was. He pulled his body on, sweating so much it was almost painful. The man on his back had calmed down, and was no longer crying out and groaning. He was hopefully thinking about Devon beaches. 'Come on, old thing!' shouted Michael. 'End is in sight!' He flopped forward, and felt a sandbag. His heart filled. He banged the edge with his hand, exhausted. 'Is anybody there? Wounded man here!' There was no reply. Where were they all? 'Bilks!' he cried. 'Bilks, where are you?'

There was a scrabbling, and a man popped his head up. 'Sir?'

'Come on, man. Get a move on. I've got an injured man here. Get a stretcher-bearer.'

The man shouted down. 'Ted! Stretcher-bearer!' He turned back to Michael. 'We don't have too many, sir. Busy day.'

'Now!' shouted Michael, summoning the last of his energy. 'Go!' He rested his head on a sandbag. 'Not long to wait, chum,' he said. 'Whereabouts are you from in Devon? My father took me down to the coast once.' The man did not reply. 'That's right,' said Michael. 'Conserve your strength.' A whizz-bang shot overhead. Sometimes, he thought, you might even pretend that they were fireworks, at a party for one of the royal family. 'Can you hear them?' he said to Glass. 'That's for Queen Mary.'

'All right then, sir,' came a voice. An MO, he supposed. Hands on his back. 'We've got you now. Let's take him.' He could feel them cutting the strings loose.

'Be careful,' Michael said. 'I think he got hit in the head.'

'Come on,' said the voice, gathering the man off his back. They moved him on to a stretcher.

Michael could barely lift his head. 'You need to take him to the field hospital! He has lost a lot of blood.'

The MO crouched beside him. 'I'm sorry, sir. He's gone. I think we lost him an hour or so ago, to be honest.'

'No!' Michael rolled over. 'It's not true!' He hauled himself to his knees, toppling. 'He is alive, I tell you! I felt him breathing! I heard him speak.' He grasped the nearer stretcher-bearer. 'Take him to the field hospital! You have to! You cannot give up on him.' The man's blood was dripping through his hair.

'Corporal...'

'I'm ordering you! Take him to the hospital. I brought him all the way back! I ignored other men. He's alive!'

'Corporal...' The medical officer put his hand on his shoulder. Michael shook it off. 'I will report you! I will report you all! You will be court-martialled. You are failing in your duty!'

'You must calm down. You should rest.'

Michael dragged himself forward through the mud. 'If you will not take him, I will put him on my back and go myself!'

One of the stretcher-bearers backed away – and that was his moment. He lunged towards him, grasped Glass by his arm. The stretcher-bearer jumped, the other fell back and the stretcher bounced on to the ground. Michael threw himself over Glass's torso. He landed on the wetness of his shirt, grappled around and pulled at it, trying to tear it open so he could feel his heart. One of the stretcher-bearers was trying to drag him off; he punched him away, grasped Glass's face. It was cool. There was no breath coming from the mouth. He straightened so that he was kneeling over him, listened again. No breath. He ducked to the man's heart. Nothing. What was it you did? One of the men at barracks had tried to teach them: pumping the chest, one, two, three. He dipped his head to Glass's mouth, did it again, pumping once more. Nothing. 'You have to help me!' he was crying as the MO hauled him off.

'Come on, soldier,' he was saying. 'We have injured men to tend to. Let us do our work.'

'But he's alive!' Michael shouted. A bomb exploded above him, a screaming, hysterical whizz-bang. In the light of it, he saw them hurrying the stretcher away. 'I'm going back for those men now!'

he cried. He tried to stand but his legs failed him, threw him back into the mud. He lay there, weeping, like a child.

That was where Bilks found him, two hours later, after searching, he said, up and down the trenches for him. 'Pie said he thought he saw you coming in. I've been looking for you, sir. You look pretty done.'

Michael lifted his head, dropped it again.

'Bad news, I am afraid, sir. We've lost Andrews, and Baker was with the padre when I saw him last. Weaver and Tiller are still out there. Injured, probably. They'll send clearing parties out to get them in the morning.'

Michael rolled on to his back. Perhaps Weaver and Tiller had been out there, begging for help, while he had staggered past. 'I hate them,' he said. 'I hate the Germans. I want them all to die.'

'Well, that would certainly speed matters up. Mind you, Kitchener might not be too pleased if they all just keeled over; wouldn't give his boys much of a triumph. Come on, sir, let's get you some tea.'

SEVENTEEN

'Look at this!' Bilks threw aside the *Daily Mirror*, beaten limp after passing through ten sets of fingers. 'Very little action on the Western Front. It's disgusting that they say that. Plenty of action, if you ask me.'

'I expect they think we're sitting about in deckchairs,' said Pie. 'Ma does, anyhow.' He was sorting through his box of souvenirs, three more German badges after the battle four nights ago, along with assorted bullets, belt buckles and scraps of shrapnel.

'Just because we haven't moved forward very much. I've half a thought to write to them and give them a piece of my mind. And you, Pie, you watch it with those things. The COs are searching bags for that sort of stuff.'

'When we return, only army property allowed,' Michael recited. Bilks had said Pie had a German watch in there, but Michael hadn't the heart to remove it. The man had been fond of Andrews; they all had.

'This *is* army property,' said Pie. 'My army property, anyway.'

'Not even any action at Loos reported?' demanded Cook of Bilks, waving at the newspaper.

'Well, a little on that. But they say it was a failure and we haven't moved.'

'Well, we ain't moved, have we?' said Pie. 'What do they know? Don't think it would go down too well if they said, another ten thousand men down, Field Marshal French's washstand no further towards Berlin.'

'His washstand won't be anywhere, if you ask me. He'll be for the chop after this fiasco.'

'Reckon he has been ever since the King fell off his horse in front of everybody. Georgie can't forgive him seeing that,' said Pie.

Michael knew he ought to stop them. *But why should I?* he wanted to shout. Fair enough officers setting an example, guiding the men, holding the line. But trotting out the usual story that they were better than the Germans, had more troops, what was the point of that? He gazed down at the pile of biscuits on the table. Andrews and Baker were dead, Weaver and Tiller missing, and still their rations were coming through. They had more biscuits than they could eat – more so because Pie refused to touch them, said he had no truck with eating dead men's food.

'Post here!' cried a voice. Meadows came around the corner dragging his heavy sack. 'Some good stuff for you lot.'

He doled out the letters. 'Ooh,' said Bilks, patting his parcel. 'Looks like Mrs B's been knitting again. See if she's managed not to put a hole in it this time.' He always joked that his wife sent scarves with ready-made rat bites, just in case. A thin letter for Michael. He recognised the handwriting. Celia. He stowed it in his pocket. He promised himself he would write back to this one.

'A soldier stuffed this in my hand for you too, sir,' said Meadows, holding out a letter. Tom's handwriting. He put that in his pocket as well. 'Oh – and I almost forgot this one. Another parcel.' He passed it over. Michael looked down at it, his heart sinking. He knew that looping, untidy writing too. It was Andrews' girl, Betty.

'Want me to do it, sir?' said Bilks, seeing his face. Michael shook his head. He took his penknife and cut open the paper. Soap, a long letter, a large box. He opened the box, hoping it would be a personal present he could send back, like a scarf. Inside was a cake. A somewhat squashed and mangled but still nice-looking iced fruit cake. He'd never known Betty send a cake before. He looked down at the letter. *I have been saving up to make you this,* she wrote. *Got the ingredients from Macys. Best fruit to be found, he said. I hope you like it – you can share it with the other boys if you like. You mustn't think about Ernie, it's just you and me. I wanted to tell you that, in case you didn't know. I know we used to be friends, but I told him we had to stop it. You're my man!*

Michael folded the letter. He picked up the cake. It was already melting on to his hands. Their orders were to send letters and items back, but to eat any perishables. He stared at the icing on the top – an attempt to spell out 'John'. He took the cake and threw it at the wall of the trench.

'Nice for the rats,' said Bilks.

'Did you want it?'

Bilks shook his head. Michael put his head in his hands.

'Good morning, sir.' A soft voice came over the side of the trench. 'Are you Corporal Witt?'

Michael looked up. A slim, blond-haired man was standing at the top. He was smiling. 'I heard you lost some men in the push. I have been sent down to join you.'

'Good morning to you,' said Bilks. 'What is your name?'

'Stuart Wheeler, sir. From C Company.' His accent was slow, country, Michael thought. Norfolk maybe.

'Well, come down here, why don't you? We are reinforcing the walls.'

Michael stared at Wheeler. The skin on his face looked soft. The blue of his eyes was very pale against the bright October sky. 'Actually, we need to collect some more wire from the stores. Wheeler can come with me.' He clambered up the side of the trench. 'Let's go.'

Wheeler nodded and followed him. Michael felt almost too shy to look at him. They walked to the stores, silently. Overhead, birds sang. You might think you were back in England. They stood in line, collected the wire, started walking back. Ten feet or so from the trenches, Wheeler dropped to his knees. 'Look at this!' Michael squatted next to him. There was a line of beetles trundling along, walking in strict formation, scrambling over a small mound of earth. 'Splendid, isn't it, sir? The way they all march so tidily, despite the mess around them. Like us.'

Michael watched the insects. The front one, the biggest, was actually rather beautiful, with its shiny armour reflecting rainbows of sunlight. After marching some way over the mound, it stopped and looked around. Its antennae waved.

'He's trying to decide where to go,' said Wheeler, entranced. 'He's got to lead them and he must get it right.'

At that moment, the beetle seemed to look up at the two men. Then it nodded and led its band on. 'He was trying to decide if we were predators,' said Michael.

'I think so.'

'We should send them over to the German side.'

'They could probably get better information than our current lot. I reckon our spies wouldn't even find the trenches – ridiculous. They arrested an old Frenchwoman over on our side for waving her washing about on the line; they thought she was signalling to the Germans.'

'Washing?' Michael could not help but smile. 'Come on, Wheeler, we should get back.' He watched the beetles trotting along and turned away. He found himself – inordinately, illogically – hoping that they would not be shelled. The other man walked on.

Michael hurried after Wheeler. 'What were you doing before signing up?' he asked.

'I was training to be a schoolmaster. I had done my college time and I was working in a school in Norfolk. Country school, had to give them all a week off every September to go to the ploughing competition. I had been reading them a lot of history.'

'That sounds interesting.'

'It was. Then the army came blowing their trumpets and looking for men. I thought I would be back in time to see the older ones finish school. Now I don't know.'

'Fingers crossed.'

'Yes.' Michael was grateful that Wheeler did not call him sir.

In the days that followed, machine-gun fire strafed through the rain and there were constant gas warnings. Michael woke in his dugout and thought about seeing Wheeler. He went to sleep thinking of his smile. He tried to find ways of standing by him and walking with him to the stores. He asked him to accompany him on visits to other captains to discuss practicalities – a job that Bilks was happy to give up because he wanted to be with the men.

Every time they left the trenches, Wheeler found something else new to show him: a spider crawling up a tree, a pair of birds hopping for worms, a weasel hunting her prey. Michael remembered being like this as a child, gazing intently at one thing, forgetful of the world outside. He'd once stared for hours at a robin in their Hampstead garden. Now, his head spun with a hundred thoughts. He tried to follow Wheeler, pick out the tiny markings on a bird, the circles of age on a worm.

It rained every day, and Michael wondered if the powers-that-be were holding off on another offensive until the weather improved.

'Fighting is summer work,' said Wheeler, when they were shovelling mud out of the trench. He had been teaching the older boys in his school about the Boer War.

'You're a one,' said Pie. 'What are we going to do until the summer? Sit about here?'

'Probably. Or they might send us off for training, running up and down some French hills.'

'What's the point of that? We might as well go home.'

'Then we'd be giving in, wouldn't we? We're a human barrier.'

It was yet another conversation that Michael knew he really shouldn't have been allowing. But what was he supposed to tell them to talk about? The football or cricket news that got to them weeks late? Their families? That upset them more.

'Not long till Christmas, lads,' he said, hating his false jollity. 'The Queen might give us a present.'

'Hmm,' said Bilks. 'That was last year. Unlikely.'

Last year, presents from Princess Mary had arrived, to be distributed on 23rd December. Cigarettes, tobacco and bars of chocolate. One of the BEF officers told Michael about the privates trotting off over to the other side in truce, one coming back saying they'd met a German who'd been a barber in Walthamstow. 'Never again,' he said. 'The papers didn't like it.'

This year, they huddled in their trenches, afraid of another gas attack, masks – useless as they were – to hand. The men swapped Christmas cards to make them feel as if they had more. Michael read his letter from Celia, even though he could hardly bear to. *Things are well. We are very well,* she wrote. *Happy Christmas!* It was littered with exclamation marks, like a sky with stars. It hurt him how hard she was trying to be happy. Still, at least she'd be able to read in the newspapers some guff about how the men on the Western Front had had a 'happy Christmas with an excellent dinner'. Bilks whistled 'Hark the Herald Angels' to keep them amused.

'I have had it with this,' Pie said. 'I might just go for a short walk. They're not going to order us out at Christmas, are they?'

Bilks looked up briefly. 'Sir?' Michael nodded. 'Okay, chaps. A quick breath of air. Keep your heads down going up. And wish any farmer you see a...' He turned to Michael.

'*Joyeux Noël, monsieur.*'

'That's it. *Joyeux Noël, monsieur.*'

They chorused it in reply. Even Bilks was hauling himself over the side. 'Just off to have a look, sir,' he said. 'Better check the locals don't bite on Christmas Day.'

Michael nodded. 'Have them back within two hours, Bilks.'

He settled back. Wheeler was standing there. 'I don't need to go, sir,' he said. 'I'll stay and keep you company. It is Christmas, after all.'

Michael smiled. 'Thank you.'

Wheeler sat beside him. 'Tell me about your family, sir.'

'Call me Michael.' He saw the surprise on the other man's face. 'Just for today, at least.'

'Tell me about your family – Michael.'

'My father was in business. Pretty normal, really. Tell me about yours. I'd really like to hear.'

Wheeler started to talk about his widowed mother in Norfolk. As he did so, he snaked his hand over to Michael's and clasped it. Michael felt his face colour. Wheeler's skin was soft in his hand. *Stuart*, he let himself think. *Stuart.*

Bilks's cheery face peered over the lip of the trench. 'Good—' His mouth dropped open. Michael and Stuart hastened to move apart, but it was too late. Bilks's eyes were glued to their hands. He stood at the edge. 'All going well up there,' he said, his voice forcedly cheerful. 'Pie found a frozen pond, they're skidding around like a set of fools.'

'They deserve some cheer,' said Michael, faintly. Wheeler had moved his hand but his body was still close. Michael could feel the warmth of it through his shirt.

The three of them stared at each other in an awkward silence.

'I say, old chap!' Captain Derreny-Mills put his head over the side. 'Happy Christmas and all that. It's quiet in here. You're not watching your men, Witt?'

'No, no. Bilks was with them,' he said, trying to make his voice loud.

'I came to beg a favour. Sorry to ask, but one of my boys has just told me he had some bad news from home in his Christmas letter. Wife expecting, not well at all, in hospital, and of course he can't have any leave yet. He's not really up to much but he was supposed to be doing sentry duty tonight. All the others have been drinking rum, sorry to say. You don't have anyone who might be able to step in?'

'I'm afraid they've all been drinking rum too,' Michael said.

'No they haven't,' came Bilks's voice. 'Wheeler hasn't, have you, Wheeler? You could take the job.'

Michael stared. He wanted to overrule – but Bilks was correct. Wheeler stood up. 'Of course, sir. What time should I begin?'

'Six, please. Thank you, old chap. And you, Witt. Good day to you. Make sure you get your men in soon. They'll start the whizz-bangs again at five, I hear.'

That night, Michael waited in his dugout, listening to Worth singing, Pie chattering about his father meeting Marie Lloyd and the other men telling them to be quiet. Finally, at half eleven, they were all snoring. He listened out for the sound of Bilks grinding his teeth – a sure-fire sign that he was asleep. After it had been going on for a good twenty minutes, he stood up. He was dressed, with his boots on – they all slept like that in case of enemy action – so it was easy to slip out and towards the fire step at the end of the trench.

He crawled along the trench, past groups of men slung over each other, fast asleep. One was lying awake, staring ahead, but did not see him. No matter; no one would challenge an officer. At the end of the trench, he pulled himself up. The land was painfully clear, lit up by whizz-bangs. Last month, one of the sentries had been taken by a German night patrol, or at least that was what they thought, since his relief had found nothing there but his badge on the fire step – they supposed he'd been fiddling with it to keep himself awake.

Wheeler was standing straight, looking outwards at the dark mass of nothing. 'Psst!' He did not turn around. 'Psst!'

He turned. 'Sir?'

'Thought I would come and see you,' said Michael, feeling shy. 'To find out how you are.'

'Not bad, thank you, sir. It seems rather quiet out there.'

'Michael.'

'Michael, then. I can't really see much, to be honest. A few of our officers walked past and that was it.'

'I am very glad to hear it is quiet. I brought you some chocolate.'

'Did Princess Mary send us some after all?'

'Sadly not. Cheap stuff I bought in the shop here.' Michael sat on the fire step. The cool air, the stars, the lack of people felt like a kind of freedom – the first he had really felt since that night at Stoneythorpe when he and Tom had discussed leaving. 'Happy Christmas,' he said, holding out the meagre bar.

'Thanks, sir. I was almost dropping off out here. Not that you heard me say that, of course.' Wheeler's breath came out frosty, little clouds in the darkness. Michael wanted to reach out and capture them in his hands.

'Of course.'

'Do you have a cigarette?'

'For you, of course.' *Anything*, Michael wanted to add, but just at the moment of speaking, he felt too shy. He took a cigarette from his packet and passed it up to Wheeler. *Stuart*, he wanted to say. *Can I – may I – call you Stuart?*

'Could you light it for me?'

Michael had to breathe in to feel the weight of what Stuart had asked. *Light it.* 'Of course!' he said, too brightly. The match flickered in the darkness. Stuart leaned in, sucked. *Oh God.* 'Let's try and ignite some German shells,' Michael said, too quickly, stumbling over the words as he took his fingers away.

Stuart blew out smoke and laughed a little. 'Yes, sir.'

'Michael. Please.' He could hear the begging note in his voice as he said the words.

'Michael. Michael and Stuart. Has quite a good sound to it, don't you think?' Wheeler blew out a smoke ring.

'Come and sit by me?' The words hung in the air.

'That would be breaking the rules. They could court-martial me.'

'I'm your officer. I'll tell them not to.'

That laugh again. *Oh God.* 'Well, if you say so. Michael.'

Stuart sat down beside him, not half a foot away, but *right beside him*. Michael could almost feel his flesh through his coat. He couldn't speak. His hands were sweating, even though the air was freezing. Tiny flares sparked up over the land in front. He stared at them, trying to see them and nothing else.

'You know, I quite like the army, never thought I would.'

'Oh?'

'The other fellows are good sorts. Beldon, in my last company, was telling me that the food is better than he can afford at home. Says that often he and his wife give their little boy the meat and they have the water it's cooked in.'

Michael looked at the chocolate in his hand. 'There is certainly food, that's true.'

'Honestly, I think it's the first place I have ever really fitted in. I wouldn't say boo to a goose as a kid. I wasn't much of a teacher. My mother wanted me to do it but the older ones ran rings around me, girls as well as boys.'

'I'm sorry to hear it.'

'Oh no, don't be sorry. I wouldn't want to be one of them,

working and the pub and then marrying some poor girl round the corner and giving her six kids. I like being different.' He blew out smoke and turned to look at Michael. His eyes shone in the gloom. A flare shot up nearer to them. 'Like you, sir. Don't you like being different too?'

Michael felt himself go scarlet. Thank God it was so dark. He started to speak but it came out as a stammer. *Breathe*, he told himself.

'I'm not wrong, am I? You are?'

Michael coughed, tried to speak. Then tried again. 'I don't know,' he managed, his voice strangled.

'I knew from when I was very small. But I had to find the right person. I did – for a while. An older fellow, new to the village. We used to meet near the canal boats, hide in the trees. Stan, his name was. Then his parents came to visit, he got scared and before you could say lickety-split, he was back in his old town and married to a cousin. I was pretty angry, you can imagine. But I think now he must be more unhappy than me.'

'Did you ever hear from him?'

'Oh, I had two letters. One telling me the news and thanking me for my friendship and telling me to be happy as a friend. Then a year or so later he wrote again, just pally, asked how I was. I wasn't going to answer. I didn't.'

'No. I can – er – see that.'

'It only makes you unhappy if you don't live for what you really want, I think, sir,' he said. 'Don't you agree?' He blew out another smoke ring. Michael stared at it, floating up to the sky. A flare rose beyond it.

Michael felt something. It was … it was Stuart's hand on his knee. *Put yours over it*, he willed himself. It was down by his side. *Do it*. He couldn't. *Oh God.*

'You know, sir,' Wheeler's voice was soft, his mouth very close to Michael's ear, 'if there is something you want to try, you should. Life's too short. *Our* life is too short.'

Michael edged his own hand on to the outside of his leg. That was all he could do. The land ahead of him had blurred, as if he had put on a short-sighted man's glasses.

'Anything you might like to try.' Wheeler's voice was still close to his ear. Michael closed his eyes. He could feel the other man's breath on his skin. His hand on his leg. He opened his eyes, turned his head. The space glittered in between them. And then Stuart moved his face closer and the shock ran through Michael as he felt the chapped patches on the soft wetness of the other man's lips, the coolness of his cheeks. He opened his mouth and let Wheeler in.

1916

EIGHTEEN

London, February 1916

'Well come on!' said Emmeline. 'I don't have all day!' She pushed Celia forward, towards a group of women in bright dresses holding up signs and placards wishing goodbye to the Westminster Fusiliers. Celia stared at them waving out, dabbing their eyes.

'Don't feel sorry for those girls,' Emmeline snapped. 'They think sending men off to fight is the most heroic thing that anyone could do.'

'Well, isn't it?' But Emmeline was charging ahead like a navy-coated comet and Celia had to break into an ungainly run, bumping along with her bags, to try to catch up. The platform was thronged with soldiers, all wearing khaki, clapping each other on the back and shouting to one another. One threw Celia a wink.

'Come *on*, Celia!' Emmeline pulled her past the lady ticket inspector into the concourse under the light of the glass roof. The walls of the station were plastered in posters calling for soldiers. One showed a sad-looking man in a brown suit sitting on a chair. A little girl with a bow in her hair perched on his lap with a history book; a small boy at his feet played with toy soldiers. *Daddy, what did YOU do in the Great War?* was the caption underneath. Celia stared at the man's face, etched with pain. Who sat down and drew these things? she wondered. What person in charge said, *Actually, make sure he looks really miserable otherwise the poster won't work.*

'I'll go without you!'

Celia hurried after Emmeline's hat and through the great entrance of Waterloo station. A team of women in long skirts carrying mops walked past her – train cleaners, she supposed. The dirty cold air hit her hard. 'Shall we look for a cab?' There was double, triple the number of people there had been last time she'd been to London, nothing but great groups of them, hurrying towards her like shoals of fish, ready to gobble her up.

'A cab!' Emmeline threw back her head. 'Things have changed now, little sister. We will get the bus. That is, unless you have come equipped with hundreds of pounds?'

Celia shook her head.

'Thought not. Come on – there it is!' She hurried towards a small crowd of people. Celia picked up her skirts and dashed after her. The bus bore a great picture of Lord Kitchener.

They clambered to the top. 'More room up here,' said Emmeline. 'Sometimes it gets so busy with all the rich people who aren't using their cars.' She settled herself into a seat and Celia balanced her feet on her case, tucking her legs under her skirts to keep warm.

'Was London really always like this?' she asked, staring out of the window at the giant buildings and the throngs of people. 'I don't remember it so busy.' She hadn't really looked at the city when they'd come to see Rudolf, she'd been so busy reading to Verena, quelling her nerves.

'Yes, well you were a child when we lived here,' snorted Emmeline. 'Not that you look like one any more.' She gave her an appraising look. 'You have certainly changed, and for the better. Your face has filled out and your hair is looking handsome. I suppose you didn't have food shortages in the country.'

'Not really.' Celia blushed at the thought of their groaning Christmas table. Emmeline hadn't changed, she thought, though she looked even more beautiful, more like a delicate fairy than ever.

'You are much improved. Although I really thought it was impossible that you could grow any taller. You're a great height, quite a giant. I suppose you are still always tripping over your feet.'

It was February 1916. Celia could hardly think where the last year had gone – a whole year frittered, she supposed, reading to Verena and hoping for letters from Rudolf, Michael, Emmeline,

Tom – even Arthur. After the most dismal Christmas she could imagine, when even Mrs Rolls cried, she had decided she should do something. If she'd been just three or four years older, she could have gone off and lived anywhere she liked. But she was too young, she was at home, she could think of nothing to do. Earlier in the month she had dreaded turning seventeen, in case nobody remembered, but in the morning there'd been a letter from Michael – and one from Emmeline. Jennie held them out to her, her face pink with pleasure. 'I kept them back so you'd have them today,' she said. Celia held them, chastised herself for still longing to ask if there had been one from Tom, then sat down, read them in order. Michael was busy with work, a lot of new trenches to be dug and organised. It was Emmeline's letter that flung the surprise at her. Celia had expected the usual words: *I am enjoying myself, I will not give you my address.* This one was different. Emmeline wished her a happy birthday – then asked her to come and visit for a few days. 'I would like to see you, sister.'

Jennie had told Verena about the letter, and when Celia went up to read to her, she asked to see it.

'She is inviting you to visit?' asked Verena, staring at it.

'It's a surprise to me.' Suddenly Celia wanted nothing more than to go to London and see her sister. 'I think that if I go to see her, I might be able to persuade her to come back.'

Verena sank back against her pillows. 'How can none of my children want to be with me? I carried you all. I bore you. And all of you want to leave me.'

'I'll ask her to come back.'

'Will you? Will you not want to stay there with her? In London, away from me?'

'I promise.'

'You cannot go alone. I shall come too.'

Celia's heart sank. 'Let's ask Emmeline first.'

A tear rolled down Verena's cheek. 'Emmeline wants you, not me.'

'I don't think it's that, Mama. Look, she says the place is very small, see. Perhaps they only have enough guest rooms for one.'

'No one wants me.'

'Oh, Mama. It's the war! If it wasn't for that, Michael would be here. Look, even if he hadn't already gone to fight, the government would force him now, with that new law. Papa too, if he wasn't in prison.'

'Celia, your father is almost fifty!'

'How old do you have to be before you're safe? Arthur should stay away, in case he gets called up. Maybe Mr Janus is going into the army and that's why she wants to see me.'

Verena nodded. 'That is a good point.' Celia could see she was coming round. 'But you can't go alone. Lady Redroad's man goes to London once a week to collect her gowns. He shall escort you. If you are so ashamed of your mother.'

'I am not!' Celia said. But there was no way to make it hurt Verena less.

After that came discussions by letter about when Celia might or might not go. Certain dates simply did not work, Emmeline said. When she finally wrote that a week on Tuesday would be perfect, in fact that was the *only* time she could come, Celia rushed to tell Verena. Her mother sat up.

'Celia, I have something to tell you. You know … well … when people are married, they have babies. Well, sometimes, people … er … have babies anyway. If there is one, you must not be surprised.'

Celia was blushing terribly. The words whispered to her in the dorm by Gwendolyn and the others came back: 'Men might kiss you and then you get a *baby*.'

'I won't, Mama.' Even though Emmeline with a baby seemed the strangest thing she could imagine.

Just before she left, Verena gave her a fistful of money. 'Some of this is for your expenses,' she said. 'The rest is to persuade your sister to come home.'

'I'm seventeen now! You would expect me to be taller.'

'Indeed. Still a child. But a huge height. You must stop growing.'

Emmeline adjusted her hat. It was a new one, dark blue with paler flowers, Celia noticed, and then reminded herself that of course it was new. Her sister had left nearly all of her clothes behind. Celia supposed she must have sold her jewellery to buy new things. She stole a look at her sister's stomach. It didn't look bigger – and surely if Emmeline had a baby, she would have mentioned it by now. Her mind struggled. What did you do with babies?

'We've been sad without you,' she said. 'Mother has been sad. I wish you would come back. I promised her I would ask you.'

'Oh Celia, you know I cannot go back now,' said Emmeline. 'Not after this.'

'Mama says that we all leave her.'

'You haven't. And Arthur and Michael will come back.'

'Do you write to Michael?'

Emmeline drew her legs under herself. 'This bus is freezing. He says France is muddy. That's about it.'

'I know. Can I see his letters?'

'Of course you can. If I can see yours.'

A lady ticket collector came to punch holes in their tickets. 'Imagine if they wore trousers,' whispered Emmeline. 'Too far, don't you think?'

'Things aren't so good at home.' Celia looked quickly at the old woman perched on the seat next to them and lowered her voice. 'You're not married?'

'No.' Emmeline stared resolutely out of the window. The houses they passed had crumbling roofs, fronts that looked as if they had lost their paint years ago. Some were boarded and covered up. They were plastered in posters.

'Is Mr Janus going to go?'

'No. His lungs are not good enough.'

Four men in uniform mounted the bus. 'Poor him. But Emmy, why won't he marry you?'

Emmeline tossed her head. 'You are so old-fashioned, Celia. Maybe *I* don't want to marry *him*.'

'Emmeline!' she cried. The old woman coughed and Celia dropped her voice. 'But what can you mean?' They turned into Trafalgar Square. Even the base of Nelson's Column was covered in posters. A fat man in a Union Jack with a stick, a line of soldiers behind him, pointed his finger: *Who's absent? Is it you?*

Her sister looked the same, spoke in the same voice – but nothing was like the old Emmeline. Every word coming from her mouth was unfamiliar: not marrying, living in London, buses, Mr Janus. Celia felt as if she was all at sea. Had this new Emmeline been there all along and Celia just had not seen her?

'Shouldn't all ladies be married? You have changed so much!'

'Celia, I feel like I am a different person to the one who wanted to marry Sir Hugh. I think, in the end, I could never be a lady of the manor. Papa always thinks so much of us all. But I'm not up to it.'

'But to go from that – to this. You could have not married Sir Hugh. You didn't need to run away with Mr Janus. I cannot understand it.'

'Well, I loved him. I love him.' Celia reddened at her words. 'It is because you thought you were the only one who wanted to have adventures. Don't lie. I heard you playing games with Tom. And now I have gone to do something different and you're jealous.'

'I'm not jealous! I just mean—'

The bus lurched and Emmeline jumped up. 'This is our stop. Come on.' Celia clambered down the steps after her sister. They walked along a road filled with shops and turned into a square of houses that must once have been handsome Georgian buildings, arranged around a threadbare garden with broken railings. Now most looked like they were uncared for: splintered window frames, doors with peeling paint.

'Where are we? Has it been bombed here?'

'Of course not. This is Bloomsbury. Very near the British Museum. Welcome to Bedford Square. Now come along in.' Emmeline unlocked a dirty black door and led her into a dingy hall.

'This is a nice house,' said Celia, looking at the damp on the walls. A bicycle was leaning against one, along with a collection of sweeping brushes. The maid must be occupied upstairs, she supposed, rather than ushering them in.

'I dare say, but we only have a flat. We are on the top floor.'

'A flat?' Celia had never met anyone who lived in a flat. 'What, you mean that there are *other people* in this house?'

'That's right. A flat. We are not in Hampstead or Stoneythorpe any more, Celia. Do close your mouth, and come upstairs.'

Celia climbed after her sister, still humping her case. The wood of the stairs was dirty and worn. A forlorn picture of Venice in an old frame hung on the first landing.

At the top, Emmeline put her key in a wooden door that hadn't even been painted. 'Here we are. Home, sweet home.'

Celia pushed in behind her, through a tiny hall and into a shabby parlour. There was a sunken-looking red sofa, a battered table and a chair. A bunch of pink flowers sat in a green bottle on the table. The walls were covered in shelves of books. Racks of canvases leant against the wall, covered in brightly coloured paint, multicoloured swirls against a yellow background, patterns of squares on rectangles, curves and lines and spots. It wasn't much warmer than outside.

She collapsed into the sofa. 'This is nice, Emmeline.' She blushed for the lie. Her sister, fair hair gathered around her face, the prettiest ballerina in the ballet, looked ludicrous surrounded by such shabbiness, standing on bare floorboards that even Celia could see were missing some of their nails.

There were three doors off the parlour. The only one ajar had white tiles and what looked like a large white bath – was it a *bathroom*? Rudolf had always talked of putting one into their house, but Verena had refused – she said that they had enough servants to carry hot water up the stairs, so there was no need for such a new-fangled thing. Celia supposed the other rooms were bedrooms. And the kitchen, she thought, that was probably down in the basement and the cook there served them all. She stole careful looks for any baby things, decided there were none.

'It is, isn't it? I did it up myself. Quite well done, Samuel says.' She shook off her coat. Celia knew she should do the same but the place was so cold without a fire.

'You mean Mr Janus?'

'Call him Samuel now.'

Celia rubbed her eyes. Her head was swimming, words crashing against each other in her mind. 'You are awfully changed, sister. You are…' She shook her head. 'I can't believe you live here,' she finished, lamely. She was feeling terribly thirsty. She wondered when the maid would come with tea.

Emmeline shrugged. 'It's very cheap; places are a good price around here. Samuel says it's because all the students who were at the university have gone to fight.'

'Like Michael.' Tears pricked in Celia's eyes – and then she could not stop crying. The tears were pouring out now, faster, dropping down on to her blouse, dampening her face. Michael fighting, Tom there too, Emmeline living with a tutor in a flat.

'Come on now.' Emmeline put an arm around her. 'Don't cry. Michael will come back.'

'And Tom.'

'He is only a servant. Granted, one who admired you excessively. But you don't need to be flattered by the attentions of a servant.' Celia felt a hot flush that he had admired her. No one had said that before.

'He is my friend. Mr Janus was a sort of servant, too.'

'Don't be ridiculous. Samuel is an artist!'

'Oh, Emmeline, everything is going wrong. Mama is in a bad way. You know I wrote to you that Papa was in prison?'

'I cried for two days. It's terrible. He has done nothing!'

'We went to see him and we thought he was going to come home. We didn't know your address or you could have come. But now they've moved him again after that ship went down.'

'Ah yes, the ship. I stayed inside, just in case. Samuel and his friend – Mr Sparks, you'll meet him – walked up to the East End. They saw a terrible riot.'

'Mama isn't how she used to be, Emmy. She gets upset. On the day Papa didn't come back, she shot the horses.' The words came out messy and broken as she repeated them to get them free of the tears.

Emmeline grasped her hand. 'She did what? She shot the horses? Which ones?'

'All of them. Moonlight is dead.'

Emmeline sat down and thrust her hand into her mouth to try to stop herself from crying.

'Mama said that you would never come back, so she shot them.'

'I cannot believe it.'

Celia knew it was wrong, but a quick impulse shot through her to make Emmeline suffer as she had. 'Well, you won't come back, will you? So what is the use of Moonlight?'

Emmeline wept then, noisily, and Celia was flooded with guilt. She put her arms around her. 'I am sorry, Emmy. I didn't mean to upset you. It is just that things have been hard at home.'

Emmeline leant her head on Celia, still weeping, and Celia stroked her hair. Eventually her sister sat up and sniffed, wiped her eyes. 'You are right, Celia, quite right. I can't come back, not yet, anyway. I would do nothing for their reputation. It's not like marrying Sir Hugh.'

'Yes, well, he was not kind.'

'I had a lucky escape.'

'Although, Emmeline, Mr Janus? How could you?'

'You don't understand, Ceels. Look, Samuel and his friends know the truth, they explained it to me. With the war, the aristocracy like Sir Hugh will lose everything. The artists will be the ones to succeed, people like Samuel. The money is theirs. One day we will be richer than Sir Hugh could dream of. We will have one of those huge houses in Belgravia and travel all over the world.'

'Artists? Is Mr Janus really an artist?'

'Do call him Samuel, Celia. And yes, he is an artist.'

Celia gazed at the canvases covered in spots. Rudolf always said of paintings he didn't like: *a child could do it!* But it was true, a child *could* do these. 'I suppose those are his paintings. They don't look like much to me.'

'Well, maybe you don't know much about art.'

'Do people buy them?'

'Well, some. He teaches art to private students too, that's how we live.'

'And what about you? What have you been doing all year?'

'It's a lot of work being a wife – well, like a wife. You wouldn't understand, Celia. I have to look after the house.' She cocked her head in the flirtatious way she always did. 'And I have been trying to draw a little too. Not like Samuel, more conventional, that's what he says. Figures, fruits, that sort of thing.'

Celia felt ashamed. 'I haven't been doing anything. I don't know why I asked. I've just been looking after Mama.'

'That is hard enough. Come now, Celia, you must be tired after all that travelling. You can lie down. And this afternoon, we have a surprise for you.' She put a hand to her head. 'So sorry, Celia, I forgot! Are you hungry? Would you like some tea?'

'Tea, please. I'd very much like some tea. Shall we call for the maid?'

Emmeline threw her head back and gave her laugh, louder than it used to be at home, still pretty. 'I don't have a maid, Celia, dear. It's me. *I* shall make the tea.'

Celia stared. 'Do you cook your own food?'

Emmeline blushed. 'Actually, that hasn't been so successful. Samuel gets us pies from one of the shops, or we go to a café. But I can certainly make some tea.'

'Really? You can make tea?'

'Come along,' Emmeline boasted. 'I will show you.' She stood up and walked to the door by the bathroom, pushed it open. Celia followed her. The kitchen was no bigger than a cupboard really, containing a tiny stove and a stone sink. Emmeline shook the kettle on the stove. 'It is already filled,' she said triumphantly. She took a match from a box by the side and struck it, lit under the kettle and a flame popped up.

'How do you know when it's made?'

Emmeline waved her hand. 'Oh, you just *know*.'

Celia watched her pour the water into a teapot, then fill two cups and add milk. 'Here you are,' she said. 'I don't have a tray.'

Celia held the saucer, balanced the whole thing on her hand, standing – she had never drunk standing before. She sipped it. Tea was much better at home, and was there something wrong with the milk? London water definitely tasted odd.

'It's very nice, Emmeline.'

Her sister beamed, ushered her through to the parlour.

'I would like to rest, actually, sister. Where is my room?'

'I am afraid you don't have a room. You can sleep here, or in our room for the moment.'

'I'll sleep here!' She would not lie down in the same room as Emmeline and Mr Janus.

'Whatever you like.' Emmeline knelt down and deftly pulled out a thin mattress from under the worn sofa. She seized a bundle of linen from a box on the floor. 'Come on, help me make it up.'

Celia gazed at her, unsure.

'Time to learn how to make a bed, little sister! You put the sheet out like this and then you tuck in the corners. See?'

Emmeline was shaking her. 'Come on, Celia, wake up!' Celia opened her eyes to see her sister propped over her in her blue gown and hat. She tugged at her arm. 'We will be late!'

Celia struggled to sit up. The light looked like that of the early afternoon. She could not have slept for long. 'Late to where?'

'Come on!' Emmeline pulled her arm again. 'No, you don't have time to change. Let's just get this dress on you, and try and smooth your hair.' Emmeline was buttoning her back into her gown and pinning up her hair before Celia could even rub the sleep from her eyes. 'You are faster than Miss Wilton,' she said.

'Needs must! Come on!' She seized the pink flowers from the green bottle and thrust them into Celia's hands. 'Hold these!' She hurried into the next room and returned with a bigger bunch of lilies and round pink flowers with yellow hearts.

'You look very pretty, Emmeline.' She did – she had rearranged her hair, and her lips and cheeks looked brighter. The white lilies set off her fine skin.

'Good. Let us go!' In a matter of minutes, Celia had her boots on, and the two of them had barrelled through the door, locked it behind them and hurried down into the street.

'Where are we going?'

'Not far. Just a few streets away. Off we go!' Emmeline caught Celia's hand and hurried her around corners, past old men in suits, maids, women pushing prams, through a square of similarly dingy Georgian houses and towards a large church on a road busy with traffic. 'Hold on tight to the flowers.'

'We are going to church? On a Tuesday?'

'Oh, Celia, haven't you guessed yet? In you go!'

The place was dark and there were a few people dotted around the pews. A man was standing at the front near the altar. Celia's eyes adjusted slowly. 'Mr Janus?' she said to Emmeline.

'Exactly so! Today is my wedding day, dear sister. And you are my bridesmaid, just as we always planned!'

'What? What are you talking about? Emmeline!'

'Come on!' Emmeline hissed. 'Walk behind me, like a brides-maid. And smile!'

Celia followed her, and saw the few people in the church turn as Emmeline walked towards them. She caught Mr Janus's eye and her face flushed red. Emmeline turned around. 'Come *along*!' Celia did her best to rearrange her face and walk, smiling, behind her sister to the altar. Mr Janus watched them approach. He was wearing a dapper yellow suit with a carnation in his buttonhole, and was smiling broadly. He had grown fatter and he didn't have the sickly look of an invalid about his face any more. Celia supposed some people might say he was handsome, in a sharp sort of way. But still. *He was my tutor!*

Celia struggled through the next hour, dizzied and confused by watching Emmeline take Mr Janus to be her 'lawfully wedded husband'. She blushed furiously when they talked about honour-ing with their bodies, and dropped her head in embarrassment when Mr Janus slid the ring on her sister's finger.

They signed the register, witnessed by a man in a pale blue striped suit and a tall, stylish woman in purple. Celia stared at her sister gazing up at Mr Janus, looking entirely in love. Now she understood why a week on Tuesday was so important.

The organ began to play, and Emmeline and Mr Janus walked down the middle of the aisle. Celia stood uncertainly until the minister tapped her on the shoulder. 'You should follow them, my dear.' She clutched her flowers and set off. The man in the third pew who had been one of the witnesses jumped up and stuck out his hand. 'You must be Emmeline's sister? Pleased to meet you. The name is Rufus Sparks.'

How do you do, Mr Sparks? she did not say.

'Don't they make a lovely couple?' said Mr Sparks as he walked down the aisle by Celia's side. 'Very happy. I like a good wedding. Especially these days.'

'This is my first wedding.' She had imagined weddings, many of them. They seemed to be something that the Deerhurst family did to which the de Witts were not invited. Verena read the announcements and accounts in *The Times*, and passed on news of cousins, uncles, second nephews, the gowns, flowers and the problems of filling the cathedral. Emmeline's wedding was to be the great one, to which they would all be invited, the one to prove Rudolf's status, the one to win the Deerhursts back.

'First wedding, first time a bridesmaid? That's good luck, you know.'

A thin little man with a huge camera around his neck was trotting towards them. 'Gather on the steps, please!' he said. Celia was pushed next to Emmeline, who gave her a beatific smile. 'I had quite a problem getting Mr Agate here,' she whispered. 'He said he was ever so busy with taking pictures of soldiers and their families before they set off to fight.'

'I cannot believe you are married. Now I see why you were so eager for me to come today.'

'Smile, Celia! Hold your flowers up and *smile*.' Celia did as she was told. There was a click and a flash and then Mr Agate called out for them to do it again. People were passing behind him, smiling at them: a wedding party, a happy young bride. Celia smiled back as they were preserved by Mr Agate's camera, stopped in time on the steps of a church she barely knew.

Mr Agate took ten more shots, telling them all to move that way, a little forward, madam, a little back. Finally he went away and left them standing there. 'Come along!' called Mr Janus. 'Let us celebrate!' The tall lady in purple seized Emmeline's arm – and then she was next to Mr Janus.

He looked at her, his face pale. 'Congratulations, Mr Janus,' she said.

'Samuel, please.'

'I hope – I hope...' What were you supposed to *say* at weddings?

'Thank you for coming, Celia.'

'Congratulations,' she said again, but it sounded poor and false. She could not help feeling that they had betrayed her. It was wrong that Emmeline was even there. It didn't matter that she herself wanted to live in Paris – and for Tom to be there too. She was different. Emmeline was supposed to be the lady of the manor. Celia wanted to seize Mr Janus by the arms and say: *Why do people keep changing?* 'I am very pleased for you.' She said the words and knew they sounded like Mary Seton, a girl who couldn't act but who always wanted to be in the school play. Everything she said sounded untrue.

She thought Mr Janus would throw the words back at her. But he didn't; he merely nodded and said: 'Thank you, Celia,' as though she had just read him a good essay on Richard III. Then he stepped away from her. 'We're going to eat now. Time to celebrate.'

Mr Sparks appeared next to her. 'Come, Miss de Witt. As the best man, or at least the closest we have to one in this last-minute affair, I should really escort you.' He offered her his arm. She shook her head but walked alongside him. He told her he was a friend of Mr Janus's from university, and talked about how they both went to art classes after their history lectures were over. They passed a swarm of men in khaki, who laughed and cheered 'The bride and groom!' as they passed.

'Poor souls,' Mr Sparks said.

'Brave souls,' said Celia. 'My brother and my best friend are in France.'

'Brave, of course. The politicians make mistakes and they send men off to kill each other in the mud.'

'Michael and Tom would not kill anyone. They are just defending their country.'

'Well.' He stopped, smiled. 'I am sure they would not wish to kill, Miss de Witt. But many others there will have to. Just because our politicians want to have more land. It is all about land. Just think, by the end of her reign, the Queen ruled a quarter of the world's population. All that pink on the globe. And achieved through what? Nothing but constant fighting, the loss of husbands, sons and fathers. God did not put us on the earth to kill.'

Celia fought for an answer. Sarah's voice was in her head. *Teach the Kaiser a lesson!* She thought of Johann. He didn't want to kill. But when he was older, he might have to. 'Maybe if they talked to the Kaiser, he would stop?'

Mr Sparks threw back his head. 'Unlikely, Miss de Witt. Britain does this over and over again. It pushes countries into an impossible position. Then they have to fight to escape and we come down hard.'

'But you will have to go to war, sir?'

He shook his head. 'No indeed. And I won't claim weak lungs like Janus. I'll tell them no.'

'But you can't do that!'

'Women don't fight. Some of you could, I'd bet. Why should we? Not till Asquith himself is in the trenches with the King will I go there too.'

They had reached a tea shop, a rather dowdy-looking place with cakes that were obviously painted and artificial in the window. Celia had not been to a tea shop since Verena had taken her seven years ago, after shopping in Kensington. Emmeline was clattering through, calling out to the staff to pull tables together and asking for their best cakes. Three sleepy-looking waiters leapt to attention and hurried off for tea. They all sat down and Celia found herself squeezed in between Mr Sparks and the smart woman in purple.

She was still reeling at the thought of Mr Asquith and the King in a trench.

'And glasses too!' called out Mr Janus. He took out from under his chair a black bottle with a golden top.

'Champagne!' said Emmeline, clapping her hands.

'Got at I can't tell you what expense,' he said. 'Secret stuff!'

'Don't wave it around,' said the smart woman. 'They might take it from us. Lloyd George will outlaw drink soon, I tell you.'

'I read in the newspaper that he said that out of the Germans, the Austrians and drink, our greatest foe was drink,' volunteered Celia.

'He would say that,' said Mr Sparks. 'Anything to deny the workers some relief.'

Mr Janus laughed. 'Anyway, no police around here. That's the good thing about war. No one to check up on us.'

'There is nothing good about war,' said Mr Sparks sternly, as a waiter placed glasses in front of them. Another brought three steaming pots of tea.

'Oh come now, Rufus,' said the smart woman. 'I imagine you have been trying to indoctrinate Miss de Witt here.' She held out her hand to Celia. 'Pleased to meet you, Miss de Witt. I am Jemima Webb. *Miss* Webb, and not about to change it. Don't listen to a word Mr Sparks says. Where would we be without the willingness of men to fight and defend what is right?'

'Why don't you start passing out white feathers now?'

'No, indeed not, Rufus. I've told you many times that men must be encouraged by fair means.'

'By which you mean romantic pipe dreams about the King?'

'Oh stop it, you two,' said Emmeline, holding up one of the teapots. 'Who is for tea before it stews itself to bits?' The waiter took it from her and she smiled her thanks, then turned her head to the two other men at the table. 'Now, George and Edward, I don't believe you have met my sister, Miss Celia de Witt?'

'Surely the young lady is Miss de Witt now that you are married, Mrs Janus?' said George, a thin-faced man with handsome eyes.

Emmeline blushed. 'That's true! Celia, you have had a promotion thanks to me.'

'It is a pleasure to meet you, Miss de Witt,' said George.

'I concur,' said Edward.

'We have heard so much about you, Miss de Witt,' said Miss Webb. 'Very splendid that you could join us on this happy day.'

Celia realised that her bunch of pink flowers was crushed on her lap under the table. She pulled them out. In front of her was a sad artificial flower in a tiny vase. She plucked it out and put her flowers in the vase instead. 'There!' she said. She could not manage any other words. She knew what Miss Webb would expect her to say: that she was happy too, that her parents would have loved to see the wedding. But she could not. 'It has been a surprise,' was all she could manage.

She thought with shame of Verena giving her money, hoping she might bring Emmeline back with her. At this precise moment, her mother was in bed – would Jennie read to her in Celia's absence? – thinking of Celia, probably picturing her arguing with Emmeline, pressing her to come home. Not drinking champagne, celebrating with people she did not know. And yet Emmeline looked so happy.

'Come on, new little sister,' said Mr Janus. 'Tell us what you think.'

Celia was blushing furiously. 'I – I always thought you wished for a great ceremony, Emmeline.'

Emmeline waved her hand. 'Oh, that was in the old days. Everybody gets married in a hurry now. That sort of thing just gets in the way.' Mr Janus put his arm around her and she settled against him, holding up her bouquet.

'Now,' said Miss Webb, putting her hand on Celia's, 'let us have no more of Mr Sparks and his ideas. We should all help the cause. Women too. Have you thought about it, Miss de Witt?'

'She is too young!' called Emmeline from across the table. 'What are you thinking, Jemima?' A waiter put down a plate of iced buns. 'Have a cake and stop talking.'

Miss Webb took a bun and popped one on to Celia's plate.

'I have signed up, Miss de Witt. I think it is our duty. I have volunteered to be a nurse, a VAD. I hope to be assigned a hospital soon.'

'So you will have a job patching up the poor souls that our government sends to war,' said Rufus. 'Smoothing their brows and making them think their sacrifice was worth something.'

'Oh stop that. The good in life must be fought for, Rufus. Like the vote; we fight for that.' She patted Emmeline on the hand.

'It's thanks to all the fighting that we got married at all,' said Emmeline. 'The minister is so used to marrying men at the last minute who don't want to go to France as single men.'

Mr Sparks shrugged. 'It's different, Jem, to fighting for the vote. By which you mean parading around the street with placards.'

Jemima turned her back on him. 'I can count on your support for that, can't I, Miss de Witt?'

Celia thought carefully, holding her glass. The last time she'd really thought of the campaigners was before the war began, when Tom had joked about her burning the tea house. All that seemed a million years ago. Now they'd called a truce with the government, no more demonstrations – and the prisons were full of Germans like her father.

'I think ladies should be allowed to represent themselves,' she said, repeating what she had said in a school debate three years ago. Miss Davis had picked her to do it, because everyone else refused. Then, it sounded lost. The other girls had looked at her uncomprehendingly and her opposition, Mary Hedges, won by thirty votes. But this time, it sounded clear, real, as if there was some sense behind it. Miss Webb nodded, smiling.

'Oh, quite. It is fine for us to bear their children, plan their meals. But decide which men are to run the country? They simply won't allow it.'

Celia swallowed her protest – my father isn't like *that* – for she might cry if Jemima asked her a question about Rudolf. 'But I thought the campaigners had stopped for the war.'

'Well, yes, you are quite right, we have directed our efforts elsewhere. But we are always *thinking* about the vote.'

'Jemima, please,' called Mr Janus. 'It is our wedding day.' He leant over with the bottle of champagne and poured a little into their glasses. 'Let's drink!' he said. 'To Emmeline and myself! And to the future!'

'To the future!' they all called, and clinked glasses. Emmeline's face was joyous, its regularly handsome features reflected in the fogged-up window of the café.

NINETEEN

'We shall go on honeymoon later,' said Emmeline next morning, 'when Samuel has sold some more paintings. In the meantime, we must see London together.' She was up in her gown and making Celia tea again. Celia's head was messy with staying up late and listening to Miss Webb and Mr Sparks argue about politics, debating with Mr Janus whether wars did or did not improve art. After the café, they had come back to the flat and talked. All of them, Celia discovered, had been at university with Mr Janus. Miss Webb had been at the women's college but, she said, had grown so bored with women's society after spending so much time with her father as a child that she frequented the library just to get some male company.

The six of them talked a lot about university, as well as general politics, and teased Miss Webb about her campaign for votes for women. She would sigh theatrically, 'Only Miss de Witt understands me,' and pat Celia's hand. The touch was like heat on Celia's spine. Miss Webb, who was like no woman she had ever met. She lived alone in her own flat, which she said was full of books, prided herself on looking 'smart but never pretty', and was knowledgeable about everything from politics to what one artist in Paris said to another at an exhibition. *How do you know so much?* Celia wanted to ask her. Instead, she tried to shuffle up next to her, eager to hear her speak, hoping that a little of her shine would rub off.

Emmeline handed her the tea, graceful, giving her a gift. 'I feel so tired,' she said, yawning.

'Do you think Miss Webb will get married to one of her friends?' asked Celia. Surely Mr Sparks – surely all of them – was desperately in love with her?

'Jemima?' Celia raised her eyebrow. 'That I doubt.'

'I think she is very brave to help the war effort.'

'They say the ladies are more important than ever. Only single ladies, though.'

'Not you.'

'No. Samuel needs me.'

'His lungs seem fine to me.'

'Celia, you forget how ill he was. With all that gas out there, he would not survive five minutes.'

'I hope the gas doesn't go near Michael.'

'I'm sure it won't. I will just go and see if Samuel is awake. Then you and I could go out while he gets on with his painting. He needs quiet to work.'

Celia sat on her bed, holding her tea. She had never slept on such a hard bed. She had woken up three times during the night. The wedding and the champagne tore around her mind. Verena and Rudolf loomed up in her thoughts and she blushed with shame. Her father had talked so often, so proudly about giving away Emmeline in marriage. And he was imprisoned somewhere they did not know, while she had watched her sister marry with no one to give her away.

Emmeline popped her head around the door. 'Actually, sister, I am going to rest again. If you want to walk out, it's only a little way to the British Museum. Turn left, right, walk straight, then left again.'

Celia gazed at her boots. She would have to go out. She pulled on her dress and her shawl and seized a book from the pile on the shelf, then pulled the door closed behind her and hurried down the stairs, avoiding the brooms and the bicycle.

She breathed in the cold, grimy air of the street and stared around her. It looked nothing like the London she remembered as a child. Emmeline's square and the next one too were empty of people. The houses were poor, some of the doors entirely lacking in paint and railings missing from the front.

In the old days, she remembered, the streets she saw from the carriage were packed with people selling things – flowers, food, books – polishing shoes or telling fortunes. Women bustled around choosing what to buy; men strode about with papers under their arms; governesses led children by the hand. Now she turned into the main road and there were just a few people shuffling past, mainly women, clutching bundles, their faces the colour of uncooked pastry. It couldn't be more different to the bustle around Waterloo. And this area hadn't even been bombed! The thought of a bomb immediately made her look upwards. She should check, she thought, she should always check! She imagined herself in Emmeline's flat, staring out of the window as the giant silver monster floated over. In Stoneythorpe, she had lain in the garden and gazed up at the sky, wondering if one would pass over her on the way to London. All the time, she had two Londons in her head: the bombed-out shell and the normal one. Neither was accurate, she thought, picking her way over a road filled with holes.

She found the British Museum, but the front gate was locked and bolted up in chains. She gazed through the railings, then walked around the other side looking for a different entrance. Perhaps she was too early. She stood gazing at the huge building, full of mummies and sculptures. Rudolf had taken her when they lived in Hampstead, just the two of them. The Egyptian mummies were his favourite; he told her stories about the Old Kingdom rulers (he liked them more than the later ones) and their gods, Isis and Osiris. She had stared at the parchment rolls, thinking how nice looking all the Egyptians seemed to be.

'No chance of going in there, miss.'

She turned to see an old man with a broom. One eye was red and watering.

'Is it closed today?'

'Shut last week, miss. Not enough men to work there.'

'When will it open?' She could hardly bear to look at his eye.

'Never, they say. You new in town?' He winked the good eye.

She blushed and turned away. She spent the next few hours wandering around Emmeline's square and the surrounding streets, wishing there were some shops to visit. The cold air blew through her coat. Finally, as the sky began to turn grey, she went back to the flat. Mr Sparks and Jemima were there with pies and a yellowish drink that tasted terribly sweet but had a strange aftertaste. It wasn't like anything she'd ever tried before. She told them that the British Museum was closed, and Mr Sparks said it was a scandal. Miss Webb asked her what she wished to do when she was older, and Celia told her that she hoped to live in Paris and write. After that, Miss Webb grilled her about Paris and which books she had read until Celia was blushing and Emmeline shouted at her to stop. 'We are naturally artistic, us de Witts. You like my drawings.'

'I do, Emmeline dear. I just wish you would apply yourself more carefully. One needs proper ambition these days – like your sister.' Celia stole a look at Miss Webb, when she was talking to Emmeline, admired her hazel eyes. She felt shy that she had told them all her plans. She felt ashamed of hardly having read much more of Freud in a year.

After Miss Webb and Mr Sparks went home and Emmeline and Mr Janus had gone to bed, Celia prowled around the flat. She looked at the paintings, great blobs of colour, yellow, blue and red, that must mean something, although who knew what? She gazed at the easel full of paper, the palette of oils. She pulled out things from the cupboards, sorting through old green bottles and wooden boxes, looking at broken pencils, scraps of paper, letters, and food that looked too old to eat. Emmeline had brought nothing with her, but Mr Janus had clearly come to the flat with the assorted detritus of years. She found his old essays from college, textbooks, and a pile of keys that did not fit the front door. After finishing the cupboards, she turned to the shelves. She opened a sketchbook and flicked through pages and pages of drawings of Emmeline. A second sketchbook underneath it bore a big 'E' on the front. She tugged it out and looked at pictures of – as Emmeline had said – fruit, Miss Webb, people in the street below. The rest were all pictures of Mr Janus, sitting, standing, looking from the window. Celia came to one of him lying down and snapped the book shut – what if Emmeline had drawn him with fewer clothes on?

She heard stirring from the next room, and jumped into bed.

Her head was dizzy from the drink. She knew she should write to her mother, but she could not bear to tell her what had happened and that she had been there – as a bridesmaid, no less. She remembered then that she had stuffed the money her mother had given her in the bottom of her case to be safe. She should give it to Emmeline as a wedding present.

Next morning, Celia woke to see Mr Janus in the kitchen, fiddling with the kettle. She pulled the cover tightly around her.

'Good morning,' he said, walking past her.

'Hello … Samuel.'

He perched gingerly on the edge of the sofa. 'Emmeline was telling me about all the things that have happened to your family. I was very sorry to hear about Mr de Witt. And now your mother is unhappy too.'

'Yes,' said Celia, thinking miserably of the notes in her case. 'She misses everyone very much.' She could smell the hair oil that made his hair slick and black.

'I am sorry for your mother.'

'Me too.'

'It's an evil thing, this war.'

'So Mr Sparks says.'

'I agree with him. Hard to get a word in, sometimes, when Rufus is talking, but he's right, don't you think?'

'We have to protect the King!'

'But would it be so bad if Germany did invade? They aren't going to kill us, are they? You know, Celia, this war is all about making profits for big business: guns, ships, the rest.'

'My father is in business. He's not making any money.' *You just don't want to fight!* she wished she could say.

'He must be, you know. Otherwise your house would have to be sold.'

'His partners are looking after the factories. Mr Lewis does a lot.'

He shook his head a little, superior. She wanted to say something, anything to prove to him that she wasn't the foolish young girl he thought her. *I am not your pupil any more*, she wanted to say.

'If you got better, you would have to join up.'

'If they say my health is good, I'll object to it on moral grounds.'

'What are you two talking about out there?' shouted Emmeline.

'Art!' he called back. He smiled at Celia. 'I should take her tea to her ladyship.'

Celia nodded. She was being stand-offish, she knew, rebuffing his attempts at being friendly. She lay back on her mattress and opened the book from the shelf she had started last night, a history of modern art. She supposed she might as well learn to keep up with Miss Webb.

She had been so busy thinking about going to London, so preoccupied that Verena might refuse to let her go, not give her any money, she'd hardly thought about how it would be to actually be there. She had just wanted to be somewhere that was not Stoneythorpe, somewhere she didn't have to bear witness to Verena's unhappiness every day. She had thought she would be spending most of the time drinking tea inside Emmeline's large house, somewhere like Hampstead. She hadn't thought they would be so central to London, that she would have so much freedom, that Emmeline's friends would be like Jemima. It was dizzying, really.

Sometimes, over the next few days, she would dream she was at Stoneythorpe and wake heavy with dread. Then she realised she was in London and relief flooded her mind – followed by a brief pang of guilt for leaving Verena alone. The days filled themselves, pleasantly; she would accompany Emmeline on a walk in the morning to buy bread from the crowded bakery on Marchmont Street and pies from the shop around the corner. They took their time about the errand, for Mr Janus painted in the flat in the mornings. Emmeline marched her quickly past the letters painted on the wall of the abandoned house on the way: MEN SHOULD FIGHT.

At lunchtime, they shared a cake on the bench in Russell Square, the cool grass long and unkempt over their feet. Emmeline would put her face towards the sun while Celia read or stared at the pigeons hopping about begging for crumbs. Usually, in the afternoon, they would go to the shops in Oxford Street. It was almost entirely full of women: the dark-haired conductress on the bus holding up her ill-fitting skirt so she would not stumble up the stairs; the tall girls serving in shops (even in the men's departments, Emmeline said); the group of women in overalls who Emmeline said were street cleaners.

'You could work in one of the shops, maybe,' Celia said.

'Imagine!' said Emmeline.

Celia looked in the long, smudged windows of a shop selling things for the home, at a pile of saucepans and a fan display of plates, wondering if she should buy Emmeline a present with Verena's money. Her mother might prefer her sister to have an actual present, a tea set or a pretty vase, maybe. But there were so many things in the shops that she did not know where to start. The money sat under her bed, burning a hole there.

In the evenings, she waited for Mr Sparks and Miss Webb to pay their usual visit. She listened to them argue about the war, or the books they had read, trying to remember every word that Miss Webb said. She listened until she was almost falling asleep on the sofa. Sometimes she would wake to find Emmeline bustling around her, making her bed and tucking her in.

One morning, after a particularly late night arguing about Mr Sparks's theory of the legacy of Darwin, Celia was awake first. After three chapters of her modern art book – she was nearly finished and felt she had learned a lot for when she went to Paris – Emmeline came out. She shuffled to the kitchen, made some tea, then came and sat on Celia's bed. 'So, Celia. What are your plans?'

Celia looked at her blankly.

'You must have an idea of what you are going to do.'

'What, today?'

'No, sister, in the *future*.' Celia stared at her. Emmeline sighed. 'I mean, when are you going to go home?'

'Home?'

'Yes. Don't look like that. You can't stay here for ever, you know.'

'Well, I know, but I thought...' Celia trailed off. She didn't know what she thought. She supposed she had expected their days of sitting in the park and passing lady clerks in shops, conversations with Miss Webb, to stretch on. 'Please let me stay.'

'Oh come now, Celia, Mama will want you home, you know that.'

'I like it here.' She knew as she said the words how miserably selfish they were. Mama was lonely.

Emmeline sighed again. 'You see, Samuel likes to paint here. And although you are not here in the daytime... you know... he finds the fact that this is a bedroom a bit – well, it is hard for him to concentrate. And, Celia, be practical, we don't have any money.'

'Maybe I could stay with Miss Webb.' The idea thrilled her as soon as she said it.

'Don't be silly, Celia. Anyway, she is going to put lodgers into her home and live in the digs for the hospital.'

'But what can I do? I can't go home.'

'Wait until you're eighteen and get married. Mama won't let you go back to school?'

'She said she thought I was better at home. That some of the girls might say unkind things because of our name.'

'At Winterbourne? I can't imagine it. Oh dear, Celia, I do feel sorry for you. There's not much to do at seventeen. I mean, it's not like you could go to work. I think it's school or home.' She patted her hand. 'But you must come back here for a holiday soon.'

'I could work.'

'What on earth as?' Samuel was coming through the door. 'Dear, Celia thinks she might go to work.'

He shrugged. 'The rate Asquith is going, he'll be sending children to work, babies to war.'

'Imagine.' Emmeline pulled herself up from the sofa, and the thing breathed out as she stood.

'I suppose I will go tomorrow,' Celia said tentatively, wondering if Emmeline would say, *Oh no, please stay for a few days at least!*

'That would be sensible. You must give my love to Mama.'

Emmeline padded back to her bedroom, holding her tea, and shut the door.

Celia sat there, the book about modern art still in her hands. She gazed down at it. She was not going to finish it. She would have to wait until the next time she came to read about the legacy of Degas. But then, she thought, when on earth would that be? Verena would never allow her to leave again. At Winterbourne, they were told that self-pity was a girl's greatest failing, outside of the seven deadly sins. She tried to hear Miss Davis's voice, but she could not fight away the pity. It swelled in her, angry.

Well, if she must go, she would take her last opportunity to see London. She decided she would go one final time to the British Museum, in the hope that they might have opened it again. Anyway, she thought, if she went out, it might convince Mr Janus she was really no trouble and could stay after all.

She tidied away her bed, dressed and tugged on her boots. She could not find her coat, so she took Emmeline's blue one – it was not as if she would be up to see – picked up the key and set off down the stairs, past the bicycle and out into the street. Two dogs were picking over the pavement – Mr Janus said there were hundreds of them roaming the city, whose owners could not afford to keep them. Without Emmeline beside her, she stopped to stare at the recruitment posters plastered over the walls: pictures of happy men and women going out to war, sad people sitting in their grey parlours. *I will look like that*, she thought, then heard Miss Webb chastising her.

She carried on walking until she reached a large building with a sign reading LADIES' RECRUITING STATION. Emmeline had made her hurry past on the other side of the road, muttering things about the war machine. 'Excuse us, please!' came from behind her. She stepped aside. Two dark-haired girls about the same age as Emmeline walked in ahead of her. They were arm in arm and laughing. *Surely a machine wasn't made up of happy people?* Celia thought.

She gazed at the posters on the front of the building, admiring the artistry. Some were of wives and mothers waving men off to war with smiles (which made her feel unhappy about how much she had cried over Michael). Most were of women doing things. A woman in a large white hat tended a man in a hospital bed who looked at her with eyes full of gratitude. Some girls hoed farmland, smiling under a beating sun. Another woman in uniform poked out her arm.

'Nice lot of pictures, aren't they, miss?'

She turned. A man dressed in khaki was standing next to her. He was smaller than her, with bright blue eyes. His accent was a strong one, London, she supposed, but she was not sure.

'A friend of my sister, Miss Webb, is a lady volunteer,' she said. 'She is going to a hospital.'

'Well, good for her, I say. They are angels, those gals. I hope I never end up in a hospital, but if I do, I'm glad that we have the best nurses there to make us well again.'

'Are you going out to France?'

'That's it, miss.'

'My brother and my best friend are there. Michael de Witt and Tom Cotton. If you meet them, tell them ... tell them hello!' She could not think of what else to say.

'I will, miss. Funny, I have a lot of ladies saying the same thing to me. I have a few messages to pass on.'

'But you won't forget mine, will you?'

He shook his head. 'I won't. See, your sister's chum will be one of that lot over there soon.' Celia gazed the way he was pointing and saw a group of young women dressed in white hats and dark capes. 'They look the same age as me.'

'I should think you are the same age, miss. Twenty-one or so, I guess. I am eighteen myself, find it difficult to guess a lady's age.'

'That's right,' said Celia, thrilling to the deceit. 'Twenty-one.' Emmeline's blue coat must make her look older.

'Well, good day, miss. I go to France tomorrow.'

'Good day.' She hesitated. What did one say? 'Good luck.'

He held out his hand. 'Would you shake on it, miss? I don't have a wife or a sister, you see.'

Celia supposed that if she looked more like Emmeline, he

might have asked for a kiss on the cheek. 'Of course.' She held out her hand and he gripped it hard. His palm was dry, and she could almost feel the lines running through it.

He let go first. 'Goodbye, then, miss. I won't forget your message if I see them.'

'Goodbye.' She watched him go, then turned in the direction of the British Museum. All over the country, she supposed, soldiers were asking girls to say goodbye to them. It ran through her with a jolt: he was the first person she had met in her life who had no idea who she was, knew nothing of Stoneythorpe, of de Witt Meats, of anything. She wanted to run after him and say: *What did you think of me?* But she knew such a question would confuse him. Instead, she watched the group of nurses walking purposefully along the street. They were not like her, wandering with nothing to do. They had work, important work. *They are angels, those gals.*

She carried on towards the British Museum. But she was no longer thinking of mummies. Instead, she played the conversation with the man over in her head. He had seriously thought she was twenty-one. Was it the case that the minute she put on Emmeline's clothes, she looked like a grown-up? If she were twenty-one, rather than seventeen, as old as Emmeline, she could do as she pleased.

Then she reminded herself that it didn't matter what she looked like. She still had to go back to Stoneythorpe and live with Verena once more, bear her grief, try to comfort her.

No choice, said the voice in her head. *You must go home.* To helping Jennie and Thompson clean the house in the morning, then spending the afternoons reading *Persuasion* to Verena. Captain Wentworth's courtship stretched blankly in front of her. After they finished it, she supposed, they would go back to *Pride and Prejudice* and start all over again.

The museum was closed still. She gazed at the white pillars at the front, the fan of steps leading upwards. She held on to the railings while ideas formed in her head, quick-fire, her heart beating so hard she could almost hear it. If Michael and Tom were out there, why should she not go too? The girls with their arms linked laughed in her mind. After all, she told herself, it was logical: the more people who helped out, the faster the war would end – and the sooner they would set Rudolf free. She could do something helpful, like writing up lists of things in one of the offices.

Verena would be furious and disappointed, and there was the fact that she would be lying about her age. But then, she could say, writing lists in an office was hardly dangerous. Miss Webb was right: it was their duty. The thought of Miss Webb and how delighted she would be at the news decided her. She turned back on herself and towards the recruiting station. She was going to see, nothing more.

Three women walked out as she stood there, holding pieces of paper and chatting excitedly. Celia breathed deeply and stepped inside. The signs pointed her past rows of books to a long hall lit by high windows. She supposed it must be a reading room or something similar. The walls were covered in recruiting posters, and two women in khaki uniforms were sitting behind a high desk. There were two queues of girls waiting to be seen. Celia joined the shortest and tried not to seem too nervous. *Just having a look*, she told herself. It was just to find out how far she could go.

She finally reached the grey-haired woman at the desk.

'I have come to enquire.'

A young woman in khaki stepped up to the side of her. 'You'll find it is great fun, you know. Here are the papers you need to fill in.'

The grey-haired woman pulled some ink towards her. Her pearl necklace quivered as she talked. 'Doing your bit.'

'I just came to ask. What I might need. So I have to fill out the papers – and what else?'

'That is it. Name, age, address, just a few questions. Then we need…' She paused and turned to the other woman, who nodded. 'Yes, dear, we need your certification of birth.'

'Oh. I don't know where it is.'

The lady with the necklace conferred with the woman next to her. 'Annoyance, I know, dear. Ladies like you are clearly of age. But still, rules…'

'I'll find it and come back.'

'Good. Annoyance having to ask for it, I know. New edict from on high.' The woman waved at the ceiling. 'Why don't I take down a few particulars now? What is your name?'

'Emmeline de Witt.' She thought of Michael. 'But really I call myself Emmeline Witt.'

The woman wrote it down. Was this adult life? Celia wondered. You could tell a lie, two lies, and *nobody would know*? She gave the address in Bedford Square.

'Age?'

'Twenty-one.'

'Excellent. Some services demand twenty-three, you know, but we are twenty-one. Our ladies are grown up enough at that age, we find. And what are you signing up for?'

'Writing things.'

The woman looked at her sharply. 'What do you mean, writing things?'

'I thought you might need some lists or descriptions. I like writing.'

The woman looked dubious. 'And do you like anything else?'

'I enjoy horse riding.'

'Horse riding? Well, we don't have any horses.' She fingered her pen. 'Has your father an occupation, dear?'

'Er – business.'

'Yes, thought so. So, I tell you what we do have. Have you ever driven, Miss Witt?'

'Oh yes. I am very fond of driving.' She had once driven a carriage, with Tom helping her. But she could learn, couldn't she? After all, she couldn't think what Miss Webb or Emmeline would be like at driving a carriage. 'I am good with horses.'

'I'm sure. But I meant motor vehicles. Do you have any experience?'

Celia looked at her blankly. Then she thought of Rudolf's expensive motor car; Michael teaching her how to drive it as they flew past Callerton Manor, laughing. 'Oh yes. Yes, I do.'

'Right then. I thought you looked like the kind of girl who

could. Many young ladies who have fathers in business are rather good at driving. Come back with your birth certificate and we can get you registered. Then we will sort out the fee you need for training, certification and uniform, ten pounds.'

Celia gazed at the woman.

'Don't be disappointed, dear. You volunteer ladies are our heroines; you don't need recompense.'

Jemima had told her that VADS did not get paid; clerks and domestics from the lower classes did. This, she'd said, was the right decision – those girls needed the money. *But so do I*, Celia wanted to cry. Ten pounds was almost everything she had in the purse from Verena. The money was supposed to be for Emmeline. She'd been going to buy her a wedding present. But Celia reminded herself, the money had been to persuade Emmeline to come back, and as she hadn't done that, perhaps it was hers. 'When will I be going out?'

'A month or so, usually. Depends on demand. First, some train-ing. Thank you, Miss Witt.'

Celia walked back past the line of girls. Not one looked at her, not one poked her friend in the ribs and said, *That one is too young*. They paid her no attention. She walked out into the sun.

Emmeline and Mr Janus were up and drinking tea when she walked in.

'I see you took my coat,' Emmeline said, raising her eyebrows.

'I'm sorry, sister. I couldn't find mine.'

'I found it stuffed under the sofa.'

'I brought you these flowers.' She held out a bunch of daf-fodils that she had bought from a lame man on the way back for threepence.

'What have you been doing?'

'Walking about.'

'Well,' said Mr Janus. 'Emmeline tells me you are going home. That sounds like an excuse for a send-off tonight. Maybe Rufus will be able to find us some cake.'

'Mama will be so pleased to have you back.'

'Actually,' Celia said, hesitating, blushing, then forcing herself to speak, 'I'm not going home. I... want to sign up for the war effort.'

Emmeline threw back her head. 'Oh stop that, Celia. You are too young.'

'But I look twenty-one. People have told me so. I want to go! I want to be a part of it.' Mr Janus shook his head. 'I want to help,' she finished, lamely.

'If you look twenty-one, how old do I look?' Emmeline threw up her hands.

'You both look twenty-one,' said Mr Janus, soothingly. 'Twins, not sisters.'

'We cannot be twins! We look nothing alike.'

Mr Janus patted his wife's hand. 'There are twins who do not look alike. But this is beside the point. Celia, you know you cannot sign up to the war. Even if you look old enough, you must prove it. Anyway, war is wrong.'

'And what would you do?' said Emmeline. 'Farm the fields?'

'I could drive things. Cars.'

'Drive a car? Celia, you have never driven in your life.'

'I have once! Michael let me drive Papa's car. And besides, I can learn. Everybody has to learn.'

'You need money to sign up as a volunteer.'

'I would find it.'

'And do they pay drivers?' broke in Mr Janus. 'I imagine it's like nurses and you're meant to do it for the glory.'

'I wouldn't take any money, even if they did,' Celia said, stoutly.

'You sound like Jemima, happily giving yourself up to the war machine for no money, when the soldiers all get paid. What is it about you lot – you demand equal pay and rights for women, but when the war comes along, you'll work on worse terms than some girl from the back streets of the East End.'

'You're right, husband,' said Emmeline. 'Couldn't you have found a job that paid?'

'Anyhow, all this conversation is immaterial.' Mr Janus stood up and walked towards the little kitchen. 'You're too young.'

'Actually, I've an answer to that.'

'You have?' Emmeline moved a book from the sofa and started scrubbing at a paint stain with her finger. 'Will you ask Lord Kitchener for special dispensation?'

'No. I will take your birth certificate and say I'm you.'

'You'll do what? What are you talking about?'

'I'll take your birth certificate.'

'This is ludicrous,' said Mr Janus, running his hand through his shiny hair. 'What is more, it's against the law.'

'That is true,' said Emmeline. 'Mind you, I don't believe that every soldier I've seen setting off to France is actually nineteen. Some of them look about twelve.'

'Tom is not even nineteen, and he's been in France for over a year.'

'That's different. Look, Celia, your parents would never allow it.'

'Samuel, wait,' said Emmeline. 'I can see a point to it. If Celia says she's me, then no one will come trying to make me sign up, will they?' She patted Mr Janus's hand.

'This is a ridiculous conversation. Celia cannot sign up until she is twenty-one. And the war will be over by then.'

'You're not being fair.'

'Celia, it is against the law. Your brother is out there. That should be enough.'

'Yes, Mr Janus,' she said, her blood boiling. He marched off towards the bedroom. The door slammed behind him.

'Never mind, Celia,' said Emmeline. 'I am sure we could find something for you to do. I hear there are tea stations where people serve those going off to fight. You could help out there.'

'Do you have your birth certificate here?'

'Of course! I needed it to get married. I mean... Celia, you can't have it.'

'But I want to go to France!'

'Oh, stop it. Anyway, on to different matters. Before you go, I have something to talk to you about. Mama never discussed this with me, and that was before she was in bed all day.'

'She only wants to talk about Jane Austen.' *You pierce my soul...*

Celia pushed the thought back in her head. *I am not reading to you*, she said.

'Listen, I saw you in the garden with Tom that night. He had his arms around you. I have been thinking about it.'

'What do you mean?'

'Celia, didn't you ever talk about this at school? When ladies let men put their arms around them, sometimes they end up with a baby.'

Gwendolyn had read a book of her father's about babies that she told them about when she came back after the holidays, but it was so muddled that Celia could not understand a thing. She smiled. 'But of course I can't have a baby, Emmeline.'

'You do not need to be married to have a baby. Celia, do you not know a single thing?'

'I know that! But I can't have one.' She blushed. 'I don't think.'

'Well, if you are thinking about going to France, then you should know this. You must not let men put their arms around you, for a start.'

'But how can that make you have a baby?'

Emmeline looked gravely at her. 'It can't. Not if you keep your clothes on. That's all I am going to say. Just keep wearing your gown and you won't have a baby.' With that, she stood up and followed Mr Janus into the bedroom.

Celia nodded. That seemed clear enough, not half as mystifying as Gwendolyn and the rest had whispered it was. And she could hardly imagine herself in a place where she wouldn't be wearing her gown. She lay back on the sofa and picked up the modern art book. She didn't have much time left to read about Monet. After all, it would be useful to learn all she could about France before she got there.

Next morning, while Emmeline and Mr Janus were still asleep, she started to sort through their piles of papers. She kept one eye on their bedroom door as she shuffled through the same boxes she had looked at before. She pulled out letters from Mr Janus's parents, his birth certificate (1896; so he was *younger* than Emmeline!), some letters about money that she tried not to look at, and then their marriage certificate, which she held for a moment, remembering the day. Then she had it. The birth certificate of Emmeline Charity de Witt, 6th February 1895. She stuffed it into her pocket along with the fistful of notes Verena had given her, put on her boots and ran out of the door and down the stairs.

When she got back, glowing with daring and excitement, Emmeline was at the door in her nightgown. 'Where have you been?'

'It's too late to stop me. I've done it. Sorry, Emmy, but I stole your birth certificate and volunteered.'

Emmeline shook her head. 'Honestly, how could you?' She bundled Celia inside, shut the door. 'What will Mama say? She will be heartbroken, you know that!'

'You started it! You left. Why should I stay if you won't?'

'That's different. Who's going to look after her now?'

'Why don't you? You're married, you can go back.'

'Don't be ridiculous! I can't leave my husband!'

There was a bang from the bedroom. 'Sorry!' Emmeline shouted. She lowered her voice. 'Celia, you're being so selfish.'

'It's not like I'm going to a picnic.' Celia wanted to raise her voice, furious with Mr Janus.

'You might as well be. You are the unmarried daughter. Your place is at home.'

'I bet Jemima wouldn't say that.'

'She has no parents and a large inheritance. She hasn't got an idea about life.'

'Emmeline, I am sorry, but I've volunteered now. I have to go.'

'What will you tell Mama?'

Celia sat down on the sofa. She hadn't thought that far. 'I'll write to her.'

'A letter! No! You must go and tell her.'

'I don't want to. You didn't tell her you were leaving!'

'She'll die.'

'What on earth do you mean?'

Emmeline shrugged. 'You have to tell her. Then you'll see.' She gathered her shawl around her nightgown, went into the bedroom and slammed the door.

'I don't think she'll mind!' Celia shouted at the door, as loud as she could. 'She'll be pleased!' She knew it wasn't true.

'We should tell Mrs de Witt you are coming,' said Mr Janus later, and went to find Mr Sparks, who had access to a telephone in one of his political clubs. He could use it when no one was looking, but the club was so busy that he didn't manage it until late afternoon, and then, he said, it was too late for Celia to get the train, so she would have to leave the next day. She stayed another night, with Emmeline red-eyed and angry and Mr Sparks berating her for being seduced into it all. Only Miss Webb was pleased, patting her hand, saying that she must have looked terribly competent to be given the role of driver, and that she was even a little envious of such an adventure. Celia swelled in her attention and promised to send her long letters – very long ones, she said.

As the train pushed into the countryside outside London, Celia thought of Verena. On the one hand, she pictured her saying *Oh Celia, how brave. Lady Redroad will be very proud.* On the other, she imagined her screaming in horror, shouting, refusing to listen, threatening to keep her inside. She reminded herself that Verena had shot the horses when she thought no one was coming home. She thought of Emmeline saying *She'll die.* Celia leant her head on the train window. Verena surely didn't want her to spend her life reading the novels of Jane Austen for hours every day.

When she had arrived at the station, Thompson had collected her and driven her back in the borrowed carriage, not saying much. Celia stared out at the fields, wintertime barren, and imagined Verena's reaction. Perhaps she would be stoical, pleased, say, *Yes, I see that the faster you all help, the quicker the war will be over.*

Two hours later, she found it hard to credit that she could have been so naïve. She had expected to go up to her mother's room to find her, but as soon as she arrived, Verena was at the door, dressed and ready like in the old days, all kindness, clasping Celia in a hug, ushering her to the parlour, where tea was laid out, and telling her how Mrs Rolls had been saving up ingredients to make a special ginger cake to celebrate her return. There, she patted her daughter's hand, told her how much she had missed her. She said that Celia wasn't to worry, that she knew she would have tried, but Emmeline had always been headstrong, and it was hardly the role of the younger sister to force the older to behave in one way or another. It was Verena's turn to go to London and try and talk her round. 'I see it now,' she said. 'It is hard for a young girl to be alone here. When I was your age, I was at home doing lessons, but now I see that things have changed. I have asked Lady Redroad, and she tells me there is a dancing class for girls in Winchester. Would you like to go to that?'

Celia sat miserably, picked at her cake, while Verena flurried around her, asking if she wanted more to eat. The room, after some time away, looked even dustier and shabbier. She supposed they should put dust sheets over the furniture. Verena poured more tea. 'You seem a little *quiet*, dear.'

Celia knew she had to speak. 'Mama,' she said. 'When I was in London, I did something.'

Verena looked at her blankly. 'Did you disagree with Emmeline, dear? No matter. I shouldn't have told you to speak to her. I will go up.'

'No, no. Actually, Emmeline is married.' Her mother looked at her incredulously. 'Already married,' lied Celia, to cover her feelings of betrayal for celebrating the wedding.

Verena shrugged. 'I'll see a certificate first, I think.'

'But, Mother, it's not that. I did something. I...' She could not say it. A tear rolled down her cheek and she cursed herself for her weakness. She was just going to have to say it. 'Mama, I signed up for the war. I am going to drive ambulances in France.'

Verena blinked, then blinked again. 'That's not true.'

'It is, Mama. I am due at training in Aldershot next week.'

Verena shook her head.

'I'm sorry, Mama.' All the arguments she had stacked up in her mind crumbled. 'I just felt... I wanted to help.'

Verena shook her head again. 'I believe none of this. I didn't hear. I won't believe it.'

'It's true.'

Verena stood up and walked towards her. Celia sat straight, tried not to flinch. Verena was her mother, after all. What was she going to do? Celia smiled at her, trying to seem welcoming. And then Verena was too close, hadn't slowed, came towards her with her hand outstretched. Celia twisted her body away and Verena landed on the sofa, face down.

Celia sat there and looked at her mother trying to bring her knees under her, ungainly, her hair escaping its labyrinthine style. It was as if the moment wasn't real; it was something in a play. In a play, how you might laugh. Now, it was dreadful, a judgement.

Verena lifted her head. Her hair dropped around her face. 'I am not listening. I won't hear it. Otherwise you would all have left me, and that would be too harsh. To have brought you all up and then for you all to go ...' She looked up at Celia. 'That would be too much for any mother to bear.'

'I'm sorry, Mama.'

The door opened and Jennie arrived. Verena rushed from the room.

'Welcome home, miss,' said Jennie, raising an eyebrow.

'I won't be staying long.'

At that moment, afraid of her mother, resentful of the others, who had gone, Celia thought only of leaving. But Jennie persuaded her to stay. 'She was so looking forward to you coming home,' she said, fiddling with her apron, worn and greying now. 'Let me see if I can speak to her.'

Celia waited, sleeping in her room, eating with Jennie, wandering around the house. She could feel Stoneythorpe pulling her back in.

'I don't think she's coming out,' said Jennie, after two days. 'She says she won't change her mind.'

Celia spent that night in bed, listening out. She waited to hear Verena walking past, bumping against the walls. She heard nothing. The house was silent. Next day, she knocked on her mother's door. There was no answer. She even thought of sitting outside Verena's room reading the next section of *Persuasion*, in case that might tempt her out. She looked into the mirror and shouted at herself: 'This way, Emmeline!' and 'Emmeline Witt, do this!' 'Turn left, Emmeline!' She tried, but still it did not feel right. Each time she shouted it, she looked for Emmeline behind her.

The night before she was due in Aldershot, Jennie helped her pack. There wasn't much to put in – they were to take only one small case of personal things, for they would be wearing their uniform most of the time. She got up early in the morning for the train, and tried her mother's door again.

'Goodbye, Mama,' she said through the wood. 'I'll be back soon. I promise.' She thought she heard a flutter of movement and pressed her ear closer to the door, but there was nothing.

She said goodbye to Jennie and Mrs Rolls, saw the disappointment in their eyes.

'You watch out over there, miss,' said Thompson, dropping her off for the train back to London.

'I'll write to you,' she said.

'That would be nice.' He carried her bag to the platform. On the train, installed in her carriage, she stared out of the window, hoping to see her mother arrive with Jennie to wave her off. As they steamed out of the station, she craned back, but there was no one there.

TWENTY

Pozières, France, Spring 1916

There wasn't much you could do about the rats, horrible things as big as cats. He wouldn't admit it to the men, but he had become rather fond of a little one who scuttled around his bed at night. Sometimes, in the morning, he woke up and saw its nose twitching, right next to his head. He was even more embarrassed to admit it, but it reminded him a little of Celia when she had been young, standing eagerly by his bed. 'Michael! Come out and *play!*'

The lice were something else altogether. One morning, Michael woke up and felt something itching on his back. Within two days they were all over his skin and under his clothes, and even when he shook them out, they were still there, because they had swarmed their way into the seams and stayed there, running up and down, making him itch. He tried to rise above it, embarrassed, for he knew that lice thrived on lack of cleanliness. The men scratched, but he would not. After one particularly bad night, he told Wheeler, 'I can't bear it any longer. Please, don't tell anyone.'

Wheeler looked at him. They were lit by just the single candle. It threw shadows on the wall, over their faces. 'Take off your shirt,' he said.

'What?'

So far they had done little more than kissing, as they had by the fire step on Christmas night. Even though they spent nearly every moment together, touching each other was almost impossible. If ever they were even close to holding hands, Bilks seemed to appear, start talking about duties. It was unbearable. At night, Michael threw himself into bed on his stomach, let Wheeler run through his mind hotly, rubbing against the sheet, ashamed of himself, unable to stop.

Four times Wheeler had been sent out on sentry duty; twice Michael had crept out to speak to him. There, looking out on no-man's-land, they had held hands, kissed again, but Michael had not stayed long. At Christmas, Bilks and the men would not have noticed his absence; by February, everyone was watching each other. So Michael crept back after fifteen minutes or so, his body flaming, hardly caring to duck when the guns fired, for he could live for ever, surely.

There were so few opportunities, the tiniest touch was enough. Michael did everything to try to increase them: offered to take over Bilks's role of distributing the rations, passed around the grog, joined the building parties just to stand next to Wheeler and give him pieces of wood. Their fingers met, and sometimes – exquisitely – parts of their hands. They brushed past each other and Michael felt the thin material of Wheeler's shirt. He thought of people in love. They got married and then they could spend every minute touching each other. He and Wheeler could not really be in love. What they had was something entirely different. He could not imagine being able to touch Wheeler whenever he liked, *all the time*.

'Go on,' Wheeler repeated. 'Take off your shirt.' It was just the two of them awake in the dugout. Bilks and half of the men were on a clearing party; the others were fast asleep. Michael could hear them snoring, especially Cook, always the loudest. Mills and Brown, who normally shared the dugout, had been sent off to do some work in another trench. For one night Michael was alone – and he was alone with Wheeler.

Blushing and fumbling, his hands failing, Michael undid his shirt and pulled it off his shoulders. Wheeler touched his back. 'Look at this,' he said. 'It's red raw where you've been scratching. You should have said.'

'The stuff doesn't seem to work,' said Michael. He had covered himself with Harrison's Pomade, but it was as if the blighters actually *liked* it; they'd got worse since he'd used it.

Wheeler ran a finger down his back. 'This must hurt?'

Michael stuttered. 'Yes. No.'

'Poor you. Well, I will see them off. Give me your shirt.' Michael felt even more miserably embarrassed passing it over. He hadn't had a chance to wash recently. But Wheeler didn't seem to care. He turned the shirt inside out and held it up. Then he took Michael's candle. 'This is how to catch them. They lay their eggs here, and that's why the Harrison's is no good.' Michael watched as he held the candle close to the shirt. 'Can you hear the crackling? That's them all right. Eggs bursting.'

Michael stared, mesmerised by Wheeler's hands. Wheeler turned the shirt around and did both sides, the back, then the arms. He curved the candle around the collar, dwelled on the cross of seam under the arms. Then he put down the candle, shook out the shirt. 'There!' he said. 'Should be good to wear now. For a while at least. You have to keep doing this.'

'Oh.' How fine his hands were, tanned brown, the nails short, the fingers moving fast.

'They're not just in your shirt, though, are they?' His eyes glittered. 'Take off your trousers.'

Michael hesitated, then bent and took them off, standing there in just his underwear as Wheeler, his face intent, took the trousers and drew them over the tip of the candle. His fingers on the material, touching where Michael's leg had been. The heat spread through his body.

'You don't have to stand,' Wheeler said, softly. 'You can sit if you like.' He was pulling the seam of the trousers through the flame, carefully, back and forth. Michael blushed. He crouched down, feeling the cool of the ground, hoping it might dull the colour in his face. He gazed at Wheeler, desperately wanting to talk to him, to hear his voice. Anything. But he was hopelessly tongue-tied, could think of nothing to say.

'I think I've got rid of all the blighters,' said Wheeler. He dropped the trousers on top of the shirt. 'For the moment at least.' He smiled at Michael through the darkness over the brightness of the flame. 'I can do the rest if you like.'

Michael nodded, hotly aware of Wheeler's eyes on him as he took off his underwear. He got his foot caught in one leg, hopped about blushing and hopeless. He handed the garment over to Wheeler, blushing at how grimy it was. Wheeler, appearing not to notice, turned it inside out and drew the seams over the flame. Michael stood there naked, watched him.

'I reckon they're done,' said Wheeler. 'That's the lot.' He gazed at Michael, unblinking. 'Do you want them back?'

Michael stared at him.

'Or I suppose I could keep you company?'

Michael nodded, dumbly. Every night he had dreamed of this, imagined it in different ways, thought of Wheeler's body, trying to decide if it would be muscled or slim, thought of the muscles of his arms. Wheeler took off his shirt, socks, shoes, then his trousers and underwear. He stood there naked.

'Come here, then,' he said, putting out his hand. Michael took a step forward, tentative as a baby, feeling the flicker of the flame as he passed it. Wheeler put his arms around him, cool, drew him to his chest.

'I don't know,' Michael began. 'I don't . . .'

Wheeler touched his hair. 'Don't worry, sir. Hold tight to me.' He reached out his hand and snuffed out the candle.

After they had done it once and then – unimaginable – again, they lay side by side on the dark ground, Wheeler's arm slung over his chest. It was all over, that impossible, marvellous thing that had transformed every inch of his body, left him torn. He wanted to bring his mind forward to preserve each feeling, but surely mind had no place in it, none at all.

'How did you know?' he said.

'What d'you mean?'

'How did you know about me?'

Wheeler gave a low chuckle. 'I could see.'

'I couldn't tell about you.'

Wheeler patted his thigh. 'You'll learn.'

He had other questions too, welling up in his mind, careering through his head. *Why, can I, when, what.* Dozens of them, all boiling down to one thing: *Can I keep hold of you? I have to.* But he didn't know where to start, felt lost in the maze, and lay there listening to Wheeler's breathing change as he fell asleep.

Some time later, he awoke to the sound of shuffling. His eyes focused through the gloom and he saw Wheeler collecting up his clothes. Wheeler looked across at him, smiled briefly. 'You should dress, sir,' he said. 'You might get cold.'

Michael propped himself up on his arm. 'You're leaving?' Wheeler nodded. 'But when will I see you?'

Wheeler shook his head. 'Why, all the time.'

But it wasn't all the time. It was no different from before, except it was worse. There was no way of touching, no way of talking, without someone seeing. Michael blushed every time he went near Wheeler, and even more because he wondered if anyone else might be able to guess. How obvious was he being? he wondered. Could anyone have *seen*? Other times, he was so emboldened by the sight of Wheeler, so excited, that he did not care who guessed. They were together – and he would never meet anyone else like him, ever.

Three days later, Bilks came down the trench. 'I have an old friend of yours here,' he said. 'Says he's a *good* old friend.'

Michael came out and saw Tom, his face thinner, shadowed.

'Hello, old man!' Tom looked delighted. 'I thought I was coming here. What luck!' Michael looked up and saw Bilks watching, his expression unreadable.

'Hello, Tom,' he said, knowing how wan his expression was, unable to fix it.

'Tom will be with us while Mills is sent to the Engineers,' said Bilks. 'Commander thinks he could learn a lot from shadowing us, learning to be a corporal. What do you think, sir? Shall we ask him to stick close to you?'

'Of course,' said Michael, hating Tom's broad grin, his genuine pleasure at seeing him. 'That would be very welcome.'

His feelings of resentment towards Tom only grew. Every time he thought he might be able to get closer to Wheeler, Tom popped up, smiling. 'How are you today?' he would say. 'I've got something to show you on the trench.' He wanted to talk late into the night, ask about Stoneythorpe, chat about the war. Michael just wanted to be alone – to lie on his front and think about Wheeler.

He had not seen Tom since that time outside the brothel. Tom was eager for news. That first night, he settled himself by Michael in the dugout. 'Tell me everything,' he said. 'How are they all?'

'There's nothing good,' said Michael, bluntly. 'Mama shot the horses and Papa has been taken away for internment.' The pain stabbed through him, one long sword, then thousands of little pins, jabbing him. He remembered learning at school that Erasmus had had to reform the early churchmen because they debated obsessively questions like how many angels could dance on a pinhead. Now the pins were bursting into him as he forced himself to say, clearly: 'He went to register and didn't come back. We never hear from him.'

Tom stared at him, white-faced. 'But that is terrible! How can it be so? It must be some mistake.'

Michael shook his head.

'Then what are we out here for if people like him are being imprisoned? I thought that we were here fighting for freedom.' He kicked the side of the trench, his boot bouncing hollowly off the edge.

'Thank you.' Michael smiled politely, trying to cover how surprised he was at Tom's vehemence. He wanted to say: *It's my tragedy, not yours! You were just a servant to him!* Instead he nodded, drawing himself up, trying to imitate the unruffled politeness of an officer addressing an inferior. 'We hope he will be set free soon.' He turned his head away, for he thought that Tom was weeping.

He tried to adopt the distant smile every time Tom spoke to him. *Do not come too near*, he wanted to say. There was no space around him. Wheeler had taken it all.

Five nights later, Tom had thankfully gone on patrol and left him to lie in the dugout. Wheeler was on sentry duty, painfully impossible to get to, since Tom was a dedicated patroller and had taken Cook with him for training. Instead, Michael got into bed, keen to devote himself to summoning every moment of their night together. He dwelled on Wheeler's body, the feel of his thigh, the gentle touch – then the hard touch – of his hands. It split him again, the act of memory, for although on one hand he was revelling in the detail, thrilling in it, on the other, he was accepting that there were some things he had forgotten, that however hard he had tried to paint them in his mind, some were already filtering away.

He was remembering the aftermath of their first session together, Stuart's sweet breathlessness, when there was a kerfuffle outside. 'Sir!' someone was shouting. 'Sir.' He buried his head in his pillow. There was a banging at the door of the dugout.

He hauled himself up – dressed, fortunately – and pulled on his boots. When he dragged open the door, Tom was standing there, holding Wheeler by the arm. Bilks and the other men were gathering around.

'What's happened?' asked Michael, dazed by the sight of Wheeler, his face dirtied, his body slumped. He wanted to prise Tom's hands off him, jealously.

Tom was panting, angry. 'He was—' he began.

'It's not true!' shouted Wheeler. 'He's lying.'

'Keep it down,' snapped Bilks. 'Some people are trying to sleep. Explain, please, Cotton. Why isn't Wheeler out on lookout? And where's Cook?'

'Cook's taken Wheeler's place.'

Bilks raised an eyebrow. 'Well that was a damn stupid idea.' Cook had the worst eyesight of any of them.

Tom pushed forward. 'No choice. I found Wheeler here slumped on the sentry post, sleeping.'

'It's not true!' shouted Wheeler, pulling his arm from Tom's grasp. 'He's lying.'

'I told you to keep it *down*,' Bilks shouted. 'Do you want the Krauts to join in?'

'Sir, he was fast asleep. Not even asleep standing. Sitting.'

'He's lying!'

278

'Why would he lie, Wheeler?' Michael knew that Bilks lived in a world of clarity, operated in black and white.

'He just doesn't like me, that's why, sir.'

'Cook was there,' said Bilks. 'I'll ask him.'

'Cook can't see a thing. You said that yourself, Sergeant.'

Bilks threw up his hands. He turned to Michael. 'You're very quiet, sir.'

'I'm listening.'

'Well, what are we going to do with them? He's right, Cook is no help either way.' Bilks beckoned to Pie. 'Could you go and relieve Cook? Send him back here and at least keep us a little safe from the Germans.' He turned back to Michael. 'Sir?' he prompted.

Michael gazed at Tom, part of his childhood, bright-eyed, indignant; and at Wheeler, his face calm, confronting him.

'Come on, sir,' said Bilks. 'You must decide. I can't. And higher up won't want this.'

They were all watching him. He had, he knew, to protect himself, to not show favouritism. And yet he must keep Wheeler safe. If he punished him, word might get back to HQ about sleeping on duty.

Michael put his hand on his gun. 'The wheel,' he said. 'Tied to the wheel, clothed, though no boots.' The wheel was the latest punishment, newly fashionable because of how many French carts they had; a man was spread-eagled over it for a night and a day, and the wheel was turned every hour. Most men were ordered to strip naked, but that, Michael felt, was going too far.

'Yes, the wheel,' said Bilks, impatiently. 'For Wheeler?' There was a giggle behind him.

The giggle decided Michael. He looked into the faces of his lover and his friend.

'No,' he said. 'We cannot tell who is telling the truth. Do it to both of them.'

He turned his face so he did not have to see Tom's eyes, crushed, the light gone from them. *What did you expect me to do? Just punish*

Wheeler? How could that be fair? He looked back, and Tom was still gazing at him, his face uncomprehending.

'Those are your orders, sir?' said Bilks, uncertain.

Michael looked at Tom, wavered, then hardened his heart. 'They are.'

Bilks nodded to Long and Ebbots to take them away. Michael knew that all the men were gazing at him reproachfully. 'We will release them tomorrow,' he said, turning back towards his dugout, blocking his ears to the sounds of coughing and breathlessness as Wheeler and Tom were pushed towards the carts behind the shacks, out on the open scrub.

TWENTY-ONE

Aldershot, March 1916

'Ladies!' the voice shouted. They were in a gym hall in a girls' school in Aldershot, lined up in borrowed uniforms because theirs still had not arrived. 'About turn!'

'I didn't think we'd be doing any walking,' said the girl behind her. 'I thought we were supposed to be driving.' Celia ignored her. She was struggling to keep up with the commands. Turn right, turn left, backwards, forwards, stand and turn. They were one great snake of girls marching around the hall and she dreaded being the part to drop out and spoil the whole. Memories of gym class came flashing back, even though she tried to force them to stay away. She saw herself, twelve again and clumsy, the last to be picked to go into the teams, getting her feet mixed up in the lacrosse classes. 'Forward!' shouted the commandant at the front. Celia felt pricklings of the same shameful thought she had had at school: the hope that someone else would fall over so she would not be the one to fail. She tried to follow the feet of the girl in front exactly, the step of her brand-new boots.

'Pause!' cried the commandant. Her uniform was sharper than any of the rest of them. Celia felt hopeful that it might be time for tea. 'About turn!'

'That's someone who enjoys her power,' said the girl behind her. Her voice was almost as elevated as Miss Ebert's, the headmistress of Winterbourne. Celia looked at her quickly: small, dark-haired, the kind of person her old art teacher Miss Quinn would have called 'elfin'. Not pretty, exactly – although it was hard to be pretty in the uniform – for the girl's nose and chin protruded too much, but her eyes were bright like clean windows. She smiled at Celia before she could look away. 'My name's Shepherd. Yours?'

'No talking over there!' shouted the commandant. 'March!'

Three hours later, they were ushered off to eat at the makeshift canteen. 'No talking on the way!' shouted the commandant. Celia marched with the other girls, trying to keep up again. They lined up in a room full of benches and tables that didn't look like any school dining room Celia had ever seen. She received a plate of stew on a chipped plate and looked uncertainly around the room. Dozens of girls in uniforms, different groups she supposed. She presumed she should sit next to the girl who had been marching in front of her, but she had been so busy staring at her feet that she had no idea what she looked like. She gazed at the spaces on the tables, feeling like the new girl at Winterbourne again.

She felt a hand on her arm. 'There's a space over there,' came the voice of the girl who had been behind her. She gestured at a table to the left. 'Let's take it before anyone else does.' She hurried forward and Celia followed her. They perched on the end of a table of girls who seemed to know each other, talking intently.

The girl held out her hand over their plates. 'Shepherd's the name, as I said. Elizabeth. And you?'

'Emmeline Witt.' So easy to say, yet it felt so wrong in her mouth, just like those nights in front of the mirror in her room. But Miss Shepherd forged on.

'And what brings you here, Miss Witt?'

'I – er – wanted to help. I wanted to do writing things. They asked me at the recruitment station if I could drive. Something about my father being in business.' Celia blushed again. It had been simple enough to fool two middle-aged ladies in pearls. But surely girls her own age would *guess*. The key, surely, was to be as quiet as possible. She had never managed 'speaking until you were spoken to' when she was a child. It was time to start.

'Ah yes, that would be right.' Shepherd spooned up some stew. 'We posh ladies know how to drive, that's what they think here. And of course we wouldn't want such a dirty thing as money. You know, there are more titled girls in here than a debutante ball. Someone needs to tell the War Office that earls' daughters get driven around by chauffeurs.'

Celia leant close. 'But I don't know how to drive. I've only done it once, with my brother. My – er – younger brother.'

'Hmm. Well, I'm sure you'll be fine. I doubt half the girls in here have ever got behind a wheel. There are probably a million factory girls who can drive better than us.'

Celia looked around nervously. It seemed a rather daring thing to say. 'I thought I might be writing things. Or maybe even chopping for cooking.'

'A cook? You? An English rose with a boarding school accent?' Shepherd smiled. 'Anyway, whose daughter are you? The Marquis of Bath?'

Celia knew she should have said, *Actually my father is German.* She blushed, didn't. 'My father is just a businessman. He – er – imports things.'

'Mine's in business too. See, we have that in common. Number one, we are both over twenty-one and not married. Number two, our fathers work in *trade*. Most of the girls here have landed money, I'll bet. Mine makes rivets for ships. He says he's never been so busy since the war began.'

Celia blushed again, knowing she should talk about the meat factories. 'We live in Hampshire.'

'Quite so. I think half of this room probably lives there, or in Kensington in some huge pile.'

'Why did you volunteer?' asked Celia, wanting to take the lead off her.

Shepherd shrugged. 'Anything is better than being at home. And I like driving. I wouldn't have done anything else. My eldest brother taught the rest of us, mad keen on it he was. We used to drive all over the land of the neighbouring farms.'

'How many brothers do you have?'

'Four. Four brothers and me. I'm the youngest. Two married. They're all in France. I tried to drive after they left, but I only cried. So I decided to come here.' She swallowed some stew. 'Ugh, gristle. I wish we would get to the driving, you know. I'd hardly call this training.'

Celia's heart lurched. Boarding the train at the station after Thompson had left her, she had been hot with excitement: she had done it. She had stolen her sister's birth certificate and she had *done* it. Then, as the green fields turned to the brown of the factories and warehouses outside London, she felt tears splattering down her face. The look on Verena's face when she said she was going, the crumbs of ginger cake on the plate, her mother fallen into the sofa, hair awry.

'Why do things have to change?' she said, out loud in the compartment, and then again because there was no one to hear. 'I am going to help my father,' she said, trying to be calm. Still the tears rolled, until they drew closer to London, when a woman with four noisy children got in next to her and she pretended to have a cold. 'There's no going back now!' she said, and reddened as they stared at her, told them she was practising a play.

'What did you say, Miss Witt?'

Celia blushed. She had spoken out loud. 'Sorry. I meant to say... my brother is in France. And my... friend. Do you think we might go near them?'

'Is that why you're here? Not a chance. There are thousands out there. All underground like moles.'

Celia looked at her plate.

Shepherd squeezed her arm. 'Don't be down. Listen, Miss Witt, I believe in saying what I think. So I shall ask you now – shall we be friends? We could stick together. I could do with a friend and you are just my type.'

Celia blushed with pleasure. 'Of course!'

'I knew the minute I saw you we were going to be friends. I had a friend just like you in school called Claire. I know we are going to do well together. I am an excellent friend, you know. I am always very helpful, I tell good jokes and I'll never laugh at you. Sometimes, though, I get a bit overexcited and can't stop laughing. Claire said it was very annoying.' She nodded. 'What about you? How are you good and bad as a friend? I think it's useful to know, we have so little time.'

'I am a thoughtful friend. But I sometimes think too much. I get stuck with thoughts in my mind.'

'Oh good. You are just like Claire. I try not to think too hard, so I'll help you.'

'I don't think we should call each other miss, if we are friends. What about… Emmy?'

'I think it's surnames only, that's the form. Why don't you call me Shep? That's what they did at school. I'll call you Witt if you do.'

Celia nodded. It would certainly be easier to be called Witt, she thought, remembering the nights by the mirror. 'Come here, Emmeline!' she'd said, and then looked around for her sister.

The bell rang and the girls started stumbling to their feet. 'Lesson time,' said a strong-looking girl next to them. 'Try not to fall asleep after your nice big lunch, new girls.'

That afternoon, they sat in a classroom at desks that were far too small and watched the commandant talk about spanners and mechanics. Then it was another plate of stew, and sleep, before the whole process was repeated. The place confused her, too many feet and people, voices. When she felt tired and cowardly, eager just to lie in bed and never get up, she thought of Tom. He had said she could never make tea, back in those days. She would show him. She would march in the right direction and learn to drive – and be good at it.

In the daytime, she clung tight to Shep, sometimes so much so that she worried the other girl would find her tiresome. She knew, of course, that it was most likely they would be split up and sent to different stations, but she could not help feeling Shep was her talisman: if she followed her and did everything she did, she would not get anything wrong – or at least would be less likely to. Shep looked like a little dark-haired fairy, but it was deceptive: she was confident, knew her way around immediately. Two nights in, she told Celia that she had been secretly preparing for the exams to study history at Oxford. 'Although I don't know how Papa would have let me. He thinks that all the world needs is rivets.' Celia said she had been thinking of going to Cambridge, but her mother had asked her to wait for a few years. 'It's true! We have so much in common,' said Shep, clutching her arm. 'Funny, though, my best friends are usually youngest children, like me. Whereas you are the third of four.'

Celia blushed. 'I often *felt* like the youngest.'

'There it is, then!'

Shep loved telling jokes, awful jokes, Celia had to admit. 'What do you do to help a lemon?'

'I know this one!'

'But I want to tell it. Lemonade!'

'That's the last time I'm listening to it.'

At night, in the dormitory, under the mass of sleep sounds, Celia listened out for Shep's gentle sighs. Then, only then, could she sleep.

In the second week, they devoted themselves to engine fixing. To her surprise, Celia found it astonishingly easy.

'No, you do it like this,' she said to Shep as she stood over her, all of them on the school playing field with practice engines on canvases on the ground. 'Put the screw in here. You know, just as she showed us in the diagram.'

'The screw doesn't go there. That isn't right.'

'Yes it does. See.' Celia pushed it in. She gazed more closely at the engine. 'Shep, what have you done? Look, this engine is *completely* out.' She began pulling off the bolts. 'Everything's in the wrong place. Let me do it.'

'I just don't understand it. How is the picture on the wall the same as this? It doesn't look similar in *any* way.' Celia smiled and began screwing the bolts back the way they were supposed to be.

'What's going on over there?' called the commandant. 'Witt, are you helping Shepherd?'

'No!' Celia screwed on the last bolt and popped her head up. 'Just admiring her work, Commandant.'

When it came to driving, Shep got her own back.

'It's just practice,' she said, over and over. 'After all, Witty, you've only driven once. I did it hundreds of times.'

'It's all right for you.' Shep could do anything: reverse, turn the car around, even take corners just using the brakes. She went fast, well over fifteen miles an hour faster than they were told. 'Stop that!' roared the commandant across the training track. 'Shepherd, stop that immediately!'

But she was blustering, for when it came to the track, Shep was her favourite. 'Oh, I give up on you,' she said to Celia. 'Why don't you go out with Miss Shepherd and let her show you the ropes?'

'Shep, it just does what you want,' said Celia as they twisted around another corner. 'It's not *fair*.'

'Pretend it's a horse.' Almost the same words Michael had used when he'd taught her to drive that afternoon in Stoneythorpe. 'Cars are like horses, you know. You have to show them that you're in charge.'

'But I'm not in charge.' Celia pressed the pedal and the thing sprang forward with such force that Shep fell back against the seat.

'Pretend!'

Celia tugged the gearstick, but it wouldn't go into the right spot. 'I can't!'

'Do you want to go home?'

Celia gave her a quick look, wondering whether she had guessed. As she did so, the car lurched out of line.

'Witt!' screamed the commandant.

Celia stopped the car and waited for the commandant to stalk over. 'Blame the engine,' said Shep.

'I don't know what I'm going to do without you. I wish we could request to be sent to the same station.'

Shep patted her hand. 'I'll write to you. Come on, better jump out and face the music. It's not as if you haven't heard it before.'

*

287

Two weeks later, Celia scraped through the test; she had a good score on the theoretical but barely got through the practical part. 'Only just a pass, Miss Witt.' The commandant sat in the office tapping her pen. 'You really are the slowest and most uncertain driver I have seen for months. Anyone would think you hadn't done it before. And at times you seem very young for twenty-one.'

Celia nodded.

'You are a good mechanic, Miss Witt, that is not in doubt. But there is more to the job than knowing which part goes where. If you were an easily flustered type, I wouldn't send you. But you are calm and they need girls out there. Don't let me down.'

Celia shook her head. 'I won't. I promise.' After all she had done, to then be sent home, not good enough, would be terrible.

The commandant took off her glasses, drummed her fingers on the table. 'Miss Witt,' she sighed, 'I don't doubt you have the enthusiasm.' She fiddled with her glasses. 'You are dismissed.'

Celia stood up, saluted and started towards the door. Then the commandant's voice. 'Miss Witt!' She turned around. 'I have an idea. I feel our best chance of success with you is if you go with girls you know from here. With some it is the opposite. I shall put in a request for you to be transferred with Shepherd if possible, even perhaps the others.' She raised her eyebrows. 'Rest assured, this is not favouritism, Witt. Far from it. Remember what I said. I am counting on you to do your job well.'

'Yes, Commandant,' said Celia, breathlessly, knowing it was wrong of her to feel so happy. She wanted to kiss the commandant on the cheek, hurried out of the room before the urge became too strong.

'We're together!' she hissed to Shep that evening. 'The commandant said we could go together! Mainly because I'm such a bad driver.'

Shep caught her hands and whirled her around the tiny space between the beds. 'You *clever* thing, Witt. I knew that your hopeless gear changes would come in handy.' They spun around again and then fell on to the bed, giggling. Someone from another bed told them to be quiet.

Shep lowered her voice. 'We are friends for *ever* now that we are going to France together. Now I will tell you a secret, if you tell me one back.' She hurtled on, putting her mouth close to Celia's ear. 'I won't tell the other girls, but father is Jewish. I know, I don't look it, do I? I put on a good show, eating the same as you lot. But I don't always feel it as mother isn't really Jewish. I could be Church of England, like you, just as easily. I'll say the prayers – but *you* know. That's the reason I am twenty-one and not married. The suitors don't like it.'

Celia's face was hot. Here was her chance to say *I am German, my father is incarcerated, I am not yet eighteen.*

'Go on. What's your secret?'

'I think I'm in love with a boy who … worked for our family. I thought we were just friends, that we'd be friends for ever. But now I think I would never want to be parted from him if we met again.' And just as she said it, the words were true. That was it. She had read about love – they were always in love in Jane Austen – but she could not grasp what it meant. The emotion they felt in books, so pure and overwhelming, was something she could not feel, because nothing was ever a total feeling to her; there was always something else peering in at the sides. And she still did not exactly feel that. But she wanted to be always with Tom, even if they never went to Paris, and that was surely a type of love, a bit like Captain Wentworth always thinking of Anne.

'So that's why you're not married. I knew there was something! Where's he now? In France too?'

Celia nodded. Her mind was flurrying with strange ideas. Did she have to marry him? Have babies with him? None of that seemed so terrible as having to *tell* him. Would she have to do that? Surely so. He couldn't be on the front line with all the other soldiers and not know. She wished she could sit down and turn herself into a list – what she felt, what she desired, written in a notebook with ruled lines. But instead she was a jumble of thoughts, scribbled all over the page. If she saw him, maybe they would become clear, she thought.

Shep laughed. 'He'd be proud of you. You never know, we *might* see him out there. Better keep up with washing your hair just in case, Miss Witt.'

Celia nodded. Maybe, after the war was over, they wouldn't come back. They would live together in Paris and be best friends and there wouldn't be any babies because she would keep her gown on.

'Will you two stop whispering?' shouted the girl from the other side. 'We have to be up early to leave in the morning. Or have you forgotten?'

They caught the train to Dover with English and Dartington, two stolid girls who had been always together in Aldershot. 'The female Tweedledum and Tweedledee,' Shep called them. None of them really felt like talking, so Shep took out her cards and taught them twenty-one, winning every time. 'I should do this for money,' she said. Celia sat there, still feeling dizzy with her thoughts from the night before. The splash of clarity, the spark of it all shocked her. She loved Tom. And if she loved him, if she felt that way about him, he must surely love her back.

At Dover, a girl called Warterton approached them in the queue. 'I hear I'm in a group with you chaps,' she said to Shep. 'I got the info ahead of time. This is Genevieve Fitzhugh.' She waved her hand at a tall girl with reddish hair and a very wide, pale face. Warterton was big too, but blonde and round-faced, the sort of person, Celia thought sinkingly, always chosen to be head girl. They all shook hands.

On the boat, Warterton alternated between talking, sleeping and eating. 'Don't you ever just sit and stare out of the window?' Shep asked, exasperated.

'Mother says people shouldn't waste their time.'

They were treated to quite a lot of what Mother thought. As they learned, Father had worked for a mining company in Africa and Mother knew a lot about life in dirty climates. There were *lots* of fleas in Nigeria, so Warterton was ready for that. Mother was a great recruiter of men, and so the minute Warterton had turned of age, she had gone to the recruitment bureau. 'Women must do their bit!' she said to them.

'Well, we are! You're preaching to the wrong lot,' said Shep.

Tweedledum and Tweedledee both whispered, one after the other, that they had brothers in France and wanted to help. Warterton said she had delayed her coming-out year so long, and now she was hoping that by coming here she had avoided it altogether. 'I look like a great dancing umbrella in those gowns,' she said. 'Much better in uniform.'

Fitzhugh spent most of the time asleep. 'She's the daughter of an earl,' hissed Warterton. 'She's Genevieve, *Lady* Fitzhugh. Says she would much prefer to be here doing something useful than on the debutante circuit.'

'But this *is* a debutante circuit,' said Shep.

Warterton shook her head. 'Nonsense. Oh look,' she said as the train rattled along. 'Chinamen.' Celia opened her eyes and saw groups of Chinese labourers building huts, three men in khaki overseeing them. She had only ever seen a Chinaman in London; three of them, near a shop in Oxford Street when she had been with Emmeline. These ones were dressed in shirts and trousers, thin shoes, piling up stacks of wood. 'We should be nearly there, then.'

Celia pressed her face close to the window, watching the men.

TWENTY-TWO

Celia drove to the station feeling as if the guns were firing inside her head, sharp stabs over and over. *Don't let me down*, the commandant had said. She could feel the ground shaking under the wheels of her cab. How could the men stand it? She forced the ambulance into gear and manoeuvred it around the corner. She felt a surge of nausea, even though – or perhaps because – she had not eaten anything other than a few bits of chocolate for two days. She was terrified of arriving and collecting her men. She pulled the vehicle into gear and cursed herself. What had she been *thinking*, signing up to do this?

'This way! Come along.' A few hours earlier, the commandant of Station 3, Division 4, Étaples, had opened the door of a large wooden building. 'Look smart. This is where you will sleep, eat, live, spend the few spare minutes when you are not with your ambulances. Your beds will be allocated to you and you can lay out your belongings.' Commandant Robinson must have been about forty-five or so. She looked jolly, Celia thought, like a butcher's wife – round red face, large chest, short legs. But she did not smile, and her voice carried around the room.

Celia and the five other women staggered into the room, exhausted after two long days of travel. A dirty, crowded boat to Boulogne, then twenty miles in the back of an ambulance to Étaples. 'Now you know how it feels for the men you'll be carrying,' said the driver when they complained about being bounced about.

Celia stared at the bare room, six canvas pallets on the floor. She cast a look at Shep, grateful that they were together at least.

'You girls are lucky,' declared Commandant Robinson. 'The other stations send the drivers out the minute they arrive. Fortunately for you, today has been quiet for us and all the mortuary runs have been completed. You will have two hours' break here. At eight p.m. sharp, you will report for duty, wearing your uniform, hands washed. You will be taken out by one of our existing drivers to see the layout of the hospitals. Then at midnight you will go out on your own.'

'On our own?' Warterton spoke first. 'We had thought we would be on probation for a month, learning the ropes.'

The commandant shrugged. 'Those were the good old days. No time for that now. Straight out at midnight.'

'But we have never driven in the dark before!'

'Well, no time like the present. You girls have it easy. At least it's not winter.'

'But what will we eat?' asked Shep.

Commandant Robinson snorted. 'More fool you, Miss Shepherd, for not bringing food with you. You have missed lunch and dinner. Breakfast is tomorrow at eight. If you are delayed while out on patrol and arrive back too late, you'll have to find something else. Most of our girls eat when they can. You would be well advised to ask your families to send food from home. Biscuits.'

Celia was doubtful about Emmeline's ability to send biscuits. And if she did, who would she write as? From one Emmeline to another?

'Your duties have been made clear to you, but I shall reiterate them. You will drive from eight p.m. onwards, bringing injured men back from the front. At six a.m., you have roll call. At eight a.m. breakfast. Then you must ensure that your ambulance is clean and the mechanics and tyres are in perfect order. I shall make an inspection at eleven. You are free for the rest of the day, but you are at our disposal if doctors or sisters require driving, or for funeral duty, and there is also housework to be done. Each time you come in you will write your name on a pencil board, and when the names preceding yours have been crossed out, it is your turn to work. You are responsible for the cleanliness of the canteen and the mess room. I will distribute those tasks. You will be allowed an afternoon off weekly.'

Celia saw Warterton and Shepherd gazing hopelessly at her, their mouths working, unable to say a thing.

'Right, ladies, settle down. Eight p.m., remember. Your beds are thus.' She pointed. 'Warterton, Fitzhugh, English, Dartington, Shepherd and then Witt.' Celia had the bed at the end of the room, which she supposed was a blessing – two walls for herself, even if she was near the door. The commandant gestured towards a pile of sleeping bags and blankets. 'Take your bedding from there.'

Celia waited in line to make up her bed, and then sat down on it. Shepherd looked as if she was about to cry.

'Psst, Witty,' she said. 'Over here.' Celia crept over to her bed. 'I've got some chocolate I kept from my last package.' Shep's mother had sent regular parcels to Aldershot, with perfumed rose petals, cakes from the cook, and chocolate. 'Don't let the other girls see.' She delved into her bag and picked out a dusty-looking bar, cradled it in her hand.

'Thanks, Shep.' Celia seized a piece and gobbled it down. She wasn't normally a great chocolate eater, found it too sweet, but right now she would have eaten anything. She regretted not buying bread from the Frenchwomen who had held it up to them at the windows of the train. 'So we go out driving straight away?'

'Why of course! We are ready, aren't we?'

'*You* are. Don't you remember? I can't drive!'

'Maggie said the food was filthy,' shouted Warterton across the room. Maggie was a school friend of hers who had come out to do the job in January but had been sent home with pneumonia. 'What would they think at home if they could see us now? Covered in mud and no dinner.'

'Do stop talking, old thing,' called Fitzhugh. 'You heard what she said: we need to be up for driving in a few hours.'

Now, heading along the dark road, Celia longed to be back in Aldershot. How could she have thought she was ready? In half an hour or so, she would be carrying dying men. For the last few hours, she had been travelling up and down the routes with a long-term girl, Johnson. She was a friendly sort, short-haired and cheerful, but Celia could hardly bear to ask her anything. She felt that the minute she asked a question, hundreds would come tumbling out and Johnson would not be able to cope with all her desperate pleading. She didn't really want to know about spanners and signs and how not to bump the men too much. What she really wanted to say was *I am afraid. Help me. I made a mistake in coming here.* She knew it was cowardice, but she could not help it. The guns banged in her head, again and again.

As she drove, she tried to recite Johnson's instructions in her mind. She was already exhausted, desperate for sleep, but she would be on duty until at least four or so. Why was it so *dark*? She knew, they'd said enough times in training, that there would be no headlights, only oil sidelights (and not even those if there was a raid on), but she hadn't grasped how black it would be without them.

She changed gear and almost hit the back of the ambulance in front of her. *Oh God.* Johnson had said that the key was to keep moving. 'No point being distracted by the chaps' screams. Just get them to the doctors, fast as you can, and try not to bump them. Things can fall out.'

'What do you mean, things?'

'Well, you know, when they haven't got any skin, they can lose bits of what is underneath.'

Celia felt sick. She had envisaged broken legs, concussion, cuts, black eyes. 'It's not what people at home think of as injured,' said Johnson, as if reading her mind. 'With a black eye, they'll keep them back to fight. No, these are burns where all their skin is off, wounds where there is only a flap of skin and their hand holding in their guts.'

'That's not possible.'

'It's nothing compared to the gas. But don't worry,' the other girl continued. 'You'll soon get used to it. And remember, they are much better off with you in here than hanging about at the station.'

Celia finally summoned up the courage to ask what she wanted to, what she had wanted to ask as soon as she signed up. 'Do you know the names of the men?'

'What, the men in your ambulance? Of course not. Why would you?'

'My brother and friend are in France. I could be driving them and not know it.'

'I wouldn't say so. Out of all the hundreds of thousands of men in France, that would be a coincidence too far, if you ask me. Now look sharp here. At the bottom of this hill, there is a really bad bend. We call it Knife Hill. One girl came off here in the winter and had to go back home for it. Bad for her, terrible for all the chaps who went over with her.'

'That's awful.' Celia thought dizzily of pictures of spanners and driving around the track in Aldershot. She had imagined herself going more or less in straight lines on neat French roads.

'Now watch carefully. Keep going down the hill at this kind of speed. As you approach the bend, drop down into first and go as slowly as you can. Don't start going slowly too early, 'cos then you might stall and the effort you need to start you up again might well send you off too fast. Got it?'

Celia nodded. 'Thank you.' She tried to focus on the practical instructions, not the terrible imaginings in her head of the girl trying to pull it back, then the whole thing overturning as men with no skin screamed.

'Right!' said Johnson, patting her hand. 'You know where you are going. You seem pretty ready to get on with it. Good luck, old thing. It's only a five-mile drive. Not even to Kings Cross from Earls Court, and much less traffic. And remember, if you cry, you can't see the road, so don't.'

After their drive, Johnson had guided her in to park straight at the station and hopped out to her own ambulance. Celia kept the engine going and set off after her towards the railway.

By the train, Celia pulled open the back cloth doors, feeling afraid. There must be thirty or so ambulances lined up, waiting. Four hundred or so men waiting inside the carriages to be piled in, one by one. She glanced at Warterton, who was beside her, but she was looking straight ahead. A few ambulances along was Shepherd, holding tight to the front of her vehicle. The train slid in and the bearers began clambering on, collecting stretchers or escorting men by their arms. 'Gunshot, right knee!' 'Head wound!' 'Shrapnel, left eye!' The orderlies read out the soldiers' tags. There were bangs and bumps, shouted directions from the MOs – and the most terrible cries, more like animals than men. Celia got back into the ambulance and reversed closer to the train. She looked at the gearstick and the pedals. *Please*, she prayed, *please let me not stall on the way out. At least that!*

There was an awful scream. 'Damn and blast you all to hell! Let me die!'

'Now come on, son, we'll soon have you well again. In you go.'

She felt a bump that meant a stretcher-bearer was loading men on to her ambulance. There was a cry and a 'Careful!' Another bump, and the sound of sliding as they pushed in more stretchers. 'Here you go!' Footsteps, which must mean a walking man was being handed aboard. He moaned out a sound that was almost worse than the scream, it was so hopeless. She forced herself not to turn around and try to look through the blinds. The back was all covered off, Johnson had told her, to make sure the men couldn't distract her. Celia supposed that some of them would be shocked that they were being driven by girls who looked younger than them. She kept her eyes forward, praying that the ambulance would do as she asked it, that she'd find the hospital in the darkness, somehow. There were more bumps. The man who wanted to die was groaning now, the same sound over and over. The back doors were closed and she put her hands on the wheel. 'Blast you! Blast you!' screamed the man. Another was coughing, horrible retching sounds. Pneumonia, she supposed.

She felt a jolt as the doors were opened again and another stretcher was pushed on, but then withdrawn. 'It's all right, mate,' the bearer was saying. 'You can hang on a moment. We'll wait till the next ambulance.'

'Please!' called the man. 'Please!'

Celia lifted the canvas curtain despite herself and glanced

behind her. A man on a stretcher, his uniform torn, was being shifted to the side. Instead, she realised, they were bringing over a man from another ambulance. He was screaming. She looked, even though she knew she should not. His shirt just covered the top of a mass of bloody bandages. He had no legs. *Oh God. God help me.* There was a bang as he was lifted in, and a dreadful shriek.

Do the praying when you get back. Johnson's voice in her head. *Out in the field, you don't have time.*

There was a knock on the side door. She opened it to a bearer standing with a tall soldier, his eyes closed. His head was bandaged and his right arm was bound up as well, his sleeve torn. He had no coat. An awful smell of rotting filled the cab. 'Here is your front sitter, driver. In the back, you have five stretchers and three sitters.' He pushed the man into the front seat. 'You new, driver?'

She nodded; no need, she supposed, to ask how he'd guessed. The man in the back moaned again and the other was coughing still.

'Give him a cigarette to get him chatting. Take your mind off things.'

'I don't have one.'

'Oh well. See if you can get him talking. Good for you, ain't it?' He gave the man a nudge. 'Don't take it too hard, love. At least they can shout. It's the ones that can't that you need to pity.'

He slammed the door – and she was on her own. She waited for the girls either side of her to drive off before she carefully turned the ambulance to go out of the gate. 'How many?' said the sergeant holding a board.

'Five stretchers, three sitters. No, four sitters.'

'You sure, driver?'

'Certain.' The smell of rotting was getting worse, she thought. What was wrong with the poor man?

'Hospital Five. Off you go.'

He stepped back and she drove forward into the night. There was a bump as she reached the road, and she heard a moan from the back of the ambulance. *Help me!* she wanted to cry. She dropped her speed, and the dim lights of the ambulance ahead moved away. She leant forward and tried to make out the road in the dark. Without a windscreen (taken out in case of bombs), the whole place loomed up in front of her, the monstrous shapes of trees, the blur of hills. A freezing draught was flapping through the thin canvas roof over the cab.

She wished that Johnson was beside her, solid and matter-of-fact, not like this man. His eyes were still closed. She could see blood running down his cheek. There was an X on his forehead marking that he had had his morphine shot. She couldn't think of a thing to say. To him, she knew, her misery would be nothing. She was uninjured, driving an ambulance, could even go back to England if she couldn't stand it. The guns boomed. She knew, rationally, that they were many miles away. *But they feel so near!*

'What did you say, miss?'

'Nothing, nothing, sorry.' She had mumbled it out, in spite of herself. Then she felt worse. Perhaps he was desperate to hear her say something.

'My name is Witt,' she said, full of feelings of treachery towards her father. 'Celia Witt. I'm from London.' She didn't have to be Emmeline for him.

He did not reply. A man cried out from the back. 'Mam!' he wailed. 'Mam!'

'Shut that!' shouted another.

Celia gathered her courage. 'Where are you from?' In front of her, the lights of the other ambulance looked like they were wavering in the darkness. That, she thought, must be terrible. What if the lights went when you were driving and you couldn't see at all?

'Birmingham.'

'Oh.' She had never been there. They were heading up the hill now, rumbling slowly. She turned the corner and the man in the back groaned. 'Is it nice there?' She was suddenly desperate for him to talk. She wanted him to tell her about Birmingham or his childhood or his sweetheart or anything. Anything so that she did not have to listen to the thrum of the engine, which couldn't drown the coughing and the moans. 'Mam! Mam!' the man in the back was crying. 'Make it stop!'

Celia kept on through the darkness, forcing herself to stay calm. As Johnson had explained, there were no signposts to the station or the hospitals. She could only go by landmarks. Hospital 5 was up a hilly road past four oak trees, number 6 after a double bend in the road. 'Whatever you do, don't miss the turning,' said Johnson. 'You can't double back; you have to find a road to turn around in and then you run the risk of colliding with another ambulance. It's easy to spot the turnings now, but not when it's raining, you know?'

'It's terrible out there, miss,' the sitter said, suddenly. 'You can't imagine.' He leant his head on the window. He knocked against it as she changed gear, but he did not flinch.

'Is it cold?' she said. He did not answer. She glanced at him. His eyes were closed. *Oh God. Please let him not be dead. Let him just be sleeping.* Surely he was not dead, she told herself. Surely someone well enough to sit up front was not going to die just like that? She had never seen a dead body before. Should she pray for him? *Oh God,* she thought, *just keep going.*

The man in the back was still coughing. It was getting worse now, as he whooped and hiccupped between coughs, gasping for breath. How long could he carry on like this? she wondered. Why had they not given him something to help?

The man who had been shouting for his mother was weeping now, huge, shuddering, pleading sobs. 'Mam!' he said.

'Shut up, you blasted bloody fool. Shut it!' That, she felt sure, was one of the sitters. There was a bump. *No!* she thought. *Has he* hit *him? Oh God.*

Another one cried out now. Then another.

'You shut up too! Can't you wait?'

Celia drove carefully around the corner. What if they began to fight? *Just keep going,* she repeated, but still. Those men on stretchers couldn't defend themselves.

'Mam! Mam!'

And then came the most terrible sound, an awful strangulated, breathless gobble. It sounded like fluid and a mouth full of foam. She knew immediately: it was the man with no legs. The orderly's voice resounded in her head. *It's the ones that can't shout that you need to pity.* She changed gear as they took the hill. Anger surged through her heart. 'Why do they not give them something for the pain?'

The sitter did not reply. Perhaps he really was dead. *Keep going.*

'Shut up, you devil.' There was another thump. And a scream.

She could feel a tear pricking at her eye. *No*, she told herself. *No!*

The man did not stop screaming. Then another joined in. And another. Three different types of noise: long, awful wails, a sharp, repeated scream, a low growl. The sitter was shouting at them, but they would not stop. *Stay on the road*, she told herself. But what could they do? Could they break out, come and attack her? It was impossible to square this vanload of men with those she had seen at Waterloo station, smart in their uniforms, singing and waving, shouting jauntily at passing women: *We'll be back soon, girls! Don't forget us!* These men in the back were another breed altogether, like animals. *And one had no legs, gobbled rather than screamed.* She cursed herself for her naivety. She had thought that men being taken to hospital would be grateful, quiet. She thought of her own teddies' hospital, set up in her bedroom, silent bears waiting appreciatively for her ministrations. *Not this*, she thought. *Not this.* They screamed and screamed and all she wanted to do was join in. There was another thump. 'Shut it, you bastards!'

Celia looked ahead and realised that the girl in front must have turned off, for her lights were no longer there. Without her, she could hardly make out the road. She did not think she could see any of the landmarks that Johnson had pointed out. How was she supposed to see a tree in this? *Oh God.* Johnson had told her to make sure she didn't miss the turning. But what if she had done an even worse thing? What if she was completely lost? These roads could be going anywhere. Her heart was banging, her face on fire. *I can't bear it!*

There was another scream, and the sitter swore again. He sounded as if he was punching the wall.

It struck her that a hearty type of girl like Warterton might have turned back and shouted something half jokey like 'Now stop that, boys! What's a girl to do in all this din?' The commandant would have threatened them with goodness knows what. Even Shepherd would probably have piped up with something. And then they would have heard her pretty voice and stopped, probably asked her to say something else, just for the sake of hearing a girl speak. So why couldn't Celia? Because whenever she opened her mouth, she wanted to cry for help.

She tried to speak, but the only thing she could say was '"Now, fair Hippolyta, our nuptial hour/Draws on apace; four happy days bring in..."'

She paused. The men were still groaning. *Come on*, she told herself. *Keep going*. Surely she hadn't missed the oak trees; how could she? She must have missed them. She recognised nothing on this road. The legless man gobbled. She wanted to drop her head and cry. Instead, she would continue and find a place to turn round. Why was there no other ambulance?

'Go on, love,' came a voice she didn't recognise. 'Keep going with the story.'

'"Do you amend it then. It lies in you. Why should Titania cross her Oberon?"'

The men must be able to sense the fear in her voice, because they were moaning more loudly. She eased off the accelerator, peering out. The ambulance tipped over a stone, and she heard the pneumonia man groan. Still no response from the man next to her. She crept forward on the dark road, feeling herself in the greatest pit of despair she had ever experienced. Surely every minute counted for these poor men, and she was hopelessly lost in the middle of France. Johnson had given her excellent instructions and she had failed to carry out even the simplest. How she detested herself!

There was another groan from the back. 'Tell us the story, gal,' called the man who had spoken before. 'Just tell us.'

'"Out of this wood do not desire to go. Thou shalt remain here whether thou wilt or no."'

And then – she turned a corner and almost slammed on the

brakes in shock. The four oak trees. There they were, ahead of her. This was surely the turning Johnson had told her about. Her heart leapt. '"Away with us to Athens; three and three. We'll hold a feast in great solemnity!"'

She swung the ambulance up the drive. The men in the back groaned at the speed but she hardly heard. 'We are nearly there!' she called out gaily. She could see the hospital ahead of her. The flaps of the canvas marquee were open, and nurses – oh God, nurses – were standing waiting for her. *Hi!* she wanted to shout. *Hi there!*

She brought the ambulance to a stop. Behind her the men were crying, great lolloping sobs. 'Mother!' called out a different voice. Celia heard the doors being opened and the voices of the orderlies taking out the stretchers.

An orderly opened the passenger door and leant in to help the man next to her. 'I think he's dead,' she said.

'Feels warm enough to me.' He fingered the man's neck. 'No, beating away. Must have just dropped off.'

Johnson had told her not to leave her cab: 'The faster you can turn around, the quicker you'll have your next load of men. Anyway, you don't want to see.' But she couldn't help it. She hopped down and watched the orderly taking out the stretchers. The man with no legs had been taken off first and the sitters had gone, so there was only the one still coughing and two men waiting quietly. They were surely the same ones who had been screaming, but now they were silent, only flinching when they were touched. Neither was much older than her, she thought.

One looked up at her. 'You were the girl reciting?' he said. She nodded. 'That was nice.'

'You've delivered us a good lot of chaps, driver,' said a nurse. 'Should keep us busy.' Her wide white hat flapped in the dark.

'They are quieter for you than they were for me.'

'I should think so. You should tell them to stop if they call out.'

'Will they live?'

'We do our best, driver. Like you.'

'And then they go back home?'

'Home? No. Not if they can still walk. Back out again.'

Celia looked at her, hopelessly. 'But they can't. How can they? How can any of them be fit for duty?'

'A lot of them want to go back. Careful there.' An orderly was pulling out the coughing soldier. His uniform was covered with yellowy-green stuff.

'He has pneumonia?'

The nurse tossed her head. 'He should be so lucky. Gas. Shrivels the lungs.' The man screamed out. 'Come along, soldier, none of that. We'll soon get you comfortable.' She turned and spoke over her shoulder. 'Go on, driver, off you trot.'

Celia stared into the back of her ambulance. Even in the dark, she could see that it was spattered in blood and grime; whatever the soldier had been coughing up; gobbets of flesh, too, probably from the man without legs. The stench of blood and urine was overpowering.

'Who cleans this up?' she asked a passing orderly.

'Why you, miss. As far as I know. Mind you, I don't think you do it until you have finished all your convoys.'

Celia gazed at the filth. She could not quite say what had shocked her more – that she had to clean it, or that she would have to fill it with men again when it was still covered in blood. The commandant had said they would have to clean the ambulances. But Celia had thought it would be polishing the outside – not this.

'Driver!' It was the nurse she had spoken to before. 'Don't dawdle! Off you go.'

Celia climbed into the cab and turned the ambulance around. On the way there, struggling with her load, she had imagined how joyously she would drive back, speeding along the roads, zipping down the hills. But although she drove quickly, there was no happiness in her heart. In an hour or so she would be back on the same road, her vehicle filled with screaming, terrified lumps of human flesh.

'I cannot do it,' she said to Shepherd, who was standing by her ambulance at the railway. 'I can't do it. Really.'

Shepherd turned to her, eyes ablaze. 'I don't think I can do it either. But you have to! You have to.'

Tears were running down Celia's face. 'I thought the one next to me was dead. The man in the back had no legs. I can't!'

Another girl looked across. 'Stop it!' hissed Shepherd. 'You'll have the commandant over. Just stop it!' But Celia couldn't. The tears were pouring down her face and her mouth was making sounds she didn't recognise. The coughing, the gas, the screams, the man with no legs. *I see these things with parted eye, When everything seems double. Help me!* She felt a crash that knocked her off balance and fell to the damp earth. Shepherd was beside her. 'I am sorry, Witt,' she said. 'I really am. But you can't cry like that. You have to go on.' She held Celia tight and Celia wept on to her shirt. 'Come on, girl,' she said, rocking her. 'We are the lucky ones. We get to stay alive.'

TWENTY-THREE

'Come on, Witt, stop daydreaming!' Shepherd slopped water at the back of her legs as she walked past. 'Commandant will shoot you if she finds you idling.' She broke into an exaggerated accent, imitating Commandant Robinson. 'If you find you don't have enough to do, Witt, then you can clean out my ambulance as well, thank you very much. Witty! Are you listening to me?' A sponge landed on Celia's head. 'Get cleaning!'

Celia threw the sponge back. 'Not with this grimy thing!' After that first night, when Shep had held her close then forced her to collect more men and set off again to the hospital, she had felt almost bound to her for ever. Sometimes she wondered if she was being faithless to Tom with Shep. She tried to imagine the three of them in Paris together, all reading books. Surely Tom wouldn't mind.

Ten o'clock every morning was ambulance cleaning. Polishing the outside, cleaning the engine was the easy part. A bit of oil was nothing to the awful blood and vomit of human misery.

She opened the back doors of her ambulance and wanted to retch. Last night she had carried cases of gangrene, and the smell was shocking, as if it had got much worse overnight. Overwhelmed with misery, she set off for her bucket of water. All over France, women like her were scrubbing, she reminded herself. One VAD whom she'd met at Hospital 7 on her third night had declared Celia lucky to be helping with the patients. 'Usually all I do is wash dishes,' she said. 'I never knew there were so many dishes in the world.'

Celia scrubbed at the bloody lumps and washed out the horrible foam. Another boy with gas. This one she was sure was no longer alive when she handed him over. She should feel lucky, she reminded herself. She slopped out the interior with disinfectant and then another bucket of water. The soiled water dripped on to the ground. She felt ill again at the sight of it.

It was her second month with the ambulances, and already Celia felt as if she was running through a routine. After that first, dreadful night, she had grown used to the work, quicker than she could ever have imagined. She had become accustomed to feeling wearied beyond measure, never undressing for bed because she had to be ready to leap out of her sleeping bag at any moment, almost falling asleep with exhaustion beside the ambulance, waiting for the next load of men. Johnson had adopted her as a sort of pet, would wave across to her when she saw her, crying 'Keep it up, Witty!'

She had come to recognise the stretcher-bearers and a few of the nurses at the hospitals. Driving through the night was still hateful, the men often terrifying, but there was nothing to beat the feeling of relief when she reached the hospital and saw the nurses and orderlies waiting there for her load. She found other sources of joy too: a sitter who was eager to talk about growing up on a farm in Wales (Shepherd had given her a few cigarettes to pass out), a man in the back who shouted 'Thank you, miss! God bless you, miss!' as she navigated a pothole. Another man shouting as he got in: 'Thank our stars we have a girl driver, chaps. They're always more gentle on the bumps.' To her shame, the sense of horror she had felt on the first night was fading as she grew used to seeing injured men. She often had to remind herself what a healthy soldier might look like.

She had even come to find a pleasure in driving itself – it was so pleasingly predictable. She knew she would never be a good driver like Shep, who sped ahead of her on the roads, weaving in and out, dodging potholes. But she was passable, as good as Tweedledum and Tweedledee, and that was enough. 'You are turning into a reasonably competent driver, Witt,' said the commandant in her second week, while she was inspecting her cleaning. 'I had my doubts about you. But I get good reports from the hospitals. They say the men rather take to you.' She patted the bonnet. 'Yes. Quite a good little driver.'

I won't! Celia cried to herself. *I won't be a good little driver! Not surrounded by all this blood and misery.* Yet she found herself becoming one, chatting with the soldiers. And she began to feel proud of herself for doing such work, and thought that even Verena would think so too – though she would never tell her mother about the cleaning, scrubbing lumps of flesh from the floor, picking up teeth and what were surely bits of bone. Celia smiled sometimes to think of how her fellow drivers were exactly those Verena had wished her to be friends with, wealthy, influential London girls – and Fitzhugh the daughter of an earl! Verena had thought she would meet this type of girl by curtseying to the Queen, then going to balls, not wading about in rubber boots, knee deep in filth, slopping out an ambulance full of grime.

And Tom, surely Tom would be proud of her, she thought, cherish and admire her for what she had done, say, *Well, I never thought you could do that!* She imagined him watching her work. *Look at me now*, she would say.

She tried to stop herself from wondering constantly where he and Michael were. She wrote them both a letter every night in her head, telling Michael what she was doing, listing the places she drove and the food she ate. To Tom she told her feelings: how each morning she was torn between pride in herself and hatred at being part of this great, awful thing. She described how the dorm room was freezing even in May and there was never enough food, how English – Tweedledee – was the most popular girl in the station because her mother sent her huge parcels of chocolate and she would go around offering her great brown package, a little like the lucky dip at the party. She told him how she dreaded the smell of the men, how she could never get her ambulance as clean as Shep's, however much she polished. She described cranking the engine, a job she liked, how she did it for the other girls when the Commandant wasn't looking. She told him everything – except for how much she was thinking about him, how when she was driving her empty ambulance to the station, she shouted out his name, so that only the trees could hear.

She had written twice to Tom care of his mother, although she didn't expect her to send the envelopes on. She had sent six letters, one a week, to Michael and received two replies – short, a lot about mud. She'd had one from Emmeline, with a drawing of herself sitting on the Bloomsbury sofa done by Mr Janus. She had to admit she found it touching, in spite of herself.

Miss Webb had written three long letters about how dull nursing was and how she envied Celia in France, and Celia had sent back platitudes because she could not bear to write the truth. Nothing from Verena, though one letter from Jennie (*not much news from here, miss, house a bit draughty but we can't stop up every gap*), and no word about Rudolf. Still, out of all the girls, only Warterton had a steady stream of letters, two a week from her mother, her sisters and her brothers, every one finished with a flourish and *Rule Britannia*. Shep thought her own mother was probably too busy writing to her brothers; Fitz said her family (she never said Papa or Mama, Celia noted) wouldn't want to know about war things.

Shep was keeping a little diary – to look back on when she was a student, she said. Celia tried to do the same but found it pained her, for it only made her go into her own thoughts: how Verena was alone, Tom and Michael somewhere she did not know, and she hadn't heard from Arthur for ages. *Some writer you are*, she said to herself, promising that she would do it after the war. Then, she thought, she would be jolly, laughing off the bad food and the rain, not tired and nervous, brought low by always feeling wet and chilly, sick of the dirt and the suffering of the men. Brave, not weak and easily cowed as she often felt now. *I have such fun with the other girls*, she told Tom in her head. *We are pleased to do our bit. The more we do, the quicker the war will end.* She said the same to the other drivers, to the commandant if she asked. And yet, you might also say (Mr Sparks, for example, might say) that she was just taking men to be patched up and sent out again, probably to be killed, and how was that really bringing Rudolf back?

Celia looked up and caught Shepherd's eye. 'No slacking,' she mouthed.

In their spare time, the two of them tried to talk about books. Shep loved history – particularly the Wars of the Roses – and Celia chastised herself for not listening more carefully to Mr Janus talk about Edward IV. And Shep told jokes; even after nearly three months, she still thought of new ones. 'Stop it, Shepherd,' groaned Fitzhugh as they were all about to sleep and Shep's slight voice came from the dark: 'What did the tiger say to the lion?'

But then, Celia thought, how could she really say she was friends with Shep? She had not told her the truth, pretending she was twenty-one, the third child of four, that her father was English. Shep had told her everything, while Celia was nothing but a fraud.

Celia walked to the front of the ambulance to start the engine, before checking the tyres and then beginning the tedious job of polishing the exterior so that it was perfect for eleven a.m. On the stroke of the hour, she stood in front of her vehicle and looked smartly ahead as the commandant crawled into the back of Warterton's ambulance to begin her inspection. Celia estimated that she would get around to her in about half an hour. She had a stock of images of Tom for just these moments, conjured up to stop herself thinking about bombs and guns: playing cards in the trenches, running races and eating Christmas dinner (she'd read the cooks brought in special beef for the day). This time she pictured him playing cards. 'King of clubs,' he said, putting it down. 'I win.'

Celia smiled at the commandant as she arrived, followed her around the ambulance.

'Not bad, Witt,' said Robinson, brushing off her hands. 'Those tyres will need pumping up soon, and you can douse out the back with disinfectant again. Tomorrow it will need to be perfect, otherwise I will have to impose a punishment.'

'Yes, ma'am.'

Instead of turning away, she remained. 'Witt. I am wondering. Your full name is de Witt, I believe?'

Celia felt a thudding panic across her chest. 'Yes, Commandant.'

'A German name?'

'Yes, Commandant, though of Dutch origin. But my mother is English.' *Oh God.*

The other girls were staring over now. Warterton was the most obviously curious, smiling at Celia and trying to catch her eye.

'Can you speak German, Witt?'

'I learnt at school,' Celia lied. She thought of her aunt Lotte teaching her the words at her kitchen table in the Black Forest. Heinrich asking her endless questions about her family and the servants in German. Hilde and Johann running around the fields, dipping their hands in the river for fish. Johann. She thought of him then and her heart was struck hard. Seventeen, now, too young to go to war. Unless he had done as Tom and Michael had and run away anyway.

'Indeed. And what sort of standard would you say you were?'

Celia could not answer. If she were to say *Good*, then she would lose everything. This was surely a trap. She stared at the commandant. Robinson looked around at the other girls and took Celia to one side.

'Let me be plain with you, Witt. We are looking for a girl with a reasonable standard of German. We have a German man brought to us in error through a mix-up at the clearing station. We need to ask him questions. Do you think you are up to it?'

Celia could have hugged her in relief. 'Yes, of course, Commandant.'

'Good. I will meet you by your ambulance today at two and you will drive us over.'

Celia returned to her vehicle and gripped the bonnet. As the commandant walked away, she stopped and turned. 'And Witt? Don't mention it to anyone, if you please. You can tell them you are driving me to a meeting at Hospital One.'

*

'If only Mother knew!' said Shepherd crossly, spooning up her stew in the canteen. 'Sometimes, when I am driving along in the middle of the night with a cart full of bloody, swearing men, I think: did you imagine it was like this, Mother? And did you have any idea we'd have to clean up blood? Or sit in cabs polluted with measles? Our brave girls indeed!' The canteen was at its fullest. Shep had to shout to get her voice heard above the others.

'My mother is probably leading a recruitment drive in Surrey right now,' said Warterton. 'Fitz's too. You're lucky, Witt, that yours is a stay-at-home type.' Celia had told them that Verena liked to knit, was not much interested in the war. Warterton's mother sounded rather terrifying, she thought. She imagined a rather larger version of Warterton holding huge meetings in halls in Cheam, calling out for young people to do their bit.

'Yes, Ma talks a lot about "my girl out in France",' Shep sighed.

'I imagine they eat buns at the recruitment meetings. Not this morass,' said Fitzhugh, gesturing at the stew. It was always a competition to see if you could find any meat under the blobs of vegetable and gristle.

'We're lucky, don't you know,' said Shepherd. 'Babb tells me that the girls at Station Two have a real beast of a commandant who makes them clean the lavatories and do all kinds of punishment duties. He says we should count our blessings that we have the Frenchwomen in to do the lav work.' Shep was a favourite with the orderlies like Babb. They loved to make her hang back and chat at the station at the end of her shift.

'I am not cleaning that lavatory!' said Warterton. 'It gets into a real state sometimes.' There was only one between forty or so.

'You'd have to if you were in Station Two.'

'How do they ever get time to sleep?' It was hard enough as it was, what with driving all night, ambulance cleaning, and then being on call all morning for ferrying doctors and nurses between hospitals, mortuary runs with miserable, bloated men, their cause of death written on tags, taking coffins to funerals and general errands. And if you were out at mealtimes, tough luck: the cook served when she pleased.

'Got one!' Shepherd held aloft a blob of meat. 'No, Warts, it's mine. Well, I don't suppose they do. Babb says that if we get offered a spell in Station Two, we shouldn't take it. Said a girl from here was sent off there for a few weeks, never came back.'

'Speaking of the commandant, what did she want with you, Witty?' asked Shepherd. 'She looked like she was telling a secret.'

'Yes, Witty, do tell all,' Warterton piped up. 'Bosom buddies?'

'She wants a ride to Hospital One to meet the director.'

'Oh come on, Witty, that's not all it is. We could see she was asking you something.'

'I said. I have to take her to Hospital One.'

Warterton shook her head. 'You're a sly one, I'll say that. Secret work with the commandant, eh? Put a good word in for us girls, won't you? Tell her we could do with a nice pud or two after dinner. A French one if she wouldn't mind.'

'A chocolate mousse!' said Fitzhugh, snorting with laughter.

'You show your poor breeding with that, Fitz,' said Warterton. 'I thought you were a lady. Mousse is for the working classes. We ladies should eat mousseline.'

'I'd like a chocolate éclair,' said Shepherd.

'I shall pass on the requests,' said Celia. 'French puddings only.'

'I would be so grateful.' Fitzhugh had been at finishing school when the war had been announced, learning about things, Celia supposed, like setting out wines, and fancy pudding recipes to give to the cook. She laughed it off when Warterton teased her about it. 'Just like boarding school, except even more dull.'

'I remember when I used to complain about our cook's queen of puddings,' said Shepherd. 'Look at me now. What I would do for just a spoonful of that now.'

'The food is terrible at the women's colleges, you know, Shep.' Warterton reached for a piece of bread. 'They think those brainy girls can live off books.' Shep had told them all she was hoping to go home to study after the war.

'Ha, ha.'

'True! They come out half the size they went in.' Warterton turned to Fitz and began a conversation about tyre pressure.

Shepherd looked at Celia. 'They're even easier to get into now; fewer people wanting to go. And I am out here.'

'Well, you can go back, you know,' said Celia. 'We can both go. We'll toss a coin for which university. We'll get rooms together and sit up late over cocoa talking about books.'

'If this war ever ends.'

'Hush.' All the girls had an unspoken pact not to mention the end of the war.

Shepherd laid her fork on her plate. 'I don't know if I could go to university, knowing what's happening out here. And what if we are fighting for ever?'

Celia put her hand on her friend's. 'Oh, Shep, you know it won't be long now. They say we are nearly there.'

'They said that even when it started. And now look at us. So many men coming through, every day. And still there are thousands out there. I don't think it will ever stop.' Her voice had risen. Warterton turned around, then went back to her discussion about tyre pressure.

Celia held tight to her friend's hand. 'What's come over you? You don't normally talk like this.' Shep was usually the one keeping everybody else's spirits up, saying that the war would soon be over, telling the jokes that made Fitzhugh groan.

'The orderly at last night's hospital said they are sending them out of the clearing stations faster than ever now; they just don't have the space for men to stay there. So they come here when they are not ready, and they die. Three died on me last night.'

Celia rubbed her hand. 'Poor old Shep. You should have said.'

'I should be used to it now, you know? But I'm not. I'm driving along and I hear another one of the men make the throat rattle that means they're for it, and I think: I can't stand it. Why do I have to see so much death?'

Celia put her arm around her. She didn't care that they weren't supposed to do it, that the commandant would shout at her if she saw. She held her close, feeling the warmth of her flesh through the thin blouse. 'Poor old Shep. I promise it will get better.'

*

'Turn right here,' said the commandant, pointing to a small road coming off the hill.

Celia cranked the wheel. 'Won't that take us past Hospital One?'

'Yes, that's the idea. Keep going.'

'Oh.'

Celia had come to be rather fond of driving in the afternoons. Going to pick up a couple of sisters at the station and taking them to their hospital was an easy job. The sisters would sometimes complain that 'you driving girls' had an easy time of it. The doctor passengers were the most entertaining, making jokes about gals in uniform and smoking out of the windows. Celia would drive them fast over the potholes and bounce them, make them laugh. 'I like a pretty girl who can find her way,' one teased her last time, nudging his friend. Celia thought they didn't look much older than her, could hardly believe they were really doctors. 'Come over to Hospital Four, why don't you, one day?' he added.

'Commandant would send me home.'

'Where next?' she asked Robinson now.

'I will tell you. It's best for you if you don't spend too much time remembering the route. Left here, Witt.'

They turned into another small road and carried on past the great canvas sides of Hospital One. A few men were being walked around the exterior by nurses, holding tight as they stumbled forward, legs in splints, heads covered in bandages. It was at times like this that Celia wanted to be a VAD, taking men for walks and giving them comfort. But then she knew that inside they were scrubbing and cleaning, her ambulance nothing compared to what they had to face. Anyway, she reminded herself, she was too cowardly to even listen to the injured men in the back of her vehicle, let alone wash them and change their dressings every day.

'Park here, Witt. That is it.' They swung in next to a parked car – an expensive one, Celia realised. The two of them clambered down from the cab and the commandant led the way to a building made of corrugated iron. A soldier guarded the door – the first uninjured one Celia had seen in weeks – and saluted the commandant. Another one met them inside.

'Follow me, Commandant Robinson.' They walked behind him along a dark corridor.

'The German ended up muddled up with our boys,' the commandant explained. 'He was thrown into one of our trenches by an explosion. It happens occasionally – things are so busy, the medics don't have time to speak to them, and his uniform was largely torn off in the explosion. He has lost an eye and has bad burns, but he is pretty much patched up now. One of the VADs knows a little German and got the impression from him that he had been in intelligence. So we wanted to ask him more questions.'

They passed through a thick metal door to a room walled in aluminium. Celia almost jumped, for in the middle of it, a man lay on a metal bed about the height of her waist. She realised he was tied there, with bonds over his chest, thighs and knees. He turned his head to look at her and then returned to staring at the ceiling. One eye was entirely covered in a black patch. There were three soldiers with him.

'Good afternoon,' said the commandant briskly. 'This is Miss Witt. She has a high standard of German. She will talk to the prisoner. What is it you want to ask him?'

A grey-haired soldier, the senior of the three, spoke up. He was small and wizened, with a peaked-looking forehead, a little gnome. 'Miss Witt. Take up position by the prisoner. We will ask you questions and you will relay them.' Celia was surprised by his failure to answer the commandant. She supposed he must be very superior, a general or similar.

'Go on, Miss Witt.' The commandant gave her a gentle push. Feeling painfully self-conscious, she walked over to stand by the man. He was very thin, his face craggy and his cheeks sunken. She thought he must be around twenty-one or so. He shut his good eye when she came close. There were red burns across his face and he had a bruise on his eye that looked fresh.

'He has injuries,' said the commandant.

'He suffered an unfortunate fall while he was being moved.'

'He looks in need of a sandwich, General,' the commandant continued.

The general ignored her. 'Now, Miss Witt, you will ask this man his name and age.'

She did so. The man stared at the ceiling and did not speak. She asked once more, trying to make her tone as kind as she could. Still he did not answer.

'Right then. Ask him his regiment and the name of his officer.'

No reply. Celia heard the commandant shift behind her.

'Is your command of the language quite correct, Miss Witt?' demanded the other officer.

Celia nodded. She almost wanted to laugh. She could have asked such questions at the age of seven. Surely there must be one soldier in the army who could speak this level of German? She gazed at the man's hand. It was so riven with scars that it looked like a sort of map. When she was younger, she had been forced by their governess to lie flat on a board in order to develop a straight back. She had found three hours of it painful. To do it for a whole afternoon must be terrible.

'Ask his name and age again.'

Still silence.

'Right then. We have tried to speak to him politely. No more! Tell him that he is from a country of despicable traitors, of people who wish to kill the innocent and will go immediately to hell.'

Celia looked back. The man's eyes were still closed. 'I cannot say that.'

'You will do so, Witt. Otherwise you would be directly contravening my orders.'

'I would thank you to remember that it is my role to discipline my officers,' said the commandant.

'She is under army orders and she must obey. Proceed, Witt.'

Celia opened her mouth but could not speak.

'This is a very dangerous man. If he were not tied to this bed, he would be strangling you. He is evil and full of violence, like a demon. Save your pity for our men at the front, dying in their thousands.'

The man on the bed was edging out his hand.

'You have a brother out here with us in France, do you not? As a driver, you must have seen cases of gas. That's what this man would like your brother to look like. His skin ripped off, his lungs full of fluid, a lump of flesh who would never come home to you.'

Celia thought of some of her gas cases – last night's man who had screamed all the way to Hospital 6. She felt a tear forming in the corner of her eye. She would not wipe it away, otherwise they would know. The man's eye opened and he looked at her.

She bowed her head and began the speech. The man closed his eyes again. She saw him clench his fist. She got as far as 'kill the innocent' and then she could not go on. She spoke fast. 'I do not want to say this. They are making me. What have you done to make them like this?' She managed to get to the end of it.

One eyelid flickered. 'You are a prisoner too, then, miss?' His voice was broken and throaty, as if his windpipe had been snapped.

'What did he say?' demanded the general.

'He said he ... does not want to talk.'

'Continue. Ask him once more about his regiment.'

There was still silence.

'You will call him a dirty bloodstained bastard and ask him about his regiment.'

'My officer will not use such words,' said the commandant, quickly. 'You asked for an ambulance driver, General, not a girl from the gutter.'

'She will do as I tell her.'

'General, Miss Witt takes orders from me. And my girls – Miss Witt included – do not have time to waste.'

The general said something sarcastic about women's participation in the war. The commandant replied angrily that they were not knitting in the depot, if that was what he thought. Celia stared at the prisoner. Then he opened his eyes and spoke to her. 'Come closer,' he said quietly.

The commandant and the general were still arguing. Celia bent down a little. 'More,' he said. 'I will talk to you if you come near.' He was whispering now, a cracked whisper that made Celia feel slightly afraid. She dipped her head. 'Tell them this,' he said. 'Tell them that I might speak to you. I might tell you something. But only if they go. All of them. Even that woman who came in with you.'

They were all watching her now. 'What did he say?' demanded the officer.

She took a deep breath and tried to look past him. 'He said that if you all go, then he will speak to me.'

'That is impossible. Tell him so.'

She shrugged. 'Chief up there says no.'

'Well they don't get any words then,' he whispered. She thought he might have winked, if he'd had both eyes.

She looked at the grey-haired officer. 'He won't speak unless you all go. Sir.' She had a sudden flash of inspiration. He surely only had the power to ask the commandant to punish her for insubordination and Miss Robinson was hardly on his side. She continued. 'And if you do not, I cannot see much point in my staying here.'

The officer raised an eyebrow. 'Commandant, is this the way you have trained your girls? To question their orders?'

'Witt takes orders from me. I have ordered her to listen and translate, which is what she is doing.'

The soldier beside the grey-haired one nudged him. 'Sir. Perhaps there is some merit in the suggestion.'

'Leave this girl with him? Who knows what he will say to her? He is a devil, Jenkins. God knows what he will do.'

'Well, he can't get free, sir. And she seems a strong enough kind of girl.'

'My girls *are* strong!' said the commandant, losing patience. 'Now, General, Miss Witt and I have been here long enough. She cannot keep asking the same question all afternoon. She and her fellow ambulance drivers are here to help the sick. This army matter is something that appears to me to be quite out of our remit. I am sure that my senior officer would agree.'

The general thought. He cocked his head at the two soldiers beside him. 'Tie up his hands and feet. Check the rest of the bindings.'

The men came forward and did his bidding. Celia stepped back and looked away as they pulled the man's hands down and tied them.

'Now you really can't get out,' said the general with satisfaction. 'Right, Miss Witt, you have twenty minutes. No more. Scream if you need us.'

They filed past her out of the room. Jenkins stopped at the door. 'Commandant,' he said. 'You too.'

'The prisoner did not mean me as well. I stay with Miss Witt.'

The man spoke up from the table. 'She must go too. All of them.'

Celia turned to her. 'He says you too. Everyone.'

The commandant looked pained. 'I cannot leave my driver,' she said to the general.

'It is too late now,' he snapped back. 'You instigated this and you must come too. Perhaps this will teach you not to interfere.'

She hesitated, and then moved around the door. It slammed behind them. The sound echoed off the tinny walls. Celia and the man were alone.

She was still back against the wall, where she had moved for them to tie him. He turned his head a little. 'So. You speak German. Forgive me, but you are German?'

'My father.' She did not move forward. The general's voice was in her head. *A demon!*

'From where?'

'The Black Forest.'

'Have you been there?'

'I've visited my cousins, Hilde and Johann.' They danced through her mind. *Last one to the river is out!* shouted Hilde. Celia wished she could keep them there, running around, held in a snow globe, never going out.

'Yet you serve on the side of these men here?' The bonds on his hand were dark leather, shiny with polish.

'I'm English. My mother is English, I was born in London.' He gave a cracked laugh. 'Anyway, I'm not *serving* like a man. We are like nurses, helping people.'

'So that is the distinction you draw. How old are you?'

'Twenty-one.'

'Really? You look like a schoolgirl.'

'Everybody says that,' she said, more stoutly than she felt.

'You know, Miss Witt – it is Witt?'

'It is de Witt, actually. I changed my name before joining. They thought it better.'

He gave a short laugh. 'Of course. Now, Miss Witt, why stand so far away from me? You do not pay attention to our dear general, surely? The man who calls me a demon.'

Celia stepped forward and then stopped. 'How do you know that is what he said? You understand him?'

'Of course. He speaks English like a peasant, so it is easy enough.'

'Well, why don't you say?'

'I choose not to. Now come closer.' She took another step. 'And again,' he said. She moved nearer. 'Let me introduce myself. I am Tibor Schmidt. I am from Berlin.'

Close up, his eye was veined and bloodshot. 'Did you really fall?' she asked.

'No, of course not. But I wish to talk of you.'

'Why do you not tell them you can understand English? Surely it would make things easier for you.'

'Miss de Witt, you do not understand much. No doubt they have told you that they need you to translate. But there are intelligence officers who can speak German. They asked for you because they thought a young German girl might soften me up. I have seen one female intelligence officer, but she was more like your commandant than you. You are a pretty girl.'

Celia just stood there. She meant to say something but could not.

'I can see I upset you speaking thus, miss. The virgin sacrificed to the Minotaur. Tell me of yourself.'

Celia wanted to rush from the room, but she imagined the general saying *I told you so. She is too weak.* She steeled herself to look into his bloodshot eye.

'Tell me of your cousins. Hilde and Johann, you said. Have they gone to fight now?' The man was fidgeting and shifting around, pulling at his hands.

'You are very uncomfortable there?'

He nodded. 'Tell me about Johann.'

'I do not know. He was seventeen in January.'

'I should think he is fighting. Some of the boys are fourteen. They look it on your side too. I take it you do not hear from your cousins.' He shifted his hands again, moved his back around.

'We stopped writing to them. Father said we should stop until the war was over.'

'So Johann might die and you would never know.'

She bowed her head. 'That's true.'

'What is your father afraid of?' He was brushing his tied hands over the leg of the metal bed.

'They have taken him away, somewhere on the coast. He is treated kindly; it is practically a holiday camp where he is – that's what they say in the newspapers. They thought he was a spy.'

'I expect they did.' He shifted again. 'Lucky that you are out here. No risk of the same thing happening to you.'

'That's not why I came! I wanted to help!'

'By dragging half-dead men around?'

He was moving so much now that she worried he was going to overturn the whole bed. 'I wish I could help you there. It must itch terribly.'

'It does. Come a little closer.' She stepped forward, and Tibor whispered, 'They have tied me so very tight. Perhaps you could free my arms slightly.'

She gazed at him. If she loosened the bindings just a little, he would still be tied and unable to get away, but they would not chafe. But then surely that was against the rules? 'I don't think I should. We will ask them when they return.'

He was shaking his right leg now. She supposed his legs, too, were in terrible pain.

'Why don't they let you stand up?'

'I imagine they think I am dangerous. They keep me like this day and night. But our side probably do the same for your men.

So. We continue. Is your father not afraid that the rest of you will be taken in?'

'My father registered as an alien, that's how they found him. But it is true that the Germans are hated. Some German shops have been attacked.'

'After the *Lusitania*?'

'Yes. Before that too. But surely, Mr Schmidt, I should ask you about yourself. I think they want to know your regiment.'

He broke into a hacking cough. It sounded like a gas cough to Celia, hard and violent. 'They have to do something about that,' she said.

'I will tell them that you said I need a cure. I should probably speak a little louder now, better for the voice.'

'You *should* take a cure! Anyway, I must ask you about your regiment.'

'What shall I tell you, Miss de Witt? One story: I was an innocent soldier who was bombed so hard that I was sent flying into an English trench and from there swept off to the clearing station. Without uniform, too shocked to speak, I was lost. I am here but I am only a lowly soldier and I know nothing of the plans. I march, I walk, I fire, I return. That is all. There is no use detaining me and they should send me to hack firewood with all the other prisoners of war.' He was shifting back and forth, clearly in pain.

'I will tell them that.'

'Or there is the other option: I am an officer who crept into the trench, injured himself, tore off his clothes as a way of getting behind enemy lines. I was accompanied by others. We were sent to work under cover of the confusion, to shoot dead as many men as we could, particularly the officers if we could get them. I had just shot an officer and then a private came around the corner. I fled, and the only way I could hide was by pretending to be a patient. I had a tube of something to take to kill myself, but I lost it and now I must remain here.'

'You would not do that.'

Tibor was wriggling his hands again. 'But how do you know,

Miss Witt? These are both explanations that they have suggested to me. I do not answer. Instead, I shall not eat.'

'Commandant Robinson said you needed a sandwich.'

'She was correct. They have offered me sandwiches. But I will not eat them. So they force me to eat.'

'But how can they force you? They push the food into your mouth?'

'No, indeed, I am too strong for that. Instead they do it as they fed your votes-for-women girls. You know how they did that?'

She shook her head.

'They push a tube up the nose and they send fluids down into the stomach. I would say it is brutal, but no doubt our side do the same to your men.'

'Why do you not tell them the truth? That you are an innocent soldier and they should send you to a prisoner-of-war camp?'

'They would not believe me. And perhaps it would not be the truth.'

'You should just tell them.'

He turned to her. 'I do not think it would matter. They do not care. I will die here.' He was shifting around more urgently now.

She reached out for his hand. 'You must not die! You're only young.'

The door opened and the general came in behind her, only one soldier by his side. The commandant was not with him. 'Good work, Miss Witt.' He raised his eyebrow. Then he began speaking to her in German. 'Very pleasing work.'

She gazed at him, her mind blurred with confusion. The man gave an awful cough behind her. 'I think Mr Schmidt is going to be ill,' she said, in English.

'He is well enough. Come. I wish to talk to you.' Why was he speaking in German? Her heart was hot, flooded. She wanted to be back at the station. Why did he not ask what Schmidt had said?

'Better go, Miss Witt,' came Tibor's voice. 'Let us say goodbye.' He was moving around, pushing with his hands.

'Stop talking and keep still!' called the general in German. 'Perhaps you should release the prisoner's hand, Miss Witt.'

'Be careful, Miss Witt. You are not in the Black Forest now. It is more treacherous.'

'Come over here, Miss Witt.'

'Where is Commandant Robinson?'

'She is waiting for you outside. Now come along, please.' The general walked towards her.

What are you going to do with him, Celia was about to say. But the prisoner broke in first.

'Take care, Miss de Witt.' And then suddenly he reared up and the bed fell clattering to the floor, one arm still attached. With the other he seized the general and they both fell to the floor. Schmidt was shaking at the restraints on his wrist. The general was on top of him, trying to stop his flailing legs. Schmidt looked up at Celia. 'You could set me free now,' he said.

The door opened and more soldiers rushed in to hold Schmidt down. They hit him and hauled him back on to the bed. The shouting echoed around the aluminium walls. Celia wanted to put her hands over her ears.

'Animal!' said the general, as he stood up and brushed himself down. 'What a way to behave in front of a lady.' He took Celia's arm. 'Come along, Miss Witt, let us depart. I am sorry you had to see this.'

When she looked back, Schmidt had turned his head to look at her. 'Goodbye, Miss Witt,' he said. 'Maybe see you in the Black Forest one day. Or perhaps again here. I think you have passed your test.'

The door closed behind them, and Celia heard him shout out in pain.

'Come this way.' The general bustled her forward along dark corridors, past closed doors. Finally he opened a door and ushered her through. It was a sparse office, piled high with files. He sat down behind a large desk and gestured at the chair in front for her.

'Where is Commandant Robinson, sir?'

'She is waiting outside for you. You will see her soon.'

Celia sat. 'Does she know you are talking to me without her, sir?'

'But of course. Now, Miss Witt, tell me about yourself.'

Celia was beginning to shake. She could not help it. *I'm actually only seventeen!* she wanted to cry. *Could I just go home?*

'I'm from Hampshire,' she said. 'My father is Rudolf de Witt. He sells meat products. I've one brother here in France and two other siblings.' Behind the general was a painting of a river, with a cart and a horse. The English countryside, she supposed. She tried to stare at it, think of the river flowing softly, to still her furiously beating heart.

'And what were you doing before you came here?'

'I was . . . at home. You know.'

'And what is your name?'

'Emmeline, sir.'

'Well, Emmeline, if I may, you are performing very well in the services. Commandant Robinson tells me you are a hard worker.'

'I try to work hard, sir.' She wished he would let her go. She gazed at the horse, tied to the cart.

'And what made you choose the ambulance division?'

'It was suggested to me, sir.'

'Indeed. But do you not feel you are rather – well – wasted driving an ambulance back and forth?'

'Not at all, sir. I am glad to help.'

'You see, our feeling is that your recruiting station missed a trick. You are clever, you are attractive and you speak German. Indeed, you *are* German. Schmidt immediately saw you as a countrywoman.'

Celia shook her head. 'I told him my mother was English.'

'Listen, Miss de Witt, perhaps I can be frank with you. We need young women like you. Pretty, clever, half-German, already serving your country. It seems to me that the entire population of Germans in England is male. We are having trouble finding girls who even *speak* German. I have no idea what schools teach these days.'

'I am happy where I am.'

'You would be serving your country.'

'I already am.' On the general's right was a picture of sheep next to a rainbow of hedges. The frame was gold and elaborate. She wondered if he had bought it, or whether such things were standard issue.

'You know, our grasp of languages is letting us down. German schools for young ladies all teach English literature. There are hundreds of English-speaking girls working for the Germans. We are at a disadvantage. So. As I say, you are intelligent. There is a lot you could do for us. You could work here, help us talk to the prisoners.'

An image of Schmidt flickered over her mind and she dismissed it. They had hit him while he was tied down, unable to respond, and if she was to talk to him, she might have to watch while they hit him again. She gazed past the general at the picture.

'I am happy in the ambulances, sir.'

'You would prefer it here. There is no cleaning and you would sleep properly, eat better. And you would be serving the war effort in a greater way. Any girl can be a driver. Those like you are incredibly rare.'

'I would miss my friends, sir.' She thought of Schmidt's face, his bruised eye.

'You would earn money here, unlike in the ambulance service. And there is more chance of medals for bravery.'

She shook her head.

He picked up his pen and tapped a piece of paper in front of him. 'Miss de Witt, perhaps you could tell me. You are German by birth. Is it that you don't want to assist us? You would rather help your countrymen? Should I report you?'

'Of course that is not true, sir. I am English by birth. I was born in London.'

He sighed. 'Tell me again, Miss de Witt. What is your name?'

'Emmeline.'

'And your age?'

'Twenty-one.'

'I do not believe you.' His words, harsh and sharp, dropped into the air.

'I am telling the truth.'

'You know, Miss de Witt, you are very plausible, but I do not think this is the case. We made a few rudimentary investigations, and concluded that you are not Miss Emmeline de Witt, but Miss Celia. This would make you too young to be on service, let alone here.'

She bowed her head. 'That is not correct.'

'Really, Miss de Witt. I am afraid the evidence bears against you. You have quite clearly lied. You understand that that is an offence? False impersonation. Did you know that?'

She had been right. It was worse than anything that had happened at Winterbourne.

'I doubt the authorities would be sympathetic. You are young, Miss de Witt. Could you really face prison?'

'I'm Emmeline.'

'Oh, come now. We both know that is incorrect. I would only have to return and ask your father. Miss Witt, I will keep your secret. But in return for something we want. You will come and work for us.'

'They need me at the ambulance station.'

'And what about your father? He is incarcerated, is he not? As a suspicious individual. I am sure the authorities would do anything to collect evidence on him.'

I won't listen to this! she wanted to cry. Something was tugging at the back of her mind. 'You can speak German. You can all speak German. You did not want me here for that.' *I think you have passed your test*, Schmidt had said. 'You wanted to watch me!' she realised, speaking it out loud in the same moment that she understood it.

'See, Miss Witt, we knew you were intelligent.'

You have tricked me! she wanted to say. 'But he was the one who said I had to talk to him alone.'

'We hoped he would. He's rather suggestible, as you might have seen. Another officer – one of our cleverest men – had a conversation before and planted the seed of thought in his mind. If he had not, I would have proposed it.'

Celia opened her mouth but could say nothing. Schmidt had been right: they weren't in the Black Forest any more.

'It is all for the good of the country,' the general said. 'As you understand.' He held out the piece of paper. 'Here! Sign this and you will not go to jail. Instead, you will come to help us. There is a lot of work you can do for us. Questioning, charming the prisoners, talking to them. And out in the field. The soldiers would think you a typical German girl. You might even get to travel there. What would you think of that?'

'But... I wish to stay where I am.'

'Look, Miss Witt, I am offering you the chance of glory, honour, and proper pay – as well as work that could stretch your intelligence. Work that might continue after the war. I thought that was what all you girls in trousers wanted: responsibility and a job. And you are saying no, you want to stay with your plump tin-pot tyrant over at Station Three, doing ridiculous tasks that anyone could carry out.'

'I like it there.'

The general sighed. He took off his glasses and wiped his forehead with his handkerchief. 'I am baffled, Miss Witt, by you young women. What else could you possibly require?'

She looked at him. He didn't seem as terrifying as he had before; instead, with his glasses off, he was more like an old man, weary, like... her father.

'I would like my father back at home again, sir.'

He laughed. 'Of course you would, Miss Witt. But such a thing is impossible. I have no power with government.'

She shrugged. 'Well then. I don't want anything else.'

He put his glasses down. 'You seriously suggest I should obtain your father's freedom? Miss Witt, he is an enemy alien, a suspected spy. Should we set them all free to go running around England, spying for the Kaiser?'

'My father is not a spy. He's no more an enemy alien than I am.'

The general raised his eyebrows. 'Indeed.'

'Well, that's what I would like. Otherwise, I go back to the ambulances. Sir.'

'Honestly, Miss Witt, I would say I am shocked by your insubordination. But this sort of independence of spirit is, to an extent, what we are looking for, so I suppose I cannot be surprised.'

'Those are my terms, sir.' Her mind was wavering. He was right: work, proper work, was what Jemima and the others were demanding. What she was being offered was men's work, surely, like doctors or bus drivers.

'They are impossible.'

'In that case, I cannot help you. Would you let me depart?'

He sighed again. 'All this debate has made me even more keen to employ you. We need negotiators who do not stir from their course. Let me look into the matter.'

'Thank you, sir.' She fought hard to keep the smile off her face.

'I can make no guarantees. I shall look into it, that is all.' He gazed at her. 'Miss Witt, this is our bargain. If I free your father, then you come to work for me. Even if it takes some time, you will come. If you are no longer at Station Three, I will find you.'

She nodded. Rudolf smiled in her head, walking towards her at Stoneythorpe. She blocked out the other pictures: men she might have to ask questions of, bound to seats or beds. 'Yes, sir.'

He picked up the paper and scribbled on it. 'Right, the adjusted forms. It is just a matter of signing. Then matters can begin as we require.'

She looked down at it, miserably. Her heart was beating painfully. She picked up the pen and etched her name. *I am doing it for you, Papa*, she said to the picture of the river on the wall.

There was a knock at the door. The general ignored it. It came again. 'Please, sir. It is urgent.'

The general sighed and rose. 'What is it?'

A soldier poked a worried-looking face through. 'Miss Witt's commandant is making a fuss outside. She says she wants her girl back otherwise she is going to the top about it.'

The general took the paper back. 'Thank you, Witt. Don't forget our arrangement, will you?'

She shook her head. 'No, sir.'

'Take Miss Witt with you to the commandant, Wilkins.'

Celia stood up, not looking back at the picture. Wilkins ushered her in front of him and closed the door. They passed down corridors, around corners, then out of a door to where the commandant was waiting on the grass.

'Come along, Miss Witt. What has been happening?'

'The general talked a lot, Commandant.'

'Let's go now. I have half a mind to report him for wasting my time.' She turned to Wilkins. 'If I get back and the place has gone into mutiny, then I will hold you entirely responsible.' She gestured towards the ambulance. 'Go ahead and take the wheel, Miss Witt.'

Celia settled behind the wheel. 'Commandant—'

Robinson held up her hand. 'I do not want to hear it. Turn right here, that's it. No more conversation, thank you.'

Celia drove, feeling the gearstick in her hand, allowing the road to take her forward, concentrating on the simple pleasure of driving, trying to halt the panicked tumble of thoughts in her mind.

TWENTY-FOUR

On 10 May, the bomb siren went off. Warterton leapt up to look out of the window. 'Hey, girls, I reckon I can see the planes.' Celia plunged into her sleeping bag. She did not want to see the things. 'They're coming,' Warterton was calling. She tore off a little more of the black paper over the window so she could peer out.

'Don't do that!' called Shep. 'They'll see us. The Kaiser is sitting up there in that thing, having a good old look.' She crouched by her sleeping bag. 'Babb said to me he couldn't understand why Fritz had been so quiet. Last year, apparently, he was going like the clappers as soon as it got a bit warmer. Too cold for him up there in winter.'

Celia had never imagined that bombs could fall so close and so loud. *Where are they?* she wanted to say, but was too afraid. She pushed herself further down into her sleeping bag, but still the bombs pounded through into her ears. The moments between were even worse, for she was so tense she was almost in pain, waiting for the next one. After they had stopped, she lay shaking for what seemed like half an hour until Warterton called, 'All clear, girls!'

Celia looked up. Tears were running down her face. Shep came over and stroked her hair. 'We will have to learn to sleep through it, I suppose,' she said. 'I thought boarding school was noisy.'

'Mine too.' Celia began rooting in her bag for a biscuit.

'How will we cope when we have to drive in it?'

Celia looked at her. 'Oh God. We will have to, won't we?' A tiny scrap of canvas between her head and a bomber.

'I'll say.'

'Don't worry, girls.' Warterton plopped herself down on Shep's pallet. 'Pass me a biccy, old thing. Safer out than in. At least we are moving about in our vehicles. Here we are sitting ducks under our big shiny roof.'

Warterton was right. At first, Celia found driving through bombs terrifying. Then she grew more used to it. Finally, she was ashamed to admit to herself, she became a sort of machine. She consoled herself that you couldn't feel fear all the time. The round of driving all night, cleaning, and barely being able to sleep was so dulling that Celia sometimes felt as if she was a vehicle herself, driven by someone else. She wondered if there was anything she could not get used to, anything at all.

She wrote letters to Verena, Michael, Emmeline, Miss Webb and Tom, telling them that she was enjoying the work, not mentioning bombs. She heard back from Miss Webb most often. There was no word from Rudolf, and Verena's only letter hadn't mentioned him, had said not much at all other than that the factories weren't making so much money these days. Mr Lewis expected things would soon improve. In the days after the afternoon with Tibor Schmidt and the general, Celia had thought constantly about her father. But after a month had elapsed, she found herself giving less thought to him. Living and working with the other girls, her time in the ambulance station seemed increasingly to be a strange dream. Her fear of the general and her euphoria at the thought of Rudolf being freed fading into something less highly coloured, a thin occasional misgiving.

One night in June, she had been desperate to talk to take her mind off the bombs she felt sure were due to fall soon – the sky had been too quiet beforehand. She asked the sitter next to her at the front about himself, and he spoke briefly about his home in the West Country, how he had fallen on his side into a trench, his fall broken by two fat rats who exploded under him. 'Rat flesh all over me.' He struck her as familiar, and finally, when they were nearing the turn for Hospital 5, she realised. 'I know you. I recognise you.'

'Oh,' he said. 'Sorry, miss. Where would it be from?'

'I met you in London, I am sure of it. Outside a recruiting station.'

'In London? I'm from Sidmouth, miss. Don't spend much time in London.' Every time he spoke, she was convinced it was him.

'It was earlier this year. Were you in London then?'

He shrugged. 'Maybe passing through. I don't think so.'

'I know it was you. A recruiting station in Bloomsbury. We talked of the nurses. And now here I am!'

He scratched his head. 'I am sorry, miss. I don't remember.'

'But you must!'

He shook his head. She shifted into third gear. She had wondered, from time to time, about the man, imagined him. And now, when she really had encountered him, the meeting meant nothing to him. He sat staring, his eyes glazed; she knew that he was thinking about the trenches, death and pain.

At the hospital, she wished him goodbye quietly as he left. He did not look back. That night, she finally took Warterton up on her offer of a cigarette. The end in her mouth tasted like poison, made her cough. 'Why on earth do you like these things?' she said.

'You will see!' And she did. Within a few weeks, she was smoking with the rest of them, hands shaking.

In the summer, the girls started falling ill. Johnson was sent to the hospital with scarlet fever. Her mother had demanded her home as soon as she was ready to travel, but word was she was determined to stay. She returned to work, sick and pale, often fainted in her cab. Five other girls had the fever as well. Fitzhugh caught pneumonia and was sent home in early July. At her goodbye party, they drank lukewarm cocoa and ate the biscuits sent to Warterton by her mother. Fitzhugh promised to come back, 'Just as soon as I have got myself shipshape.'

'I doubt she will,' said Warterton later that night while they were queuing for the WC. 'Once the countess gets her hands on her darling daughter and hears what has been going on, we won't see her for dust.'

'No, Fitz will come back,' said Shep. 'She's different.'

But now it was the end of July and another girl, Shaw, the

round-faced daughter of a Manchester mill owner, had taken Fitz's place in the dorm.

There was still no word from Rudolf, and Celia told herself that it was hardly worth thinking about. The general was right: he simply could do nothing about it. Rudolf would remain in prison whatever she did. It was almost ridiculous of her to have imagined that she was worth enough to exchange for him, insignificant as she was.

You must be pleased over there that the weather has cheered up, wrote Emmeline. Celia replied saying yes, of course. Not adding that the downside of early summer was that the air raids had become so much worse. A clear, sunny day always filled them with dread, for it made it much more likely that by nightfall the bombs would be falling.

The bugs and lice had got worse as well. Celia woke to find cockroaches crawling over her hands, if she fell asleep with them outside her sleeping bag. The few times she had lain awake, she heard the rats scraping at the walls. She was always itching, sure that the lice had got into her uniform. Worst of all, they were in her hair. Poor English had scratched so much that the side of her head was bleeding. Finally, after a night convoy when she was so infuriated by them that she could have screamed as loud as her soldier cargo, Celia had had enough. The next day, rather than go to lunch, she took Warterton's scissors from her bag and used her fusty little mirror to pull straight her hair and cut it. She gave up trying to get it straight and snipped willy-nilly. She began to enjoy it, conjuring Verena's voice in her mind: *I would be heartbroken if I lost my hair! Well, Mama*, she wanted to say, *I'm losing my hair and I am going to be happier!*

Shep appeared at the door. 'Witty! What are you doing?'

Celia looked at the hair all over her legs, her feet, on the floor. 'I couldn't stand it any more. I can't keep it clean.'

Shep came over and touched her hand. 'Poor Witty. But your hair was lovely.'

'It wasn't really. My mother's lady's maid said I would lose it by the time I was fifty.'

'Cooper and Mill would scream.' Cooper and Mill were new girls, out for a month and already the man-hunters of the station. Warterton had even seen Mill sneaking off to meet one of the orderlies after the end of duties. She said they would get them all into trouble. Celia knew she should disapprove too, but she watched them sometimes, creeping out, and wondered if it might make you happier to be like that.

'They might like it. What do you say, Sheppie? I can do yours if you like?' She held out the scissors and snapped them at her. 'Come along!'

Shep screamed, laughing. 'No!'

Celia advanced. 'Come here! I will make you look splendid!' Shep dodged out of her way. Celia snapped her scissors again and Shep reached down, caught up a biscuit and threw it straight at her. Celia ducked. 'I surrender! Biscuit attack!' She dropped her scissors and put out her hand to shake.

Shep grasped her in a rough hug. 'Don't cut it again, will you?'

'You'll never get a husband like that,' said Warterton, sauntering into the room. 'It's far too short!'

'I'm not looking for a husband.' Tom came into her mind, and she put him away at the back. Shep released her from the hug. 'Anyway, what husband wants a girl with fleas in her hair?'

'You'll never find a lover either, Shep. Not like Cooper.'

'I don't want to be like Cooper!' Celia blushed. Shep and Warterton both disapproved of Cooper. Celia would never admit that she sometimes lay awake at night wondering what the other girl was doing, out around the back of the station.

Warterton sat on her bed, pulled out another packet of biscuits. Her mother had started to send them regularly, now, along with letters about how there was *nothing wrong with coming home, dear, you are always a heroine to me.* They all supposed that some of the other volunteers had started describing how things were, blood and death.

'Cooper'll have us all sent home sooner or later, the longer she carries on trying to take men into her ambulance.'

'I would have been shocked by that sort of talk a year ago, Shep,' said Warterton. 'In fact I don't think I would have understood.' Celia still didn't understand. Not what Cooper did in there – she had pieced that together, more or less, she thought, from what the other girls had said. What she wanted to ask Cooper was *Why are you happy?* She seemed to shrug off the war.

'Hmm,' said Shep. 'What did the captain say to the virgin VAD?' They shook their heads. 'Court martial for not doing your bit for the war effort!'

'Shep, you are *terrible.*' Warterton threw her pillow. Celia patted her hair, tried not to think about Cooper. It would grow back, she supposed.

Dear Sis,

How are you gals getting on out there? The chaps here are thrilled when I tell them that my little sister (twenty-one, of course!) is out there working. We know we romanticise you ambulance ladies. As I told you, Belton's cousin's friend said it was hard work and a lot of housekeeping too. I look forward to hearing all about it when the war is done.

Not much to report from out here. We are still keeping Fritz on his toes.

Another letter from Michael. He had written two, both sent to Emmeline to forward to Celia. She supposed he thought a letter to a girl out serving might be looked at more zealously by the commanding officers. But the letters didn't seem much different to her whether they were sent to England or the ambulance station. He was always so jolly, said she must be having a splendid time too. The words sounded nothing like him, her nervous, shaky brother with his head in a book. It was another man, practical, cheerful, like Johnson before she fell ill. With his early letters, she had thought he was merely pretending; now, after seeing so many soldiers, she thought that he had actually come to be that man every day, simply because it was the way he had to be.

'Another secret admirer?' called Shepherd.

Celia shook her head. 'My brother.'

She had been hoping to sit and read it in the back of the dorm hidden from everyone, even Shepherd. Letters were like chocolate or cakes from home, there to be shared out among all the girls. Those from men out fighting were highly prized.

'Give it me!' Shepherd cried, rushing forward, her hands out. 'You know I'm in love with your brother.'

Celia held it away from her. 'Stop that! I haven't finished it yet.'

'Oh, not fair! He is my future fiancé, remember? I come first.' Shepherd always teased that she was going to marry Michael. 'We'll live happily ever after,' she said. 'Occasionally we'll allow you to visit us in our castle.'

She lunged again for the paper and Celia batted her off. 'I will show you *later*. Patience.' Her friend shuffled off to the stove to boil up some water, and Celia settled back to the letter.

Michael was continuing being jolly.

We had a good little concert last night. We still have our chap who was an actor, pretty invaluable man to have. The other battalions want to take him, but our senior has said he is ours. Mind you, the other battalions don't like us much anyway. We have got a reputation for giving Fritz a pounding, so the chaps who come after us think they are going to get a battering in return.

We are pretty busy here and things are getting busier.

'That means they are gearing up for a push.' Celia jumped. Shepherd was standing over her. 'That's all they can say, but it is what they mean. Busy! I know it's true. I heard one of the MOs talking to the commandant about it. They have been told that the expectation is of low casualties, but to be prepared just in case.'

'Shep, you shouldn't listen in on conversations.'

'It is important for us to know. And how else would we? From letters like this? Anyway, they like to put it around, if you ask me. Otherwise we would all be asking, two years at war, and what have we done? Moved forward a couple of inches.'

Celia nodded gloomily. Emmeline had sent her a leaflet that

338

was being handed out around London, full of pictures of shops empty of sweets and bread. *The war will go on for another ten years*, it read. That had made Celia cry when so much had not. She had sobbed on Shep's shoulder. 'Another ten years of this. We'll be old by the time it is over and all our youth will be lost.'

'What rot,' Shep had said, tearing up the leaflet. 'Your sister is a silly thing. My father says we'll be home by Christmas.'

'People said that last Christmas.'

'This time it is true. Fritz is taking a battering.'

'Come on!' Shep was saying now. 'Hand over the letter! I need to read the words of my beloved fiancé.'

Celia passed it over and smiled. 'You are right, Shep. You are always right. I suppose a push is a good thing.'

'It is. But that's why we're getting so many men with handies.'

'Handies?'

'The orderly told me last night. You know, they seem fine, except for a shot through their hand. As if the wound is self-inflicted. He said others have started eating cigarettes soaked in vinegar to make themselves ill, can you imagine?'

Celia covered her ears. 'We shouldn't say any more! We'll get in trouble.' They were supposed to tell the commandant of any suspicions about men with pretended or self-inflicted wounds.

'No different to all those girls trying to bury their heads in Johnson's pillow, trying to catch the fever.'

Then followed three weeks in which Celia forgot how to sleep. The trains were so full that they went on all night and then late into the morning, started again by seven. Thousands and thousands of men, sitters crammed into the trains so tightly that they couldn't move, stretchers balanced on each other. The injuries were terrible, legs, arms, faces. Most of the sitters shook, teeth chattering like a child's play skeleton, all the way to the hospital. Those who didn't told her terrible things: queues of men at the dressing stations, their wounds festering in the sun, dying because all the morphine was saved for the operations. One man with a shattered arm said they were so low on doctors that the padre was anaesthetising the men for operations, and asked him to help hold them down with his good arm. They wouldn't talk about the fighting. The commandant was hysterical with panic, sent two girls from the san who were half dead with the flu out to drive. Shepherd fainted at the wheel and had to be revived by her sitter.

By the second week, Celia was weeping with tiredness at the wheel, not caring that the men could see. That same week, the commandant gave them all an hour at lunch, said Station Three would cover. Warterton called them over to look at a newspaper. 'Keep quiet, girls, but look at this story. One of my brothers sent it. Thousands dead on the Somme.' She unfolded *The Times*. 'Thank God Richie is further south.'

'I don't know where Mick and James are,' said Shep.

'I don't know about mine either.'

'That's why we've been so busy, though. And why leave has been cancelled.'

They stared at the article, holding hands. Celia felt it then, how torn they were. On one hand, she was a sister, a friend, her body frozen with terror for Tom and Michael, as it always was with news of such a great battle. On the other, she was an ambulance driver, feeling the clunk in her mind as things fell into place, like solving a puzzle in the old days.

'Lucky Fitz went home when she did,' said Shep. 'They'd never let her go now.' She took her special box of Milk Tray – solely for emergencies – from under her bed and offered them each a stale-looking violet cream.

'Look at this,' said Warterton, clutching a biscuit. 'The newspaper says the soldiers were told the wire would be cut and that they should walk forward slowly. They got there and it wasn't.'

Celia looked at the words. 'But isn't that what they tell them to do in every battle? Walk forward slowly till they reach the wire. The men say it's never cut. What's the difference here?'

Warterton nodded. 'You're right, Witty, that's what they always say.'

Shep pointed to the paragraph at the bottom. 'No, girls. The whole point is the size of it. This wasn't just a little battle. It was thousands.'

'It says here they're making a film about it.'

'Who wants to see a film about that?' said Warterton. 'I'd prefer to watch Vesta Tilley, awful as she is.'

'Strange that you despise her so much when we're all a set of Vestas ourselves. We'd do well in the music hall with these outfits on,' said Shep. 'Anyway, you might feel different if you were at home. Your mother will be first in the queue at the pictures to see *The Heroic Sacrifice* or whatever they're going to call it. Then she will write to you all about it, along with another box of biscuits.'

Summer rolled into autumn. Celia received a letter from Michael after the big push, saying that he'd been sent elsewhere (and that Tom had too). Shep's brothers were still alive, but Mick had been taken prisoner. Her mother wrote to say that the Red Cross had been to inspect his prison and it was passable. The food at the ambulance station grew worse, and there was even less meat. The commandant apologised, said that rations were going down fast and there was nothing she could do.

Celia had never eaten so little. It made her feel cold, chill hands, her stomach a hollow late at night. In the old days, she had eaten meat at lunch and dinner, and in the holidays extra sausage rolls. At school, she thought, hunger had been that half-hour before the lesson broke for lunch, staring at a map of Europe wondering whether they would be eating beef casserole or lamb hotpot, pondering how many spoonfuls of potato she might get from the servers. Now, she was hungry all the time, even if she woke in the middle of the night. Only the smoking made her forget.

She watched Cooper smiling to herself in the canteen. A few times Celia had gone to the WC in the middle of the night and seen her wandering out. She knew she was being disloyal to Shep, but still she wondered about Cooper, what happened outside. The kiss from Tom had driven deep into her heart. Surely, when Cooper was touched by these men, she felt the same.

Every day, it got colder. Celia dreaded driving in the snow.

Already her hands felt as if they were iced to the wheel, and no snow had yet fallen. The men screamed much more in the cold. 'The only compensation for winter is that the enemy stops bombing,' said the commandant, when she found Celia rubbing her hands on the bonnet of the ambulance to get warm. 'He'll take a holiday soon, Witt.'

But he didn't. Every night they told each other it would be his last, and then he did it again.

The commandant's whistle blew. 'Ambulances!'

'Come on, girls,' called Warterton, stumbling to her feet. It was three a.m. and they had been sent to bed after an afternoon of driving. 'Station Two have clearly given up. Once more into the breach and all that.'

'We will follow you, King Henry.' Shep was pulling on her trousers.

'Come on, Witty.' Celia felt weighed down by tiredness, as if she could barely move her legs. She wanted to lie back down again. 'Come on, old thing.' Shep tugged on her arm. 'Your secret admirers are waiting for you at the station.'

Celia rolled out of bed. 'I'm coming.'

The shriek of the alarm sounded. 'Oh God,' said Shepherd. 'Here we go. Double the fun.' She squeezed Celia's hand.

'Don't look up at the monsters,' called Warterton. 'That will give you the willies.'

'You can talk! You gaze at those planes like they're the second coming.'

At the station, the bombs were falling, but once they had loaded up, the skies went quiet. Still, just in case, Celia kept her sidelights off. She craned forward to see. The men were nervy, dreading the next bomb, crying out at every bump. She forced herself to be like Warterton. 'Don't worry, chaps!' she called. 'Not much further to go now. Hold tight! Here comes another pothole!'

The moon came from behind a cloud, so she accelerated. It was a curse and a blessing in one – easier for her to see, yet much easier for pilots to spot her. She pressed on. Her shell-shock case gave a terrible scream, but he would have cried out at anything – the opening of the back doors, the change of gear if it was particularly creaky. She had stood at the back as they loaded him in, staring ahead, his hands and legs twitching, his face all fear. He had shrieked hysterically as the doors of the neighbouring ambulance closed. 'He landed on a dead body that burst,' said one of the men dispassionately. 'Poor fellow.' He was screaming over and over. 'Don't worry, son,' the older sitter said. 'Our boys will beat the Krauts back.'

She hurtled over the pothole, and as she did so, she saw another ambulance ahead of her. She admired the driving: swift, neat, avoiding a pothole by swerving on to a verge. Over the trees, the moon was hanging, low and gibbous. Plenty of light to drop bombs on the right target. There was a flurry of bombs and a huge crash. It didn't sound too far away. 'That's practically over in Belgium,' she shouted at the men in the back.

'I think Jerry's nearer than that,' said the sitter next to her. He had a bandaged head and arm and had been smoking silently since they set off. 'I reckon we'll be able to see them overhead soon.' Celia dropped one wheel into the pothole the driver in front had missed. The men groaned.

'It's the ambulance station they want,' she said, braver than she felt. 'They don't care about us.'

She turned the ambulance towards Hospital 5, accelerating hard to get up the hill. The nurses were waiting for them outside. 'All right, love,' said the stretcher-bearer. 'Good girl, getting the chaps here quickly.' Three were still screaming as they were taken out.

'Don't think they liked your driving much, Witt,' winked the nurse, Tibbets. She was a pretty girl, with brown curls and a small nose. The sitter was gazing at her. Celia thought she could tell the soldiers who were going to recover soon – they perked up at the sight of a good-looking nurse.

'Might get them to send you out in my place, Nurse Tibbets.'

Tibbets smiled. 'Safe journey back, Witt.'

Celia wanted to seize her hand and say, *Let me stay with you!*

Please! But the canvas roof of the hospital was no protection. 'See you next time,' she said. She backed the ambulance away from the stretchers and shot down the hill. The bombs were still falling. Now to keep going, so fast that she'd be back in her bed before she knew it. She went over a bump so quickly that she felt as if she might take off. In front of her, another ambulance joined the road from Hospital 2. Celia waved, but the driver wasn't looking behind her. It had the same bloodstain on the back as the one she had followed earlier – and still she was not sure whose it was. The other girl was going at top speed too. 'Race you!' Celia shouted into the air rushing past. They bumped past the woody copse that led to Hospital 3.

Another bomb dropped behind her. Celia threw herself over the wheel. It was so close. Then she pushed down on the pedal. The ambulance shot forward. It was the fastest she had ever gone in her life.

She did not look up in case there was a flying machine over-head. Instead, she kept her eyes forward, catching up to the other ambulance, racing along the road. Another bomb crashed behind her and she swerved in shock. She pulled back on to the road and pushed on, her ears numb. She felt sure that the thing was above her, aiming for the station. She gripped the wheel and, in spite of herself, glanced up. The great body of a plane hung over her. She slowed down immediately, slamming on the brake. She thought she could see the figure of the gunner at the back. *I can see you!* she could have cried to whoever he was, some boy her own age. *Stop!*

She slowed to a crawl and watched the aircraft move forward. Then another bomb, smashing on to the road ahead. She stopped dead and dropped her head to the wheel. There was a crash and a flash of flame. The ambulance in front swerved off the road and fell on its side. 'Stop! Stop!' Celia screamed. The plane swooped upwards, off into the sky, the trail fizzing in its wake. She leapt down from the cab and hurried forward. The road was on fire. She crawled down into the grass, around the side of it, feeling the heat flame her skin. In front of her, the wheels of the ambulance were moving helplessly, like the legs of a dying fly. 'I'm coming!' she shouted. The fire swallowed her voice.

She carried on crawling, called out again. The driver's side of the cab was facing upwards. She reached for the door and pulled. The girl had fallen against the other side. Her dark hair was spattered in blood. 'Hello?' Celia said tentatively. 'Hello.' She heard a rasping breath. 'Hold on,' she said. 'I'm here now.' She had no idea, she realised, how she could help this girl at all. Maybe she shouldn't try to pull her out, but surely it was more dangerous to be in? The fuel might blow up. 'You're fine now, dear,' she said. 'Don't worry.'

The girl gave a groan. Something about the voice struck horror into Celia. *Oh God.* She reached her hand forward to the girl's head, brushed the hair back, exposing the face and the deep wound in the forehead all at once. She screamed out the word before she could even think it. 'Shep! Shep!'

Shep's eyes gazed upwards and closed. 'Don't go to sleep,' Celia begged. 'Please.' She clutched at her, tried to cradle her, but she could reach only to stroke.

'Witt,' the voice croaked. 'Witt.' And then her head dropped, and Celia could feel the flow of blood slowing, stopping.

Soon there were voices and someone's hands on her. Johnson and another girl – Cooper. 'All right there, Witt, we've got you. Keep calm now.' Celia kept screaming. She felt one of the girls pulling at her. 'Let's take you back. The doctor can give you something. Come on, Witt.'

'What rotten bad luck,' Cooper said. 'The two of them were as thick as thieves.'

'Rotten,' said Johnson. 'I'll take her back. Do you think you can stay with Shepherd – I mean Elizabeth?'

In the ambulance back, Celia was placed in the position of a sitter but could not sit. She flopped over, bumping her head on the dashboard. She did not want to sit up straight, ever again. Back at the station, Johnson hurried her inside. A doctor came to where she was screaming in the canteen and jabbed her. She felt warm liquid flooding her body, gave in to the relief.

TWENTY-FIVE

Pozières, Summer 1916

It was the big push. That was all they had been talking about over the past days, the big push. It had even filtered down to the men. A thousand commands going up and down the telephone lines, letters being issued, withdrawn, inspections, discussions. You got caught up in it, the excitement of what was going to happen. Then another command and you were all supposed to do something different. Michael had decided that it wasn't worth devoting too much thought to one command; best just to say, *Of course the men will be ready, sir*, read the instructions and then file them away. He had a box under his bed for such letters, the pile growing bigger every day.

New posters were stuck up reminding them that speaking loudly on field telephones was a court-martial offence. There was detailed talk about barrages and wire-cutting and the rest. Michael went to three meetings at HQ, in which they looked at reports, maps and proposals. Each time, he felt sure (though not entirely, since he could not take any notes) that it was exactly the same plan that they had gone over before, with only the odd detail changed, here or there. Still, they debated, nodded, discussed, and considered the possibilities, ending – always – in agreement. It would of course be an excellent way to proceed. The men were quite ready, eager to go forth and engage. They were in good spirits, keen to progress. Another general would then talk about what really mattered: the mood at home. His wife was feeling a little persecuted at the first aid committee; the other ladies demanded to know if anything was really being done out here. There had been a letter to *The Times* in which one lady suggested she might take her stock of white feathers out to France and distribute them there.

Each meeting finished with the same conclusion. Something must be done. HQ would improve things, create a new and unique plan, something that would fix the matter once and for all. They had to keep even this quiet: that there would be a plan. So Michael could not speculate with Bilks about what might or might not occur. He did not tell Wheeler, instead applied himself to wondering what the unique plan might be. Perhaps they might bring in a new bomb or type of gun.

The night after making the judgement, Michael had lain in bed, listening. He had not seen what happened, for after the two men had been hauled away, Bilks had found some military policemen to tie them to the wheel. So he imagined it. In the cracks of silence between bombs, he heard Tom scream.

Tom came to him after they took him off the wheel and spoke looking at the floor, promising he would not make the same mistake again. Michael tried to smile at him, say, *I forgive you!* But Tom would not look up.

'Was it so very terrible?' he asked Wheeler, three nights later, when they were alone.

'Not so bad, not really. He was the one who was screaming. I know you had to punish me,' Wheeler whispered, stroking his back. 'But you punished him too and that was fair.' Michael turned around, moved towards him, but Wheeler ducked away. 'I should go. Bilks will be here.' He winked.

It was back to normal with Wheeler, better even. But Tom was angry. He avoided Michael, would not meet his eyes, stayed as far as he could from him when they went out on clearing parties or rebuilding trenches. *Being in charge is a lonely job*, Michael told himself, and similar platitudes. But it was not so simple, for some of the other men were fighting shy of him too. They were afraid of talking to him in rest breaks and they did not invite him to play cards at the end of the day. Who minded? he said to himself. Who minded what Cook or Pie thought? Wheeler was content and that was all that should matter. But he still could not tell Celia what he had done. He wrote her letters, enthusiastic, talking about the food. Every time he picked up his pen, he saw Wheeler's face gazing at him, imploring him. If he had punished only Wheeler, it would have made him liable to be picked out again by higher command. He put down his pen and answered the voice in his head: what else did you expect me to do? He had meant to show fairness. Instead, he guessed he had exposed himself even more.

Tom would forgive him, he was sure. Already the passion of Tom's feeling seemed to have thinned, and when Michael asked him to do something, he looked at him with resentment only. He would understand in time. Sometimes, though, Michael thought back to the moment of standing there in front of the two of them, and an odd flush of feeling came to him, a recognition that what he had experienced then was not an endeavour to justice but a desire for cruelty, to crush Tom's appealing gaze and stop his puppyish need to follow him around. *We are not friends*, he wanted to say. *I barely know you. You were my servant.*

Then, two weeks before the July push was to begin – still no plans – word came from on high that Michael's men, along with the rest of the battalion, were being sent south for a different endeavour. They walked, caught the train, carrying their packs, disembarked somewhere near Boulogne, he thought, occupied a trench that was wider than their old one had been and more makeshift – the sandbags were made from coloured material, flowers, stripes, checks, that he presumed had been local bed-spreads and curtains. The men there before them had even left old cigarette boxes around. Michael stood there, gazing at the muddy trench. What on earth were they meant to do here while the big push was going on in the north? Tidying up and pushing sandbags into place for the next load of men to come? He supposed so, presumed that after the first push had succeeded, they would come south and do the same here.

'Come on, men,' said Bilks, slipping down behind him. 'Let's make ourselves at home.'

*

348

Five weeks later, Michael and his men had made their trench as wide as they could. They had shored up the sides and reinforced the edges and the bottom. More men had arrived from other parts of the country and the trenches resounded to explosions, thanks to big teams of miners from the west. It seemed to Michael that the whole lot of them were being run from the HQ near Pozières. Their CO turned up with letters and read them out. 'Continue your excellent work, men,' he said. 'Making ready.'

The area was pristine in a way Pozières had not been: houses still standing, even churches; farmers walking their cows across no-man's-land. There was a wide stretch of ground between them and the enemy, and the Krauts on the other side barely shelled them at all, but still they went through the motions of guns, sentry posts, raiding parties. They gathered together their grenades, counted their ammunition, discussed with the gunners how they might bring over the cannons, prepared for attack, even though, Michael knew, nothing was going to happen. The Germans were no different: they were two sets of toy soldiers walking in and out of position, shaking their guns, never shooting, all of them waiting for the grown-ups to come and play the real game.

The men were getting hard to motivate, he and Bilks had agreed. They were frustrated that the big push was being planned up north and they were doing housekeeping in the middle of nowhere. Pie kept saying that he spoke for all the men when he said they wanted to go back, that they felt the other fellows were fighting hard out there and they wanted to join them. 'We have to obey orders,' Michael told them, while they were playing cards at lunchtime. 'I don't like it any more than you do.' He looked at Tom staring into his cup. Bilks raised an eyebrow at him. It was wrong to say it, he knew, a cheap way to garner popularity, but what harm could it do? The CO was too busy reading letters from high command to listen to what the men might say.

'When can we go back?' demanded Pie. He had already been out hunting for souvenirs over no-man's-land, and found very little. He said the stretcher-bearers must have picked them all off and sold them.

'We will await orders. Perhaps we will stay and the other men and the battle will come to us.'

'Let's start our own. I'll go over and hit Jerry on the head with my mug.'

'That's enough, Pie.' Bilks shot Michael an angry stare. 'Command order us correctly, thank you.'

'If they did, we wouldn't be here.'

'That's enough, I said.'

Michael looked over at Tom. He was still gazing at his cup.

'I will go to see the CO,' he said. 'I'll try to find out what he aims to do.'

Three days later, Michael was in the CO's office, a fine room in the local town hall, newly commandeered. 'The men want something to do, sir,' he said. 'They're not happy.'

'That is a coincidence,' said the CO. 'There is something I need done.'

Michael almost smiled. He had expected some variety of fight with the man, and here it was, simple and solved. The CO said there was a line of trenches ten miles to the west that the Germans had entirely deserted, yesterday, after a massive bombardment. HQ wanted information about the layout and so Michael and his men should lead a raid on the line tomorrow. They were to stay an hour or so, with half of them drawing the layout – if he could find that many who could draw – and the others collecting up abandoned weapons for testing: guns, ammunition and grenades. Once they had surveyed the area, the CO, said, the gunners were going to go in and bomb it to bits. He said he was sorry but they were to expect a lot of bodies, since the German stretcher-bearers hadn't managed to get in.

'It's not fighting, I'm afraid. I expect some of that in a few weeks or so, just between us. Keep their spirits up, Witt, and we'll have them back in action before you know it.' Michael supposed Pie would be happy at least: good opportunities for hunting for badges and whatever else down there.

That night, they were occupied in planning. Michael would

head the drawing team; Bilks gathered together the men to collect up ammunition. Michael took Wheeler – after all, a schoolmaster must be able to draw – along with Long, Ebbots and Porter, who all claimed they could handle a pencil. Bilks told him to take Tom, said he'd oversee Pie and the others. 'Pick up the bullets first, Pie,' he said. 'I'll inspect your pockets.'

They walked west, Bilks navigating, and took lodgings in a barn belonging to one of the farms on the way. When they all bedded down that night, the men were restless, excitable. Bilks had to tell them to stop talking, otherwise it would be a washout tomorrow, but even he was excited: his voice wavered when he spoke. It was impossible not to feel a thrill, Michael thought. They would be entering a German trench – and they would find out how different it was from their own. It was their reward for these weeks of drudgery.

Once the men were asleep, he gave the signal: three short coughs, then another. He stood and crept out of the barn, as if he was going to relieve himself. Outside, he leant against the wall and waited. He watched his breath ruffle the air, imagining how it might billow out if the weather were cold. After five minutes had passed, he heard Wheeler's step. He waited, enjoying the hard thrill of anticipation. The pain of the early days had dissipated into contentment, but there was nothing of the complacency he supposed must happen if you lived together and could be sure of always lying by the other at night. Although even then he could not imagine his heart failing to fill with excitement when Wheeler was near. Still, they would have a chance to find out. After the war was over, they were going to live together in Paris. It was easier to hide there, they'd decided.

He heard Wheeler's footsteps, heard him breathing before he came near. He turned, looked at him, opened his arms. They clung to each other. If you were watching from the outside, he thought, you might imagine they were two people holding on, saving each other from drowning. Afterwards, they didn't allow themselves much time. Two or three minutes together, not long to talk. But

Michael knew that they were thinking the same thoughts: Paris together, the house they might have, their love.

Next morning, they left the barn and occupied one of the French trenches near to their target. Bilks handed round the rum flask – although what they were doing would hardly be dangerous – and they readied their guns to walk over. They assembled their packs as if they were going out properly, with drawing paper and pencils, containers to hold the bullets and samples they found. At eight, they went over, walking sedately across the grass of no-man's-land. Michael permitted himself a brief squeeze of Wheeler's hand when no one was looking.

As they approached the German trench, the men hung back – of course you would. Michael and Bilks went on ahead, guns in hand, and peered over the edge. The trench was smaller than Michael had imagined, narrower than on the other side and stacked high with sandbags made from curtain material. There were bodies strewn on top of each other where they'd fallen, already decomposing in the heat. Bilks clambered down and extended his hand for Michael. 'Looks clear to me, sir,' he said. The two of them began to check the corpses with the end of their guns.

'I wish we could bury them,' said Michael.

'If they would do the same for us,' replied Bilks, turning over another with his gun. 'Anyway, if they are going to bomb it tomorrow, they'll have a grave of sorts.'

Michael gingerly poked his gun at a body. He didn't share Bilks's relish for the job. His second was turning them over enthusiastically, jabbing at their hearts. Michael couldn't bear it. He told himself it was out of respect for the dead. Really, he dreaded them. They were already bloated with fluids. He feared prodding one and being hit with an explosion of the stuff. He nudged one whose face was swollen and yellow. 'I think they're pretty dead,' he said.

'I've got a few more to get through,' Bilks puffed. Michael leaned against the wall as Bilks turned over the rest against his side of the wall, prodded them for life, let them fall back. At last he stood up. 'We're clear.'

'Bring the others down.'

Bilks moved aside two of the bodies to give the men enough space, then clambered up the side of the trench and called them down. 'Here we go!' Michael heard Pie shout. They jumped down one after the other, all of them looking around gleefully. Cook whooped and Michael gave him a hard look. 'Come on. We need to get started.' The men were delighted, he saw, wildly light-hearted, casting about for souvenirs, wide-eyed at the thought of entering the most forbidden place.

'This isn't a party, men,' said Bilks, sharply. Cook was leaning against the side of the trench, laughing hysterically. 'Stop that. Over here, please, Wheeler, Ebbots and the rest of you. Let's get started.'

Cook straightened his face, walked over. Michael's group pulled out their paper and set about the near side, the one he had just checked, drawing out the size of the trench and what they guessed what would be its overall plan. Michael watched Wheeler as he bent to pick up a bullet, then looked back at his own work. Birds spun overhead.

They had nearly finished their drawings. Michael could feel the men growing restive, as if he had taken a group of children to a party and then refused to allow them to play.

'Stop that!' he shouted. Cook was prodding at the eye of one of the corpses with his finger. 'Have some respect for the dead.'

'For Fritz, sir?'

'We are here to do a job. Get back to it.' Cook bent his head to his paper.

'Finished, sir.' Ebbots moved off to another section of the trench. There was now no one between him and Tom. Michael watched. He could see Tom's face registering their closeness. He moved nearer and raised his finger to Tom's paper. 'That is a good likeness.'

Tom lifted his eyes briefly, then returned to his paper. 'Thank you, sir.'

Michael glanced across at Wheeler, but he was some way along, on the other side of the trench, and did not see. He looked back at Tom. There were a dozen things he wanted to say. 'Yes,' he said. 'An excellent likeness.'

There was a clatter behind them. Michael turned to chastise Cook for fiddling again – and then felt his whole heart still. Along from them in the trench, near where Wheeler was drawing, a man in khaki was sitting up from under one of the corpses. His face was covered in blood. That was the side Michael had checked. He opened his mouth. *You're supposed to be dead*, he tried to say. The others were not looking. The man held up two grenades, smiled. 'Good morning,' he said.

There was another movement, someone else scrambling to their feet on the other side. 'Run!' Tom was tugging him, shouting. Then it was all about battering up the side of the trench, Tom climbing out first, grasping his hand. 'Come on, Michael.' Then pulling him hard, running fast. And an explosion behind him so powerful that they were both thrown forward, flat on their faces. That was when he remembered. 'Wheeler!' he screamed. 'Wheeler!' He struggled to his feet.

Tom seized him. 'Get back here, Michael.'

'Let me go!'

'They're all dead! Don't! There might be more of them.'

'I don't care!'

He flung himself back through the smoke to the trench, coughing, his eyes watering, fighting through with his hands. He could hear Tom coming behind him, shouting for him to stop. He skidded to a halt at the side of the trench. He could see nothing but blackened bodies, limbs, blood. Tom's hands were on him, pulling him back, begging him. 'They're all *dead*. We need to go *now*, sir. Michael.' He felt nothing then, blackness over his mind as he fell back into Tom's arms.

'You have to get better,' the CO was saying. 'You must. Awfully bad luck what happened to you chaps. But the Germans caught us out.'

Michael did not reply. Over three months later and he was still in the French convalescent hospital. They said he was resting. He lay in bed, staring at the sky.

'Look, Michael,' the CO was saying. 'I know it was a hard blow. It's always sad to lose men. And I know how friendly you were with Bilks. He's a loss to the service, no doubt about it. A most reliable chap. But you were lucky to survive. To think, two Germans with grenades, and you and Cotton lived. I suppose, being in the middle, you were farthest away from both of them, but still, it was a lucky escape. God has spared you and there is nothing wrong with you. We can't let you stay here much longer. You must go back. Cotton is already there.'

Michael gazed up, heard the man's voice but could not see his face.

'It's nearly December. We need you. I've found you a new second, Orchard, you'll like him.'

Michael shook his head. 'It was my fault,' he said. 'I didn't check every one.'

'What? I can't hear you, man.'

'My fault.'

The man brushed back his hair. 'Now you know that's not correct, Witt. It was the fault of the Germans. Look, thousands of men have been killed this summer. It is no one's fault but the enemy. You should know that.' Michael had read all the reports, the thousands of men, falling in front of the enemy, the dressing stations overwhelmed with the dying, the guns firing into the air, the search for bodies that still went on. He knew, rationally, that if they'd stayed in Pozières, most of the men might have died anyway. But the rational part of his brain wouldn't work.

'Why was I not beside him? We could have been together.'

'Look, man, you have to stop this. You have to pull yourself together. HQ have been merciful so far.' He lowered his voice. 'Not the best idea to have sent you to that place, of course.' Michael closed his eyes. 'But you have to pull yourself together. No more of this. We need every man. Too many have fallen ill over the winter. Properly ill.' He stood up. 'If you'd never come here, you wouldn't be like this. Should have got straight back into the saddle. I am going to put in for your transfer out next week. You'll meet Orchard. We'll put you on offensive quite soon; Orchard will help you. Take a run at the Germans again. We'll get the better of them.'

Michael stared at the ceiling. Wheeler was projected on it, like a film. He was smiling, holding out his hand. *Meet me in five minutes*, he said. *At the back of the barn.* They stood together and held each other until you could not tell where one ended and the other began. He breathed out.

Two weeks later, he was on the back of a lorry heading south. He'd said goodbye to the nurses and the MO, taken his new uniform and gun and practised with the gas mask in front of the instructor. He sat shivering under his greatcoat, his head spinning, dazed. He didn't talk to the men around him, just felt the lorry bump as it drove forward, further from Wheeler, closer to the front.

TWENTY-SIX

Étaples, December 1916

'The commandant wants to see you,' said the nurse, carefully. It was Celia's fifth day in the hospital – not that she would have known if they had not told her – and her first day free of the drugs that made her sleep. She lay in bed in a room with six other girls, the injury ward rather than the infectious diseases. Two other girls had been hit that night, but escaped with a broken leg each and bruises. Celia watched them, reading in bed, and tears rolled down her cheeks. The nurse had told her that Warterton was coming to see her after cleaning her ambulance. Celia did not know what she would say to her. Warterton, always so cheerful, practical. She would remain untouched by the war; in fifteen years' time she would be the mother of six fine boys in the country, organising jolly running races, the ambulances forgotten apart from the odd day when the local ladies' group asked her to give a talk about her experiences. Warterton would sit at the end of her bed, hold her hand and tell her that Shep would not have wished her to be so cast down.

'Ask the commandant if I can see her tomorrow,' she said. 'I do not believe my health is up to it today.'

'She says it is very important. Come now, I will take you down. Let's get you out of bed.' Celia pushed her legs over the side; they were weak with underuse. 'I have shoes here,' said the nurse. 'Easier to wear for the walk.' She wrapped a dressing gown around Celia. 'Let's go.'

The commandant's office was sparse. 'Thank you, Nurse. You may remain. Witt, I think it is best that you sit down.'

'I can stand, Commandant.' The commandant's pity was much more painful than her sharp words.

'All the same, I suggest you sit down. Nurse, perhaps you could help her.'

Celia folded her body into the seat. This was what normal people did, she reminded herself. Sit down. Stand up. She put her hands in her lap.

The commandant picked up a piece of paper. 'I have a letter here from your mother. She would like you to return to your home. I believe it is in Hampshire.'

'I don't think I wish to go home. I'm up to the work, I promise.' She didn't want to go home. She wanted to lie somewhere cool and dark and not have to think.

'It is not that, my dear.' Behind her head, Celia heard the nurse shift. She had no time to consider it, for the commandant was hurrying on, talking, sending out words. 'There was a great advance of troops. Many men were sent over. Thousands have been lost. We have been trying to keep up here with the injured. But the lost…'

I don't understand, Celia wanted to cry. *Stop talking like this. I just want to sleep.*

'The medical staff did everything they could for him,' she was saying.

For who? Celia was confused. Then suddenly her mind cleared. 'Tom!' she whispered. 'Tom!' The nurse put her hand on her shoulder, because she was shaking.

The commandant looked across the table at her, confused. 'Tom? Do you call him Tom? It is your brother, dear. Michael.'

Celia felt her face crumple and drop into nothing. She fell to the floor. There were strange noises in the room, great bellowing sobs that did not sound like anything human. They bounced off the walls, echoing in her ears. *Stop!* she wanted to cry at the person who was making the noise. Then she realised that it was her.

TWENTY-SEVEN

Isle of Man, December 1916

It was morning. Rudolf walked twenty-five times around his cell. He walked around it twenty-five times at lunchtime, and twenty-five times more at suppertime. Each round usually took him fifteen seconds at average pace. Sometimes he would go faster, Thus he would keep himself fit and ready, not like the other men near him, who he supposed sat down, felt hopeless, saved all their energy for shouting out for the warders. That wasn't him. He had no time for such weakness of spirit. Eric, his father, was watching him from above, and he wished to make him proud. Even imprisoned, even without liberty, even subject to indignity, he would not lose his soul.

He marked off the days on the wall, telling them by the change of the light in the window overhead. Then, after the dinner tray, he recited great works until the light faded and the guards started shouting for quiet. He had started out intending to recite English works. He would practise Shakespeare, and after he had recited everything he could remember, he would move on to Marlowe and then Jonson. When they finally decided to let him free, he would be like a butterfly, still healthy, knowledgeable. But when he came to it, he couldn't do it. He couldn't recite *Twelfth Night*. Or *Macbeth* or *As You Like It* or any of them. He found himself wanting to declaim German works instead: Goethe, Schiller and his mother's favourite, Sophie de la Roche. He spoke the words quietly, under his breath, so that no one would hear. He used English only when the guards shouted to him, came to empty his pail or took him out for his weekly exercise up and down the corridor. Otherwise, he spoke German. *I am becoming what you think I am,* he said softly in his mind as they hauled him out by his arm. *German, not English. I can't stop.*

One morning, Jervis, one of the guards who was less rough when he took him out, came to his cell and opened the door. He pulled paper and a pen from his pocket, hissed in Rudolf's ear: 'You've got three minutes to write to your family. Quick.'

Rudolf stared at him. 'What do you mean?'

He hissed again: 'Hurry.' Then raised his voice. 'Brief cell inspection, Witt. Turn over your bed, please.' Rudolf went to his bed and Jervis pulled him back. 'Write!'

'But why?' Rudolf gazed at the man, sweating in his uniform. It had to be some sort of trap. They had chosen Jervis because he had thought him kind.

Jervis dropped his voice. 'Look, favour from some friend of yours. Lord Smith or someone. Quickly.'

Rudolf looked at his paper. What to write. At the beginning, he had scribbled to his wife in his head, over and over. But after the months elapsed and nothing changed, he found his mind too full of the words of his books to write.

'It's your last chance!' said Jervis. He raised his voice and started shouting something about the pillows. Rudolf bowed his head and began writing.

Dear wife and children,

I hope you're all well. I hope, Verena dear, you have heard from Michael. And that Arthur is home now. I'm sure Emmeline is also once more friends with us all. How is the house? Does the ivy need cutting back? I wish I were there to do it. How is my little Celia? Working hard at her lessons, I imagine. I am well, wife, taking exercise, keeping my spirits up. I hope that I may

Jervis snatched the paper. 'Right, that's it. Time to go.'

'Please,' said Rudolf. 'Please let me sign it.' He felt a tear at his eye.

Jervis handed him the letter; Rudolf scribbled, gave back the pen. Jervis shouted out loudly about the inspection and how Rudolf should keep his cell tidy from now on. Then he slammed out of the door. Rudolf sat there staring at it. The words he'd written resounded in his mind, simple, childish. He felt full of shame. Next time, he would think of something better. He would practise, not spend every night reciting German. He would be ready.

Verena repeated Rudolf's words in her mind. Taking exercise, keeping up spirits. She had written back, sealed it, but Lord Smith's man had told her there would be no chance of a reply. She left the envelope on her bureau, just in case.

She turned over in bed, reminding herself to tell the girls to change the sheets. Every day for the last week she had forgotten to ask them. And now they were dirty. Even worse, she hardly noticed. Why, she wondered, why were you supposed to wash sheets? It was one of the routines of Stoneythorpe. But what would happen if you didn't? Perhaps it was all just a great lie to keep everyone occupied, women, servants, the people who made sheets – who did that? – filling their time, over and over, because if they stopped, they might want to ask questions. Well, she wouldn't allow that. She pulled herself out of bed – no need to dress, since there was no one to see – put on a shawl for the cold and padded downstairs.

Her mother had been very fond of cleanliness. 'Next to godliness,' she had said to all the servants, dismissed plenty for not measuring up. She spent hours training Verena in the standards that she desired her to keep in her own future home. Lady Deerhurst had great hopes of Verena's future.

How many years? Verena pondered. Nearly twenty-five years ago she had stood in Buckingham Palace waiting to be presented to the Queen. Mama was particularly concerned about the ostrich feather. They had hunted all over for one that protruded properly from her hair. But still the feather of the girl in front of her billowed out much higher than hers. And, she realised, gazing at the others, her diamonds were a little dull. Other dresses were a more brilliant white. How could it be, she thought, that after all her mother's efforts, still someone else's dress was a brighter white than her own?

They progressed forward. The room was incredibly hot and bright and there were dozens of girls ahead of her. She could just make out a tiny black-clad figure with a pile of hair. 'No crown,' whispered a girl somewhere. She waited, hot in her dress, sure that when she reached the Queen, her ostrich feather would have sunk and her dress would be sticking to her throat. After an hour or so, she was three girls away from the throne. The girl ahead of her with the perfect ostrich feather was still looking quite pristine. The flowers in the room were terribly pungent and the lights were so hot. The diamonds scratched her neck but she didn't dare move them. Men in swords surrounded the Queen and someone was giving out names.

She had been told hundreds and hundreds of times that this would be the most wonderful day of her life. Presented to the Queen! As Lady Deerhurst had told her, thousands of girls were not presented. Their families were not deemed proper! Now she was here. Afterwards, Lady Deerhurst had promised her, a great vista of wonder would open and her life would begin. All the dancing lessons, the French, the careful schooling, the dressmakers' bills and the creams ploughed into her skin would now prove their worth.

Lady Deerhurst herself had been presented to the Queen when she was nineteen, a group that became special, as it happened, because it was the last one before the death of the Prince Consort. 'They looked so happy,' Lady Deerhurst said, shaking her head. 'He was a great support to her.' She was fascinated by the Queen's widowhood, talked at length about whether one should set aside a special room for one's late husband if the Queen did. The question of how to be a dignified widow was one that she found constantly occupying. Verena's father was some way from death yet, but *still*. One had to plan.

Verena didn't think that her mother ever believed the Queen might die. And yet here they were, years later, governed by her son, at war with her nephew. She had not thought much of the Queen when she met her. Perhaps Her Majesty was tired; she supposed it was even harder under all the lights for such an old person. Verena gave the deep curtsey – which she had practised probably a thousand times – and looked up into the tiny eyes. She smiled, and a flash of something crossed the Queen's face. She recognised it with a jolt: displeasure. It was exactly the same expression that crossed her mother's face when she had said something wrong. She flushed miserably and stumbled up, ungainly. Still, years later, the memory of it made her blush.

And then afterwards it was as if everything she did was slightly wrong, a little shadowed. She went to the balls of the daughters of friends of her parents in cold country houses, talked to men who were as bored by her as her father seemed to be, ate cold meat and cake. Her parents hosted a party for her with musicians and singers, the Great Hall decked with greenery that took the servants a whole week to bring in and put up. Her mother set up six fittings for a special gown for her, pale yellow with pure gold thread running through it. She watched them pull it around her too-tall figure blushingly, knowing it would have suited her mother so much better. Gold and lemon were her mother's colours – she had worn them to her own coming-out ball. Verena felt clumsy and ill at ease, and was quite sure that every girl who arrived looked prettier than her. Some of them she barely recognised, even though she had been going to the same parties as them for the past four months. She danced with some men who trod on her gown, heard some of the mothers discussing her father's renovations to the hall, wondered if it was just her imagination that there were fewer people at her ball than anyone else's – and pretended to have a quite wonderful time. At the end of a whole year of balls and gowns and cold meat and cake, not a single man had asked her to marry him. 'No one,' said Lady Deerhurst in a voice full of doom, 'has even come *close*.'

Rudolf had rescued her from it all. The strange, tall man who danced like a jerky puppet at the ball of a friend of her father's. Lord Deerhurst had attended under sufferance, because many of the guests were *in business*. His banker had begged him – and friendly favour from a banker was always useful to have, he thought. 'Don't worry about dressing her up too much,' he said to his wife. 'We don't want to look as if we have *tried*.'

'Would you care to dance?' Rudolf had asked her. He had come over, hand outstretched. As he took her around the room, she only wanted to laugh. His movements were so untidy, and he grasped her so hard that she thought his fingernails might pierce the back of her gown. After a brief wrestle, she took to more or less guiding him. He tried to say something about the room and she shook her head. If he spoke, he would surely not be able to dance at all.

'Thank you, Miss Colebridge,' he said, when it was over, escorting her to her seat. 'The Honourable Miss Colebridge, I believe.'

'Quite correct.'

'Your parents must be very proud of such a pretty and graceful daughter.'

'I am sure, sir.' She jerked his arm to swerve him out of the way of a couple that he hadn't seen.

She had not thought anything of him, then, other than that he was a jolly man who could barely dance. She didn't think he would be her saviour, the man who rescued her from what she now realised had been her future: to keep going to balls and receptions with all the other girls who had failed to get a husband, over and over until she managed it – or, she supposed, everyone gave her up as a lost cause. But he was. Next morning, he paid a social call on Lady Deerhurst, and her. They talked inconsequentially about churches.

'What an odd man,' said Lady Deerhurst. 'I think we shan't be in when he next calls.'

They were not. But still, he wrote, sent letters via servants that Lady Deerhurst did not see. Verena met him in the park when she was meant to be riding, at the portraitist and even when she said she was visiting Charlotte Sutherland for tea.

'When did you fall in love with me?' she asked him, in bafflement, after his proposal.

'On the spot. I knew you were the one. I could see I would have a fight. I saw your mother's face. But you were my princess, like in those Arthurian myths. I had to capture you and set you free.'

And free she became. Free, she thought, and much richer than some of the other girls in that line for the Queen. Charlotte Sutherland had married the most dreary old marquis, who turned out not to have a bean. Not many of them probably lived in a house like Stoneythorpe now. And yet although she loved Stoney-thorpe – and all the more because Rudolf did too – the time when she had been happiest was when she and Rudolf were first married: poor, cut off by her father. Rudolf was working every hour for the factories and they were living in the house in Hampstead where each one of their children was born.

Verena had come to decide that she was fondest of children when they were about four or five; no longer babies, but still close to those early days of childhood where they lived in their own odd world. Babies muddled her; she worried why they cried. Arthur had wailed whatever they did; she and the nurse picked him up, put him down, fed him, didn't feed him. Nothing worked. Everything seemed to send him into a temper, his face bright red with fury. So she was happiest, perhaps, when he was five, Michael three and Emmeline two – and she and Rudolf had decided she would have a year before beginning another child (their *last* child, she said).

June 1897, the summer of the Queen's Jubilee. Arthur perched on Rudolf's shoulders near the Mall to watch the tiny Queen go by. 'Mama met the Queen,' Rudolf said with pride. Now the Queen received her tributes outside St Paul's, because she couldn't walk up the stairs.

Verena thought of her as she lay under the oak tree in the Hampstead garden. Not even so old and a widow. She watched the play of light through the leaves. Sarah, the nurse, took the older children on long walks, Rudolf was out working all day and she had the house to herself, padding around it, gazing at the shafts of light through the windows.

After an afternoon of lying outside, the children would return with Sarah, and at seven or half past or so, Rudolf would come home. It was perfect. Until his tedious cousin, Heinrich, arrived from Bavaria for a visit. He wanted to see London, hauled Rudolf off to walk along the Thames and demanded dinner at the club.

'How long will he be here?' Verena had hissed after Heinrich's stay stretched into a second week.

'Oh, Verena dear. Not so long.' And then she felt churlish, because Heinrich was Rudolf's dearest friend – practically a brother really. He had a new wife to support and hadn't found a proper line of work. She did feel sorry for him, really! But when Rudolf came in late, night after night, smelling of drink (and sometimes, she worried, smoke), it was hard to feel the gracious sympathy she knew was the preserve of a true lady. And Heinrich sometimes sent her rather odd looks, extraordinary, even.

'What a lovely-looking lady you are,' he had said, brushing against her that morning.

But complaining to your husband that his cousin was too complimentary – what sort of behaviour was that? Lady Deerhurst – who Verena often imagined in her head – would have been very firm: *That sort of behaviour belongs in the schoolroom, dear*, she would have said.

Well, Mama, replied Verena, *it's not just me.*

It wasn't. She had seen Heinrich following Sarah around with his eyes. And even – worse – Maria. Sarah was a plain girl, with popping eyes and a pug nose. No one could seriously be in love with her – apart from the children, who climbed all over her in flushes of adoration. Maria Cotton, their upper housemaid, was beautiful. Lady Deerhurst would never have employed her, but when she had come for her interview, Verena had felt ashamed of her instinctive reaction – that such a pretty girl would be trouble – and determined to give her a chance based on her abilities. *Oh, just stop talking, Mama*, she had said to her mother in her head.

Maria was a good maid, quick, obedient, respectful. But she was so painfully attractive, which was always more upsetting when one knew one was only a year away from getting so *large* again – and all the rest of the indignities that went with it. Even Rudolf, who was the most tactful soul alive and as devoted to one woman as the Prince Consort had ever been, had mentioned three or four times what a fine-looking girl Maria was.

I do not imagine things! said Lady Deerhurst. *Neither do you.*

Should I consult my husband on the matter? Verena wondered. On the one hand, he had told her she should always feel she could confide in him. On the other, this was surely something she could address herself. And he loved his cousin so, he would hate to hear any aspersion. Even worse, what if talking of men and housemaids put an idea into his head? Rudolf was an innocent, that had been almost immediately clear to her. She had to preserve that state.

Mama? she tried again. *Should I tell Rudolf?*

But Lady Deerhurst, normally so garrulous, was silent.

In the end, Verena decided not to say anything. Instead she engaged in a quite excruciating interview with Maria while the girl was dusting the mantelpiece.

She walked into the room and shut the door. 'Maria, I wondered if we might speak.'

'Of course, madam,' said the girl, turning around smartly. Her face was so docile that Verena was covered in shame at what she had thought.

'I just wondered if you … were happy here?'

'Of course, madam.' Her answer rang with surprise.

'Oh good.' Verena sat down to support her back – aching *already?* 'I am glad. Yes. Very glad. It is … well … if you ever felt that you were not, you should say.' She stumbled on her words. The girl was staring at her. This was not going as she had expected. *Mama!* she cried in her head. *Could you help me?* Again Lady Deerhurst was silent.

'Well, if you were not happy here. If there was anything you might wish to … talk about. Yes. I hope you might … tell me.' The girl stared at her. An awful blush spread over her face.

'I am very content here, madam.' She bowed her head. When she looked up, her eyes were dark beads. 'Has anyone said I am not?'

'No, no.'

'I am most content.' She tossed her head. 'Of course I won't be here for ever.'

Verena nodded, dumbly.

'I have learned a lot here about how to run a household. It will come in useful for the future.'

Verena heaved herself to her feet – the girl did not offer her a hand, she noticed. 'Thank you, Maria,' she said. 'You may continue.'

Maria nodded, perfectly obedient. And yet, as Verena watched her turn back to the dusting, she had the curious sensation that positions had been reversed in the oddest fashion. The girl was the one telling her to go away; it was her house and Verena was the maid.

Verena felt dizzy, clutched the arm of the chair.

Oh, what nonsense, rang Lady Deerhurst in her mind. *You need to lie down, Verena. The child in you is making you imagine things.* She had never been so grateful for the appearance of her mother in her life.

And Lady Deerhurst had been quite right – as usual. The summer had rolled on. At the end of August she came down to breakfast and Heinrich was telling Rudolf that he simply had to leave that day. Urgent business, he said.

'We will be so sorry to see you go,' she said, holding his hand. She did not say, however, *Please visit again soon.* Maria was more sullen in the days afterwards, but she took it as simply the effect of the sun. And perhaps, she thought, she had not been the most *pleasant* mistress. *You must set an example of behaviour to your servants*, said Lady Deerhurst. *They are like children. They follow you.*

Verena realised she had been sitting on the marble seat in the hall of Stoneythorpe for nearly an hour. Her legs were cramped under her in the cold. She stood up to stretch them. That was when she saw the letter by the front door. It was from France. Not in Michael's handwriting. She leapt forward, full of joy. They were telling her he was finally coming home.

TWENTY-EIGHT

Stoneythorpe, December 1916

Four years ago, the whole village would have come to Michael's funeral. Now, apart from the vicar, the church held just them and the servants. Arthur had written to say that travel was impossible. Celia thought she hardly knew what he looked like any more. She thought of him in terms of the photograph in Rudolf's study – the dark hair, thin face, too long nose, the mouth she knew was handsome but too narrow – for there was no other way to remember him.

Emmeline and Mr Janus, Verena and Celia stood in a row in the chill church. The greenery up for Christmas was a mockery, Celia thought. Last night had been the first time Emmeline and her mother had met since that dreadful schism – and this morning had been the first time that anyone had seen Lady Deerhurst, thin and pale, hobbling in with her maids, since long before the war. She was accompanied by their cousins – Verena's sister said she was too unwell – Matthew and Louisa, looking respectably sad and neatly dressed. Sarah, their old nanny, had arrived in a car paid for by Verena. Last night, Celia had come by train from London with Emmeline and Mr Janus. Verena had surprised them all by grasping Mr Janus and weeping on his shoulder. 'At least I still have three of my children,' she was saying. 'Some would tell me I should feel grateful.'

Celia looked around and a big tear rolled down her face. Michael would have expected more. When she was younger and feeling as if she had been unfairly treated at school or by Verena, she would luxuriate in imaginings of her own early death and funeral. The pews of a grand church in London would be full of weeping, all sorts of people she had never met. Every girl from Winterbourne would be standing there looking miserable. The church would not be nearly empty, as this one was. She felt Emmeline clutch her hand. The vicar began talking of peace and charity. Verena was still standing rod straight. Celia felt more tears falling from her eyes and did not try to stop them. She supposed that her father had been told, but how could you know? She imagined him sitting alone in his cell, receiving an official letter from somewhere. *Your son is dead.* He wept alone, maybe wrote a letter, even though no one would ever see it.

The bearded man had come to them while they were waiting outside for Lady Deerhurst to arrive. He held out his mittened hand to Verena as his breath pooled in the cold air. 'Professor Punter.' He looked, Celia thought, as everyone would think a professor should look: dirty grey hair falling past his ears, pale skin and an old navy jacket over baggy trousers. He gestured to the young man beside him. 'This is Dr Green, lecturer in classics. He cannot fight due to his lungs.'

'Thank you for coming, Professor. Dr Green. We are very grateful.'

'I was very fond of Mr de Witt. An excellent student. We had hopes for further study for him.' He smiled sadly. 'I go to more and more funerals these days.'

Emmeline pushed Celia forward. 'My sister is interested in study, Professor. She likes literature.'

Celia blushed furiously. Professor Punter gave her a distant smile. 'Well, miss, young ladies might soon be the only ones left remaining to study.'

Celia could not talk to him. Nothing seemed real, nothing was right. She felt as if she could see every tiny particle in the air and they made a mass around her. She could not push through it. She was not properly there, properly alive. Professor Punter was an invention. In a minute, Michael would walk around the corner, throw back his head and laugh.

The Professor shook his head. 'Mr de Witt was an excellent

student. I was not surprised to learn he had died such a brave death.'

Verena looked up. 'Oh really, Professor? We have little detail. My daughter has written to the War Office but we've had no reply. All we know is that he died in the course of his duties.' Dr Green was looking at the floor. Celia supposed he was embarrassed because he couldn't fight.

'One of my students told me that he died saving a friend of his, a young man in the same division. In the heat of battle he stopped to help him, drag him back to safety, and that's when he was shot.'

Celia could feel her mother stiffen. 'Which young man?'

Professor Punter was still talking, looking into space. 'Such a brave act, is it not? I knew I could rely on my boys. I believe they are told not to stop for fallen comrades. And yet Michael was determined to do so. The Ancient Greeks would be proud. It makes me think of the words of Seneca.'

As he talked about Seneca, Celia could feel her mother growing jumpy beside her, not wanting to interrupt him out of politeness but worrying that Lady Deerhurst was about to arrive.

'Professor, do you know the name of the young man he saved?' she said, in the midst of a monologue about *Plutarch's Lives*.

He broke off and looked at them vaguely, as if they were his students. 'Why yes. I believe his name was Tom Cotton. A friend of the family, is that not correct?'

Verena's face was pure fury. Celia said, 'Mama—' to stop her from speaking. But then Lady Deerhurst arrived and they all curtseyed and bowed to her, progressed into the church.

The day after the commandant had given her the news, Warterton took her to the station. 'Tell me you'll come back, Witt,' she said. 'Please.'

'I will try,' said Celia. She couldn't see past returning home and the funeral, couldn't imagine the world moving after that. 'I don't know.'

She travelled back from France with another girl, Bligh, who was being sent home for pneumonia. She coughed all the way, so much that Celia sometimes thought there must be no sound left in her. On the boat over, a few soldiers tried to engage them in conversation, not put off by Bligh's terrible coughing, but Celia ignored them. She came into Charing Cross and went straight to Emmeline's. It was six o'clock. Emmeline put her arms out and held her close.

And now here they all were in the church, watching as the vicar ploughed through the words. Celia had turned her head, looking for Matthew and Louisa. Instead, she saw Tom. Her blood froze. She could not speak. He was wearing uniform, his arm in a splint. He was taller, she thought, thinner, his face was browner – but it was *him*. She tried desperately to catch his attention, but he did not look. She smiled. He ignored her. Emmeline had noticed her shuffle around and saw, drew in a sharp breath. Then Verena turned to see what was happening and Celia saw her face blanch. Verena poked Emmeline in the ribs. 'Look forward!' she hissed at Celia. Celia did so, staring at the vicar, listening to his words. After a fit amount of time had passed, she turned again. Tom was not there.

Panic spread through her. She clutched her sides. Surely he had just walked out to take a little air and would be back. But when she looked again, he was still not there. She put her hand to her heart and felt it grow cold. She could not bear it. She pushed past Mr Janus, on the end of the pew, and hurtled down the side aisle and out of the door. There was no sign of him outside. 'Tom!' she shouted. 'Tom.' The village green in front of her gave back her call, mocking. She waited for a few minutes. It was the singing of 'Onward, Christian Soldiers' from inside that pulled her back. So few people were singing. The thin, broken sounds filled her heart with pain.

After the service, they went to watch Michael's gravestone being erected. They buried a few of the belongings that had been sent back – a belt, a buckle, one of his letters – but of course no body. The vicar had said it was irregular but allowed it on account of Michael's great sacrifice for his country. Celia tried not to think of the corpses she had seen in France, the tattered remains of men. Her mother had been spared that, at least.

At the graveside, she craned and craned, turned around repeatedly to see, hoping that Tom might be there, but he did not come.

Lady Deerhurst, Matthew, Louisa, Professor Punter and Dr Green came back to the house for a dismal tea with the vicar. The Professor talked loudly about Seneca and then the rituals of Sparta, how they suffered for bravery. Lady Deerhurst stared at the room, its new shabbiness, and said it was much changed. Celia was grateful for Cousin Matthew, thin and bespectacled, who talked about his interest in painting and admired the portraits of Arthur and Michael on the walls. At fifteen, he was already taller than her. Louisa sat and gazed around the room, clutching Lady Deerhurst's hand. She had very pretty dark eyes, Celia noticed, and the upright posture she herself had never managed. She supposed Lady Deerhurst would be planning a marriage for her to someone terribly grand. After a proper amount of time had elapsed, they all made their excuses. Lady Deerhurst clambered up into her carriage, waving gracefully.

After the others had gone, they sat in the sitting room, surrounded by the cakes Mrs Rolls had made. Her heart had not been in it and the seedcake had been sour. 'How could you have engaged in such an exhibition?' Verena was furious. 'How could you, Celia?'

'She was just trying to get some air,' broke in Emmeline. 'That's all, Mama.'

'Emmeline, you know that is not true. She ran out of the service in front of everyone.' They were speaking as if Emmeline had never gone away. Celia supposed Verena was saving her words for Emmeline until later. Michael's death had taken everything and turned it around.

'There weren't that many people to be in front of, Mama.'

'Don't say that,' said Emmeline.

Celia hung her head. 'I'm sorry, Mama. I just wanted to ask him about what happened.'

'We all know what happened, Celia. There is nothing more to

know. Your brother died saving... that man. *He* should have been the one to die.'

Tom had written. A letter had come after the one from Michael's CO – he had said that Michael had died bravely in an enemy attack, but gave no details. 'My whole world is lost,' he wrote.

'He didn't even have the honesty to tell us!' said Verena.

'Maybe he couldn't,' said Mr Janus. 'They don't let men write that much in their letters. And it seems like he was the only one to survive.' They had expected letters from other men in his company, but nothing had come.

Emmeline dropped her head into her hands and wept. Celia put her arms around her and her head against her shoulder. She could think of nothing to say.

That evening, when Emmeline and Verena were safely in their rooms, Celia left her room and hurried down the stairs. Thompson was at the bottom, still clearing up after the tea.

'Where are you going, miss?'

'I need some air.'

He held out his hand. His eyes were reddened and sore-looking. 'Don't go out, miss.' He shook his head. 'I'll call Jennie, we could talk. She had a letter from Smithson last week. He's in Mesopotamia now, says days aren't too bad if the water cart turns up on time.' He was talking fast at her. She didn't want to hear it, not about the men who were still alive when Michael was dead. Marks was with the Hampshires and she felt sick with herself that she hated him for being alive.

'Just wait one moment, miss.'

'You can't stop me.' She pushed past him towards the door and ran out around the side of the house. It was dark, but she followed the route she knew towards the side street of low houses. One of the lights was on in the Cotton house. She knocked on the door. No one came. She knocked again. The door opened a crack. Mary's face appeared.

'Oh, not you.'

'Tom is here.'

'No, he isn't. Please. Go away.'

'He must be. I've just seen him.'

Mary opened the door a little. 'What are you talking about? He's not here.'

'I saw him.'

'I don't believe you. Go away.' She started to close the door. 'Your brother dragged him off to war. Now he's in hospital some-where, we don't know where. All thanks to your family.'

'My brother died saving him!'

'I'm sorry for your loss. But Tom's not here.' Mary closed the door as she was speaking. Celia knocked again but there was no answer.

She walked back home. Tom had come to the funeral but not seen his family. She might think she had imagined him – or it had been someone else – but Verena and Emmeline had seen him too. Then she remembered. Michael was gone, dead in a cold trench in France, and they would never see him again. She walked back, overcome with desolation.

1917

TWENTY-NINE

London, February 1917

It was early February. Celia had been staying with Emmeline ever since they had left Verena at Stoneythorpe a week after a miserable Christmas. Most days she had spent lying in Emmeline's room or on the thin cold grass in Bedford Square, looking at the dreary winter sky. She never knew which was worse. The nights full of Michael, catching her hand as they ran together to the stream, there to pick her up from the station in Cambridge, swinging her up into his arms even though she protested she was too big. Or those when he was not there and she saw only endless dark space, aching as she prayed over and over for the dawn.

She knew she should not, but despite herself she loved the dream that came to her often, that Michael had returned, she had awoken and he was beside her, sitting on the bed, smiling and tanned, putting his hand in hers, saying he was sorry that he had been away so long, he had been lost in France, but now he was back. She cherished, clutched the joy, trying to prolong it, even though the realisation of the truth when she opened her eyes was thick with pain. She knew that doting on the dream made the pain worse, but she could not stop herself. She spent her days trying to imagine over and over how it had been, how Michael had saved Tom, what could have happened. She wished she'd run after Tom at the funeral.

She was lying in Bedford Square when she felt a shadow fall over her. She looked up and Emmeline was standing there. 'You can't spend your days like this,' she said.

'Emmeline. Would you leave me alone?'

'We have all lost something. We are all without Michael. Not just you.'

'Please, Emmeline.'

'I think you should do some war work again. Something in London.'

'I don't want to do that any more.' Celia wanted to reach up and hold tight to her sister's hand. 'Please understand.' Emmeline was trying to help her, she knew, but Celia just wanted to tell her how wrong she was. 'I can't.'

'Well, perhaps you will have to. I need you to. You need to do something if you are living here. We don't have money to spare. You know Samuel lost that pupil, Christopher, because the parents couldn't afford the lessons, and he isn't selling many paintings. And Mama doesn't have any to give us. So you should work or go back to Stoneythorpe.'

Celia propped herself on her elbows, screwing up her eyes against the sun. 'I can't go back there!' Verena, wandering around the house, her eyes full of pain, begging for conversation, worrying over the placement of a vase, the space for a table. Celia knew she was wrong in not wanting to go to her mother, but she could not help it. 'You were trying to persuade her to come to London.' Verena had been complaining that the factories were doing badly, that a man had come and said that Stoneythorpe needed a new roof but Mr Lewis didn't think he had the money to give her.

'Yes, but she won't agree, you know that. Anyway, we are talking about you. You could go and be a driver in London. I've read all about this WAAC lot. Something you'd get paid for. And you're eighteen now, no need to pretend to be me.' A week ago, Emmeline had invited Jemima and Rufus for a birthday tea. They sang to her and Celia could only cry.

Celia looked up. 'You're being unfair. You didn't see it. Shep died and then Michael died!' Saying the words out loud scarred her throat. She felt hot tears running down her face.

Emmeline swept her skirts from under her and sat down. 'I know, Celia. But you're still alive.'

Celia cried into the bright winter sky above her. 'I don't want to be. I don't understand why I am.'

Emmeline patted her hand. 'You don't have a choice. And while you are waiting to die, you have to live. Come, Celia, let's go. I will take you to the recruiting station.'

Within a week, Celia was back in uniform again as a driver for an officer, Captain Russell. He was youngish, dour-looking, spent most of the time with his head buried in papers. That suited her well. She drove him from meeting to meeting, moving between gears, not thinking. She put on her uniform, cleaned the car, collected him and his papers. While he was in his meetings, she huddled in her greatcoat, trying to keep warm by burying her hands under her legs. She dodged patches of ice, roadworks at Piccadilly. After work, sometimes she took a parcel that Emmeline had given her for delivery to one of Mr Janus's artistic friends. It was against the rules, but Emmeline begged and it was easier than saying no. In the evenings, she came back to her bed at Emmeline's and pretended she was asleep. She wrote to Tom at his family's house, only twice, but in her head she was always writing. She let her hair grow back, thinner and wispier than it had been before.

Once she went to the works canteen, but the ringing tones of the other girls made her shrink back in fear. The waitresses carrying bowls of pudding were so full of life, the men laughing around the tables, the groups of women in uniform patting their hair – she wanted to say, *But why are you so happy?* They all looked a little like Jemima: slim bodies, round red cheeks, girls who could never be knocked to the ground.

She tried to avoid Jemima when she came around, pretended to be asleep on the sofa so they would not have to talk. She knew that Jemima was a little hurt, and it was her fault, for she had changed and the woman she had idealised had not. Jemima had been so pleased to see her back, hugged her violently, told her how glad she was to see her and asked to hear all about France. But Celia couldn't tell her. Every time she opened her mouth,

Michael and Shep loomed up in front of her. *They are dead, while we are alive.*

Everything made her feel bent down, as if she had been pushed over and could not get up. The word 'fight' made her feel sick, and who cared about the vote, she wanted to say. *What difference will it make? They will still go to war.* When Jemima came to her, her eyes bright, offering a pie or a cake that she had found at great expense, Celia felt a failure, hopeless for not being able to give her what she wanted. Tom was the only one she wanted to see. He had the answer to the puzzle. She thought of him lying in no-man's-land, thinking that no one was coming to help him, giving himself up to the gunfire. And then Michael bending over him. 'I'll help you,' he said. He pulled Tom up into his arms, dragged him forward.

Warterton had written twice since Celia had been home, saying she hoped she would come back soon. Her writing was large, round, neat. The food was worse, she said, but HQ had demanded a review of why so many girls had left, and so orders had come in to give them an extra hour's rest in the morning. Cooper was on warning for sneaking out, might be sent home. Celia hadn't replied. She couldn't bear writing to Warterton; what would she say? *I can't come back. I don't have the courage to face death again. If I see a man screaming because his leg has been blown off, I will think of Michael and I will feel as if I want to die myself. I would stop the ambulance and cry. And if a Zepp came towards me, I'd get out and stand under its silver sheen and say why don't you take me now, like you did everybody else?*

She had even received a letter from Commandant Robinson, who'd passed on Shep's parents' address and suggested they might like to hear from her friends. That made Celia cry hard, for Robinson had called her Elizabeth, the name Johnson had used after they knew she was dead. *She's still Shep!* Celia wanted to cry, but she knew it wasn't true. Shep was dead, buried in France in a grave near the brave soldiers. And girls who gave their lives were not Shep or Sheppie, but Elizabeth – dignified, graceful, truly English.

She stared at the letters from Warterton, the commandant, three from Verena. She picked up her pen to reply, and then could not. She knew the words she should have written: *how are you?* to Warterton, *thank you* to the commandant, and then a fond anecdote about Shep to her grieving parents, an enquiry about Mick in the POW camp. Warterton would have done it straight away, ticked off her list, written something general and kind about how *everybody loved Shep*, and then a pleasing detail like *she always had biscuits to spare*. Every time Celia thought about writing, she wanted to scream. She would have to say that Shep was brave, good, *doing her duty*, as you always had to say, not that the war had taken her and there was no plan to it. She could not bear to write *Shep was, Shep had*, for then that would make it real.

One day in early March, Captain Russell came in holding a map. 'A different route today,' he said. 'I need to collect some documents from a house in Hampstead, near the Heath. Do you know the way?'

It was the first time they had diverged from the usual route around Whitehall and the War Office. Celia nodded. 'I know the way.'

They headed past the stations and north through Camden. Women, bent over around tiny fires, sold piles of belongings near the roadside, saucepans, clothes, tables and chairs; some, she supposed, after their houses had been burned down, some simply desperate for money. Dirty children sat beside them, selling off their toys. Ragged newsboys ran around shouting about the next big push. 'Fritz on the brink of collapse!' they cried. 'Buy the paper!' Nursemaids wheeled out prams. Celia found it almost shocking that people were still having children. Houses were missing their roofs, the garden squares were without their railings, windows were dirty. The only men she saw were elderly, women hurrying around them. There were no spring flowers.

Celia shivered as she arrived on the borders of Hampstead. She had not seen their old home for years. Already she was recognising the houses, dully noticing how they did not look grand any more. There were broken window panes, grimy doors, skeletal perambulators abandoned in overgrown gardens. The place looked like it had been bombed, even though she knew the bombs had not come close, at least not yet. 'It is Prince Arthur Road I want,' Captain Russell said.

'I know it.'

He raised his head from his papers. 'You are familiar with this area, Miss Witt?'

'I lived here when I was a child. In one of the nearby streets. John Road. Keats lived there once.'

'Did you really live here? I did not know you were from the area.'

She gazed out at the road. 'My father was a meat importer. He wanted to move to the country to buy a big house there. It was a beautiful house, but my sister and brothers preferred London.'

'Are they still in the country now?'

'No. Only my mother.' She manoeuvred to avoid a pothole.

'The rest are here?'

'Not in Hampstead. Other places.' She changed gear and turned the corner.

'I have a great admiration for you war girls, you know,' he said. 'Coming from all sorts of backgrounds, buckling down.'

She could not think of a reply and kept her eyes on the road. She knew he was treating her with more respect and interest because he thought she was rich.

'You must have left a lot of your old life behind in the country, I suppose. Friends, your family. Your sweetheart.'

'I don't have one.' The words rose and glimmered between them. She could have got out of the car and walked to where Tom's house once was.

'A young girl like you. Surely you must.'

She turned into Prince Arthur Road. 'What number, sir?'

'Sixty-five.'

She drew up outside, pulled on the brake. 'Won't be long,' he said, manoeuvring himself out of the passenger seat. 'Don't feed the strays.' The previous day, while she was waiting for him, she had broken off a bit of her sandwich to throw to a scrawny-looking pigeon, and he had come around the corner and caught her. 'Don't you know it's illegal?' She did know about the law, of course, but hadn't really associated all those dire warnings and advertisements with these few puny things, scrabbling for grain at the tail end of winter. She didn't know, hadn't realised that you could be fined for feeding pigeons or stray animals, wasting food. She hoped that no stray animals would come near; she would only feel too much pity for them.

She sat and looked at Prince Arthur Road. She was strictly forbidden to leave her vehicle unattended. But she could hop out now and run to their old house, just a few streets along, and Russell would be none the wiser. A woman walked past with a pram, two small children at her side. That decided Celia. There was no threat here, just mothers and babies; it was the safest place she could possibly leave the car. She leapt from the cab, locked the door and ran at top speed around the corner, turned past the house that used to train orphan daughters of Crimea soldiers for service, her favourite house in the old days.

She slowed as she saw their house. The trees at the front had grown taller and wilder. The roof was missing tiles and there was a broken chair lying by the door. She stepped on to the drive and walked slowly to the door, the knowledge that she should not pulling her forward. She knocked. A scruffy-looking maid answered.

'Yes? Oh, we don't have anything for the collection, you know.'

'I am not here for that. I lived here once. I wondered if I could see inside.'

The maid shook her head. 'Of course not! Whatever next?' She started to close the door.

Celia held out her hand. 'Please. Could you ask your mistress?'

'They're all out. You'd better go. Come back tomorrow, she might be in then.'

'I can't. I am only here today. Please.'

'I will call the gardener if you don't go.'

'I would give you money.' Celia put her hand in her pocket and brought out some notes. 'After all, if they are not here, no one would ever know.'

'Miss, I told you. I can't let anyone in!'

'You can take this.' Celia fiddled with her purse, brought out more notes.

'You're trying to bribe me.'

'I just wanted to offer you something. Listen, please let me in. I have lost a lot. My father and brother are dead in the war.' How terrible she was for lying. 'I would like to remember the times when we were all happy.'

The girl looked at her and hesitated. Celia held out the money. 'Please. You are my last chance. I won't be able to come again.'

The girl's voice softened. 'Which battle?'

'The Somme, that's what they said. He was near the Somme.'

'Mine too. He was only sixteen. Told them he was nineteen and they believed him, even though he looked like the skinniest thing alive. My mother half tried to murder him when he came back from the recruiting, but it was done. He only had two leaves, four days each. The second one, madam here wouldn't let me go, so I never saw him.'

'I'm sorry.'

The girl shrugged, rubbing her eyes. 'No point crying over spilt milk, though, is there? He wanted adventure, that's what he said. Well, he got that all right.'

'My brother ran away too. He knew we would try to stop him, I suppose.' Celia was still holding the door. 'I'm sorry your mistress didn't let you go.'

'Your work here is more important, that's what she said. She goes out and helps at the canteens. It's all for show – she'd do better to send me and dust her own vases. I'd like to be in the factories. Good money.'

'Those girls get bright yellow faces, you know, from all the chemicals around. And their hair. I don't think they can ever get it out. Haven't you seen them?'

She pulled open the door. 'I'd like blonde hair. Still, but they're doing something, aren't they? And it's better pay than sitting around here cutting the ends off flowers to try and make them last that bit longer.'

Celia followed her inside. The hall looked woefully dusty, and cobwebs were hanging from the doors. She almost tripped over a trunk in the hallway.

'So what do you want to see? Dining room? Parlour? Those are the doors. Although I suppose you know that.' The girl gestured around.

'I will put my head quickly in the sitting room,' said Celia.

The girl pulled open the door and Celia peered around. The chairs were covered with sheets and the low table was lopsided. She could not bear to look further at the place that Verena had so loved. 'May we go upstairs?' The girl nodded and the two of them trotted up to the cold first landing. But Celia had only one place she wished to see. 'Up again,' she said. 'Please.'

On the top floor, she pointed at her door. 'This used to be my room.'

'Oh yes?' said the girl, bored. 'It's just a room for old boxes now. You had better hurry up, you know.'

Celia pulled open the door. The girl was right. The place was piled high with boxes. She pressed some more notes into her hand. The maid nodded and shut the door. Celia stood there in the light of the windows. There was nothing to look at. Her old room was gone. She put her hand on the wall where her bed had been, where she'd once leant her head before going to sleep, whispering to the fairies hiding in the crevices behind the wallpaper. The new owners had stripped it off, painted it over with white. She fought down the tears. *After all this*, she wanted to say, *you cry over wallpaper?* She looked at the floorboards. She had once known every inch of them, every crack, mapping out the world she saw there. She thought about all those knights of the Round Table that you never read about because they never found *anything*. There was nothing here to see.

She heard sounds on the stairs. The maid burst through the door. 'What are you doing in here? I heard moving about.'

'I wanted to stand where my bed used to be.'

The girl reached forward and patted her pockets. Celia jumped at her touch. The girl shrugged. 'Don't think you have anything.

Although what there would be to steal, I don't know. You should go now.'

Celia followed her out of the room and down the stairs. She thanked her as she left. 'You should sign up to the factories, you know. If you want to.'

'Maybe I will. Put madam here in a spin.'

'Imagine,' said Celia, knowing she sounded like Emmeline. 'Why not?' She hurried out of the door and down the drive.

Russell was waiting for her by the car, tapping his fingers.

'Ah, sorry, sir.' She ran to him. 'I thought I saw... er... I... a runaway dog.'

'You weren't feeding it?'

She shook her head.

'The city is full of stray dogs. You know you should not leave the car under any circumstances.'

She nodded. 'Yes, sir. But this one looked particularly fine. I thought he must be cherished.' She was aware that Russell could have her sacked. 'And he reminded me of the pet dog I had as a child.'

'Well,' he said, shrugging, a smile she could not read on his face. 'You're here now. Come along, Miss Witt, let us depart.'

Her heart filled with relief, she climbed into the cab and started the engine.

'So you're not going to report me?' she said, as they turned on to Queensway.

'No. You are a good driver. Quiet. The girls before you were always trying to talk.'

'Thank you,' she said. 'Sir,' she added as an afterthought. Her heart swelled with gratitude. She stopped to let a group of VADS troop by, holding tight to their headdresses to stop them from flapping in the breeze.

'I suppose you went to look at your old house,' he said.

The VADS passed and she geared up. 'I haven't seen it since I was a child. I thought I might – well, remember things there.'

'And did you?'

'No. It was just a house.'

'A lot of things have been lost in the war.' He dropped his papers on his lap and stared out of the window. 'You said you had no sweetheart?'

She blushed furiously. 'No, sir. As I said, I don't have one.' She wondered if the previous girls had really been quite as talkative as he'd suggested. He seemed eager to ask questions. 'I have a friend, though.' The words were out before she could stop them.

'Is he out in France?'

'Maybe. I don't know where he is. He was in hospital at Christmas, I suppose he might still be there. I don't think he wants to see me.'

'Has he said so?'

'Not in so many words. But he ran from me at . . . an event.'

'Men like that are often afraid, in my experience. They have suffered such injuries that they cannot bear for anyone to see them. Don't be put off.'

She slowed to turn the corner, looked out of the side window. A passing soldier gave her a wink.

'You know that as soon as he is recovered, he will have to return to the front, Miss Witt. You should visit him now, while you have the chance.'

Celia nodded. 'Perhaps you're right. But I don't know where he is. He may have been sent back already.' She swerved into a line of traffic heading into town.

'Well,' he began, then paused and thought. 'I suppose I could look him up for you. Let me know his name and battalion, and I'll see what I can do. But you are not to mention this to anyone. Let it be our secret.'

'Thank you, sir. That is very kind of you, really—'

'Let us say no more. Now, drive on.'

That night, she meant to write to Tom in her mind, but Rudolf came to her every time she tried. The image of him was painful, for it was the one from the party that had failed. She saw him standing there, encouraging Missy to the lucky dip. The rest of them were all sitting around him. They had changed. Emmeline was wider, paler, did not fuss so with her hair. Verena looked tired. Tom wore a scar across his face. Rudolf, though, was still the same, the great owner of Stoneythorpe, hosting a party. But surely, she thought, surely he had been altered more than any of them. She could not see him, could not imagine him. And did that mean she would never see him again? No, she told herself, they would be reunited, all of them, at Stoneythorpe.

She clung to the picture, ignoring the voice that said it was as hopeless as wishing for a fairy when she was a child, that everything had been so taken apart that it could not be put back together again. Tomorrow, she vowed, she would write a letter to Rudolf and send it to the government, and she did not care if he received it or not.

THIRTY

Number One War Hospital was a building that fitted the word 'utilitarian'. Over the days since Captain Russell had told her that Tom was there and found her the address, Celia had fingered the paper, touching the scribbled words, trying to imagine what kind of place lay behind them. She had imagined – in the way she had once dreamed of Stoneythorpe – a Victorian fantasy, pale stonework around the tops of the walls, large bay windows looking out on to the garden, a heavy door with a porch. Instead, Number One was huge and flat and bulging, sitting at the top of a hill, simmering under the early April sun like a giant red-brick saucepan. It had once been a workhouse, someone told her on the train.

Celia walked through the quiet gardens, trying to picture Stoney-thorpe as a hospital, men being escorted by nurses around the rose garden, in rows of beds in the dining room. She approached the doors, wiping dirt from her eyes. The train to Reading had been full of soldiers, and she had stood all the way next to a window that billowed dust into her face. She had borrowed one of Emmeline's gowns and put her hair up, but after the train, she was covered in grime and her hair was blown out of place.

She found the reception area and a nurse who directed her along some corridors to Tom's ward. An extraordinarily pretty dark-haired nurse, barely older than Celia, was at the desk. Celia felt her heart swell with envy.

'Mr Cotton?' she said. 'Sorry, miss, no. He's told us before: no visitors.'

Celia gazed at the sprinkling of freckles on the girl's neat little nose. 'I've come such a long way. Couldn't you just ask him?' The hallway smelled of disinfectant. She felt grimy, as if she could never be clean enough to come into such a place.

The nurse shrugged. 'We have to respect the wishes of the men.' Her voice was hard to place, Celia thought. Midlands, perhaps, but not much of it. She supposed she had joined from school too. She had precisely the kind of beauty Emmeline had envied in the old days, thick dark hair and creamy pale skin; looked like the kind of girl who should be in evening dress, not working in a hospital in Reading. Her hands were those of a nurse, though, scrubbed raw, the nails bright red around the rims where she had scoured them with disinfectant.

'Please.'

The nurse nodded and whisked off to a door. She returned shrugging again. 'He's awake, miss. But he still says no visitors.'

'Did you tell him it was me?'

'I gave him your name, yes.' Celia hated her suddenly then, this girl, smaller than her, younger, who got to touch Tom's hand, speak to him, ask him if he wanted visitors. She could imagine her tone: *There is some* person *here to see you.* Celia knew she hardly looked impressive in her old gown and boots.

'Tell him I have to see him.'

The girl put on her best look of weariness. 'We have patients coming in all the time. I can't run messages all day.'

'I know that. I was in France too. I delivered men in pain to the hospitals. Please let me in.' She could feel tears filling her eyes and hated herself for the weakness.

The girl shook her head. 'He's in good hands here. You of all people should know that. After the operation, he will be on his way.'

'What does he need an operation for?'

'Oh, you know. A minor wound. Recovery won't take long.'

Celia turned away. The door just ahead of her surely contained Tom's ward. She was so close. She took a breath. 'Tom!' she shouted, as loudly as she could. 'I am here!' Then she turned and ran, barrelling past the girl.

She had got ten or so paces down the corridor before another

392

nurse seized her arm. 'It's all right,' said the dark-haired nurse. She put her arm around Celia, and carbolic soap and linen filled Celia's nose. 'Come along, miss. You know we can't have this.'

A burly orderly folded his arms at the massive wooden door. Celia knew without having to ask that beyond him was the room where Tom lay. 'Come on now,' said the other nurse. 'Let's go back. There are unwell men here.'

Celia looked at the orderly and let the nurse take her arm. They walked back to the front door and the desk. She flushed with shame at having made such a fuss.

'This is a hospital,' said the second nurse. 'We can't have this. I could ban you, Miss...?'

'Witt,' said the dark-haired girl. 'She was in France.'

'All the more reason she should know. She has seen men with shell shock. They need peace and calm.'

Celia felt a stab of remorse. 'I know.'

'Mind I don't see you again.' The other nurse swept away.

Celia looked back at the dark-haired girl. 'What's your name?'

'Rouse. Nurse Rouse.'

'Thank you for looking after him.' She fought for composure, found herself imitating Verena. But she could not hold it. 'Please,' she said. 'Please let me see him. It would mean so much to me. Michael, my brother, died, and Tom came back. I've been waiting for him. All I want to do is see him.' She felt herself weeping again.

The nurse raised an eyebrow. Celia could not read her expression. Perhaps, she thought, miserably, she did not think her pretty enough for Tom. It was true, France had made her skin duller, her hair more stringy and her lips so dry that no amount of Emmeline's creams could make soften them. *He kissed me!* she wanted to cry out. *He kissed me in the garden.* But here, she knew, being Miss de Witt of Stoneythorpe Hall did not mean anything, and perhaps in this new world Tom could find a million girls like her and she would be alone.

'Why do you think he won't see me?' Celia put her hand on the wall. Freshly painted, she guessed. So many houses in the country must be newly painted to be hospitals, or newly built. It was good for the men. She wondered how many of the soldiers she had driven had ended up in places like this. A door opened some way behind them and a smell of custard wafted through the air.

'Lots of them don't want to see anyone. What they have experienced out there – you know better than me, Miss Witt – it is too much, I think. They can't make conversation any more.'

'But I have seen it too. I could help.'

Nurse Rouse turned away, smoothing her apron. The custard smell filled the air again. 'I've work to do.'

'Well I have nothing else to do and the day free. So perhaps I will sit here and wait.'

'You can't,' said the girl, flatly. 'This isn't a café, you know. I'm sorry. You will have to go.'

Celia suddenly could not bear any more discussion. 'I will go,' she said. 'I will be outside.' She turned and walked hurriedly out of the door. Perhaps Tom might come out for a walk, escorted by a VAD.

The door closed behind her and she stood against the brick wall, feeling the sun move over her face. On the far side of the building was a larger spread of garden, with steps leading down to what looked like an ornamental fountain. It reminded her of Stoneythorpe. A stab of guilt ran through her. Rather than driving Captain Russell around London, she should be at Stoneythorpe, encouraging Verena to offer it as a hospital. She gazed at the path, and her thoughts began to spiral. Really, she told herself, they were no better than the mistress of their old house who went off to do war work she was no good at, leaving her servants to arrange her flowers.

She leant against the wall, wished she had a cigarette. Across from her, a VAD came into view supporting an older man. His entire face was bandaged, two gaps left for the eyes. He walked slowly, deliberately. Celia could see the nurse talking to him, but he did not respond. She felt her hand twitch, the legacy of the shaking ground in Étaples. She slid to the floor and sat on the grass, and no one came to move her on. A family walked past clutching flowers. They returned minutes later, the mother trying not to cry. Two girls arrived separately. One came back quickly, the other stayed an hour. *See*, Celia wanted to cry, *some of the soldiers can take visitors. Why not you?*

Three hours or so later, when the sun was burning high in the sky, Nurse Rouse emerged. 'Oh,' she said. 'You are still here.'

Celia nodded. 'I took the day off. I thought he might come out.'

'We've told him to. But he hasn't yet. They have to understand that they are not ill, they can walk around. If I was in their state, I wouldn't want to stay in bed.'

Celia felt pressed to defend him. 'I suppose they don't have the strength. I saw so much death in France.' The ambulances full of screaming men, the terror, the pain, the crosses on their foreheads, the moment when the morphine wore off in her cab and they cried out, begging, shouting, 'Nurse!'

'But that's war, isn't it?' Nurse Rouse patted her hair. 'I have to go over to the store block for some gauze. You can walk with me if you like.'

They set off across the parched ground. 'Tell me about him, please.'

'Not much to say. He has been here four weeks, transferred from somewhere else. He doesn't say much. He will have an operation soon. As I said, only a minor wound.'

'I'm glad it is only minor.'

'Yes.' The girl paused and brushed non-existent dirt off her apron. 'Fortunate.'

'But why an operation if it is only minor?'

'The doctors here are thorough. This is the store, Miss Witt. I must leave you here. You should go before the sister finds you.'

'When should I come back?'

'I don't know.'

'Next week?'

'You could try, I suppose. Now please go before Sister comes back. If Nurse Priddle tells her, we'll both be done for.' The door of the store block closed behind her.

Celia turned to gaze at the hospital. No sign of anyone. She set off on the long walk back to the station.

Next day, she told Captain Russell that she had decided against seeing Tom. 'He will contact me when he desires to do so,' she said.

Celia came back to Reading three Fridays in a row, telling Russell that Verena was unwell and needed her help. Each time Nurse Rouse met her and told her that Tom would not see her. She learned that after the second week he had been in for his operation and it had proceeded well.

The fourth week, Russell was called to an urgent meeting on Friday, so she had to come on the following Monday instead.

'I was wondering where you had got to,' said Nurse Rouse.

'I didn't think anyone would miss me,' Celia said, surprised.

'Not *miss*, exactly. I have got used to you coming. We have a lot of visitors here, not many of them as polite as you.' Rouse had violet smudges around her eyes and her nails were red raw around the edges.

'You should have a rest from this,' Celia said.

She shrugged. 'You sound like my mother. There is no one else to do the work if I do not. We are short staffed as it is. Anyway, wait here. I will go and ask Mr Cotton if he will see you.'

Celia stood by the desk, brushing at her hair. Her appearance had been too long lost to really improve, but if Warterton was here, she would tell her to pinch her cheeks and look sharp. *The war won't last for ever!* Celia could hear her saying.

Some time elapsed. Nurse Rouse came back. 'He's still refusing to see you.' There was something about her face, though, that prompted Celia. She felt she saw a small smile – and that made her want to leap at her. 'I don't believe you,' she said. *I can't go on like this* was in her head. She pushed away from the desk and ran – and this time there was no orderly. Nurse Rouse did not shout after her, and so she burst through the wooden doors into the ward. Two nurses looked up from cleaning a wound on a man's arm. For a moment, she stood there, confused by a room full of bandaged men.

'Celia,' said a voice to her right, tone resigned. 'I am here.' She spun around, and there was a man in a bed, his leg suspended on a wire, his head bandaged.

'Tom?'

Rouse and an orderly charged in and caught Celia's arms roughly. The same smell of disinfectant, soap and linen.

'Don't,' he said tiredly, from the bed. 'There is no need to pull her around. She can stay.'

The matron bustled through the door, Nurse Priddle behind her. 'What exactly is going on here? Young lady, what do you think you are doing?'

'It's all right,' Tom said, quietly. 'She was upset. Let me talk to her. She won't stay long.'

The matron turned to Celia. 'What selfish behaviour. When men are trying to get well here.'

'She didn't mean it,' said Tom. 'She doesn't understand. I will talk to her.'

'Very well,' said the matron. 'But no more than ten minutes. And Nurse Rouse – I will see you in my office.'

They swept off and the door banged behind them. The other two nurses got back to work. Celia hesitated, then pulled up a chair next to Tom. It was hot in the ward, even more so by his bed.

'Hello, Tom,' she said, the words catching in her throat. 'How are you?' He was wearing hospital pyjamas. His bedside table was empty except for two books, turned spine side away so she could not see what they were. She realised that the whole of his neck and chest was bandaged. She blushed at the intimacy of sitting so close to him.

'What happened to you?' she said. 'You were well when I saw you at the funeral.'

'There was a gas attack after I went back. I lost a lot of skin and my lungs are a bit damaged.' He opened his eyes. Then he closed them again.

'But…' Celia's mind flashed with bloody jaws, bombs, the

screams of the men. 'I thought it was just a minor injury. That's what Nurse Rouse said.'

'Well of course she did.' His voice had changed. The burr of his accent had gone. He sounded more like an officer. Celia could see his hand, almost as raw as the nurse's, resting on the coverlet. Easy to reach out, touch him. He coughed again. 'We ran out of masks and they told us that if we wet our handkerchiefs then the gas wouldn't come near. It wasn't true. How did you find out where I was?'

'A friend is… er… a nurse.' She thought of gas billowing up. The men in her ambulance who had taken the gas were the worst off, coughing up green stuff. She knew what Tom meant by 'wet' but was too polite to say: some men in the ambulances had told her how they urinated on cloth and tied it around their faces. One of the orderlies had told her that the gas formed foamy stuff in the lungs and then it drowned you. He said he'd seen men tearing at their own throats in fear. Celia remembered when she had gone underwater in the sea for the first time, the panic as the water closed over her. She gazed at Tom's face. She could not imagine being drowned in herself.

'Have you told my family?'

'No.'

'Don't.'

'Are you in pain?' How stupid and empty her words sounded when she said them. All the other men were probably laughing behind their hands.

'They give me things for that.' He shuffled himself up to a more upright position. The bandages bulged a little over his chest. 'Look, Celia, I don't want you to come here any more. I have met a girl. I'm going back to marry her after the war is over. There's no reason for us to see each other.'

'What kind of girl?'

'It doesn't matter.'

'In France?'

'No, here.'

'But how could you have met one here?' The new girl danced in her head, dark-haired and shiny-lipped, a little like Nurse Rouse.

He coughed again, longer this time. 'Celia, I did.'

'I want to be your friend,' she lied, a lump in her throat as she forced herself to speak. 'We are friends.' She didn't say, *I realised when I was in France that I was in love with you. We could get married, that's what people in love do.* The other men around her were probably listening to every word.

'It seems a million years ago, you and me in Stoneythorpe. It's all over now. I've a new life.'

'In the garden, before you left—'

'It doesn't mean anything. That's all in the past. Celia, I wish you would listen to me. You have a new life now as well.'

She wanted to scream but forced herself to be calm, reminding herself of the gas, what he must have seen. 'You said we would be friends for ever.'

'I was wrong.'

She felt the tears pricking at her eyes and fought to push them back. 'You're all I have now.' The girl twirled in her head, laughing.

'You have your family.'

'All the time I was in France, I thought of you. I drove the ambulance and I wondered if I might see you. I thought that I was helping men like you.' He put his head back and stared at the ceiling. 'Did you never think of me at all?'

'No.'

She glanced down at her hands in her lap. The floor under her feet was spotlessly clean, black and white marble tiles, arranged in neat squares, sharp lines cutting them in two, four and eight. She raised her eyes, even though he was not looking at her.

'What happened to Michael?'

'He died. Like so many of them.'

'But you were there. Professor Punter, Michael's tutor, came to the funeral and said that he had heard from another of the men that Michael saved you. Tell me.'

'We pulled each other up. I can't remember any more.'

'You must!'

He looked at her. 'You want to know? Yes? Well, I'll tell you.' He lowered his voice to a whisper. 'Crashes, explosions, blood, screams, commands to go forward even though they were firing on us. Keep going, they said. Keep moving. If you turn back, we'll shoot you. That's what they said. So we kept moving.'

'And that is how Michael died. He didn't save you?'

'Something like that.'

'An enemy shot, then he fell – and then what?'

'I told you, Celia, I can't remember. Nobody will know. Stop trying to make sense of it all. It was war.'

'We thought we might receive other letters from men in his company. But no one wrote to us.'

'Most of them died. Now, we shouldn't talk of it any more. It's not fair on the others here.'

She was crying now, wiping away tears with her arm, feeling them soak her sleeve. 'Why are you so angry with me?'

His voice came out a little softer. 'I'm not angry with you, Celia. I am just trying to tell you that things have changed.'

'I haven't changed. You haven't.'

'I have. I've done things you wouldn't forgive.'

'No, Tom! I'd forgive you anything. And I'm sure there is nothing to forgive.'

He shook his head. 'Oh no. There is much to forgive. Celia, I wish you would stop it. You have always idealised things, and now here you are idealising me. It doesn't work. I'm not who I was.'

'Yes you are!'

'Sssh!' hissed the nurse from across the ward. 'Keep your voice down.'

'I'm going to marry this girl. There will be no reason for you and me to see each other.' He dropped back on the pillows. 'Celia, it's time for you to go.'

'I'll marry you!' she said, her words coming out more loudly than she could have imagined. She thought she heard one of the men behind her laugh. 'I will marry you!' Her heart flooded with emotion. Miss Celia de Witt of Stoneythorpe, her father's hope to be a great debutante, now the ambulance driver who would marry

Tom! What would the Cottons think? They would be stunned, excited. Grateful.

Tom sighed. 'I don't want to marry you, Celia.'

Her heart dropped. 'The other girl.' Sitting close to him, holding his hand.

'Even without her, I wouldn't want to marry you.'

She knew her hands were twitching, her face too, as if there were a hundred twigs inside her waiting to burst out of the tree. 'Emmeline said you admired me.'

He gave a hard laugh. 'Your family thinks everyone is in love with them.'

'Your sister said something similar, said we expect admiration because we have money.'

'Mary does not know a thing. Celia, we were childhood friends, no more. Now we are older, and I'm sorry, but I do not want to marry you. I don't know why you ever thought I did. I'm sorry you've been thinking of me. There was no point to it.'

She stumbled to her feet, her head ringing and tears blurring her eyes. 'I'll marry you!' came a voice from one of the other beds, and her heart burned with humiliation. An arm caught hers. 'This way, miss.' One of the nurses helped her to the door. Celia wiped her hand hard across her face, and then took one last look behind her. Tom was weeping. She wanted to reach out for him – and then in a moment she was out of the door, into the corridor, and Nurse Rouse was taking her arm.

'Sorry, Miss Witt,' she was saying. Celia flung herself against her chest and wept. The nurse patted her hair. 'Come now, miss. Some fresh air would do you good.'

She half pulled Celia forward to the door and tugged it open. Celia bent double and took great gasps of air. 'I can't!' she said.

'Don't try to speak, Miss Witt. Just breathe.' The nurse patted her back.

Celia fought hard – against her tears, the desire to scream, the desire to throw herself on the floor. Finally she managed to stand. 'It's you, isn't it?'

'Who?'

'The girl he's going to marry.'

Rouse raised an eyebrow. 'He hasn't told me, Miss Witt. I'd expect I would know if I was.'

'You're pretty.'

'And I'd be dismissed if Sister thought I had been talking like that to patients, don't you know that?'

'Oh yes.' Celia blushed. 'I feel... I feel...'

'Don't feel. Try not to. Just think about putting one foot in front of the other. That's what you have to do.'

'I am sorry.' She leaned against the wall, holding her side. In front of her, another VAD was pushing a man in a wheelchair around the grounds. He was holding his hands against his face, as if the light was too much.

'I had a fiancé, you know. He was killed by a bomb. At least you still have the man you love.'

'He doesn't love me back, though.'

'He's alive. And the doctors think he should make a complete recovery from the gas.'

'That's good news.' She reached out a hand for Rouse. 'What's your name?'

'Virginia. Don't tell the chaps, though, or I will cop it.'

'Sorry about your fiancé, Virginia.' The nurse was turning the wheelchair around and beginning the slow walk back to the hospital.

'Just another war story, isn't it? They tell us we have to buck up, get on with it. No use in crying, that's what my mother says. Crying is what the Germans *want* you to do. Every tear shed by me is a victory for the enemy.'

'Your mother knows what she thinks.'

'She certainly does. She runs fund-raising committees at home. Money for our brave boys and girls. Sometimes I think she is almost pleased, deep down, that I lost George. Means she has something to talk about when other women start on about sacrificing their sons.'

'Surely not?'

Virginia nodded. 'No, you are right. I am being unfair to her.

I just cannot bear all that talk of bravery. George is dead, and all for what?'

Celia shook her head. 'I don't know.'

'And here I am, a VAD, one of the lucky ones, used Father's money to pay for the uniform and lecture fees. At my last hospital, I did nothing but wash up all day long. I hardly ever saw a patient. On breaks, they got me to cut up squares of paper for the WCs. Mother would demand stories and what could I tell her? That the proper nurses had been beastly to us again? After my first day, I took my apron back to the lodgings and scrubbed it for three hours to try to make the cross less bright, so I'd look like I had been there longer. Didn't work. Here we see the patients, at least. Anyway, I should go in.' She turned away, then came back. 'You know, Miss Witt. He shouts out your name in his sleep. Quite a lot. He told me once in the midst of a morphine shot that he had a girl back in Hampshire.'

'But now he has someone else.'

'Who knows? They say odd things, soldiers in hospital. Some of them try to make their family suffer, so that they feel the same misery as them. Others want to pretend everything is perfect. Some don't want to see people at all. Listen, what I am trying to say is don't give up. He might change his mind. I don't know; things will be different. When the war ends.'

'That might be another twenty years.'

'Listen, Miss Witt, I should go.'

Celia grasped her hand. 'Give me your address. Your mother's address. I will write to you. Not about him. Just things.' She held out her pocket notebook, kept with her even though she wasn't in uniform.

Virginia hesitated, then scribbled out an address in Macclesfield. 'But don't write to me, really don't. What would we say? If you get married, maybe I'll come. If the Germans haven't bombed us to bits before then. Now go! I can't tell you how much dishwashing I will get tonight, thanks to you.' She waved her hand and disappeared back into the building.

Celia turned away, gazed at the brick walls and glittering

windows to imprint them on her memory, then began her walk back to the station.

'Oi, darling, waiting for me?' said a soldier on the platform at Paddington.

She shook her head. 'I'm sorry, Sergeant. I've devoted my life to votes for women.' She ran into a fug of people heading to the Underground, and let London take her up.

THIRTY-ONE

'Where have you been?' Emmeline was by the door when she opened it. 'You're wearing a dress.'

Celia looked down at herself. She had been so caught up in her thoughts on the way home that she had forgotten to change into her uniform.

'You told me you were driving Russell to Bournemouth,' said Emmeline, tugging her inside.

'I ... er ... changed in the canteen.'

'I think you are lying. You have been crying, I can tell.' Emmeline threw herself on to the sofa, legs stretched out in front of her, in a way she would never have sat in the old days.

'Why do you care?' Celia perched against the bookshelf.

'Because you are my sister, that's why. Because we can't afford for you to lose this position by truanting off.'

'I am not going to lose my position.'

Emmeline pulled herself upright. 'Really? He sent a minion looking for you today. They said you had gone to visit Mother. He came to check.'

'Oh.' Celia sat down on the sofa.

'So where have you been?'

'Actually, I went to see Tom.' The words fell into the quiet room, splashing like someone falling into a pond. Emmeline recoiled, then came forward, furious. 'You did what?'

'Tom is in hospital. I went to see him.'

Her sister's face flamed. 'I do not believe it. I cannot. How could you?'

'He's ill, sister.'

'That ... that servant! The man who took Michael to his death? How could you? I cannot believe it.'

405

'He did not take Michael to his death. They were in it together.'

'Oh yes, but he survived and Michael did not. Why do you think that was? Because Tom pushed him forward, I would say. I always knew he was no good. He's infatuated with you, always was.'

'Emmeline, stop this. Listen to yourself. Don't you know how many thousands of men died out there? You can't blame Tom.' She wished she had not sat down next to her sister. All she wanted to do was escape.

'You see him wrongly. You always did. You thought he was perfect. Not a killer.'

'Oh, Emmeline. You are being ridiculous now. I'm not listening to this any more.' And yet a small, sharp splinter of doubt was weaving itself into Celia's heart. What had Tom said? *I've done things you wouldn't forgive.* He did not want to talk to her of Michael. She put her head in her hands.

Emmeline inched towards her. The sofa sighed under her weight. 'And what did he say to you? I wonder. I know. Not content with pushing Michael forward to take the bullet, he thought he might ruin you as well. He wants you to come to him when he is free.'

'Not true. Actually, *I* offered myself to *him.*'

Emmeline let out a small scream. 'You did what?'

'As I said, I offered myself to him. I asked him to marry me.'

Emmeline dropped back on the sofa. 'I want to die! How can this be true? You offered to marry him?'

'Yes, I did. He turned me down.'

Emmeline put her hands over her face. Celia felt like saying *Who helped you when you really wanted to die?* Emmeline sat up. 'I can't understand this. But we shall say no more about it. You will not go to see him again.'

'You don't have to command me. I won't. Because he has told me not to.' *I don't want you to come here any more.*

'Celia, I came to you when you were sad in the gardens. I spoke to you. I did not tell you that you must live so you could try to marry Tom Cotton.'

'So what did you tell me to live for?'

'For us.' She moved to Celia and took her hand. 'You need to live for your family. And I have something else to give you purpose. You must keep working for Captain Russell.'

'What do you mean?' Celia asked the question, but something was creeping up inside her, words that might come together to make a sentence, an answer. Tom flooded her head, turning her down, moving his face away. *Your family thinks everyone is in love with them.*

'Haven't you guessed? Have you not understood what is going on? Celia, we are helping people.'

It was there, but through a thick fog. Celia could not reach it. 'What do you mean?' she repeated.

'Those parcels I give you. Do you not wonder what they are?'

'I'm delivering them to a friend of Samuel. Artistic things.' As soon as Celia said the words, they sounded hollow, untrue. She wished then that she could stand up, leave the room, run out into the square. But she was held there by a spell, unable to move.

'And there is no one better than you to do it, the driver of Captain Russell.'

'What are you talking about?'

'Do you know, Celia, what they do to men who will not fight?' The front door banged shut and they felt the walls wobble.

'They have to do other war work?' Celia had seen articles in the newspapers about the Quakers, who were working hard as stretcher-bearers, factory workers, building roads. They said they were happy to tend the sick and help the men. She supposed some of her stretcher-bearers in Étaples had been Quakers.

'I know what you're thinking. Not the religious men. What if you won't help the war effort at all, because even raking the land or driving a bus helps a great plan of aggression? Samuel does have poor lungs, but not that bad. Not really. He could certainly go out as a driver like you did. But he chooses not to, for that would be to participate in a great evil.'

'He chooses not to?' The men in her ambulance, crying out. Those who had shot through their own hands so they never had to return. Tom flashed through her head, his lungs full of gas, set to go again once he was fitted up and ready. *Things have changed,* he was saying. Michael bending down in no-man's-land, taking Tom's hand, saving him.

'The deaths of those masses of men are a sinful waste. Germany and England will go on fighting until there are no young men left. Samuel says that one day all young men will choose not to go and instead the politicians will understand that they have to make peace, not war.'

Tom's lungs full of gas, told to hold a handkerchief to his nose. Celia gazed around, her eyes taking in the room, the books, the paintings, the geranium on the table. The bright stabs of colour entered her pupils; she could feel them, but she could not register what they meant. 'Mr Janus might be arrested.'

'He might be. But he is down as sick. Soon they will expect him to go to do some sort of work. But we have work here. As I said, what do you think happens to men who object to the war?'

'Taken to prison.' She pulled her mind from the screams of the men in her ambulance, fixed her gaze on the poor geranium, its leaves browning no matter how much water they gave it. Mr Janus had found it in a market, said it would cheer the place up a bit. Now it was sitting listening to Emmeline with her.

'And what do you think happens to them there?'

Celia shook her head.

'They are treated in the worst way you can imagine. They are given no food, no water, no covering; their clothes are taken from them. If you were to murder ten women, the government would treat you more kindly. We have to protect these men.'

Celia felt the panic rising in her chest, tightening her lungs. 'And these are the parcels I am delivering.'

'That is right. Food, clothes, water. These men are hidden behind panels, in cellars. You are perfect. No one would suspect the driver of Captain Russell, formerly an ambulance girl in France.'

Celia put her head in her hands. 'Emmeline. What are you doing? What will happen to you if you get caught?'

'Us, you mean. We will all go to prison. Jemima and Rufus too. They will beat us and force us to eat, I suppose.' The excitement in her voice bubbled through. She didn't understand, thought Celia, she didn't know what it would be like. Tibor Schmidt was in her head. *You're not in the Black Forest now.* She looked up at her sister.

'Emmy, while I was in France, they tried to use me to interrogate a German. I said no. The man there told me that they would always be watching me.'

'Oh, just words.' But Emmeline looked less sure.

'And we are German! They have Father. They are watching us.'

Her sister's face clouded. Then she stood up and clapped her hands. 'Well, we will just have to stay careful, won't we? Look out for informers.'

'The risk is too great. I don't think you really understand what prison is!'

'It is too late now. You're already involved. You've done it enough times. We're going out tonight. You will come with us.'

Celia gazed at the geranium again, all the things in the flat, looking back at her. It was her price for being here, she saw this. Her mind was full of Michael, dying in some muddy field in France, Tom, his head bandaged, lungs scarred by the gas. 'I can't leave you to do it alone. But Emmeline, what has happened to you? You would never have done such things before. You wanted to marry Sir Hugh Bradshaw.'

'Well I was wrong, wasn't I? Samuel has shown me the right way to live.'

'How did you get the *idea* to do this?' *Tom*, she wanted to cry, *you could take me away from this.* No answer came.

'I don't know much. Neither should you. But Rufus comes to tell us where we should go and what to do. That is enough for us to know.'

That night, Jemima and Rufus came to the flat at eleven o'clock, Jemima straight from her shift at the hospital. They were wearing dark coats with hoods over their heads. Emmeline made Celia wear the same. The five of them hurried out carrying boxes, bags of food, clothes and bottles of water. They split up at Bloomsbury Square – Celia was with Jemima, Emmeline with Samuel, and

Rufus went alone. Jemima and Celia visited six houses, delivering food, dropping off water. They walked in the darkest parts of town, skulking through the shadows at the back of houses, on the edges of squares, one fifty paces behind the other, first Celia, then Jemima, taking it in turns to look behind them. Jemima took the bundles upstairs and left Celia to wait and keep watch at the bottom. 'Best you don't come,' she said, when Celia asked. 'The less you know, the better.'

'How long would we be in prison?' Celia said.

Jemima shushed her urgently. 'Never! Don't say that. Anyway, they will be kinder to us because we are women. Not that it will ever come to that. We are careful. Come on. Last one now.' They were standing outside a row of hotels in Paddington. They did not have a list. Rufus had given them six slips of paper, one for each address. When they had made the delivery, they had to tear the paper into little pieces and throw them into a drain. Now there was only one left. 'Gloucester Terrace,' she said. 'Not far. Off we go.'

Celia thought miserably of Tom. In France, driving, she had told herself that he would be proud of her. But she could not see him being proud of this, letting men avoid what he went so keenly to do.

They cut up past Paddington station, still busy with people. Celia felt relieved, light-hearted even, that they had finished nearly all of their addresses. Jemima moved forward to lead the way. 'Then to bed!' she smiled at Celia over her shoulder, before pushing ahead to increase the gap between them. They passed through a flurry of girls who looked like VADs. One of them smiled at Celia. Celia could not smile back. *I am saving a few men – but what about the rest? You will have to clean them up, patch up their wounds and listen to them as they scream.*

It was when they were about ten yards past the station that Celia began to think that there was someone behind her. It was not that she could actually see anyone. It was just a feeling that she had. He – or she – seemed to be walking in time. When Celia stopped, so did he. She set off again. He did too. She could not tell

Jemima, for then he would know. She could not run away, for that would leave Jemima on her own. She carried on walking, hoping that he would turn off, just be another workman on his way home. He did not. Jemima was walking quickly now. Celia supposed she wanted to get home. She picked up her own pace and felt sick as the man behind her did the same. Then she realised. It was the house they were going to that he wanted, not Celia. She had to tell Jemima not to stop there. But how could she? She walked on in miserable indecision. She had no idea where they were, but surely they were not far away now. Jemima trailed the hand that meant left turn. Celia heard the man cough behind her. She knew then, as sure as she could ever be, that she had to act.

Two men rounded the corner towards Jemima, working men who looked as if they had come straight from the public house. Celia took a deep breath, gathered her coat around her and ran, her heart in her mouth, her feet pounding the cobblestones. She fell on to Jemima from behind, barrelled her forward into the men. 'What the hell?' shouted one of them as he fell. Jemima was screaming and his friend was shouting too. 'Muggers! Police!' The fug of alcohol fumes rose from them both.

'Stop it!' hissed Celia to Jemima. 'Stop it!' She looked up to see a man – it had to be him – in a grey coat sauntering past. He tipped his hat. 'May I help?'

'No!' spat Celia. She met his eyes, pale blue, mocking.

'Call the police!' the man on the floor was shouting.

'Very well,' said the blue-eyed man. He squatted down and reached out his hand. They all stared as he pinched a little of Celia's sleeve, then Jemima's. Then he stood up once more. Celia stared at his legs. 'I shall tell the first policeman I see.' He raised his eyebrow. 'I suggest you all take care. Especially you ladies.' He sauntered on, turning once to look at Celia and doff his hat again.

'What the hell is happening here?' said the bigger of the two men. 'Who the hell was he?'

'I am sorry, gentlemen,' said Celia. 'I am really terribly sorry. I meant to run into my friend here to play a joke on her. I had simply no idea that you two gentlemen were here. I do apologise.'

'I should think you should apologise,' he said. 'Knocking over law-abiding citizens like that. I should call the police on you.'

Jemima was sitting up. She pulled back her hood to reveal her hair. The moonlight made it shine brightly. 'I'm so sorry,' she said, in a majestic voice, 'that my friend was so boisterous. But you must allow her one last moment of play. We are to become nuns next week. We are here delivering food to the poor.'

'Nuns?' The younger of the two men dropped his hand from Jemima's thigh.

'That is correct. We are about to dedicate our lives to God. My friend here has great high spirits at the thought. She was a little overexcited. I do apologise, gentlemen.'

The men were scrambling to their feet. 'No, no, miss, no need to apologise,' one was saying. 'Don't give it a second's thought. An honour to meet you ladies. We must go.'

The younger one looked at Celia. 'Tell the boss up there I didn't mean to call you muggers. Hope he won't hold it against me.'

'Oh I am sure not,' she said, quite as sweet as Jemima. 'God is all forgiveness. And we are all sinners.'

'Yes, miss. We must be going. Give our regards to him upstairs.'

Celia watched them hurry off. 'Come,' she said to Jemima. 'We must get back to the flat.'

'That man was following you?'

'He was.'

'Oh, God. When did he start?'

'Somewhere after Paddington.'

'Has he definitely gone?'

'I can't tell.'

'Let's run.' Jemima seized her hand and they set off, bags bumping against their waists. They looked behind them all the way home. Celia was startled by the shadows, jumped when she saw an animal. Her heart was full of fear.

'Emmeline!' she cried, coming into the flat the next evening. The day of driving had been a long one. She wanted to prop open her eyes with matchsticks.

'I'm in the bedroom.' Emmeline was crouched down by the bed, packing up boxes with scarves.

Celia sat on the bed. 'I've had a letter from Mama.'

'What's happened now?' Emmeline barely looked up.

'Lady Redroad wants to make Stoneythorpe into a hospital. Mama says that if she does, she wants us to go back and help.'

'Mama couldn't oversee a hospital, even at Stoneythorpe.' Emmeline disentangled a mass of grey wool from a black scarf.

'No, I think Lady Redroad would be doing all that sort of thing. Anyway, I think it would be more a place for men to get better than have operations. But it would be good for Mama, don't you think?'

'Of course! Lady Redroad should use her own house, though.' Emmeline looked up briefly, her handsome eyes smaller than usual, the edges bloodshot with tiredness.

'I think there's some reason why, Mama says. Not suitable. Too big.'

Emmeline threw a green scarf into the box and laughed. 'Samuel would say she wants us to bear all the costs while she gets the glory.'

'True. But it *would* be good for Mama. And she would be useful. After all, she did run a whole house once.' Celia leant down and pushed a knitted hat into the box.

'Once. I think it's a good idea, especially if Lady Redroad is doing all the work. But I won't go back.'

'Don't you think you should?' Celia watched her sister close the box, move it to the side and take out another one.

'Let's see if it really happens first. Anyway, you can go.' Emmeline's smile was so innocent it made Celia think of the old days, when she was about to marry Sir Hugh. 'My work here is more important.'

'But they're following you. They followed us.' In a second, she was back there, heart thumping with fear, hurrying down the street, all blackness.

'Everybody is followed in London.'

Celia watched Emmeline pack more scarves, her hands working neatly. She tried to imagine Stoneythorpe as a hospital, the dining room full of wounded soldiers, doctors and nurses bustling through the corridors. Instead what came to her was an image of her mother, locked in her room, lying in bed, back turned when Celia peered through the keyhole, bumping through the corridor at night. She could not imagine Verena inviting Lady Redroad to set up a hospital there.

'You and Jemima can take these tonight,' said Emmeline, breaking into her thoughts.

'I can't! Not tonight! Last night was too much. I am too tired.' All she wanted to do was lie down and sleep for ever on the sofa.

'Tomorrow night, then. We must do it!' Emmeline clapped down the lid of the box like a full stop.

Celia sat at the table and wrote to Verena. *When you begin to make the house a hospital, I will come.* Stoneythorpe, turreted, ivy-clad, was pulling her back, and who knew if that was only to wander around the corridors and read *Mansfield Park* aloud, while the possibility of the hospital was endlessly discussed, never happening. She tried to throw aside the picture of it as it was now – dull, deserted, dust settled on every surface – replace it with the time before the war, the whole place quivering with bustle and anticipation, readying itself for the descent of the children and the party. But she couldn't see how it could ever be like that again. Verena's need for them had echoed through every word in her letter, but Celia was fighting it away. She folded up the letter for posting, feeling ashamed of herself. To try to make herself feel better, she wrote to Tom, telling him about the weather and her driving job. She only felt sadder at the end of it because she knew he wouldn't reply.

As the weather improved, the bombs got worse. The newspapers said that the Kaiser was aiming to knock London down (although avoiding Buckingham Palace, so as not to hit his relations). 'Don't think about it,' said Jemima. 'You can't let them know you're afraid.' But Celia couldn't help it, craned up out of Emmeline's window to look for the fat silver body of a Zepp, kept her eyes on the floor when they went out delivering at night. Bombs fell on Chelsea

Hospital, Pancras Road, the Strand, the Royal Academy, St Paul's and the Bedford Hotel, not far from them. The Sphinx on Victoria Embankment stayed upright, propped on rubble. The street lights were wrapped in brown paper and Emmeline was reported for showing a crack of light from her house. Even Captain Russell was jittery, told her to drive fast at the end of the day. She begged Mr Janus and Emmeline to come to Russell Square tube for the night, but they refused. 'Government propaganda,' Mr Janus said. 'Trying to scare us.' Emmeline nodded. 'Anyway, if a bomb hit the tube and it fell in, we'd be much worse off. And there are rats down there. Big ones. You can go if you like.'

'I won't leave you,' said Celia. Instead, every night, she lay in bed, waiting for the sound of the policeman ringing his bell, the distant fire of anti-aircraft guns, the baby-like shriek of a shell falling somewhere near. She longed for winter, when Mr Sparks said they'd probably stop.

After six nights of bombing in September, the planes came less. Emmeline stepped up her demands, asking Celia to deliver larger and larger parcels. Celia refused. Emmeline accused her of mooning after Tom. Celia told her the truth. Number One War Hospital had sent back her last letter, said that Tom had been sent out to France again and they couldn't forward post. Sometimes, at night, she decided she could hear the guns resounding in France, imagined Tom lying in a shell hole, coughing. The thought of offering herself to him raked through her and tears ran down her face.

'I can't,' said Celia, thinking of Tom, Captain Russell, the general. 'I just can't do this for you.'

'Excuses,' said her sister. 'Think of these poor men.'

Eventually, Celia agreed, hiding the parcels under coats in the back of the car. Then, finally, when Jemima and Rufus were at the flat, they told her that she had a new task.

'You must help us take people. We need men to be moved around.'

'How on earth can I do that?'

'You will drive them,' said Mr Janus, smoothly. 'You will put them in the boot of your car when Captain Russell is in the front, and you will drive them.'

Celia looked at him in horror. 'What are you saying? That's completely impossible! How can I do something like that?'

'We need you to do it,' Jemima said. 'Without you, these men will die. They will go to prison and they will die. They will have everything taken from them, their clothes, everything. You know, one of them told me that if you are not what they deem "cooperative" in prison, you even have the privilege of a bed taken from you. Your arms are tied to the wall, splayed, and you have to hang there. Whenever they come in, they beat you.'

'I know, I know, it is terrible. But I cannot put men in the car. Captain Russell will check. I am supposed to inspect it for bombs every day. Sometimes he checks under it too. What if he decided to look in the boot?'

'Well, you'd have to put him off.'

Celia felt tears behind her eyes. 'Why can't you do these things? Why does it have to be me?'

'Because you are the one no one would ever suspect,' said Mr Janus.

'That's not true,' she said. 'I told Emmeline. A general in the ambulance station said he'd watched me.'

'Oh yes, I heard. Idle threats.'

She stared at him, her old tutor. 'Please.'

'You drove through battlefields and you can't do this?'

'It's because of the battlefields that I can't. Don't you see?'

She tried to catch Jemima's eye, but the other woman looked away.

Mr Janus shook his head. 'We need you. But perhaps if you can't do this small thing for us, then there's no room for you here.'

'Samuel.' Emmeline put her hand on his arm.

He paid no attention to her. 'I mean it, Celia. You might have to find somewhere else.'

THIRTY-TWO

'Hey!' A voice behind her. 'Hey there.' Celia was used to men's voices calling her in the street. She made a play of looking down and carried on walking. It was mid-afternoon in Leicester Square, late November and already growing dark. Captain Russell had told her to drop him at Westminster and leave the car behind. She'd decided to walk the long way home. Ever since she had told Emmeline that she would not transport men in her car, her sister and Mr Janus had been furious with her. Most nights they barely spoke.

'Miss!' She pretended to be studying the billboards as she walked, identical groups of beautiful women waving their men off to war. There was the sound of footsteps running behind her, then a hand on her shoulder. 'Miss de Witt!'

She turned. She barely recognised the man, tanned and tall, blond-haired, handsome, a little faded, thick coat over his khaki uniform. 'It's me, Celia,' he said. 'Jonathan.'

She stared. 'Why... so it is.' He was holding out his hand. She took it, tentatively. 'You look so different,' she said. His face had widened somehow, his eyes become brighter blue. His hair was cut short, like a soldier's. Most of all, he had grown older, she thought, thinner, his cheeks more sunken.

'I guess we all do. You have grown up, Cel— I mean, Miss de Witt.'

She blushed. 'The war.' Around them, people were hurrying, men and women, nurses in uniform, groups of workers, mothers, men in suits. They stood still. She reminded herself that if she thought him terribly changed, she must be more so, much older, creases around her eyes, her hair a darker blonde, the strands so fragile that they looked like they would snap if you touched them.

His words in her head. *Not my style of broad. Little German fräulein.* Well, he wouldn't think like that any longer.

'You are in the women's corps now?' He looked at her uniform. 'Very smart.'

'Not really.' The nurses' uniform was pretty; hers was all baggy green. She wished she had scrubbed her boots and brushed her coat that morning. 'I'm a driver for an officer. It's easy work.' She took her hand from his. 'I thought you'd gone back to New York.'

'I'm in the Flying Corps. Me and a whole bunch of chaps from Canada. I'm based in Norfolk. Marham, do you know it? Going back there tomorrow. I wear my uniform about, though, makes things easier with the white feather brigade.'

'Michael is dead, you know.' She said the words out loud and wished that the whole of Leicester Square would stop dead, frozen, not start again until she gave the word. Like a princess in a fairy story, waiting to be woken by her. The people carried on around her. She gazed at the poster again. How could those women really say *Go!*

'I know,' he said. 'Professor Punter wrote to me. He said he had lost a few chaps.' He put his hand on her arm. The ring on his little finger glittered. 'I was in Egypt when it happened, or I would have come to the funeral. I wrote to your mother; I hoped you might see it.'

She shook her head. She had hardly stayed long enough at Stoneythorpe to receive letters, hurrying off with Emmeline as soon as it had been decently possible. She blushed with guilt.

'I was shocked to hear it. I am sure he died a very brave death.'

'I don't know. There wasn't much about it in the letter from his CO. It just said he had been on active service. Professor Punter said he died saving another man in his regiment, Tom Cotton. Do you remember him?'

Jonathan shook his head.

'You know. He was at Stoneythorpe. He was the groom.' She hated saying the words out loud. Tom in bed, lungs thinned by gas. *I don't want to marry you.* She felt her throat tighten, pushed the picture away.

'Oh yes. I think so. He was in France too?'

'That's right. They were together. I went to see him in hospital. He didn't want to see me.' How easy those words were to say. If she kept saying them, over and over, perhaps they would no longer hurt. *My brother is dead, my father is in prison. Tom told me he never wanted to see me again.* He might even be dead now, she supposed, like Michael, in no-man's-land somewhere.

'Lots of chaps don't want to see a soul when they are laid up.'

'I asked him ... I asked him how Michael died. He wouldn't be clear. He said there were shots, shouts, that it was war.'

His hand was still on her arm. 'Hey,' he said. 'Why don't we go and sit down? I found a nice coffee shop just around the corner from here.'

'I can't.'

His face fell. 'You are due back?'

'No – no, not exactly. The captain has discharged me for the day. I am just ... well ...'

'Oh, come now. Some tea will do you good. I doubt the captain feeds you up, does he?'

'Not really.' She realised that she felt terribly hungry. Miss Webb hadn't come round with a pie last night, so there'd been nothing for breakfast.

'Come now. Just for a minute. It can't hurt. Please, Miss de Witt. You would be doing me a great favour. I don't have a girl, it's just me. I don't think I can face another evening in my hotel.'

'Michael should be here. It shouldn't be you and me. It should be the three of us.'

He squeezed her arm. 'I know. But we are alive. Please. It's my last day. I go back tomorrow.' She looked at him, the pleading in his eyes, and something in her heart turned over. Cambridge loomed up next to Leicester Square, its spires glittering over the patchy grass, Michael in a punt, laughing.

'I will, then.'

'Come. This way.' He winked at her. 'Not a single chap here wouldn't want to be escorting a gal in uniform. Especially a tall, pretty one like you. You know they use English girls in the French clubs as dancers, because the French girls haven't got the height?'

She tried to smile.

'I am sorry. I shouldn't be flippant. Bad American habit. It was terrible news about your brother.' They sidestepped a gaggle of skeletal pigeons fighting over breadcrumbs. 'The war has taken a lot of men.' He put his hand on her arm again and she felt its warmth even through her coat.

'Some of the girls think it's great fun. I wish it would end.' Two women passed, both eighteen or so, their hair beautifully golden, their faces bright yellow.

'I hear they can't even get that colour off in the bath,' he whispered in her ear. 'Yellow for life. At least you're not that.'

'No.' She smiled. 'Munitions girls get paid more than me, though.'

Ladies and gentlemen walked arm in arm, too finely dressed to care about war, she supposed. The King might pop out any moment, she thought, wave them back to the Palace. 'Our house is all different now. My father is in prison, my mother is sad. It isn't much of a place any more.'

'Yes, I heard about your father from Professor Punter as well. That is terrible news. Do you hear much from him?'

'Never. That's a good thing, though, we think. They would write to us if he were dead, so he must be still alive.' She listened to this voice coming from her, this almost cheerful voice, the kind of girl who belonged on the recruitment posters, being brave and bright-eyed about everything. She expected him to say *Oh come now, Miss Witt, surely you are angry.*

'That's true. This way.' He pointed her to a pretty café with windows draped with gold and red curtains. A great stack of cakes adorned the centre.

'Oh!' She fell back. 'We cannot go here!'

'Why not?' His face clouded. 'You don't like cake?'

'No, no. I do. But … it is far too expensive.'

He smiled. 'I have plenty of money left for my leave. And

no one to spend it on. As you know, my family are so far away. Indulge me, please, Miss de Witt.'

'Well, all right then.' He held the door open for her. Two immaculately suited waiters standing just inside the blue drapes welcomed them. The gold-painted walls were swathed in blue velvet and hung with paintings. At the tables were beautifully dressed women straight from Emmeline's magazines, and a few men. One elaborately frilled little girl sat next to a woman who was perhaps her grandmother. Celia hung back. 'I don't think—' she began, but Jonathan was already striding forward after the waiters. The three men stood by the table. Celia gazed at them for a moment, then blushed as she realised she should choose a chair. She sat and felt the expensive linen of the tablecloth fall over her knees.

'Tea for two, please,' Jonathan said. His voice was so loud, she thought the whole restaurant could hear. 'And a selection of cakes for the lady, if you would.' He turned to Celia. 'A little coffee, perhaps?' She nodded. 'Coffee as well as the sponge,' he directed.

Celia watched the waiters and bent close to Jonathan. 'I don't think they like uniforms here,' she whispered.

'Oh, they should welcome us. They are a little snooty, but, hey, same way that the meanest nurses slap you down and shout at you for trembling, but they get that needle in and out faster than you can say jack rabbit. The nice girls fret and miss the vein. This lot have the best cakes. In fact, I don't trust any restaurant that doesn't have snooty staff. Polite waiters, shocking food. Anyway, last time I came here, I was with three other chaps. They much prefer to have gentlemen if they are escorting ladies.'

'The last time I came somewhere like this, it was for a ... wedding. But it was a much poorer place. You wouldn't think there were food shortages, being in here.' She had read in Captain Russell's *Times* last week that the government was thinking of going one step further than last year's edict and restricting lunch in restaurants to one course, dinner to two.

'No, indeed. There's plenty of sugar, if you can pay for it.'

The waiter returned and poured the tea.

421

'I don't feel much of a lady any more,' Celia said as he left.

'You will always be a lady. Anyway, times are changing. I am sure most chaps are looking for a wife who can change gear and fix an engine.'

'That I can do.'

'Well, there you go.' He winked, a hint of the old, confident Jonathan, the one she had seen before the war, imagined hosting parties. She began to smile but dropped her eyes, not wanting to meet his gaze. She looked so much older when she smiled these days, Emmeline said.

He was regarding her carefully. 'You know, you really have grown up, Cel— I mean, Miss de Witt. Forgive me, but you were a girl before; you were – how shall I say it – not grown into your height.'

'I'm still not beautiful,' she said, cutting him off. 'That's Emmeline.'

He smiled quickly. 'I wouldn't say that was true. But now you have really... come into your features.' She could see him scrabbling for words as the colour rose in his face. 'Very appealing.'

She pushed down a desire to giggle. 'Thank you.'

The waiter placed a great pile of cakes in between them. Celia suddenly felt the hunger curling in her stomach. She was desperate to grasp one. Verena's strictures on manners ran through her head.

'Come on, ladies first.'

She blushed and pulled out a dark brown rectangle sprinkled in what looked like caramel. She felt her fingers sink into the icing.

'I can't bear to start it. The faster one eats it, the quicker it will be gone. I rather want to look at it.'

'Well, the faster you finish, the sooner you can have another one.'

She shook her head. 'I saw the prices! Some of these cost nearly a week's wages.'

'All the more reason to have two. Now, start it, or I can't!'

Celia looked up and saw that the little girl was staring at her. She gave her a great smile and held the cake up to her mouth. She did not want to use a fork, would use it for the next bite. Her teeth touched the caramel icing, then the sponge. Her mouth filled with the taste, and she realised she had not eaten anything like this since before the war. The party that had failed – although Mrs Rolls could never make a cake as light as the one she was eating. She wished she wasn't so desperately hungry, that she could enjoy the taste rather than merely fill the emptiness in her stomach. She could have eaten them all, told herself that she must force herself to behave. Jonathan took a slice of sponge.

She put down her cake. 'Did Michael tell you much in his letters?'

'I got the same from him as the other chaps out in France. Busy out here, lots of good chaps, mud, French friendly. I wonder if they gave them a set list of things to say. Michael would have been going through his men's letters, making sure they didn't give anything away.'

'They didn't want us to know the truth.' The ring on his little finger had a tiny white stone in the right corner. She wondered that she had never seen it before. She pulled her eyes back, aware that she was staring.

'Would you have written the truth?'

She fiddled with the silver spoon by her teacup. 'No.'

'War is a terrible thing, Miss de Witt. No logic.'

'Tom didn't really explain it. He said guns and shooting and going over the top, that's all.'

'I think that is pretty much how it is, you know. The men can't see a thing. They are sent over and it is all they can do to keep their heads down. You know, it seems to me that the newspapers, the government, they make a heroic story out of it, but there really isn't a story. It's not like a book. Not that I've seen much combat myself, but from what I hear, a thousand men are sent over and nine hundred of them are shot. The German who shot Michael wouldn't even have known he was doing it; he was just firing into space.'

'I can't believe that.' She looked at his eyes and quickly glanced away. She thought of him in the garden saying that Sir Hugh would come back *for as fine a girl as your sister*. He had been wrong then. He liked things short, she realised. He liked to summarise and know things in a concise way. *Sir Hugh will come back.* But that wasn't enough; there were layers and shades now that made things impossible to understand with a few words. There were thousands of words out there, words in the past tense confused with the present, and no matter how many of them she conjured, she couldn't get close to the truth, not yet.

'Really, Celia, I think that's the way it is. With the Flying Corps, we spend more time cleaning the planes than using them. But what I have seen is horrible stuff, no logic to it, a mess.'

'When I saw Tom, I felt he was hiding something. I did not believe the letter either. Killed in the course of action. Surely someone could have given us more details than that?'

He picked up the jug and poured more milk into his tea. She watched his hands, waited.

'I think if I had lost a brother, I would be like you, searching for an answer. But there isn't one. The men went over and the shooting was random. Thousands died on the Somme.'

'But why would Tom hide something from me?'

'You don't know that he is. But I suppose that if he saw Michael die in front of him, he wouldn't want to remember the details.'

'It seemed more than that.'

The waiters were pouring tea again. Celia tried not to stare at them, to pretend she was in this sort of place all the time. She fiddled with the side of her plate.

'I really think, Miss de Witt, that it is only the horror of war.'

'I was in France for nearly a year. I saw some of it.'

'Good for you. Were you nursing?'

'Ambulances.' One word, one simple word, and she wanted to cry it out: the bodies of the men, the coughing from the gas, the screams as the morphine wore off. Shep dying as she reached out to her, Johnson calling her Elizabeth.

He whistled. 'They really do breed some gals in your family. Tell me – if you don't mind – where were you?'

'Étaples. Although I didn't really have much idea where I was.

I was always driving. The food was awful. Nothing like this.' She pointed at the stack of cakes.

'Have another! But see – you're doing the same. You're talking about the dreadful food because it's easier. You don't want to talk about what you really saw.'

'No. You're right. I can't really think of the words to fit. I think we need new words for it all.' She took another cake. Warterton was still out there, driving doctors and coffins around by day, dreading the night and the bombers. She had written again two weeks ago, saying that none of the old lot were still there; she missed the girls she had gone out with. She said that perhaps Celia might like to visit her mother in Winchester if she got a moment, since she had told her mother all about her and she was very eager to meet her. *She'll talk a lot but she'll give you a good meal!!* Warterton had written. The exclamation marks hit smartly at Celia's heart, Warterton trying hard to seem jolly, to persuade her to go. Celia had not replied, still had not written to Shep's parents, telling herself it was because it hurt too much. And here she was, tucking into soft cakes and drinking tea.

Jonathan broke into her thoughts. 'You were a great reader when I last saw you. Do you still keep up with the intellectual trends? You were deep in Freud, I think?'

'Not so much, no. The war takes up everything. I look at the books and they seem to belong to an old world where everything was safe. I don't even know if I want to go to university after the war is over any more.' The picture of Cambridge she'd always dreamed of floated in front of her: a sunlit table in a library, cycling to lectures, giving the other girls cocoa in her room. She pushed it away.

'You should go. I'll be there too, and the ladies' colleges let us call round for tea.'

Little German fräulein, he had called her. 'I might not let you visit me.'

'I would expect not. You'll be one of those serious lady students, no time for fun.' His hand was near the milk jug. She knew he wanted to reach for her fingers. 'The war will not last for ever, you know,' he said.

She wanted to push those words from his mouth and replace them with her mass of confused letters: no sentences, no verbs, nothing but a fog, as if, she thought, she was looking at signs but could not read. 'Everything's changed at home. We've only seen Papa once, when he moved prisons.' She put her hand in her lap, so he could not reach for it. He left his where it was for a moment, then took it back to his cup. The ring glowed gold in the lamplight.

'And when was that?'

'Middle of 1915. I spent the year after you all left with my mother. It was terrible. Michael went to France, and it seemed like Arthur was never coming back. And Emmeline disappeared with my tutor.'

He put his teacup down abruptly, so that it clattered in the saucer. 'She did what? What about that stiff old stick?'

'Sir Hugh changed his mind because of the war. So she came to London with Mr Janus.'

He whistled through his teeth. 'I never would have thought it. What a gal, after all.'

'She's married,' Celia said hastily. *And telling me to deliver objectors around London because she thinks we won't get caught.*

'Another war widow then, poor gal.'

'He is not well enough to fight, actually.'

'Poor chap. I don't remember much about him. Colourless sort, wasn't he?'

'I suppose so. He is different now. I live with them. So you were wrong that Sir Hugh would come back for her, forgive us all.'

'Did I say that?'

That shocked her. 'Yes! Have you forgotten?'

'Well, clearly she didn't want him, did she?'

Celia shook her head. She had found in general that people's memories of the time before the war were unreliable. Even Emmeline's were quite wrong sometimes. She supposed that the war was such a great, dividing thing, you spent so long thinking about it, that the time before became some kind of muddle. Except for her, that was. She had every moment entirely clear.

'Anyway, after Papa was detained and Michael and Emmeline left, Mama grew upset. She said there was no point to a house like Stoneythorpe. Then she shot the horses.'

Jonathan shook his head. 'That's a lot of bad news. I had no idea. I imagined you still living there just as you did before. I thought of you doing lessons. I thought that your mother would be the type to keep things going.'

She blushed at the judgement of Verena, unfair, she thought. Surely thousands of women were not behaving like those ones in the pictures, making tea and waving their men off. And yet still it rang a small bell inside her, the one that said her mother should have tried harder. 'I shouldn't have told you.'

'No, no, of course you should. And I asked.'

'Anyway, she might make it into a hospital.'

'That would be a fine thing.' He smiled nervously, as if he knew he had said too much.

She thought she should try to be polite. 'What do your family think of it all? Your father.'

'I don't write to them much. They want me to come back to New York.'

'Why don't you?'

He played with his cup. 'I am here now, that's the thing. I feel like I have to stay to see it through to the end.'

'If there is an end.'

'Of course there will be.'

'I am glad I have no more brothers in the war. Arthur is still in Paris.'

'And mine is in America.'

She supposed she should remember her manners. 'You had older siblings, I recall. A brother and a sister, I think, Mr Corrigan.'

'Call me Jonathan, please. Yes, one elder sister. She is married to a New Yorker. My brother has just finished at Harvard.'

She nodded and picked up her teacup. There were so many words, millions of them – she had after all been trying to learn

427

them all before the war began. But she could not think of a single one to say. She took a sip of tea, nearly cold now and greasy with milk.

He sighed. 'I have kept a memory in my mind of you all preparing for the party. I did not think things would have changed so much.'

'The party was a failure. At least you didn't see that.' With those words, she remembered something forgotten, so important to them all at the time. 'And you too! Why did you leave so suddenly? Mama's feelings were hurt.'

Jonathan looked around. Most of the other people had gone. 'I think the café may be closing.' He summoned a waiter for the bill.

'Why didn't you stay?' Celia tried not to look as he counted out notes and coins as shiny as the ring on his finger.

'It is hard to explain. I just couldn't. I told them I had business.'

'They didn't believe you. Who would? You promised to stay for the party.'

He stood up. The waiter arrived with Celia's coat, engaged in a creditable attempt at not seeming disgusted by it. She supposed he was used to furs.

'You know, you were the beginning of it all. Once you left, nothing went right.'

He shook his head. 'I couldn't stay.'

'Why? You saw the fight with Sir Hugh and you left. Were you so horrified by us?'

'Of course not! I just couldn't.'

'Well,' she pushed ahead of him, 'I suppose that is that. You just didn't want to.'

The waiter held the door open for her, smiling. 'Madam.' She ignored him and continued out into the biting wind. People were hurrying, collars pulled up against the weather. She thought it would probably snow soon; maybe it was snowing already in France.

'Thank you, Mr Corrigan,' she said, holding out her hand. She was being cold but she could not help it. 'It was a very nice tea. I am sure you send your regards to my mother and sister.'

He grasped her hand. She wanted to tug it away. 'Don't go!' he said. 'Please.'

'I have to get back.'

'You're angry with me.'

She shook her head. 'It was because we were German, that was it. You didn't want to be seen with us.'

'No.'

'You were just like all the rest of them. You liked us enough in the good times. But then you dropped us overnight.'

'That's not true. What are the royal family, after all? They changed their name in July. Did you know they had six choices of name? Windsor was the best, don't you think?'

'The King wouldn't make room at the palace for the Tsar, even though they're cousins. Now they're going to put him on trial.' His attempt to make her smile only infuriated her. 'You know, this afternoon, when we met, I should have said that if my family were not good enough for you, then I'm not either.'

'Celia, it wasn't like that. Let me explain.'

'What could you possibly say?' She tugged her hand back and stuffed it in her pocket, where he couldn't reach it.

'It was a mistake,' he said. 'I know it. I just thought ... if the war was going to begin, I should get back to America. And, if I am being honest, then yes, I felt as if things were not simple at Stoneythorpe, with Sir Hugh and the rest. I was only making it more complicated.'

'You knew what the war would be like, then?'

'No. I didn't expect anything like this.'

'And what you did to me before you left was wrong. I dreaded seeing you in the morning. I didn't know how I was going to speak to you. I was glad you had left.' Instead of freezing London, where the ground was dark with dirt, early grey snow dropping on the slabs, she was back in the garden in Stoneythorpe, and he was putting his hand out for her face. He was kissing her. His cigarette glowed in the darkness, silhouetting the roses.

He ran his hand through his hair. 'Was it so terrible of me? It was, wasn't it? I am a cad. I frightened you.'

'No, you didn't. Or maybe a little. Not any more. It's all different now.'

'I shouldn't have, Celia, I know. I had heard so much about you from Michael. I was always predisposed to like you. And then I met you and you were so engaging and said such odd things. I only found myself liking you more.'

'Everybody else who came to visit admired Emmeline.'

'Not me. I told you that then.'

'Oh yes, I remember.' *Not my style of broad.* 'Why did you call me a little German fräulein?'

'Oh, I did. I am sorry. I don't know why. But you were little, you were a fräulein… Look, I know it was wrong. I trespassed on the kindness of your parents. I wish you would forgive me.'

'I suppose I do. You know, it might have been the thing I remembered, how awful it had been, if so many other things had not happened later. After Michael went, I forgot about it.' She blushed. 'Until… well, until now.' He was standing by her in the shrubbery, running his hand over her cheek, reaching down to kiss her.

'I am sorry. And I ran away. It was cowardly. I never thought that Michael would go to war.'

'Don't think he went to war because of you.' A drop of something freezing landed on her nose.

'Did he leave me anything to say goodbye?'

'He left something for me and Mama, Papa, Emmeline. We found paper in his room on which he had started letters. Dear Mama, Dear Celia, Dear Papa. There was one for you. Dear Jonathan. It stopped there. He put a comma.'

'I wish I could have it.'

'Mama threw them away, I think. We were expecting him to come back, you see. If someone is coming back, you don't need bits of paper saying Dear Jonathan.' She had told herself this a thousand times; said that was why Verena hadn't kept them, all those pages with Michael's writing on.

'I wrote to him care of Stoneythorpe. Did you forward the letters?'

'I think so. But you know what war is like. Things get … lost.' She blushed. Thompson had sent on two, after all, after the one she had destroyed.

'I didn't receive anything from him.'

'Well, he was occupied. Being brave. He was so brave, that's what they told us. He gave his life for his country.'

'It's getting cold. I have kept you out long enough already. I should escort you home.'

'You don't have to.' She brushed another drop of freezing rain from her eye.

'It is the least I can do, after keeping you out. As I said, I'm very grateful that you could spare time to take tea with me. Where are we headed?' His voice was newly stiff and formal, like the girls at school when they were rehearsing for their drama exams.

'Bloomsbury.'

'Come then.' They set off north. He had his hands buried deep in his pockets. The first flakes of snow fell around them as they walked.

THIRTY-THREE

By the time they reached Tottenham Court Road, shops shuttered, cheap stalls along the road, she could not bear it any more. She stopped dead near a dirty-looking church. 'I'm sorry,' she said. 'I've spoiled everything.'

'What do you mean?'

'Everything was so nice, the cakes, meeting you out of nowhere. And it is all spoiled now. It's my fault.' For so long, two years really, she had thought of Jonathan with hostility, imagined that he had escaped the war and was happy while they suffered. She had torn up his letter. And now, standing in scraps of snow, two street cleaners shivering as they threw salt onto the road for the buses, she was afraid of him going. She didn't want to be alone; she wanted to stay and talk about Michael, as if by sitting together, sister and friend, they might make him alive once more.

'No, you were right to ask. I acted wrongly in hurrying away. Listen, Celia – Miss de Witt – don't be down. Please. I couldn't bear to think I had made you unhappy.'

'The war makes me unhappy.'

He held out his hand. 'I tell you what. Don't go. You must still be hungry. Let's get something to eat.' He hesitated, and she could see the fear of her saying no pass across his face. 'There are some nice places for dinner.'

The other choice was the saucepan of old soup bubbling in the damp flat, or the smoggy café around the corner, since she didn't get many of Jemima's pies these days. 'All right, then. On one condition.'

'Which is?'

'No talking about the war.'

'That is a good idea. Come,' he said. He put his arm through hers and led her onwards. She felt the press of his flesh through her coat. The warmth spread through her. Strange, she thought, that such a touch meant nothing from Emmeline, her mother, her father. With Jonathan, though, it seemed significant, as if she should remember how it began, how long it lasted. She pushed the thought down, almost shocked by herself. She couldn't think that way about Jonathan. She was in love with Tom.

They walked back the way they had come, past the Trocadero, dark and closed up, and on to Piccadilly. Cars careened around the statue of Eros, greying and chipped, not cleaned for four years. She stopped to shake the flakes of snow from her hat before they melted.

'Let's go in here.'

'But this is the Ritz!' The gold doors rose in front of her.

'Our money is as good as anyone else's. Come on, Celia, let's go.'

The restaurant was full of men in suits and smart women in gowns of pink, blue, yellow, as perfect as jewels in a shop window, untouched by the greens and browns of war. Celia blushed, thinking of her uniform, her hair pulled back, wished she had spent nights rubbing cream into her face or wax on to her lips, washing her hair in oils and rose water. The place had thick white tablecloths, mirrors on the wall and a heavy carpet that absorbed her feet as she trod. As they sat down, she tugged nervously at her uniform.

'I don't think people like me should be coming here,' she whispered.

'Oh don't be silly. I'll tell you what will make you feel better.' He waved to a waiter. 'Champagne, please.' The waiter nodded and whisked away.

'We can't!' she hissed across to him. 'Jonathan – Mr Corrigan!' Lloyd George boomed in her head. Drink was evil, enervating the nation, bringing down the working man. She remembered the champagne at Emmeline's wedding. But it had been *legal* then. Even the royal family had vowed not to take drink until the war was over.

'Why not?' he said. 'Why can't I treat a hard-working young lady to a drink or two?'

'It's illegal, Jonathan. You could get arrested.' The girls in Étaples had passed round flasks of alcohol against the rules. One of them had been caught, and let off with five mornings of extra cleaning after she'd said she kept it for the most desperate men.

'They only care about the working man or woman, you know. It's only Joe round the corner who will be fined five pounds for buying his wife a sixpenny beer. Although how they can afford it any more, I don't know. Look around you: don't you think everyone here is buying each other a drink?'

'I don't know.' The women all had long glass flutes, some of the men the same, others taking small tumblers of what looked like whisky. 'What if they catch us?'

He winked. 'I'll tell them I'm a rich Yank and didn't know the law. Actually, the base is pretty dry these days. CO hates the rum. Says it makes us slower on the controls. All the more reason to stay here.' He grinned.

Celia nodded. If the police were to come, they would have to arrest the whole place. 'But this will cost a *fortune*. I can't.'

The waiter had returned and was pouring from a dark bottle.

'Allow me to treat you, Miss de Witt. As I said, I have this money and nothing to spend it on.' He held up his glass. The ring glinted. 'Cheers!'

She took a sip. It was bright and sugary, tasted like the golden colour it was. She felt the bubbles billowing into her head. It was much sweeter than the stuff at Emmeline's wedding, and there was no comparison, really, with the horrid rum they used to pass round in the flask. But the wedding was before, and overseas was different. This was in London! She was doing something that not even the *King* was allowed.

'Why don't you have a girl?' she found herself asking as another waiter put leather menus on the table.

'Never found the right one.' He grinned, fingered his glass. 'Maybe I was waiting for you.'

'You can't have been.' She wanted to laugh, but she was blushing. 'You would have written to me if you were.'

'I did write.'

'I didn't see the letter you wrote after Michael's death.'

'No, I wrote again after that. And then three more times. I wrote from Egypt.'

'I never received them. You sent them to Stoneythorpe?'

'I did. I suppose they got lost on the way.'

'Perhaps.' Or maybe, she thought, there was a pile of letters at Stoneythorpe from Jonathan and who could guess who else, letters that Verena had not given her.

'I wrote to tell you that I was thinking of you, that I felt for you in your loss. I know I had already said that in the first letter, but I wanted to say it again. I wanted to ask if we could meet but I did not dare. Instead I wrote about Egypt, a little. I remember you talked of travelling. I wrote again, but there was still no reply, so I thought I should leave you alone.'

'I would have liked some letters about Egypt.'

'I wrote to you about what I saw. I told you about everything, the sand outside, the heat, the odd local fruits they bought us, the language of the servants. I wrote about other things too, Michael and Cambridge and our studies, how life had been there, what I hoped for the future.' He stopped, drank some champagne. 'Actually, I wrote to you before as well, before Michael died. I thought of you at home. It wasn't much, just things about Cambridge and how I missed your brother. I didn't know who else to tell.'

'I would have been interested.' She was lying: before Michael's death, she would have put such letters aside. Now she reached out for the words, for he had seen her as the Celia she had been before the war. No one else but Verena thought of her that way any more. 'Tell me about America.'

The waiter appeared behind them. 'Have you made your choice, sir?'

She had barely looked at the menu. 'What do you think?' Jonathan said. 'Sole followed by steak?'

She nodded. 'Are we allowed three courses here?' she whispered.

'Just about.'

She could not think when she had last tasted either sole or steak. The very thought of them made her feel so hungry she thought she might faint, even after three cakes. Jonathan held up his glass. 'To us!' he said. There was something oddly intimate in the touch of their glasses. She blushed and looked away. All the people around them were in couples or pairs of couples. They were married – or perhaps lovers. They must think the same about her and Jonathan.

The sole was placed in front of her by a waiter who whisked his hand away immediately. She waited for Jonathan, then followed him in cutting into it. The fish fell on to her fork, the test of a good one, she knew. It tasted delicate, of whiteness. She took another sip of champagne, felt it dancing up into her head and behind her eyeballs. 'We have a whole bottle to finish,' he said. 'Now, we are not to talk of the war, or of the past. So why don't we play a game? Spot me something beginning with Q.'

Three hours later, she fell against him as the doorman ushered them outside. 'Oops-a-daisy,' he said. 'Come on now, Celia.' She grasped his hand and thought how funny it was that he had said her name. She started laughing, and soon she was bent double, unable to stop, like a child. Snow was falling around them, dusting her shoulders. A spot dropped on his nose and she laughed even harder. She leant against him. The centre of her felt weak, like a puppet that had collapsed in the middle. She kept laughing. He gripped her around her shoulders as she bent over, laughing still.

The door behind them opened and two people came out.

'We should walk on,' Jonathan said. 'We are getting a bit in the way here.'

Celia tried to step forward, but found herself laughing again. She held on to his waist to stop herself from falling. 'Let's go this way,' he said, pulling her to the side. She looked up and took a deep breath. 'I can't,' she said. 'I can't!'

He was smiling at her, but it didn't matter that he wasn't laughing too. She knew he saw how funny it all was. She felt him put his arm around her shoulders. 'Let's not go home,' he said. 'Would you like to go dancing?'

That made her laugh even more. 'I can't ... I can't ...' Finally, she managed to say it. 'I can't go dancing in this!'

'Plenty of war girls go dancing.'

She laughed again, thinking of glamorous women in high heels and shiny dresses. 'I can't!'

'Well, why don't we try?'

She tried to stand up straight, and fell against him again. She put her arms around him. In a moment, he was grasping her close, holding her to him. 'Let's stay here!' she said.

'We can't stay here. We'll freeze. Come on, I will find a taxi.' He held her arm as he steered her forward into the road and hailed a cab. She dropped against him in the warm interior. He put his arm over her and stroked her hair.

At the door of the club, she watched him count out notes – much more than he needed. She knew from the look of the man in the booth that she was the problem. Two pretty women in sequinned gowns spun past her as she waited. One had a white fur wrap draped over her shoulder the way Mrs Rolls used to hang a tea towel over hers. The other had gold high heels on, buckled low over her feet. They both stole glances at Celia, laughed as they did so. She looked back calmly. The waiting in the cold air had steadied her head.

'You had to pay a lot for me,' she said. The club was down a dark set of stairs. He let her go first and she was tentatively finding her way, clutching the wall with her hand, edging her feet. 'I am not dressed correctly. Those other girls were very smart.'

'You are dressed fine. You are serving your country. Those girls were probably tarts.' He had to shout over the music filling the corridor.

'What do you mean?'

He took her arm as she pushed open the door in front of her. 'You know.'

Celia gazed at the club. She thought she must be in some sort of play. Everyone was beautiful. She could not see the two girls – it was as if they had disappeared into a mass of loveliness. Her eyes were dazzled, gazing at the bright gems. Men and women were dancing to a band at the front, drinking together at low tables. She gazed at a couple in front of her. The girl had a butterfly ornament in her dark red hair.

'This way, sir, madam.' A waiter showed them to a table just to the side of the band. Celia tucked her knees under the white tablecloth, feeling less self-conscious seated. The waiter put a glass of champagne in front of her. The band were playing an upbeat song. The music coursed through her. She gazed at a couple on the dance floor, moving together quickly to the beat. 'They do it well,' she said, admiringly.

'Some people come here every night.' Jonathan took a sip of champagne and sat back.

'Do you come here a lot?'

'Not now,' he said. 'I used to. I met a girl who ... used to come here. I wanted to see her. She made a fool of me, of course. Looking for a man with more money than me.'

'I'm sorry.' Her words came out clipped, and she felt a spark of anger with herself. The thought of the girl stung. 'Was she very pretty?'

'Of course. All those types of girls are.'

'Like the ones at the door?'

He shook his head. 'No, she wasn't like them, not really. She just liked dancing. She wasn't a tart. Listen, let's not talk about her.'

'What do you mean by a tart?' The couples came dancing past her, hands on each other's arms. The lights on the dance floor looked like little stars.

'Oh Celia, you must know. They go with men for money. Surely you aren't ignorant of that?'

'Oh.' Warterton had told her that the men at the front queued up to go with Frenchwomen. She had driven through Covent Garden late at night and seen gaggles of women standing on corners who she supposed might be looking for men. But she had thought of such women as poor, dirty, lying in grimy rooms. These ones looked like they must be duchesses, in glamorous evening gowns, their fingers sparkling with rings. 'I didn't think they would be so ... rich.'

'Smoke and mirrors.'

Celia gazed around and saw that the red-haired woman with the butterfly ornament was on the dance floor. She was wearing a bright gold gown, jewelled over her back. The man's hand was around her waist. They turned with the music and she saw his face. He was gazing at his partner in naked adoration. Celia's heart sank. She could not imagine someone feeling so strongly for her.

'These people look very happy here,' she said. 'I suppose they chose the right husband.'

'I don't think many are married. Quite a lot are here with some-one else's husband, I daresay.'

She stared at him, shocked. This was worse than Cooper. Why get married, then, if you wanted to be with other people? But perhaps all their husbands were fighting and they felt terribly lonely. Still, surely Jonathan was wrong. She took a sip of her champagne. She was getting used to the stuff now, she decided; it was barely going to her head at all. 'Are you still in love with her?'

'Who?'

'The nightclub girl.'

'Naomi? Of course not.' He laughed, then softened his voice. 'Listen, I shouldn't have talked about her. I'm here with you.'

All the men here are looking at women and you're not looking at me, she wanted to say. She reached out and caught a spot of wax dripping from the candle on the table.

'You know,' he said, 'when I wrote to you, these ideas kept forming. I told you about Egypt and the things I saw. I said how much I missed your brother. I thought of you reading my letters. I thought maybe . . . I don't know . . . maybe we might be closer friends than we were. Or something like that. I had this image of you in my head, the girl I saw last.'

'I'm not that girl any more.'

'No. You're more.'

The band finished the quick-paced song. A woman in a blue dress stepped forward and began swaying as the violins played. She had a low voice. It was a love song from a woman to a man who had deserted her.

'Let's dance,' Jonathan said to Celia.

'I don't know how to.' All the lessons with Miss Gillieflower had been about the type of dancing you might do at court. Not this.

'I'll show you. Just follow what I do.'

She folded her hands in her lap.

'Don't think about those other women, Celia. You are much more beautiful. Their faces are just caked in paint, you know.' He stood up. 'Come with me. I want to dance, and there's no one else I want to dance with.'

He put his arm through hers as they stepped down to the floor, and then held her close. She realised he was stronger than she had thought as he whirled her around, spinning her across the floor, taking her from side to side. They danced past the singer, and Celia felt herself flush. *Don't forget me, why did you go away, you broke my heart and oh why would you not stay.*

'You know,' he said. 'This is the champagne talking, Celia, but sometimes, since Michael's death, I have thought of you and me dancing together. I thought we would do it well.'

'What?' He was swinging her in a turn then and didn't answer. She asked again, but the music was too loud to hear what he said. As they turned once more, past another beautiful woman, she told herself that perhaps she hadn't heard correctly. She had muddled what he said with something the lady in blue had been singing.

'Again?' he said, after the song finished. The band were fiddling with their instruments. Celia looked up, and one of the sequinned women was casting her a mocking glance. That was it. His arms were still around her. Why not? she thought. Everybody else was doing it. That was what war made people do. She thought of Cooper, smiling to herself in the daytime, creeping off from the dorm at night, even though it might have got her fired.

'Where did you say your hotel was?'

'I didn't. Knightsbridge.'

'Why don't I go back with you?'

'What?'

'I said, why don't I go back with you? To your room.'

He gripped her hand. 'Celia? What are you saying? You don't mean that!'

She was flooded with shame. 'You don't want to.' First Tom, now him.

'No ... no, it's not that. It is just ... Celia ... you are ...'

'That's what everybody else is doing around us, isn't it? They dance, and then they will go back to each other's hotel rooms or apartments.'

'Yes, but Celia, you are not like them. That's not ... not what I want.'

'You don't like me. I'm too plain.'

'No!' The word exploded from him. 'Listen, come back to the table. Then we can talk.'

She sat down next to him, her heart hot with misery.

'It's not that I don't like you, Celia, not at all. Not that. Of course I do. I just ... you know ... that's not what ... those girls, they are not like you. They are different.'

'They're beautiful.'

'So are you. And all the more so because you haven't spent hours before a mirror, primping yourself. You are like ... something else. I shouldn't have brought you here. I suppose ... I don't know what I planned. There wasn't really a plan. But if I could look into the future, I wish we might write to each other and do this again when I'm next back, and ...'

'And?' She was wrong to demand, she knew. But she wanted to hear his explanation.

'Oh dammit, who cares.' His voice was all irritation. 'You could be my girl. Walk out together. You know. And I suppose ... I suppose ... You know, all the chaps are doing it. People get married after knowing each other for a few weeks! Why not us? Eventually.'

Celia felt as if she was going to shake so hard she might fall from the seat. 'You don't know me. Not really.' She fixed her gaze on his eyes. The colour in them was sweeping, the same thing she had seen after the morphine shot as the relief plunged though the soldier's body.

'I do. Michael told me all about you. I know enough; I want to marry you. How much longer do we need? I am back in four months, we could do it then. I would say let's wait until the war is over, but why should we? We shouldn't let the war win. We can do it wherever you want. You can pretend not to be married if you want to carry on driving, I don't mind. And then we can... I don't know. You could come to America just to see, and if you don't like it, we'll come back.'

Celia gazed at the candle, still dropping hot wax over its saucer. 'I don't know what to say,' she managed. It was an answer, she thought, something like the morphine that meant she didn't have to think. And yet that didn't make it less true. How she had hated America before. Now she thought: there is no war there! The woman was singing another song, about the sea. The drink was dancing in her head. And Jonathan's kiss outside Stoneythorpe, the glow of his cigarette in the darkness... 'I just met you by chance and now you ask me to marry you.'

'It was by chance, it's true. But I've been thinking about you. I wrote.'

'I can't comprehend this.' The picture of the flat in France floated into her mind, the pile of books by her window looking out on to the Seine. Cambridge slipped in behind it, so the two were mingling. 'Marriage.'

He patted her hand. 'I'm sorry. Sorry.'

'Well, people are getting married quickly in the war, you are right. I read about it.' *Do you love him?* Shep would have asked. *I don't know*, Celia wanted to reply. *How will I know? I can't tell!* And then Tom rose up in her head, his head covered in bandages. 'I am...' she began. *I want to marry another*. But then, *I do not want to marry you*, Tom had said. Him and the other girl, living in a cottage somewhere, her serving up food that she had cooked herself. Celia had always thought of spending her future with Tom, exploring, visiting the world, talking, riding around the countryside together. That future she could see. But maybe, she told herself, that was because it was not real, never could be. This possible future with Jonathan was something quite different, lost behind a foggy glass. A great boat going to America, dance clubs like this – and then what?

Jonathan poured more champagne into her glass. 'Please don't try to speak. I was wrong in springing this on you. Let's write to each other, meet up again next time. Don't think about the other things I said.'

She nodded. 'I would like to write.'

'I shouldn't have said it like this. I should have had a ring and a bunch of flowers and the violins behind us should shoot into song. We should be in a park surrounded by people dancing. I should write it in the snow.'

What would Emmeline think of Jonathan? Celia supposed she would probably like him. Only three years ago she had said *I am never getting married!* Tom had laughed at her, said she would be a grand lady. Emmeline had got married in the blink of an eye. She and Jonathan could do the same. And then she would be his, every night. Her head was spinning.

She tried to speak again, could not.

'But I haven't thought of the most important thing,' he said. 'You probably don't like me. You're just being kind to me as the friend of your brother.'

'No,' she said. 'No. I do.'

'You're not promised to someone else?'

'No.' It hurt to say the words. 'I'm not.'

He put his hand over hers. It glowed in the lamplight. 'I'm pleased.'

She felt the warmth of his hand. She didn't want him to take it away.

'I'm so happy,' he said. 'Really.'

I am too, she was about to say. It didn't matter about Tom not wanting her, Michael under the ground, Rudolf in prison, Verena's sadness. Here was happiness; this was what it was. You had to catch it and hold tight to it. She held his hand.

The candle darkened. She realised there was someone standing above them. 'Hello, Corrigan, old chap!' It was a dark-haired man, tall, smartly dressed in an evening suit, small eyes in his wide face.

He was smiling. 'Fancy seeing you here. I thought you were out in the field.'

'Back on leave. Hello, Burlington.' Jonathan's tone had dropped low. His voice was weary, displeased. But the smartly dressed man, Celia thought, was too drunk to notice.

'What a pleasure to see you, old thing. And who is this little lady?'

'A friend. Miss de Witt.' He mumbled her name so no one could have heard it, let alone Burlington. Celia blushed. Was he ashamed of her?

'Charming, charming. Lovely to see a war girl out enjoying herself. May I sit down?'

'Well, we, er, were just talking actually.'

'Splendid. I will join in! Budge up.' He folded himself down on to the seat and squashed up against Celia. She felt the pressure of his thigh and her blush deepened.

'Aren't you here with anyone?' Corrigan said. 'Surely they'll wonder where you are.'

'Oh, some chaps over there.' Burlington waved his hand. 'They won't miss me for a tick. Had to come and say hello to my old chum. We miss you now you are gone off to be a hero.'

'Hardly a hero. I see you've avoided it.'

'Oh, I went for a month or so. But I'm needed at home, don't you see. My old man bought a munitions factory, told the powers that be that he needed me to run it. It's good money, that sort of thing, you know. He made me promise I would return to college after the war was over, but I prefer living in London. Don't fancy going back to the wet old fens.' He squeezed Celia's arm. 'No pretty girls like this young lady here, I can tell you. You Yanks always get the beauties. Now, tell me, what are you two drinking? Champers? I will get some more.'

'Really, Burlington, we were just leaving.'

'You can't refuse me one night with my old pal and his lovely lady.' He waved his hand at the waiter. 'More champagne over here, Christopher.' He squeezed Celia's arm again. 'Christopher is a good one, you know. Can't do enough for you.'

'You come here a lot, I suppose.'

'Every night, some weeks. Gets a bit dull, same old scene. Although not as dull as Cambridge. But still, same old guys, same old gals. That's why I couldn't believe my luck when I walked in and saw you two on the dance floor.'

'We really are just leaving.'

'Oh, one more won't hurt.' He moved his hand up Celia's arm. 'You are very quiet, old thing. What are you in the forces? Not a nurse, I can see that.'

'I'm a driver.'

'Oh, wonderful! Trust you, Corrigan, to find a girl with a car. Now tell me, how do you know our big Yankee chappie here?' Celia almost jumped; under the table, Jonathan was digging his nails into her leg. She turned to him in shock. *Don't!* he was mouthing. He reached across her and pushed away the bottle of champagne. 'We really need to go now, Burlington. Sorry we don't have time to stay. Come on, Celia.' He pulled her to her feet.

'Why! Just when we were getting acquainted. We can't have that. What did you say your name was again?'

Jonathan was grasping her arm so hard she felt tears come to her eyes. How could he treat her like this?

'De Witt,' she said. 'Celia de Witt.' She heard Jonathan groan over the music.

'We have to go now, Burlington.' He was almost shouting.

But Burlington was staring at her. 'De Witt? As in Michael de Witt? Of course! You are a relative of his?'

'I am his sister,' she said proudly.

'Oh God!' she heard Jonathan say. 'Celia, please.'

'Of course you are! I should have seen the resemblance. What a guy. It was a pleasure to know him at Cambridge.'

'Thank you.' Jonathan was pulling at her but she would not go.

Burlington put his hand on her shoulder. 'So sorry about his passing. So very unfair. I couldn't believe the news when I heard.'

'We miss him very much. I wish he'd never gone to war.'

'You are right. Pretty brutal stuff if you ask me. You would think

445

there were enough Fritzers killing off our chaps without the Brits doing the same to their own men.'

Jonathan was tugging at her so hard she almost fell against him. 'We have to *go*!' he said urgently. She ignored him. Burlington's words were shaping in her head. 'Doing the same to their own men?'

'Yes, just terrible. You would think they would be sympathetic. Not *shoot* them.'

The music flashed around her head. The candle was flickering. 'What do you mean?'

'Celia, please.'

Burlington's big bear face crumpled a little. 'What happened to him. You know.'

'He was shot by a German when they went over the top.'

Burlington looked at Jonathan over her head. 'She doesn't know.'

'I don't know what?'

'Celia, come on, I'll tell you outside.'

'I want to hear now!'

People were turning to look. She could hear Burlington saying, 'I am sorry, old chap, I had no idea.' Jonathan was trying to pull her forward. 'Come on, Celia, let's get some air.'

'I don't want air!' A man in a suit was coming towards them. 'Is something the matter, sir?' he said to Jonathan.

'No, no, we were just leaving. Celia, let's go.'

'I want to know! Tell me!' The man in the suit gestured to the band and they played louder. Burlington, face wracked, was muttering urgently to Jonathan. 'Tell me now!' she cried.

'Let's talk about it outside.' Jonathan was still holding her arm.

'No!' she said, gripping Burlington's arm. 'You tell me!'

Burlington stared at her, his face frozen in horror. 'I . . . I am sorry,' he said.

Tears were pouring down Celia's face. 'Sir, I really must insist,' said the manager.

'Come now, we're going, Celia. We have to go. I promise on everything I have, on my life, that I will tell you outside.'

'He will,' said Burlington. 'I'm sorry.'

She loosened herself and let Jonathan lead her away. The tears were blurring her eyes. She could not see any of them, not the beautiful girls, the waiters with champagne, the musicians in the band. They were probably all laughing at her.

Outside, the cold hit her like a slap. Her boots crunched in the snow.

'Tell me,' she said, seizing his collar. 'Tell me now.'

'Celia...'

'You promised! You promised!' She knew the tears were dripping off her chin, didn't care. A couple passed them, laughing, arm in arm.

'You don't want to hear it.'

'I do! Don't treat me like a child.' She let go of him, stood staring up at him.

He stared at the frozen ground. 'I shouldn't know it. One of the chaps from college was a friend of an officer in the next platoon. Michael was ill, Celia. He was ill from the bombs, from the misery of it all. You must have seen the men with shell shock.'

'Michael didn't have shell shock. He wrote to say how well he was.' She could have almost smiled at how wrong he was.

'Of course he did. That's what they all did.'

'He wouldn't have been fighting if he had been ill.'

He looked up briefly, then dropped his gaze again. 'You know that's not true. They fix up the bodies, send them back. Who cares about the minds? Celia, you were out there. You know that all sorts of men fall prey to it. It is an illness. He wasn't weak. It's like the flu.'

'What did Burlington mean, *doing the same to their own men?*' She stared at him, willing him to look at her.

'That's what I am trying to tell you. Michael was ill. I think that the sound of bombs echoed in his mind until he wasn't sure what was real and what was not. He was desperate. And when he had the order to go out over the top, to lead the men, he couldn't. He couldn't go.'

Two women came out and pushed past them, talking loudly about the cold. 'What do you mean, he couldn't go?'

Jonathan looked up, and she saw tears in his eyes. 'He tried to get up over the trench but his legs wouldn't carry him. He collapsed to the ground. The men had to advance without him.'

'So the Germans shot him when he was down like that?'

'No. Listen, Celia, you know it is a hard world out there. Sometimes they send the military police to shoot anyone who tries to hide behind in the trenches.'

'He was shot by the *police*?'

'No.'

'Thank God. That would be terrible.'

'I am sorry, Celia, but what happened was worse.' He put his head in his hands. 'I can't do it. Tell me that's enough, you don't want to hear any more.'

'What?' The darkness was creeping up on her. 'I want to know.' She stared at the gold ring on his finger.

He dropped his hands. His face was clotted with tears. 'They make the officer stand in front of his men. Each of his men has a gun. Then they are told to shoot.'

Celia was captured by it. She could not hear. The buildings around her were turning and she could not hear. The guns, a row of them. *Tom!* 'I am sorry,' Jonathan was saying. 'We were supposed to be keeping it secret. But Burlington always forgot things like that. I knew it! Why did I let him near you?'

Celia straightened up, wiping her mouth with her hand. Her mind ran red with blood. 'The men shot him? But Tom was one of his men. That can't be true.'

'You should have been told. If you were the family of a private, they would tell you, I think. But one of the officers in charge of it all was a chap called Ardle, who was a few years above us at Cambridge. I never liked him much, but we have him to thank: he said that Michael was a good man and did not deserve the stigma of cowardice, and that the family would be told something else. He put it about among the college lot that Michael died saving another man. He wrote to Professor Punter too.'

'Professor Punter told us that,' said Celia, dully.

He held out his hand. 'I hoped you would never know. Come, Celia, please. I will take you home.'

'So your friend from Cambridge told you?' *Killed in the course of his duties.*

'He told another man, who told me.'

'Everyone knows, apart from us?'

'No. Only a few. Let us go now. You should rest.'

She walked a few steps with him, like a wind-up toy. Then she snatched back her hand. 'I hate you!' she cried. 'How could you not have told me? You *knew* and you never said.' She shook her head. 'I will never see you again!' She turned and ran. And then pain stabbed through her head. 'Help me!' she cried. And the world went black.

She woke up to Emmeline splashing water on her face. 'Celia!' She was lying on the sofa in the flat. 'Oh, thank goodness. I thought you would never wake up. No, don't sit up. You'll only be sick again.'

Nausea rose up. 'Actually, I am going to be sick.'

'Oh God!' Emmeline seized a bucket from behind her and pushed it under Celia. 'Have you been *drinking*?'

'Where is Jonathan?'

'Gone. You were almost completely collapsed. But when he laid you down, you opened your eyes and told him you would never see him again. Then you fainted. What on earth has happened? Are you *drunk*?' Emmeline was wearing her dressing gown and one of Samuel's pullovers over her nightdress. 'In public? You could have been arrested.'

The blood was in her head. Michael was crying out. *They forced him to his death.* He had to walk tall, upright. Pale. He said to the men, *I don't blame you.* Or perhaps he was crying out, screaming, begging not to be taken. *Oh God.* She bent and was sick again.

'Celia, what were you doing? Jonathan said you met him in town by chance. And then you started drinking with him?'

'Emmeline, please stop.' Celia lay back, nausea in her mouth. She was freezing. 'Can I have another blanket?'

Emmeline bustled off and returned, tucking it around her.

'It must be late. I'm sorry.'

'It is three in the morning. Lucky Samuel sleeps through everything. I hope downstairs do too, otherwise I will have some complaints tomorrow.' She stroked Celia's hair. 'Dear me, Celia, you know you shouldn't drink with men.'

'We were talking of Michael.'

'Yes. It was strange to see Jonathan. He was very fond of Michael. But even though he was Michael's friend, you have to be careful on your own! He said he found your address in your pocket. Why did you say you would never see him again? Did he try something with you?'

'No, no. We just had an argument.' Celia struggled to pull herself up, blushing at the thought of Jonathan rummaging through her pockets. 'Listen, Emmeline, you should go back to bed. Jonathan treated me properly, I promise. You are right, I shouldn't have drunk.'

'Well, I shouldn't think it took very much. Look at you.'

'I had some champagne at your wedding. And some stuff out in France.'

'The stuff at my wedding was more like lemonade, frankly. You have learned your lesson now, though, haven't you?'

'Yes.'

'Anyway, what was Jonathan saying that kept you so interested all night? I always thought him rather dull.'

Celia blushed. She couldn't answer. If she talked about him asking her to marry him, then she would have to talk about Michael, what Burlington had said. Her heart lurched at the thought of it. She could not tell Emmeline, she would never tell any of them. *I will die first*, she said to herself, knowing it was melodramatic but thinking there was no other way to put it.

'Yes. Honestly, Emmeline, I will be fine now. You go back to bed. If you could just get me some water, I'd be grateful. I need to sleep it off.'

'You don't want me to sleep beside you? Are you sure you feel well enough?'

'I promise.' Emmeline walked off to get water. As she did so, Celia tried to formulate her thoughts. 'Emmy,' she said, 'I have changed my mind on something important.'

'Oh yes?'

'I am going to go to Stoneythorpe. Mama needs me. I was wrong to leave her alone for so long. I wish you would come too.'

'You won't stay to help us?'

'No.'

'How can you desert us? How *can* you?'

'Mama needs me more.'

Emmeline threw herself to her knees. 'Please, Celia. Please. Just once more. We need you.'

Celia gazed at her sister, her blonde hair glowing as she knelt, like some kind of picture of a saint, devout in a book of Italian art. Her mind flashed back to the time on the roof. *That's my heart tearing*, she wanted to say, did not.

1918

THIRTY-FOUR

Stoneythorpe, September 1918

The ivy across Stoneythorpe was wild and unkempt. It had grown around the front, up to the chimneys, even over the windows. It was like some strange sea monster's hair, Celia thought, curling its tendrils into the bricks. Rudolf would say it would pull the house down. All his painstaking work in cutting it back lost, as if it had never been done. It was so grown in that Thompson told her it couldn't be pulled out or else the mortar would crumble.

Celia stared up at the house, the autumn sun burning the roof from behind, backlighting it with sharp white, as if God had taken a great pale pencil and drawn around it. Rudolf might not even care, she reminded herself, when he came, since he would finally be free. But she knew that they had let the house fall into a sad state, that he would be disappointed in them.

Celia had set off on the train five days after telling Emmeline her decision. She did her duty, took one last delivery, a man in the boot, shook as she drove, terrified when he knocked in Knightsbridge that everyone would hear. She delivered him to Paddington, where a man in a pulled-down black hat took him from her boot and told her to turn around.

'That's it,' she told Emmeline that night. 'I can't do it again. I should go to help Mama now. And I'm too afraid.'

She gave in her notice to Captain Russell, who said he would take her back any time, a good, efficient worker like her. Her sister cried at Waterloo.

Thompson collected her from the station and told her Verena was much changed: up and receiving Lady Redroad and the

Dowager Lady Redroad at that precise moment, engaged in final discussions.

The four of them took tea together. 'The government will take care of everything,' Lady Redroad said.

Celia saw her mother bloom under Lady Redroad's attention, nod and smile as the other woman made proposals for the hospital. Celia pushed down her resentment that Lady Redroad was only friendly to them when it suited her, for her mother was better than she had seen her since before Michael left.

In the ensuing days, the Dowager Lady Redroad and a matron sent from Winchester did most of the planning, wrote the lists and hired the staff. Thompson put the furniture in the attic, and he and Jennie moved the sculptures and the rest to a storeroom. The next months were a bustle of activity: nurses and doctors arriving, beds being delivered, people making plans. Celia plunged herself into moving stores of bandages and measuring the distances between beds. It saved her from thinking about Michael, shot by his own men, Tom, his lungs full of gas, never wanting to see her again, Emmeline carrying boxes through dark streets, Rudolf alone in a cell. Instead, she thought of her mother, watched her change, grow taller, bolder, become what she had been before the war. She felt grateful to Lady Redroad, a sensation she wouldn't have thought possible.

The day after she arrived, Celia helped Jennie to pack all the sculptures and paintings from the storerooms in cloths and paper. They laid them in Verena's old trunks and carried them out to where Thompson had dug a great hole in the frozen garden. Matron had said they needed the space. Thompson stood in the hole as they passed him the wooden boxes full of the artwork Rudolf and Verena had bought in Rome, the treasured landscapes of the English countryside, the bronzes that Lord Deerhurst had left Verena. Only a few of the family portraits remained in the house: Rudolf and Verena in Rudolf's study, with little ones of all of them around; the big portrait of Michael before he went to Cambridge in what had been the sitting room. 'We'll have to remember where they all are,' said Jennie. 'What if we forget? We can't dig up the whole garden.'

'We won't forget,' Thompson replied. 'Not all three of us. They're in between the rose gardens.'

'I won't forget,' said Celia. It was where Tom had kissed her. 'I'll find it.' Every time she walked over the area, she tried to tiptoe a little, so that the ground would not press down on the trunks, squash the Roman nymphs and flatten the paintings. She walked lightly, greeted them as she passed.

Celia wrote to her sister, describing the difference in their mother, asked her to come to Stoneythorpe. Each time Emmeline refused, said she was engaged in work that was more important.

Then, in July, she replied in a different tone. Two men had attacked Samuel in the street when he was out delivering and told him they would do much worse if he didn't stop. On the next night, Rufus had been attacked so severely that he'd decided to return to his parents for a spell. Samuel decided it wasn't safe for Emmeline to remain and so she came, grudgingly, to Stoneythorpe.

'I won't stay a day longer than you, Celia,' she said. 'When you go back to driving, I come too.'

'I won't go back to driving.'

Celia meant it. London, everything about it, seemed a million miles away already. She moved boxes and beds, scrubbed stairs with Jennie, and every day the girl who had driven Captain Russell around London was left further behind. Jonathan had written twice to Stoneythorpe, once apologising for getting carried away, asking her to write back. The second time, he said that he hoped he hadn't upset her, that they still remained friends, and could she just write back to set his mind at rest? But every time she picked up her pen, she thought of him telling her in the snow of how Michael had been shot, and she found that she couldn't write a word. She'd tried to tell her mother that Professor Punter got it wrong and Michael didn't die saving Tom, but she wouldn't listen.

Stoneythorpe wasn't theirs any more. Thanks to Lady Redroad, the Dowager and Matron Reed, the stables were full of hospital supplies and spare beds were propped around their furniture in the attic. Thompson kept the grass short so that the men could walk on it, and the only flowers surviving were the ones that could pretty much take care of themselves. Soldiers flowed around the front hall or sat on the hard marble benches that had only been ornamental before. Rudolf's study was now the operations room, occupied by the doctor in charge, Verena and Lady Redroad, the Dowager, the matron and any of the other neighbourhood ladies who came to help. The dining room, the sitting room, the ballroom and the parlour were all wards.

Upstairs, the soldiers occupied all the bedrooms except for Verena's and Celia's – she and Emmeline were sharing, Emmeline's bed crammed against the wall. Michael's room, too, had been left untouched. Verena had locked the door and forbidden it even to be used as a store. Celia supposed the aeroplanes still flew from the ceiling, unmoving in the airless room. The nurses slept on the floor above, in the guest rooms, and the ones above that which had been occupied by the servants. The downstairs offices next to the kitchen were filled with bandages and supplies. Thompson sat there, for he was the supplies man, as well as fetching, carrying and tending the lawn. Only the kitchen was the same, except Mrs Rolls and Sarah had two other girls to help them full time. It was the only way to get thirty-nine lunches out on time, Mrs Rolls said.

Jennie was a volunteer nurse, like Celia, with some other girls from nearby families. She and Celia poured over Smithson's whereabouts with the Westerns on a map of Mesopotamia, tracing out Baghdad and Jabal Hamrin. 'He'll come back,' said Celia, knowing how hollow her words sounded. But men did survive, of course they did. Marks was still alive somewhere or other, Jennie said, had come back to the village on leave and thrown his money about.

Three or so years ago, Celia had wandered the corridors, prowled alone, trying the doors and gazing from the windows. Now every spot was occupied: soldiers, nurses, women trying to visit. Janey from the village mopped the footprints off the floors all day long.

They would never really go, Celia thought; they would always be there, however much Janey scrubbed.

And yet, although Stoneythorpe was different on the surface, it was the same. The garden where the children had not come, and Michael's room unchanged, his umbrella in the stand by the door. Every day, Celia worked to keep her remembrance of him at the forefront of her mind, determined not to allow the portrait of him in the parlour to become the truth. She forced herself to hold on to the memories, replaying pictures of him at Cambridge, before the party, even outside the pub on the green, gazing at the recruitment station. The two of them as children running in the garden. She rehearsed them over and over in her mind, knowing even as she did so that the very act would make them even more false, repeating the same actions like wind-up dolls so that soon, whatever she did, he would become indistinct, his edges dropping away from her mind, and she could reach out her hand for him but see only her own palm. Sometimes she stood outside his room, clutching the doorknob, wishing she dared ask Verena for the key.

Standing looking at the house, Celia could just see her sister, her arm linked through that of one of the soldiers. He was shuffling forwards, stumbling. Celia knew from watching that he wished to fall to the floor and never get up again. She hadn't thought how difficult it would be to accompany men into the garden. Her vision had been of them gently leaning on her as she led them forward, asking about their sweethearts or their wives and children, just like the white-clad women at Number One War Hospital, wandering over the grass. Instead they were angry, begged her not to take them out, and then when she did, shuffled and struggled, clutching at her arm.

Only yesterday a young soldier, shot in the leg, fell against her when they were walking, almost pulling her down as well. He sat on the ground, crumpled, staring up at her. 'I don't know why you're always telling me to walk,' he said, in a low voice, Norfolk accent. 'What difference does it make? You just want to make it heal so you can send me out there again.'

She stood there, staring at the sun glittering on his scarred face. 'That's not true, Roberts. We want you to get well.'

'To be shot at again.'

'Come on,' she said. 'I will help you up. Let's go back.'

'And there might be a music group or some kind of craft that I could do? Something to keep me *busy?*'

'Why not?' she said, losing patience. 'Wouldn't you rather be here than there?'

He gave her a furious stare.

'Sorry,' she said. 'I was out in France for a while. I saw some of it.'

Celia held out her hand and knew he wanted to brush it off, but he had no choice but to take it. He gripped hard. 'It's all very well for you ladies,' he hissed. 'You get to stroke our brows, take us for walks in your fine country home, tell us how brave we are. It's easy for you. Sending us back out so that we can fight and die for one square inch of French land.'

She pulled him up as he hoisted himself.

'When the explosion hit me, I fell against another man. He let out a groan. I saw he was still alive. He had a hole between his eyes where the brain was coming out. I saw it, grey stuff, curved like something you'd get out of a tube. I should have shot him. But I couldn't. I left him there for the bearers.'

'I'm sorry. Come, let's go back.'

She linked her arm through his and they made their way back to his ward. She helped him into bed. 'Women will be the next to fight,' he said, as she took off his dressing gown and settled him in. 'You wait.'

I nearly did, Celia wanted to say. *They wanted to send me out spying, and that would be a sort of fighting, would it not?* The general flared up in her head, smiling at her, handing over the paperwork. *Well,* she wanted to say to him, *you didn't get anywhere, did you? So I'm free of you.*

'You probably think fighting is rather jolly. Like giving over your grand house to sick soldiers.'

Celia nodded. She knew, she had been told by the doctors, to ignore such talk, that it was really just the pain speaking, nothing else. *It's not that grand any more*, she wanted to say. The hospital had proved to be more expensive than they had imagined. In fact, Celia thought, when they had been discussing it, they had not really thought about money at all. She'd thought the King and the government would pay for it all. Certainly Lady Redroad and the Dowager had been confident, waved their hands, said Mr Asquith would provide. Now, the solicitor, Mr Pemberton, couldn't balance the accounts. They were taking the men that the health authority sent them, but the grants they received were not enough. Already, he had told them in a financial meeting yesterday, the hospital was eating up thousands of pounds. It was September now, he said. They had until December to improve matters.

'Well, I cannot think of anything to cut,' said Verena. 'The men will protest if the food is worse. There is nothing we can do, do you not agree, Matron?'

Mrs Reed nodded. 'There is nothing extravagant in what we give the men.'

Lady Redroad waved a hand. 'We shall write letters. And apply to the authority for more funds.'

Mr Pemberton gazed at her. 'Might there be funds from another location, Lady Redroad?'

She blanched and drew herself up. 'All of Lord Redroad's funds are entirely tied up. We shall ask the government.'

Mr Pemberton snapped his book shut. 'Well I suggest that you do, Lady Redroad. Otherwise Mrs de Witt and whoever wishes to help her will have to take on debt.'

Celia was so lost in her thoughts that she did not see Jennie.

'Hello,' she said, touching Celia's arm. Jennie somehow managed to get her uniform whiter than anyone else's. Celia's hands and apron were dirty almost the minute she walked into the ward. Jennie was above all the grime. She smiled at Celia, her face perfectly clean, her hair shiny under the pristine hat, the map of Mesopotamia stowed in her pocket. 'We have a new patient transferred over. He has been recuperating from head injuries. I think you would like to see him.'

Celia shook her head. 'I can't do anything with them, Jennie. I've tried. They don't cheer up.' The sad soldier yesterday had been just another one of the same. Emmeline tossed her hair and talked of her husband, and the men liked her, teased that they would take her dancing when they were recovered. Jennie was cool, brooked no nonsense. Verena largely hid in the study. Their favourite was Nurse Lloyd, a dark-haired girl from London with huge eyes who reminded Celia of Nurse Rouse. Some of the men said Lloyd had a French look about her. But Celia wasn't like her sister or Nurse Lloyd, she couldn't find the touch to make the soldiers think well of her. She always seemed to say the wrong thing, words that made them silent or angry when they had just been laughing with Emmeline. She cleaned their wounds, helped them to eat and drink, tidied their hair, changed their beds, encouraged them to walk, bend their fingers, wriggle their toes or whatever else the doctor had told them to do. But they did not like her. She worked better in an ambulance, she thought, sitting behind a curtain, reciting Shakespeare.

Sometimes she even wished for Jonathan. He at least thought she was brave, clever, strong. She had written back to him only once, with the news that the house was now a hospital. She'd told him that they were all well, and that she'd tell no one about what he'd said. She couldn't think what else to write. When she thought about that night, her mind snagged around it: her offering herself to him, his proposal of marriage. She had decided that he'd done it because he felt sorry for her. He had done it out of pity, and that made her shrink from the thought of him.

'Celia, stop looking into space. Come and see this patient. The girls are making up a bed for him. He's waiting down there.' Jennie pointed at the marble benches. Celia could see the scattering of men moving around in blue pyjamas and gowns. One man was sitting on a bench alone, his head in his hands.

'Let's go then.' She followed Jennie down the stairs. As they walked, she thought she saw the man's head move slightly. His hand touched his ear. She strode towards him. She knew before he raised his head.

'Tom,' she said, standing in front of him. She didn't have to turn around to know that Jennie had gone. 'Tom. It's me, Celia.'

He looked up. His eyes were scarred, the eyelids thick with lotion, his face flushed with patches of red from burns. There was grey in his hair. His head and arm were bandaged.

'They told me I was just coming to a country house. I never thought in a million years it would be here. I suppose it makes sense, though. Near my mother.'

She charged on, wanting to keep Mrs Cotton from her mind. 'We persuaded Mama to give it up. It was right, don't you think?' If he moved up, she could sit down beside him. But he did not, and she could not find the courage to ask.

'You've changed it a lot.'

'It's a hospital now. I hope Papa would approve. I wrote to you that he was taken away, but I don't know if you got my letter.'

'No. Michael told me anyway. It was a shock.' His face darkened.

'You didn't receive my letters? I sent some to your mother. I don't suppose I really expected her to send them on.' The soldiers ambled around them, limping on crutches, clutching bandaged heads. She saw them out of the corner of her eye, silently begging them not to stop and ask for tea or help with medicine. She hoped Tom would not ask how many letters exactly. She had written so many hundreds in her head, but in the end not even a dozen on paper.

'Perhaps she did. Letters went missing. Have you heard from your father recently?'

'We never do. We have to think that it's a good sign. He's still alive. What has happened to your eyes?'

'I went out again after the last place. Passchendaele. It was hell. More men died in mud than were shot by the Germans, if you ask me. A grenade splintered up into my eyes. I keep them closed most of the time. Some of it went into my head too. I think they want to watch me to see it doesn't move around too much in there.'

463

'Are you in much pain?' she said. How weak her words sounded. 'Sometimes I forget it.'

'Have they given you something?' She stood there, still willing him to ask her to sit down.

'I don't want anything. I want to feel it. I hate seeing the rows of medicated men. We might as well be dead animals.' He dropped his head back into his hands.

'I'll find out about your bed,' she said, for something to do.

She hurried down the hall, pushing her way through the men, burst into the office. 'When will Tom Cotton's bed be ready?' she demanded. Matron looked up from her papers, one eyebrow raised. 'If he has just arrived, two hours, like everyone else.'

She slammed the door and hurried back. 'Let's go outside,' she said to him. She could not bear to see him sitting for another minute. He got slowly to his feet. She linked her arm through his unbandaged one. She tried to imagine him as one of the other soldiers, with whom the touch of skin meant nothing at all. But the thought that his bare arm lay under the sleeve was almost painful. They walked through the door.

Outside, she felt the sun pool on her face. She gripped his arm more tightly. 'I've been thinking a lot about you,' she said. 'I've missed you.' Jonathan burned through her mind, her pleasure with him at the restaurant. She pushed him away.

'I don't know what I have been thinking about. War, I suppose.' The grenade splintering up into his face, breaking into his eyes. He must have screamed terribly in the ambulance, she thought, hoping they got him the morphine quick.

She was about to ask about the other girl, then pulled herself back. She would be coming to visit him soon, and that was that. The memory of offering to marry him was one that raked over her, made her want to wake up and moan. She would pretend she hadn't.

'There was a man in my ward who screamed, always at the same time, midnight. He screamed for as long as it took for them to get to him to sedate him. The nurses said he had been found under piles of dead bodies.'

A group of men were sitting watching two others playing draughts. Celia and Tom walked past them. She realised they were heading to the rose garden.

'I heard something about Michael. I was out with … a friend of his and another man came up and started talking.' She watched Tom pale and stare at the ground. 'He said he'd been shot by our own side.' She stopped, surrounded by the paths that once had been Verena's homage to Versailles. A nurse ahead of them was pushing a soldier in a wheelchair.

'I'm sorry, Celia.'

'It's true then. He was shot as a coward.'

Tom coughed roughly. 'Not a coward, Celia, no. Don't say that. He was ill. He heard the shells all the time, even when they weren't falling. He had lost so many men. What happened was wrong. We were there to shoot Germans, not English.' He started walking again. They were almost at the fountain, crumbling and musty with leaves, so stoppered up it might never work again. She reached out to touch it, the stone comforting, secure.

'You were there.'

'No, no, I didn't mean "we" like that. I was sent away a month before to fill … The signallers had lost a lot of men in a shelling. I heard that it had happened. I am sorry, Celia.'

'Professor Punter said Michael died saving you. But you weren't even there when he died.'

'That's right. I'm sorry.'

'You knew when I came to see you. You didn't tell me.' She watched him gazing at the grass. As a child, she had spent hours lying on it, attempting to be the same size as the insects, trying to tell which ladybird was which from her book: harlequin, two-spot, Adonis. She wished she could be back there now, hold tight to Michael and say: *Don't go! You mustn't go!*

'I couldn't. Don't you see?'

She held on to the fountain, feeling the grit of the stone, clutching it so hard that it might have crumbled away in her hand. The scars looked even darker on his eyes. 'Who shot him?'

'I don't know. They chose men from the regiment. I heard it

was a group of thirty or so. I don't know who … You know, if I did know, maybe I would have killed them. If I'd known, I'd have stopped it.'

'How could you have done that?' But her heart swelled at his bravery, at the thought that he might have stood up to majors and generals and pulled her brother free.

'I would have found a way.'

He took his arm from her and held his head in his hands. She put her other hand on the fountain. Her heart was falling away from her chest, she felt, miserable at the thought of Michael, yet big with pride that Tom might have saved him. It was too much feeling, she thought. She thought again of the awful grenade, thrown into his face, she supposed, the flame and the heat; he must have felt his skin was on fire.

He looked up at her. His face was wet with tears, the burnt patches scarlet. 'I hear that gunshot every hour. It's in my head. He's there, in front of them. I know he was brave until the end.'

'I think so too.' She did. Tom was right. The army was in the wrong, not Michael.

'I wasn't there for him. They sent me away to another battalion. If I'd been there, I could have helped him go over to fight. I would've encouraged him.'

'I've tried to imagine it. Over and over. I can't think how he must have felt.'

Tom pulled a handkerchief from his pocket and blew his nose. 'Best not to think that way, Celia. He died a terrible death, it's true, but being in the trenches meant awful death also. Some men in my regiment died because they could not get out of the mud. We had to leave them to be sucked in.'

She let go of the fountain. The smell of the dead leaves was too strong. 'Come, let us walk on.' She stepped on to a new patch of grass. They had the same stuff in France, little seeds pushing through the soil, turning green. 'I wanted to die when I heard about Michael. I thought – how am I supposed to bear this? I thought of you. I knew it, you know, I knew you weren't there. If you'd been there, you'd have tried to help him.' She felt a rush of shame that she had ever doubted it.

Tom looked down. 'Yes.'

'When I think of it now, it still makes me want to die.'

'Don't say that. He fought bravely, honestly. Have you told your mother?' He reached out – she thought for her arm – then drew back.

Just ahead of them was her dell, the small entrance to it over-grown with thorns. She had only been in it twice since she had been back. Both times it had not been the same: too damp, cold, and there was no longer any charm in being alone. 'None of them. I never will. Mama couldn't bear it. She talks about his heroic fighting with his regiment.'

'He *was* a hero, Celia. He didn't deserve such a fate. He wasn't a coward, you know. It was the shock. He should've been in a hospital.'

They had reached the rose garden, the stems bent under the weight of their thorns. She supposed they wouldn't flower next year if no one had cut them back. Tom crouched down on the grass. She sat next to him and felt his body quiver as he wept. The tears poured down her face too. He put his hand on her knee. 'I'm sorry,' he was saying. 'I am sorry.' She wanted to hold his bandaged head, touch his scarred eyes, stop the splinters from moving around in there, make him well.

There was a cooling as a shadow passed over her head. She jerked up to see nothing. 'It must have been a bird,' she said. 'We should go back, Tom. If you aren't there, your bed might be given to someone else.'

'We were so young here,' he said. 'I thought... well... I expect you know what I thought. I thought things were going to be different.'

'We're not so old now.' She was staring at one of the rose bushes. That once sported yellow flowers, she felt sure of it, though maybe no more, the blossoms lost under thorns. She looked back at Tom, his poor eyes swollen from crying.

'You know that's not true. I feel old.'

'I suppose so.'

'You wanted to write books in Paris cafés.'

'So I did. I don't want to now. I don't know what I want to do when the war ends. If it ends.'

'Of course it will. One day.'

'Come, let's go back. Before I get in trouble for taking you out without permission.' She thought of taking his arm again, did not. 'No wonder you didn't want to see me when I came to the hospital. You knew about Michael.'

'I wished I could have said to you that I was there, I tried to stop them, helped him run away. But I didn't arrive back until weeks later.' He put out a hand, touched the tip of one of the bushes, avoiding the thorns. 'What they did was wrong.'

'You know, I even wondered if you were ashamed of me, if that was why you turned me down.'

'There was something…'

'What?'

'I can't tell you.'

She was suddenly impatient. 'Well maybe it can wait, then. Come on, let's go back.' He would have saved Michael and that was enough to know. She wanted to run, but it wasn't fitting for a nurse. Instead, she walked beside him, head bowed, slowly. Stoneythorpe rose up in front of them.

THIRTY-FIVE

Ten days later, Tom and Celia were out walking together. He let her take him out most days, although he barely uttered a word.

She watched him carefully for signs of improvement, a quicker walk, eyelids less bowed down perhaps. So she didn't hear what Tom said when he first spoke. She had to ask him, and he repeated: 'Someone's coming towards us.'

She glanced up. A shabby-looking old man was walking their way. It must be a relative of one of the men, wandering in the wrong direction as they often did. Where were they going to put this one? He was wearing a pulled-down hat and he had a long beard. He was weaving towards her, his feet tripping unsteadily. Even though she could not see his face, there was something oddly familiar about him. She stared harder, trying to make it out. He put up his hand and waved. She stared again.

'That's your father,' said Tom, just as the thought was crystallising in her mind. 'That is Rudolf. My—'

She didn't stay to hear what he was saying, for she was running, dashing towards her father. 'Papa!' She hurried over the flower beds and the grass, holding her skirts out of the mud, rushing towards him, her heart in her mouth. She flung herself into his arms. 'Papa!' She smelt old clothes and tobacco as he held her. She looked up at him, and he was weeping. 'You came back. They set you free.'

'My Celia,' he said, holding her by the shoulders. His accent had got even thicker. His face was almost obscured by an unruly grey beard, his hair grown wild and long. He looked like one of the poor men who sat on the corners in London, unkempt, holding blankets over their shoulders. 'You are a grown-up now.

A lady.' Tears ran down his face. 'My little girl. I wanted to be here for it.'

'Three and a half years, Papa. A lot has happened.'

'I know.' He stroked her hair. 'I cannot think what you have seen. But I am here now.'

'Yes.' An icicle struck her heart. 'Why did they set you free?'

'Medical grounds, they said. Who knows? Some of the other gentlemen said they thought the war is soon to be over. I don't know. Never look a gift horse in the mouth is an English saying that I was always very fond of.'

'Yes, of course.' The general reared up in her mind. She had signed herself to him in France, flourishing his pen under the portrait of the country stream. He had fulfilled his promise. Now she would have to go to him. He could ask her to do anything, hold down soldiers, tell them evil words. She could not hide.

'Come,' she said. 'Let us go in. You must want to sit down. Have you seen Mama?'

'No. I arrived and I saw you first, walking in the gardens. I left my bag by the door.' Celia was flushed with panic about her mother. Verena would be in shock, she wouldn't be able to bear it. She might have a heart attack.

'They drove you here?'

'I came by train like anyone else. I didn't write. I think I could not quite believe it was true before I arrived here. After all, they could have taken me back at any time.'

'Yes.' They still could, if she did not go to the general.

'Father...' She hesitated. 'You received Mama's letter? About Michael?'

He ruffled her hair. The gesture that had felt so natural before he was taken was odd now.

'Yes. I received it. I cried to the wall. And now it is just a sharp ache – here.' He held his hand to his chest. 'My poor Celia. You loved Michael so. And now he has left us, taken from the fields along with thousands of other men's sons.'

She leant against him. His voice sounded strange to her, not the one she knew. The years had changed him, she thought, or else she remembered him differently. The picture she had of her father – tall, kindly, patrician – was not the man in front of her, who was sunken, shabby, not even clean. She felt a stab of remorse for noticing the dirt under his fingernails.

'His body may be in France, but Celia, you know he is in heaven now, with the angels. God is looking after him. He is safe there, happy.' He patted her hand. 'Let us pray for him.'

'Now?'

'Yes. Let us kneel and pray.'

Celia blushed. She had gone to church with the rest of them before, bowed her head, prayed and sung the hymns. She had not given it much consideration, except to think that she would not do that sort of thing in Paris. Now, the very act of praying seemed wrong. If God existed, he was sick and ill and not looking at his humans at all.

'Come, daughter—' Rudolf broke off. 'Is that Tom behind you?' He shaded his eyes. 'That boy over there? My eyesight is not what it was.'

She turned. Tom was sitting on the grass, watching them.

'Yes, Papa. He's been injured, quite badly.'

'Poor Tom. I did not know it.' He held up his hand. 'Tom, my boy! Hi there!' He began shuffling towards him. 'How are you?' Tom was standing up and holding out his hand to be shaken when Rudolf grasped him and hugged him. 'My boy!' he was saying. 'My dear boy.'

'I'm sorry, sir,' Celia could hear Tom saying. 'I'm sorry.'

Celia watched them as though they were actors in a play. Eventually Rudolf waved her over. 'Now,' he said. 'We will all three of us pray together. For Michael.'

He held their hands and they knelt on the grass. Rudolf began to speak. 'Our Father, we commit your child, Michael, to Your care. He died bravely, trying to save others. He is with You in Heaven. Have mercy on our souls.' Celia squeezed her eyes shut, unable to look.

Tom replied. 'Have mercy on our souls.'

She heard footsteps behind her. She turned, and Verena was

471

standing there. Her mouth opened, but no words came. Rudolf and Tom started from each other.

'Wife! I was just coming to find you.'

Verena's mouth quivered and her eyes leaked tears. Rudolf hurried to her, held her in his arms. Celia stared at them and looked away. It was too painful to watch them, her parents, now two old people, holding each other, buffeted by the wind. She gazed back towards the house. The general danced in her head, smiling as she signed the papers, handing them over. *You will come*, he said. *Even if it takes some time*. She saw the future: Rudolf and Verena living content in Stoneythorpe, Tom too, while she was sent to Germany to ask soldiers cruel questions while they were tied down to boards.

That night, they had a family supper in Rudolf's old study to celebrate his return. Thompson got out the silver plates from the cupboard, dusted them off and found three bottles of red wine in the stores. Verena had lit some candles. Celia found an old gown at the back of her wardrobe that was only a little too short. Usually, she, Verena and Emmeline ate at different times, sometimes in the study, usually on the wards, hurrying through their meals so they could help the men eat theirs.

'Don't make Papa talk,' Verena had pressed Celia beforehand. 'Don't ask too many questions.'

'I'm not fifteen any more,' Celia said. 'I know.' But she did need to be told, really. She wanted to ask him everything: how life had been there, whether he had suffered. Anything so she did not have to think about the general. Her mind reeled. What would he make her do?

Rudolf and Verena, Emmeline and Celia balanced their plates on the desks in the study. It was such a long time since she had eaten properly, Celia thought, she could barely remember how to do it. Mrs Rolls served up the same casserole and suet pudding as the men had – no time to make anything other – but added swirls of top-of-the-milk to the casserole and some special jam to the pudding. Thompson passed the food and drink around, his hands shaking. Jennie and Mrs Rolls came up too, sat with them on Verena's special invitation, accompanying, not eating.

Celia spent every moment covertly gazing at her father. Thompson had shaved off Rudolf's beard and cut his hair before dinner, but it only showed off how small and wrinkled his face had become. He had grown thin and sunken, smaller in height. His eyes were a yellowy colour. She saw that he barely spoke, instead was constantly opening his mouth and licking his lips because they were so dry. He stopped in the middle of eating to pitch himself double and cough for what seemed like nearly a quarter of an hour. He looked like he had been away for twenty years, not close to four.

Celia reminded herself that he probably thought she looked older too. Jonathan had flattered her when he said she had got prettier. She was taller, thinner, her hair dull, tiny lines around her eyes, shadows in her face where once there had been plump skin. The rest of the family too, she thought, staring at them all as they ate. Verena would pass as twenty years older than she was, no longer upright, plumper around the middle because she hadn't worn her corset since Rudolf left, her hair still long, but dry and straw-like. Celia supposed she should cut it off.

She looked up at the portraits of them around the fireplace, her sister smiling out. Emmeline did not strike as hard as she once did. Her skin and hair were paler and her eyes were grey in some lights. The men teased her because they found her amusing to talk to, not because she was a rare bird to be goggled at, as she had been before the war. For real beauty, most of them preferred Nurse Lloyd.

Celia wondered if Arthur was the only one of them who might look as he had before the war. She could barely even remember his face – when she thought of him, she just imagined versions of the few photographs that were still displayed over the mantelpiece in the study. She supposed he was the same: tall, black hair falling over his forehead, smiling when he had a new plan he wanted you to enthuse about. Paris was a city of pretty girls, and restaurants like the one she had been to with Jonathan. She supposed Arthur occasionally thought of his family, brushed them out of his mind.

'You are deep in thought, Celia dear,' said Rudolf.

'Oh no. I was listening. I am just … so pleased to have you back, Papa.' He was right, she had been paying only half attention. They had been talking about the house and the arrangements. She had drifted away when Verena was describing in detail the plans of the Dowager Lady Redroad and the matron, the new routine of the servants, how each room was used, the renovations they had been told to do to make the place fit for a hospital – a ramp for the wheelchairs, extra cleaning for the places where there might be operations.

'Everything has been so well planned, my dear,' Rudolf said. 'I am very impressed.'

Verena spooned up the last of her casserole and smiled. 'Thank you, husband.' It was all over: the dead horses, the anger, the padding around the empty house crying after the ghosts of her absent family. Celia wanted to cry out: *Is this it? Is this all we are going to say? We have all seen the worst of our souls and we are sitting here discussing the timings for luncheon and the storage arrangements in the cellar. Men died on me.*

She knew that she was being childish. She was the youngest once more, cross at the conversation of her parents, not speaking out.

She looked across at Emmeline, bowed over her plate. 'Emmy,' she said, under cover of further conversation about the cellar. 'Do you wonder what it was like for Father in the camps?'

Emmeline opened her eyes wide. They looked paler than ever. 'I thought Mama told you not to ask questions. Why do you want to? He is back, he's alive and that's enough, thank you. I don't want to know.'

'Don't you think he might want to tell us?' Her gaze flickered up to the portraits over the fireplace, Rudolf and Verena, then one of each of them. Celia had been ten, remembered hours of her legs itching as she posed, wanting to leap up.

'No. I wouldn't if I were him. He wants to look forward. You're always the same. Forever dwelling in the past.'

'What is that, girls?' Rudolf called across Verena.

'We were just discussing how pleased we were to have you back, Papa,' said Emmeline. 'We're very lucky.'

'Yes,' said Rudolf, smiling widely. 'We are together. Thanks to the mercy of God. I always hoped He would reunite me with my beloved family. And now He has done so.'

Celia hung her head. A leprechaun little God with pale eyes and hair brushed over his forehead. The general took off his glasses and sighed. *What do you girls want?* Verena smiled at her, the first true, open smile that Celia had seen her mother give since returning home.

'The house is much changed,' Rudolf said. He was standing with Celia at the back of Stoneythorpe. 'I cannot sleep without walking now,' he had said, asking her to come out with him. 'In the camp, I used to walk thirty times around my bed at night.' So they were walking ten times up and down the back of the house as a replacement. They had managed five and he was stopping for breath. The sky was darkening, the first bats looping overhead.

'Everything's changed, Papa.'

'You did what you could. You cannot keep a house in wartime, I suppose. I do not think there is much to do to improve it at the moment.'

'No, Papa. After the war.' Although they couldn't, she thought, not really. All their money was going into keeping up the hospital, and she couldn't think what would be left. Though, now her father was free, he could manage the factories himself, so more money would come.

'Lady Lenley begged me to keep her roses. I think they've just about survived. I wonder what she would think of the rest of the house.'

'We should invite her back to see.'

'If she's still alive. I expect she probably is not. I wish I had brought you a present, Celia. I thought of all the presents I might have given you for your eighteenth birthday. So many things I have not seen. I have not been here.'

'That's not your fault, Papa. It's war. We're lucky we have each other still. Come, can you walk again?'

He took her arm and moved forward. 'My poor Celia. All the things I wanted to give you. Everything I wanted to tell you. Do you know that when buying a book, you should touch the ends of the last page, to see if they're quite sharp; then you will know how long it will last. You know that now, I suppose.'

'No, I don't know about buying books.'

'I think you are being kind to me.' They stepped around a plump squirrel digging unafraid in the soil. 'I lay in my bed in the cell and thought of what I would like to buy you. Dresses and ornaments, books. I had such plans for the birthday ball. We would invite the finest families, you would be the belle of it all. Stoneythorpe would be admired. Even your mother's family would come.'

'We still could hold a ball.'

'Of course we could.' It hurt her that she could see him saying things to please her.

'Now we have you back, we can do anything.' They were halfway along the house. Only four and a half laps to go, thought Celia, then chastised herself. She was disgusted that she could want to hurry up time with her father, escape him, when she had yearned for him for so long.

'I wanted to add a lot to the house. I hoped to give it a whole front entrance.'

'We could start planning it. Easily.'

'I am so tired now, Celia. I feel tired almost as soon as I get up. I am not a young man any more.'

'I can be young for you. Come, Papa. We should go in for the service.' Since the hospital had started up, they had asked the vicar to give a service at twelve and again at eight, after his duties in the church. 'You'll like it, Papa. It is beautiful to hear the men singing.'

She turned back and he was weeping. She threw her arms around him. 'Papa, what is it? Was it the service? I'm sorry. Don't be upset.'

His face was buried in his hands. 'No, no, my dear, really. I just remembered the other men I have left behind.'

'What was it like there, Papa? Was it very hard?'

'We tried to sing to keep our spirits up, but sometimes the guards would not let us even do that. There was so little food. Sometimes I could hardly sleep, I felt so hungry. And other things, little things really. We had to hand in our mattresses and blankets every morning, receive them back at night, you had nothing that was your own, not even that. But I should not complain. It is nothing to what our soldiers have gone through every day, nothing to what Michael had to endure on those battlefields before he died. And you, my dear, things were not easy for you with the ambulances.'

'No, but I could go where I pleased. I could have come home if I wanted to.' She was glad, so far, that he had asked her little about the ambulances. No one ever really had, she thought, apart from Miss Webb. And she always disappointed anyone who did ask because she had no easy way of summing it up. Warterton would, she supposed, say something like *terribly cold but jolly good fun. Formed friendships for life with the other girls.* She had written again recently, saying that Cooper had been dismissed and sent home, although she hadn't seemed to care much. Celia could hardly believe, really, that Warterton was still there.

'There are many men still there. My friend Mr Jozef, the tailor from Hackney, and Mr Wehrer, the music teacher – we always called each other Mr, not Herr – I cannot see how they can get out. I am so happy and they are still locked away.'

'Maybe they'll set them free too, Papa.'

He clutched her arm. 'I do not think so. I know I have been fortunate. Someone pulled strings to let me out.'

'Yes.' She stared at the house, the glass in the windows shimmering back at her. The men would be seating themselves, ready to sing now.

'Someone had influence. Someone succeeded.'

'Papa—'

'I know it was Lord Smith. He – well, his man – wrote to me

not long after I arrived and asked if I would sell my factories to him. I knew what he meant. He meant that if I sold to him for a good price, he would get me out. I was wilful, Celia, I resisted. I was wrong. And then last year, I relented.'

'Oh Papa, you didn't!'

'I told Mr Lewis and Mr Pemberton to sell him all but two of them. Those I kept, my favourites. He has the others.'

'Mr Pemberton didn't tell us.' The lights at the back of the house gleamed into her eyes, all, she knew, using dozens of candles and jugs of oil. They didn't have the money for it, not really.

'He kept it secret, as he should. But see, Celia, it has worked. Lord Smith has got me out. I am here now. And yes, I am less without them. But I shall build up again.'

'It wasn't Lord Smith, Papa.'

'Of course it was, my dear. I shall write to him soon; I will leave it just long enough for it to be discreet.'

'What if it was someone else and you sold the factories for no reason?'

'Who else could it be? Come now, Celia, let us go inside.'

Celia followed him in. Perhaps it *was* Lord Smith, she thought, briefly, then dismissed the notion. What power could he ever have had? It was the general, and he would be coming for her soon.

They joined the service at the back of the room. The men were singing: 'Dear Lord and father of mankind, Forgive our foolish ways.' Captain Campbell from B Ward played the old piano that Celia and Emmeline had thumped on as children. Celia tried to sing, but the tears were hot behind her eyes. *How were we foolish?* she wanted to cry. *What else could we have done?*

THIRTY-SIX

Celia did not always have time to read the newspapers. The men asked her to buy them from the village, along with cigarettes, sweets, books, and they would occasionally squeeze her fingers when she handed them over. Most days she passed the papers to them as untouched and unopened as the boxes of cigarettes and bags of sweets.

After six weeks Tom's eyes had improved enough that the doctor allowed him to read, and he began to ask for the newspaper. Sometimes, when she delivered it to his bed in what was the dining room, he asked her to read aloud to him. 'We are moving forward on the Western Front,' she read. 'The German army are exhausted. The British have victory within their sights. Belgium awaits our advances – and will thank us for our long efforts in freeing it from tyranny.'

'I don't believe it,' he said. 'They'll be in the trenches for ever. Tell me something else.' He often broke into a dreadful cough, retching, tears coming to his eyes. He sent her to burrow into the social columns, give him anything but war. But the royal family had little to report – Ascot and the balls were still suspended until peace arrived, and the King was talking to Lloyd George while the Queen visited hospitals.

After a while, she began to make up stories to tell him, describing balls at Buckingham Palace and the marvellous gowns worn for the latest presentation to the Queen. He lay back with his eyes closed. She sometimes thought he was not listening, imagined that if she read out recipes and bridge reports, he would not notice. She wanted to touch his face.

When Verena and Emmeline had realised Tom was in the

hospital, they were furious. 'He wasn't there!' Celia told them. 'Honestly. Professor Punter got it all wrong. I promise you!'

Emmeline shrugged, said it was true that no one had officially said it, and Professor Punter had always struck her as rather wavering. Verena shook her head and refused to listen. But she had to treat him as a patient. Generally, she tried to avoid him.

So far, Tom's family had not been to see him. Most of the men didn't want visitors, it was true, but their families were further away. Tom had told them not to tell his mother, said he would go to her when he was recovered. Celia sometimes felt a stab of guilt about Mary, the gentleness in her face as she offered Celia Tom's letter to read, all those years ago. It would be easy enough to call at their house next time she was in the village. She didn't; walked twice past the end of their road on an errand for Matron and did not turn down.

So far, the girl hadn't visited him either. At night, she danced through Celia's mind, laughing and throwing back her hair. She dared not ask Tom about her, expected, one day, to walk past the room and see her there.

When she read out the news from the Western Front to the other men, they asked her to repeat it, shouting it out. 'The German army are exhausted!' they called to each other. The idea of peace was spreading fast. They talked intensely but quietened as she entered the room. 'You just need to hang on until it's over,' she heard one telling another. 'That's it, just pick a hole in it so it won't heal. Who wants to be sent out to clean up after them all?'

'First in, last out,' replied the other, his voice thick with the exertion of tearing at his scar. Celia supposed she should report them. In France, one of the nurses had told her that they practically had to glue the dressings to the men, to stop them from tearing them off and trying to pick the wound open.

Emmeline had become caught up by the news. She sang around the ward, talked of shopping in London, told Celia to smile. She was getting plumper, too, even though there was less food than ever. She had been up to London twice to stay for the weekend in Bloomsbury, but Mr Janus said it was more unsafe than ever and she had to return to Stoneythorpe.

Celia didn't know if she could believe that the war was going to end. Too many times before, everyone had said it was nearly over, or that it would go on for ever. Rudolf had been with them for a month, and she still hadn't heard from the general. Every day, she dreaded a letter being handed to her by Thompson. 'Something from the War Office, miss.' Perhaps, she thought late at night, when the general's pale eyes were in her mind and would not let her sleep, perhaps she would be terrible at the job and he would let her go. She was painfully aware that she hadn't asked him how long he would need her for.

'Do you think we could run away?' she said to Tom, in the middle of reading him an invented court report. The room was quiet. Three of the soldiers had gone out to take the air, and the others were asleep. 'Could we go to France or something? After it's all over. We could find Arthur in Paris.'

His eyes opened. 'What are you talking about, Celia? Run away? How can I go anywhere? And why would you want to leave? You are happy here.'

'Wouldn't you like to go to Paris?' She had last sat here properly as a family on that night with Sir Hugh, when Michael had fought him and Verena had tried to give them all French sauce on the food, to make Sir Hugh like them better.

'Probably not any more. I suppose it's as bombed out as every-where else.'

Then she remembered. 'You have a girl.'

He flushed. 'Celia, you know there was never a girl. Yes, of course I met girls. But there was never one I loved. I lied to you.' He looked quickly around him. The men were still asleep. 'Sorry.'

'Why did you lie to me?'

He shrugged. 'I am sorry. I couldn't think of another way. I couldn't tell you about your brother. And there was another thing. When we were younger, we talked of running away together, of living in Paris. I thought we could. But we can't, you know.'

'We are grown up now, yes. But I don't know. Paris is always there.' She gazed at the bandage on his arm. Sir Hugh had sat just where Tom was now, talking about the Callerton game.

'We can't do that sort of thing. Or not in the way we thought it. We could go as brother and sister.'

'I'm too plain for you, is that it?'

'No, Celia.' He looked around the room. 'You're beautiful. But... listen. Have you never thought about my father?'

'He left your mother when you were small. You have not seen him since. Your mother remarried, had the other children, he left too.'

'She was never married. Never.'

'Lots of women don't marry,' she said, stoutly, the new knowledge she had gained from the war. 'It's no crime.' She was whispering, afraid of waking the other men. She had to hold on to the conversation, she knew. Matron might come in, commanding, or Nurse Lloyd looking pretty, and Tom would go quiet.

'She couldn't marry. My father was already married.'

'Oh. How do you know?' She leant forwards towards him. She could smell the thick ointment they still had to plaster on his face and chest.

'She told me. And I know him. I have always known him.'

'So you see him? He acknowledges you?' The man in the next bed stirred. *Don't move*, she wanted to say. *Don't wake up.*

'Yes. Very much so. Although not as his son. As a... friend.'

'As a friend?' She heard the words, but the meaning behind them was blurred. 'Does your mother mind?' She felt a stab of guilt thinking about Mrs Cotton.

'Not really. She has never talked about it. I just know.'

'I think he must be very wrong to love your mother when he was already married. And leave her alone with you. He is a man of little moral fibre, I think. I said this to you before, I remember. No man who deserts a woman thus can be a true man.' She enjoyed the standpoint that came from being right. It made her speak clearly.

'Celia—'

'Men should be answerable for that sort of thing. I think things will change after the war. I really do. I mean, if he had acknowledged you properly, your life would have been different.' She was warming to her theme even more. It was so much easier to talk about this than her own feelings, a little as if she was winning a debate at school. It was so exciting, hearing about Tom's father. If she spoke well, she told herself, the conversation would continue.

'That's true.'

'Don't you ever want to challenge him and say... You should stand up in front of the world and say, "I'm yours".' Her voice was louder now, but she didn't care. She was right!

'How can he? It would hurt his family.' Tom turned his head and looked square in her face. His direct gaze made her feel shy, but she kept her eyes on his.

'They should know what kind of a person he really is.'

'Sometimes things aren't made better by telling the truth.'

'The truth is always the most important thing.' She was almost floating on the excellence of her argument. This must be what it was like in Parliament, when you knew you were winning the point. Tom would agree with her and the two of them would be bound together in this new endeavour – and the whole world would know about his father.

'Really?'

'Yes.' She smiled, almost shouted the word.

'You really think that I should tell everyone who my father is?'

'I do.'

He coughed, dreadfully, turned to the side as it ended with a retch. It was the gas cough, she knew. He gathered his breath. 'Even though it would hurt people.'

'The truth is more important.'

'Even though it would hurt you?' He averted his eyes from her gaze, began fidgeting with his hands.

She shook her head. 'Why would it hurt me?' But something was creeping up on her, a slow, cold feeling, like water rising around her feet in a bath that was filling. She looked at his face, turned away from her, and her heart dropped.

'Why do you think?'

'I don't know. I don't know what you mean.' *Come back!* she wanted to say. But all her clarity was gone and she was lost in a mist again, couldn't see through.

'Well, if you don't know, can't even guess, I shouldn't say.' One of the men turned over and yawned loudly. Tom lowered his voice to a tiny whisper. 'Listen, Celia, you must have other duties.'

'I want to hear,' she hissed. 'I want to know. You have to tell me now.'

'I don't think I do.'

'You must. Why can't you? Please.' She put her hand out to his. He pulled it away.

'I can't.'

'Please.'

He looked away and sighed. She watched him. The moment stilled between them. This was her chance to say *Stop!* She didn't. 'Go on.'

'Celia, have you never guessed? It's your father.'

She stared at him. 'What are you talking about? You're joking.' She wanted to throw back her head and laugh, the idea was so ridiculous. 'It is not true! You're mistaken. It is lies. Your mother told you lies.' The man in the next bed raised his head, looked confused.

'It is true, Celia. Think about it. I promise on my life.' Rudolf coming to greet him first. *My boy*, he had said.

She dropped her voice. 'I've never heard anything like it. Why tell these lies?'

'It's true. The night before I left for France, I told my mother what I was going to do. I tried to tell you too, do you remember? Well, anyway, she was so angry. She started telling me all these things. She told me about your father. She told me everything. I'd talked of you, you see, and she laughed at me and said that even if I wasn't a servant, I couldn't ever think of you.'

She stared at him, her eyes dropping and head rushing.

'Everything. And it all made sense. That's why your father has done so much for me. He's mine, too. So you see, we can't go to Paris together. We're brother and sister.'

She stood up. 'It's not true. You're telling me lies!' She leapt towards the door, the chair clattering to the floor behind her. The man in the next bed was sitting up now. She ran from the room, not looking back.

'What is it?' said Emmeline. 'Celia, it's two o'clock in the morning. Why are you looking out of the window? I have to get up at six.'

'I can't sleep.' Three days since Tom had spoken, and she was looking at the rose garden in the gloom. The place where Tom had kissed her, four years ago. It was their fault. They had dug up the ground to put in the sculptures, disturbed it. Now it was coming for them, spreading its curse around.

'Well, try. I'm so tired. This is the third night you've been padding about here. It is too much. Samuel is coming to visit soon. Thanks to you, I'll be too tired to talk to him.'

'You're always sleeping. And you're sick in the mornings. You should go to the doctor.'

'I am quite well, thank you. Well, I would be if you would settle down. I could sleep in the middle of one of the wards and get more rest than this.'

'I can't sleep. I really can't.'

The days since Tom had spoken had been dreadful. She could not sleep or eat. Every time Rudolf came near her, she ran away, refused to be in the same room as him. She demanded Jennie's cleaning duties so that she would not have to go into Tom's ward. Her mind went wild with remembering and inventing. Rudolf and Mrs Cotton falling in love while she was a maid in Hampstead house. She felt sick with panic all day long. The voice in her head drummed insistently. *You have brought this terrible thing on us all.*

'I'm afraid, Emmeline,' she said. 'Awful things are happening.'

Emmeline sighed. 'The war's nearly over. The Germans are losing. Haven't you heard?'

'Yes. If they do! Anyway, it's not that.' She'd calculated. Tom was almost a year older than she. 'Do you remember much of the summer of 1897?'

'What, when I was two? Of course not.'

485

'Do you remember Father then?'

'Not a thing. Celia, what's this about?'

'Nothing. Sorry.' Celia got into bed and pulled the covers to her chin. She lay there staring at the ceiling, her heart crashing in her chest.

The next day, Celia was hurrying through the corridor when she saw Rudolf ahead of her. She turned off into a side room. 'Celia,' he cried. 'Celia. My dear.' It was a small room, once used by the servants for items from guests. Now it was just full of things moved out of the main house that weren't precious enough to be buried outside. She backed against the shelves full of ornaments and a pile of lampshades.

'My dear, what is it? Are you ill? I have not seen you for three days.'

'I'm well, Papa. I've just been busy. There is so much to do.' She put her hand on a lampshade. It wobbled a little, broken, she supposed.

'I have not seen you. You were not at dinner last night.'

His face was furrowed, forehead lined with worry. She couldn't look at him. 'I was tired. I had much to do.'

'All the days in the camp when I thought I would be there for ever, I thought of you. My little Celia. I thought of how happy we would be together.' He put out his hand. 'How you have changed.'

She blushed, looked down. 'I grew up. The war came.' She didn't take his hand, and it hovered there, in the air. He took it back.

'I know. It is sad for me. I hoped to see you grow up. Now those years have been taken from me.'

'I thought of seeing you too, Papa.' She pushed past him then, and hurried out into the corridor. Tears were blurring her eyes.

Celia was tidying the storeroom behind the study. The door opened behind her. She whirled around. Tom stood there, blocking the light.

'You are not supposed to be out of bed on your own.'

'I know. But you've been avoiding me.'

'No I haven't.' She stared at his face, his eyes, his mouth, his hair. 'I haven't.' Could she see Rudolf there? She thought that she could, the dark eyes, the thick hair. Older, with a beard, would he look like her father? She supposed so. They had kissed. She had thought of marrying him – and spending her nights with him. She felt sickened.

'I think you have.'

Celia turned back to the pile of bandages. 'But what is there to talk about?'

'I shouldn't have told you. I'm sorry. I know how much you love your father.'

'I asked. I asked you and you told me.' She was squeezing a bandage in her hand.

'I'm sorry, Celia. Have you spoken to Rudolf?'

'No. He doesn't understand why I don't want to talk to him.'

'It isn't so bad, what he did. It happened. He and my mother fell in love. And he has always looked after us. More than most gentlemen would.'

'It should never have happened. I thought he loved us.' Clutching the hand of Mrs Cotton, coming close to her, smiling. Emmeline and Michael tiny children, abandoned as he held Mrs Cotton in dark corridors, the way Cooper had done with the soldiers in France. She threw the bandage into the pile. Dozens and dozens of them, being used, thrown away, piling up again. The war must have gobbled up a million bandages, thousands of millions. She wished she could sit down and surround herself with them, so nobody could find her.

'He still does, Celia.'

'He betrayed us.' Her father holding Mrs Cotton, closer than he held her mother. She told herself to stop. Her father betraying them, forgetting them all, laughing with her. Tom's birth. *I shall look after him for ever.* He had talked of his joy at the birth of Arthur, Emmeline, Michael and Celia. Then he bent over the crib, saw Tom, cried with happiness. Mrs Cotton smiled at him from her bed. 'He lied to us all.'

'I think your mother knows. She doesn't like me. She suspects.'

'Maybe. It was cruel to her. And us. And you. All of us. I never thought my father was like that.' She thought of the men in the nightclub with Jonathan. He had told her that they were probably married, there with other women. She had felt ashamed of them. And now she should feel the most ashamed of all. She had kissed someone who was her brother, even if only partly. She leant against the wall, her hands buried in bandages.

'You're the proof. He betrayed our family.'

'It wasn't anything bad. Why shouldn't he fall in love with my mother?'

She fought to push down her response. *Because she was a servant.*

'And now you're back here. Have you said to him "Hello, Father!" when we are not looking?'

'No, of course not.'

She turned fully to look at him. 'Why not? That is what he is to you, isn't it?'

'We don't talk about it in that way.'

She picked up another bandage. 'What do you mean? You don't refer to it?'

'No. We've never referred to it.'

'You never call each other father and son? You never speak to him of it?' She was raising her voice, but she didn't care.

'No.'

'How *do* you speak to each other?' She wanted to grasp him by the neck.

'He is kind to me. He asks how I am. You saw. He's pleased to see me.'

'But he never calls you "son"? He never refers to it?'

'He asks after my mother, wants to know how she is.'

'That means nothing, you know. He's a kind person. How do you know he's really your father?'

'I told you what my mother said the night before I went away. And Rudolf is kind to me. He always has been.'

'He's kind to a lot of people. Maybe your mother is lying.'

'My mother's not a liar.'

'I might ask her.'

He seized her hand. 'You mustn't! You must never do that.'

'But I don't believe it. Why shouldn't I find out the truth?'

'Rudolf is too good for me, is that it?'

'No, no, that is not it.' She felt painfully ashamed of their positions, he bandaged, injured, while she was free.

His face was dark with anger and pain. 'I couldn't possibly have your father, is that what you mean? Not someone like me. I could never be the son of Rudolf.'

'I'm sorry.'

'So your father was only ever kind to me out of pity?'

She couldn't bear the expression on his face. There was such a small gap between them, half a foot. She could reach her hand over and touch his, just a tiny space. But she didn't, held her hand still. Everything was crumbling. She didn't know what to believe.

'You're like your brother. He pretended to be friendly, but really he wanted me to see that I was his servant.'

'That's not true.'

'Leave me alone. Just go.' His voice was cracked, like that of an old man.

'Tom, please.'

He shook his head. 'Go away now. I don't want to speak to you any more. I mean it. I'll call for a nurse if you don't go.'

'Please, Tom.'

He closed his eyes. Tears rimmed his cheeks under his eyelids.

She put out her hand.

'Go,' he said. 'Now.'

Celia ran from the room. Outside the door, she held her head and wept. Then she crept up to her room and flung herself on the bed. Emmeline was already sleeping, as she always was by eight these days, lying on her back, breathing heavily. Celia gazed out of the window into the darkness, the night mist coming down over the dead roses. Tom's words there, four years ago. If only he hadn't said them, had never kissed her, then maybe she wouldn't have imagined things about their future together. She knew that wasn't true, though; she had always thought of them together, right from the start. Now all of it was broken, taken away, and there was nothing to put in its place.

Next morning, she was polishing a banister – she had asked Jennie if she could do it, so that she had easy work, no chance of seeing the men or having to talk to them – when she heard footsteps coming towards her. She looked up, scrubbing hastily at her eyes. Mrs Cotton and Mary, escorted by Emmeline. Mrs Cotton was nervously pulling at her coat. Mary was looking straight ahead, dignified.

'Hello, miss,' she said.

Celia tried to smile. 'Hello, Mary. Tom is much improved, you know.' She glanced at Mrs Cotton, her round, rose-cheeked face, careworn. Twenty years ago, she supposed she had been young, giggling. Could Rudolf have loved her? She shook her head. Impossible.

'Tom will be very pleased to see his family,' Emmeline said. 'He's been in good spirits, has he not, Celia?'

'Indeed he has.' She could hardly look at Mrs Cotton.

'Come on through.' Emmeline ushered them onwards. The door closed behind them. Celia leant against the wall. Emmeline swished out again. 'Still here?'

'Just catching my breath. I am tired today.'

'You shouldn't spend your evenings staring out of our bed-room window then, should you?' Emmeline shook her head and departed.

Celia pressed her ear against the door. She could hear the low rumble of voices. Mrs Cotton was crying. She waited. After a while, the door opened and the Cottons emerged. Mrs Cotton was red-eyed, holding Mary's hand. Celia scurried after them. 'I wanted to ask you something, Mrs Cotton.' The pair hurried on, out of the front of the house. Celia rushed around them. 'I wanted to ask you—'

Mrs Cotton stopped. 'Yes?' Could she have been beautiful? Celia supposed so, gazing at her face.

She couldn't say it. Couldn't ask the question. Tom was in hospital, injured and she couldn't ask it.

'Nothing, Mrs Cotton. I'm sorry.'

Mrs Cotton pulled Mary's hand. 'Come along. Goodbye, Miss de Witt.'

Celia stood there and watched them hurry away.

That evening in her room, wanting nothing more than to escape Stoneythorpe, she went to her desk and picked up her box of letters. Emmeline was downstairs, waiting for Mr Janus to make his weekend visit. She opened the lid. Hilde's letters were near the top, and she took them out, smoothed her hands over the pages. The early ones were decorated with pressed flowers that Hilde had found in the forest. The ones from the beginning of the war were plain: *I have not heard from you in some time. Things are different here.* Celia pushed them to the side, feeling guilty. She wanted the very first letters, those written when Hilde was seven.

She scanned through the early letters. *My father,* she wrote. *My father is taking us fishing. Will you come too?* Hilde's letters were on white paper, blue paper with scalloped edges, unevenly cut pink paper drawn with flowers, the handwriting growing and changing until the neat script of the most recent ones. She thought of the years before the war, playing outside with Hilde and Johann, eating bread at the table.

She picked up her pen. *Dear Hilde,* she began. *It is some time since I wrote. I have wondered how you are.*

Before she knew it, she had filled two sides of paper. She told Hilde of her work with the ambulances, of Michael's death, of the change in the house to a hospital. She tried to describe it. She folded the page in two and pushed it into a drawer.

'I've written a letter to Hilde,' she said to her father, that night at dinner in his study. They had grown used to each other now, no more silver plates or candles, and Jennie and Mrs Rolls were downstairs. Thompson still served, less nervously now. 'I have not written to her since the war started. What news have you had of them?'

'Not much. Heinrich wrote to Mama to say that Johann was fighting in Belgium. Hilde is still at home, I believe. Remember, Celia, the government sees them as our enemies now. We're not supposed to correspond with them.'

'I wish we could see more of them. It has been so long.'

'When the war is over, you can return to visit them,' said Rudolf. 'That might be soon, after all.'

'After some time has elapsed,' cut in Verena.

'Indeed so. We can all be a family once more.' With three people missing, Celia thought. Arthur unseen for years. Michael lying in his grave in France, a book somewhere marking him out as a coward. *Executed for cowardice*, she supposed, must be written in it, signed off by some clerk. And would Johann be there, or had he been killed as well? But above all Tom, lying in his bed instead of sitting with them at the table.

THIRTY-SEVEN

Celia stood by the door and watched Tom walk slowly around the rose garden. Frost was touching the stems of the roses and the soil. Emmeline had told her he was out here, having refused the escort of a nurse. She picked up her skirts and hurried to him.

'I know it's you, Celia,' he said, without turning around. 'Don't come. There's no point in talking.'

'I'm sorry, Tom. I really am.'

'I said I didn't want to talk.'

'I'm sure that Rudolf would not do such a thing.'

'You don't know for certain, either way. Have you asked Rudolf?'

'No. I don't need to. I just know.'

'And I know too. Mother wouldn't lie.'

She gazed at him, and then came a bell, ringing clearly somewhere in her mind. He was so certain. What if he was right? She shook the doubt away.

'I think I might go to Germany after the war is over. Would you come too?'

'Go to Germany...?'

'Why not? We'll be at peace then.'

'We'll never be at peace. We can't go there.'

She looked down. The soil was mulch under her feet. The vases and sculptures were beneath them. After the war, she and Tom could come to the garden and dig them up, return them to the house.

Turning to him, she put her hand out. 'Are we friends?'

He paused, then took it. 'I can't have expected you to be happy about what I told you. I tried to hide it when you came to the hospital to see me.'

'I see why you did. You were kind to do it.' The words caught in

493

her throat. But it was worth having, this moment of forgiveness, slight though it was. She had to keep it, having lost so much. They began to walk back to the house, an uneasy truce settling between them.

As they came closer, Emmeline was waving. 'Celia!' she cried. 'Celia! Come here! Quickly!'

Celia broke into a run. Her heart was in her mouth. The general was here for her. She was to be taken away. 'What is it?' She flung herself at her sister. 'What's happened?'

Emmeline grasped her hands, crossed them over and swung her around. They were small girls again, twirling in dress-up nurses' uniforms. Celia's skirts swung out behind her. Emmeline was laughing. She pulled Celia and the pair of them toppled over on to the cold earth. She was laughing. Celia had not seen her move so quickly for months.

'What is it? What's happened?' Celia punched her shoulder. Surely the general was not here if her sister was laughing.

Emmeline rolled over to lie on her back. 'You'll get green on your uniform,' Celia said.

'It doesn't matter! We will be able to afford new ones.'

'What?' Celia sat up, shading her eyes. Tom was limping towards them.

'Can't you guess? Mama has got the money! We have the money for the hospital. The authorities sent some and the Dowager Lady Redroad found a friend in Scotland who wanted to help. We have all the money we need!'

'That is happy news.' Celia tried to smile. The general was still in her mind. They would get the money for the hospital and it would not matter, for she would still be taken away, forced to do his will.

'Mama wants us to go in. Papa has found some champagne in the cellar. Tom! You must come too.' She shot him a smile, all shiny teeth and bright eyes, just as beautiful as she was in the old days. 'It's too cold out here to walk.'

She linked her arm with Celia and pulled her along, tugging

her towards the back door. Two soldiers in the garden gazed at them, surprised.

'Come on!' Emmeline cried, hauling her along the kitchen passage and out into the hall. The three of them burst through the door of the study. Rudolf was there, with Verena, Matron, Mr Janus, Jennie, Mrs Rolls and Thompson. They were all laughing, and Rudolf was pouring champagne into the glasses as Jennie held them. 'I don't think I have enough!' he was saying. 'We'll use these, then!' replied Verena, holding up two cracked teacups.

Rudolf turned. 'Welcome! Celia, Emmeline – and Tom! You have heard the news? We have the money we desire!'

Celia watched the bright stuff glitter into the glasses. 'How happy I am with the news, Papa.' She waved across the room at Mr Janus. Jennie passed her a teacup.

'Just in the nick of time,' Emmeline was saying. 'We were close to the edge, Papa.'

'So here we are,' Rudolf said. 'All together again.'

'Nearly all,' said Verena.

'Yes.' Celia looked down and saw Tom do the same.

'But we should toast what we still have,' said Rudolf. He held up his glass. 'To Stoneythorpe!' he said. 'To our great house and its continuation.' The wintry sun from the window struck his face.

They all lifted their glasses. 'To Stoneythorpe!' Celia smiled at them: her father looking younger than he had since his return, her mother clutching his arm. Emmeline was over by Mr Janus, holding his hand. Jennie was smiling in her uniform, next to Thompson, Mrs Rolls and Matron. Behind her she could hear Tom breathing.

Rudolf clapped his hands. 'To family!' he cried. They lifted their glasses again. He was about to repeat the toast when the tinkling of the telephone broke through the air. They all turned to stare at it, the receiver bobbling a little on its support. It was so unexpected, as if a zebra had suddenly appeared in the room. Celia felt sure she had not heard it ring since she had returned. 'Shall I, sir?' said Thompson.

'No, no, I shall take it,' said Rudolf. He stalked over to the table and picked up the receiver. 'Stoneythorpe,' he said into it, stiffly.

They all stood silently as he nodded. 'I see,' he said. 'Right. Yes. Are you quite sure? Yes. Well, thank you.'

He put down the telephone and looked around the room, opened his mouth. Celia saw her mother's face pale. And then he smiled. 'The war is over,' he said. 'It is over. The armistice was signed in a railway carriage in France this morning. The Kaiser has surrendered.'

Verena gave a little scream and dropped to the floor. Her teacup clattered to the side. Matron and Rudolf were immediately beside her. 'Give her air!' Matron was commanding.

Emmeline had come across and was clutching Celia's arm. 'The war is over,' she was saying. 'Sister – the war is over.'

'What about Berlin?' said Tom. 'No great push to Berlin?'

Rudolf stared at the telephone. 'I suppose not. But that is better, all the same.'

'Well then, we are giving in. If we don't go into Berlin, we are surrendering to them. They'll be back. It will start all over again.'

Matron was still fanning Verena. 'Mrs de Witt will come round.'

'But the war is over!' said Celia. 'Now we're free. We should toast that.'

'Yes, quite so,' said Rudolf. 'Let us raise our glasses. To the end of the war!'

'To the end of the war!' they all repeated, their voices ringing out, echoing around the walls. Rudolf's smile was frozen to his face.

Emmeline seized Celia's hand and pulled her out of the study. 'The war is over!' she cried breathlessly at a group of soldiers in the hall, laughing at their surprise. She battered through the door of the dining room. 'The war is over!' she shouted into the ward. Celia dropped her hand and ran around to the parlour. 'The Kaiser has surrendered!' Emmeline tugged her away, laughing, and they ran towards the ballroom. But word had spread now, and everybody was shouting it, the soldiers cheering and even strict Nurse Black crying out, 'We've won!'

Celia and Emmeline ran back into the hall. One of the men caught Emmeline up and danced her around. Celia hung back. She watched them all cheering and laughing, raising their crutches in the air, and her heart sank. She looked up to see Tom limping out of the study. He gazed at her, his face pale. Her heart switched and she felt like a ship trapped in a bottle, as if everything she could see and hear was kept away from her by a pane of glass. The day they had desired for so long – and it barely seemed any different to the others. Some man had signed papers in a railway carriage with another man and now they would not be fighting. But the men were still injured, Michael was still dead, Rudolf was wrecked, things with Tom were broken and the house was ruined. She watched the men laughing with Emmeline, holding up their hands, others shouting to the patients still lying in the wards. 'What are we going to do now?' she asked them. But the glass was in front of her and no one could hear.

'You are sitting out here alone.' The frost had covered the roses entirely. 'It's very cold.'

Tom looked up. The whites of his eyes glittered. 'Looking at the stars. Thinking.'

'May I sit down too?' Celia didn't wait for an answer. She folded her legs under herself and sat on the cold grass. She wanted to push the general out of her mind. Now that the war was over, he surely could not come for her. What use could he have for her now?

'Does it feel strange that it's over?'

Tom shrugged. 'I don't believe it is. I think it will come back.'

'Surely the Germans have given in?'

'You know them. They might have tricked us. We aren't in Berlin, after all.'

'You're right.' That thought was so miserable that she couldn't even address it. That today they'd been dancing and tomorrow they might be at war again. She looked out over the grass, just lit by the house behind them.

497

'You kept your secret about Papa for a long time,' she said. 'Must've been hard.'

'I don't know what to think now. I was so sure, but now I'm back at Stoneythorpe... Maybe Mother just wished it was so.'

She wanted to console him with something. 'I don't know him any more, my father, not really. I didn't expect it to be like this. I thought it would go back to how it was. Sometimes I wonder if he thinks more about the men who were in prison with him than us.'

'Don't be silly.'

'That's how it feels.'

He put his arm around her. 'It's bound to be hard at first. You've grown up. Think what you've seen since he left.'

'Not much good.'

He squeezed her and she blushed with pleasure, grateful that it was dark. 'Tom, I...' She wanted to tell him about Jonathan but could not find the words.

'I think that if the war's really over, we should try and forget about it. Not think about it. I imagine that after a year or so, people won't want to hear about it any more.'

'I can't imagine not talking about it.'

'You'll have to find new things. You could go to Paris now, see Arthur.'

'I'd be lonely there.' She hesitated, forced herself to say it. 'Would you come too?'

'Maybe I would after all.' His arm was still around her. It was burning her shoulder.

'Are you sure there's no other girl?' She was smiling as she said it, teasing him. Clearly, she thought, clearly he couldn't believe she was his sister if they were talking like this. Mrs Cotton must have been lying.

'Of course not. When would I have time for another girl?'

'Nurse Rouse was pretty.'

He gave a quick laugh. 'All the men are in love with nurses. It means nothing.'

'I said I'd write to her, but I didn't in the end.'

'You won't now the war's over. You'll want something else to think about. I do.'

'Like what?'

He shook his head, coughing. 'What am I talking about? I'm sorry, Celia.'

His eyes shone in the dark. She thought of Jonathan, her invitation to him, felt a wash of shame.

'Did you meet girls in the war?'

'Not many. Let's talk of something else.'

She looked up, and the stars were hiding behind frosty clouds.

'What about the girl you talked about?'

'I told you, I made her up.'

'There was a girl at the station, Cooper, who kept going out to meet men. I guess that was why she did it. Maybe I should have done that too. She seemed happy.'

'Maybe she was.'

'Oh.' She could think of nothing to say. 'Can you tell me about it?'

'No. You'll find out when you're married.'

'I will never get married.'

'So you say.'

'It's true.'

She looked at him. He seemed about to speak. Or even do something. His hand was a white light on her shoulder, hot, sharp. Go on, she willed him. *Say it*. The second trembled, waiting. She could feel it.

He stood up, held out his hand. 'Come on, Celia. Let's go inside. They'll be looking for us.'

The moment was gone. It broke free of her hand, flew into the dark sky. She clambered up and they walked together towards Stoneythorpe. Yellow light fell from the windows, throwing thin shapes onto the unkempt lawn.

THIRTY-EIGHT

Only a month later, and Stoneythorpe was quite changed. Nearly all the soldiers had gone home or to other hospitals; just a few remained, the cases that Matron said could not be moved, the few she had a soft spot for, who, she said, were gentle boys not suited to hospitals in town. The dining room was theirs once more. Celia decked it with garlands of ivy and holly brought in by Jennie from the village, Emmeline standing at the bottom of the ladder, ordering her to put it higher and arrange it better.

They were planning a big Christmas party for the men remaining. Rudolf had even pondered inviting the village, but Verena shook her head and told him the idea was impossible. Perhaps, she said, perhaps in the future they might consider it. Once real life began again. Celia had shivered with shame, for she agreed with her mother; even though the war was over, the village still wouldn't come.

When Celia woke – late, like the daughter of the house rather than a nurse – she walked down into the hall and smelt baking. Mrs Rolls and Beryl, the new kitchen maid, were making mince pies in the kitchen. There wasn't enough sugar or butter or fruit for a Christmas cake, so they were having a kind of Victoria sponge, made with a ground-down sort of flour. Celia felt almost faint at the thought of it. She hadn't eaten cake since she had had tea with Jonathan, and then she had been so hungry that she had wolfed it down too quickly; probably bread and cheese would have done as well. This cake, she vowed, she would really enjoy.

By mid-afternoon, she was caught up in the bustle of it all, carrying the plates of food upstairs and setting out the decorations as her mother instructed. It would be their first proper Christmas since the dreadful one in 1914. The year after, it had been an empty day, when Verena had risen for an hour and they'd sat in the parlour together, unable to think of anything to say, Verena declining to play snap. They had spent the Christmas of 1916 together at Stoneythorpe, a week after Michael's funeral. Mr Janus had talked a lot of how he didn't celebrate Christmas because he thought it an instrument of repression of the poor, and that had been welcome to Celia, for she had been moving through a long, dark tunnel after Michael and could not see how she could ever escape it. The next year had been jollier: she had travelled up from Stoneythorpe to spend the day with Emmeline, and Jemima had come round with three pies, and a bar of chocolate given to her by a grateful soldier in her ward. Jemima had refused to listen to Mr Janus, and had sung 'Hark the Herald Angels' so loudly that the people in the flat downstairs banged on the ceiling. She had told Celia that 1918 would be quite different, that the new year would see a new world of peace.

Tom had been wrong. It didn't seem as if the war was coming back at all. The Germans had kept to the treaty and the soldiers had started to return home. Celia thought of them, thousands of them, living together, sleeping in the same holes, protecting each other, dragging each other through the mud. And now they were separated, thrown back into the world, sent back to live different lives, alone, isolated. She couldn't imagine seeing Warterton, Fitz or the rest again, what they might talk of other than old times, and you weren't supposed to talk of those any more. *Look to the future*, that was what the newspapers exhorted. *We need to begin again and forget.* She imagined the last soldiers left out there in France, coming back over the mud, past the abandoned tanks and guns, staring at the places where they had once fought – which now had to reflower, grow houses, trees, people again, the spots where a hundred men had fallen becoming a vegetable patch, a children's playhouse, the site of a home.

She told herself it was her own fault, not the war's, that her thoughts were so out of place. The newspapers and magazines were telling everyone how to celebrate: deck all the rooms with pictures of the King and General Haig and hang curtains to celebrate red, white and blue. There were patterns to show the children how to make St George and the dragon out of newspaper. Celia stared at the recommendations. When she'd thought of peace it had been all about things going back to how they were. She could not have imagined that they might not change back, that London would still be bombed and men still blinded or lamed, the things they had put up with because of war still remaining.

By early afternoon, the table was laid. Captain Campbell was practising on the piano and everyone was ready. Tom was out in the garden, directing two soldiers digging up the statues and ornaments. She went out to join him. She padded over the frozen ground and towards the bent figures. Tom waved at her, and she smiled back.

Since that night after the end of the war, they hadn't come out to the rose garden together. He had avoided her, she admitted to herself sadly. He was always polite to her, friendly even – but he didn't want to talk to her, tell her anything, not any more. He rested, walked, read like all the other patients, seemed more eager to talk to Lloyd than her.

Mrs Cotton and Mary came to visit most days, and Celia avoided them. When Matron asked if she could escort them to Tom's bed, she said she was indisposed. That wasn't always far from the truth. She found herself feeling tired and unwell, a little weak. She told herself it was low spirits, a heartsickness that she knew many others were suffering after the war.

At six o'clock, Thompson lit the candles and Mrs Rolls brought up the last of the food. Captain Campbell sat down at the piano. Thompson passed round glasses and then came around with wine, and Rudolf stood up. Celia remembered his habit of speaking for hours in the old days, waited.

'Merry Christmas!' he said, his voice low and wavering. 'To a new year, 1919!'

They held up their glasses. 'To 1919!' Their voices all sounded so sincere. Celia felt ashamed of her doubts.

By eight o'clock, she was dancing in the arms of a patient called Peter, who had only just learned to walk again. Emmeline was swaying with Mr Janus. The whole hall was waltzing: Mrs Rolls and Sarah danced together, Thompson whirled Jennie. Rudolf and Verena stood by the side, smiling. 'It is my birthday ball,' Celia said to the soldier. 'I am having my birthday ball after all.'

'What?' he said. 'Sorry, miss, I can't hear much. Bomb at Ypres.'

'Nothing!' she shouted back.

He whirled her around. They stopped to catch their breath. She laughed, just because she could. A voice behind her. 'May I?' She looked up, and it was Tom. 'May I have this dance?'

'Of course!' She flushed red.

He put his arm on her back and they began to dance. She felt his hand through her dress, struggled to force her feet to follow his. She glanced away, too shy to look into his eyes. 'Tom,' she said. 'I'm sorry about Papa.'

'Don't,' he said. 'Let's not talk about it. Not today.' He gave her an expert turn around a nurse dancing with a soldier.

I love you, she wanted to say. *I don't care about any of it.* Instead she said, 'The war is definitely over.' He smiled and held her closer.

The door slammed open. Captain Campbell stopped playing, and they all turned. A tall, dark-haired man stood there. He wore a smart suit and carried a black and silver stick. He looked astounded by the scene in front of him.

'Arthur!' Emmeline screamed. She ran across the room to him, threw herself into his arms. Celia stared. It was him – taller, more handsome, richer. Arthur.

'Good evening, everybody,' he said, his voice as loud and commanding as ever. 'How's tricks? Just back from Paris and I thought I would drop in.'

'You've been away for so long,' Emmeline said.

He laughed. 'Doesn't look like too much has changed. Even the old piano is still in decent nick.'

Verena was crying.

'Don't be sad, Ma. I am back now. And' – he turned to the pianist – 'I don't wish to stop the party. Carry on, dear fellow. I will dance with my beautiful sister here. Even if she is – as I see – a married lady.'

Captain Campbell lifted his hands, not quite sure what was going on, looking at the family for confirmation. 'Please go ahead, Captain,' said Rudolf across the hall. Campbell swooped down on the keys and began playing once more. Arthur whirled Emmeline around, her skirt flying out, and all the other couples began to follow suit. Tom let go of Celia, and another man, Captain Wood, took her solemnly in his good arm.

'It is my birthday ball,' she said again.

Captain Campbell pounded out 'Shine on Harvest Moon' and they all danced on. Behind them, the door drifted open, letting in splashes of light from the lamps in the hall. Celia smiled at Wood, the dancing partner she barely knew. Out of the corner of her eye, she could see Tom, standing there, watching.

EPILOGUE

December 1916

Tom pushed his rifle up into the mud. He could not see a thing through the early-morning mist. If he heard a command to shoot, he would not have the faintest idea what at. The men either side of him were looking ahead, although God knew at what. It was his bet that there was no one there. After all, that was what they had told them in the first place. Entirely deserted of Germans, even the trenches. And then they had gone into that trench and the story had been different. After four days of having turpentine rubbed on his chest for the gas, here he was, back at the empty front line, with a group of men he didn't know. Michael was still in the field hospital, he supposed. He'd asked to visit him, but they'd told him it wasn't allowed. He'd see him soon, he hoped. They couldn't send them to different battalions now.

He had a new gun, one he didn't much like. He rather missed his old one. He had looked after it for two years, after all, spent more time on it than on himself – although admittedly, keeping a rifle clean and dry was easier than doing the same for a man. Guns didn't get trench foot, that was for sure. He had laid out the ammunition, polished it on a groundsheet, taken up the grease and rubbed it over the whole thing, getting right into the cracks. Then bayonet ready at his waist, one cartridge in the chamber, cocked, safety catch on, ready to go over. He had decided his was a lucky gun. It seemed to have kept him safe until now. Secretly, not telling anyone, he called it Celia – sometimes Cordelia if he thought anyone might hear. Some German had the thing now, probably kept as a souvenir, or passed to HQ as a sort of curiosity, and he had this new gun, which he supposed had been the possession of some poor devil who'd died. It really wasn't up to the standard of Celia; you could tell the chap who'd had it hadn't looked after it very well. Perhaps that was why he'd been killed.

'Cotton!' An officer was standing above him. 'You're needed.'

Tom wrinkled his brow. 'I was told to wait here, sir.'

'Yes, but now we need men. Orders from HQ. Quick smart.'

Tom nodded and scrambled up out of the trench.

'What is it, sir, another raiding party?'

'Come along with me, Cotton.' The officer ushered him forward. A group of fifteen or so men were waiting by a barn. 'Right, chaps, we need riflemen. You all have your guns?' They nodded. It was a rhetorical question, really; of course they would have their weapons, or they would be court-martialled. They trotted after him down a path, through some farmland, until they came to a large field flanked by hay barns.

'There's been a German spy found out here in our uniform, chaps,' said the officer. 'Awful thing. Very clever man, English so perfect you'd think him one of ours. He stole a lot of secrets, passed them back to the enemy. We think he gave information about our plans for the Somme, resulted in many casualties on our side.'

There was an intake of breath. The officer continued, telling them about the horrors the men had undergone. Tom watched him speak. Cutting the wire, he thought; you could have done that and you didn't. The Germans didn't need to pass on intelligence.

The officer commanded them to arrange themselves in a line, fiddled them backwards and forwards until he was happy. He shifted their feet around with his hands.

'Now, check your guns for ammunition. All set?'

'Yes, sir,' they chorused.

'When the spy comes out, he will stand in front of you.' The officer stepped to the side of the spot he'd indicated, too superstitious to stand there, Tom supposed.

One of the barn doors opened and a figure came out wearing a British uniform, a brown sack over his head. Two military policemen held his arms. He was stumbling, staggering against them.

Tom felt a painful pity. Surely this was hardly fair, fifteen of them against one. The chap next to him was trembling, he could feel it. He wanted to put out his hand to him, but didn't dare.

The man came closer. An X was painted on a white hand-kerchief stuck to his chest. He was crying, a muffled, pleading cry that Tom couldn't bear. He'd spent two years listening to grown men cry, of course, weeping into their pillows, calling for their mothers. But nothing like this: a hopeless cry, like a dog begging to die.

'Guns raised,' called the officer. He stepped back as the military policemen pushed the man into place. Tom raised his gun. He would shoot the other way, he vowed, past the prisoner. The officer was too close for him to fire at the floor. If he shot at the man's foot, would that only be worse, prolong the agony?

A bird sang as it flew overhead. Tom wanted to pull it down, gather it to him and say: *Why can't we stop?* It soared on.

The military policemen lifted the sack from the man's head. Tom noticed first that he was wearing a gag – that was why his cry had sounded so odd – and a blindfold. Then he saw the rest of the face and knew.

'Sir,' he said desperately, turning, grasping the officer's jacket. 'Sir, that's not a spy. He's English. That's my corporal.'

'Ready!' shouted the officer. The military policemen were adjusting the positioning of the second handkerchief, the blindfold, marking the man's forehead with an X like his heart.

Michael stood there, knees wobbling, tears pouring from under his blindfold. He was hiccupping, shaking, with his hands tied behind his back.

The officer brushed Tom off, like a fly.

'Raised!'

'Sir, we can't.' He tugged hard on the man's jacket. 'We *can't*.'

The officer's face was blazing with fury. 'Stop this, Cotton!' He lowered his voice. 'He wouldn't lead his men over, like a weakling.'

'He was ill.' Tom's mind flashed with the sickness and horror he had felt when Michael had told him in the trench that Rudolf was in prison. He had kicked the wood in fury, knowing that Michael

507

was looking at him in confusion, not caring, wanting to say, there and then, *You don't understand. I'm more like you than you think!*

'Cotton, he is a coward. Now if you won't do it, we'll find men who will. Think what you're doing to those around you. They think they're executing a spy. How will they feel if they hear this?'

Tom hung his head. He could hear Michael crying.

'Do you want to be shot next?'

'No, sir.'

'Well get back in line, raise your gun and fire.'

Tom nodded, shuffled back to his place. The nervous man next to him glanced at him. One further along the line was staring at him, angry at him for delaying things.

Michael was trembling, his shoulders wobbling. 'Keep still, prisoner!' called one of the policemen. Tom prayed, desperately that Michael hadn't heard his voice. *Oh God.*

'Prepare!'

Another bird careened overhead. Could something happen, anything that might stop it? General Haig or the King appearing and demanding they stand to attention? A wild horse running through them? Tom held his gun, his fingers shaking.

The command came. Tom squeezed the trigger, pulled back, fired.

AFTERWORD

I've wanted to write about a family in the Great War since I went on a school trip to the trenches of Flanders, aged ten. I was shocked by how small the trenches were. I struggled to imagine how grown men could have lived and fought there. I thought I'd understand when I was an adult. Even after years of research and writing, I am still amazed by how men fought and survived in those tiny, muddy holes in the ground for years on end.

Ever since then, I've been thinking about the human stories of the War. I'm fascinated by the women – like Celia – facing disease and death daily, and the people at home, their possessions destroyed by bombs, waiting for news about their loved ones.

In writing about the War, I've had the incredible privilege of reading the letters and diaries of those who were there. There are so many fantastic diaries of the men, the nurses, the drivers and the people at home. Every word they write strikes home – they're unforgettable. The De Witt family are fiction, but they are based on the spirit and sentiments of those real people who refused to ever give up.

Arguments about who was responsible for the war still rage and politicians call for each other to resign over it. But I know from talking to people all over the country that what they really want to know is – what was it *like*? How did it feel to be there? That is the story that I wanted to tell in *The Storms of War*. If I've achieved that at all, it's because of the words of those men and women who lived through those dark times, and spoke or wrote of their experiences.

While writing on Queen Victoria, I became fascinated by the links between Germany and Britain. If she had been male, she would have ruled Britain and Hanover jointly from her accession in 1837. But Hanover forbade female monarchs and her uncle Ernst went off to do the job instead. The two countries were bound together by the tightest of social, cultural and indeed blood bonds – and then expected to simply separate and move on. Wars are still fought on the basis of seemingly easy divisions, between countries, ethnic groups and indeed within families. Such separations rarely go well.

On 5th August 1914, a day after the announcement of war, Asquith and the British Government passed the Aliens Restriction Act. Suddenly, thousands of Germans who had lived in the country for years were branded the enemy. They had to register almost immediately (by 17th August) at local registration stations, couldn't live in 'prohibited' areas on the south and east coast and were not allowed to travel more than five miles without a permit. The permit would only be issued for twenty-four hours. They had to give up their cars, motorcycles or cameras.

For years, thousands of Germans had lived happily in Britain. They worked as butchers, barbers, tailors, waiters, music tutors and governesses, surrounded – and welcomed – by the English. They had a reputation for being the best barbers and waiters; sure hands, people thought (and they were known for working for less than their British equivalents). The top London hotels such as the Ritz and Savoy employed nearly exclusively German waiters. The Prime Minister himself had a German governess in his family. Two members of his cabinet had German chauffeurs (they were swiftly naturalised after the announcement of war).

These Germans had married British women and fathered children – and now they were hated. The press was bursting with stories of the evil of the German race. Spies were everywhere and everyone was expected to report them. Formerly, the press had been wildly occupied by the question of Irish home rule, suffragettes and working-class strikers. They were all forgotten in the rush to demonise the Germans. Their British wives were extended no mercy, for they were seen as having taken on the nationality of their husband. Advertisements were displayed in the press to say that there were no German or Austrian subjects in the *employment of the Savoy, Claridges and Berkeley Hotels, the Strand Palace Hotel, the Frederick Hotels, Messrs J. Lyons and Co, and the Palmerston Restaurant.* In August, the *Daily Mail* suggested *if your waiter says he is Swiss, ask to see his passport. The Times* published headlines about THE ALIEN PERIL.

Despite the cries of the newspapers, wholesale interning of German citizens was slow to take off – there was nowhere for the government to put them, to start with. Anyone arrested could be released if two British citizens vouched for them. By May 1915, after the terrible sinking of the *Lusitania*, wholesale internment of men between seventeen and fifty-five began in earnest. Many German women were deported, although those who had children between five and fifteen were exempted. In *The Storms of War*, Rudolf is taken away but Verena escapes, partly due to her aristocratic background.

These Germans were crammed into various unsuitable places across the country – in London, Olympia and Crystal Palace were commandeered – and camps were swiftly built. Rudolf is in the most notorious: Knockaloe in the Isle of Man.

I was fascinated by this: what were the lives of these people – these twilight people, half English, half German – really like? Many saw Britain as their homeland but now they were hated and excluded. How did they survive, in their homes and communities, when everybody was on the lookout for spies? Did their neighbours pretend they 'weren't like other Germans' or just revile them? Even Ralph Vaughan Williams, sitting down in Margate to write notes for the *Lark Ascending*, was arrested as a spy by a zealous Boy Scout in early 1914. Everyone was under suspicion.

I've based this book on the letters and diaries of our wartime ancestors – and it's been an incredible privilege to read their words. Stoneythorpe is based on Bramshill House (although in my version, it's a little smaller than the vast original!), a Jacobean house built in the early seventeenth century by Edward de la Zouche, 11th Baron Zouche. It was used as a Red Cross Maternity Hospital in the war and, since 1960, it has been our National Police

Training College. It's currently on the market for £25 million – a price just outside the budget of the pre-war Rudolf de Witt!

Michael and Tom fight with the 7th Suffolk Regiment, formed at Bury St Edmunds and landing at Boulogne in May 1915, fighting at the Battle of Loos, then Pozières in the Somme in 1916 and remaining in France until after the end of the war. Smithson is with the 13th Hampshire Regiment who fought at Gallipoli and then went to Egypt to defend the Suez Canal in 1916, then spent the rest of the war in Mesopotamia, occupying Baghdad in March 1917 and fighting in Jabal Hamrin in October.

ACKNOWLEDGEMENTS

Thank you to the Archivists at the Imperial War Museum, the British Library and the National Army Museum for their assistance – and research gems. Thank you also to Frank McDonogh, Saul David, Roger Moorhouse, Paul Reed and Gary Sheffield for advice on historical accuracy and military matters. Any mistakes are mine, not theirs. Among my favourite books for research has been *War Girls* by Janet Lee and the invaluable research by Richard Van Emden – especially *The Soldier's War*, *Meeting the Enemy* and his work with Steve Humphries, *All Quiet on the Home Front*. Max Arthur's *Forgotten Voices of the Great War* was a great help. I have found invaluable Lyn MacDonald's work (especially *Somme* and *The Roses of No Man's Land)* and the innovative work of Panikos Panayi of De Montfort University on Germans – especially *The Enemy Within*. Winifred Smith's diaries formed the basis for Evadne Price's *Not so Quiet* – a very moving book. Jeremy Paxman's *Great Britain's Great War* is a brilliant piece of work. Max Hasting's *Catastrophe* is excellent, along with Saul David's work. Kate Adie has written superbly on the home front and women in her *Fighting on the Home Front*. I recommend them all as fascinating reads.

I'm incredibly grateful to everybody at Orion for their help in the process of telling this story. Jon Wood has been an impossibly amazing editor, full of thrilling inspiration and wonderful ideas, so generous with his time. He's made this book what it is now and it has been a true and great privilege to work with him. Jemima Forrester has been fantastic – gone above and beyond the call of duty with quite brilliant points and such kindness and patience and splendid attention to the detail – I'm lucky to have access to her talent. I'm so very grateful to them both.

I'm grateful to Susan Lamb for all her imagination, kind support and generosity – and a brilliant point about horses, which would have put me to shame if it had stayed in! Susan has given me and the book so much fantastic guidance and really amazing ideas – I'm so thankful for all her time and care about the book. Thank you to Lisa Milton for everything – and to David Young for his support and kindness. Thanks to everybody else who has given me so much, including Mark Rusher, Gaby Wood and Graeme Williams for fireworks of ideas – and Mark Stay for knowing everything about everything. Sherif Mehmet taught me how to organise our Christmas lunch, and made sure everything about this book ran smoothly. I know there are a plethora of Orion staff, booksellers, reviewers and readers who will make this book come to life, so thank you in advance, and I'm sorry I don't know you yet. It's been brilliant to work with Orion.

Thank you to Gillian, Darren, Emily, Sophie and Charlie at Gollancz for making life fun (I'll put a spaceship in a book one day...). Simon Spanton was instrumental in making this book happen, from the first glimmerings of an idea to the final result. Thank you.

I'm very grateful to my wonderful and very generous agents, Robert Kirby and Ariella Feiner, for everything – they must have felt they were living in the wrong century with all this! They are always there for me and full of ideas, even late at night...

Thank you to my colleagues over at Royal Holloway, Professor Sir Andrew Motion, Professor Jo Shapcott and Susanna Jones. Andrew has read my earliest fiction and has improved it beyond measure – I'm very fortunate.

Thank you so much to Marcus and Persephone for putting up with living in 1914 rather than the twenty-first century!

And, above all, thank you to my readers – especially to all those who write to me. I couldn't do it without you! The story of the de Witt family will continue next year, following their fortunes from 1918 to 1927. I hope you'll join them again.